LAURA MARTIN

REGENCY
Australian
Bachelors

MILLS & BOON

Published by
Harlequin Mills & Boon
An imprint of Harlequin Enterprises (Australia) Pty Limited
(ABN 47 001 180 918), a subsidiary of HarperCollins
Publishers Australia Pty Limited
(ABN 36 009 913 517)
Level 19, 201 Elizabeth Street
SYDNEY NSW 2000 AUSTRALIA

Printed and bound in Australia by McPherson's Printing Group

MIX
Paper | Supporting
responsible forestry
FSC® C001695
www.fsc.org

CONTENTS

Courting The
Forbidden Debutante

Laura Martin writes historical romances with an adventurous undercurrent. When not writing, she spends her time working as a doctor in Cambridgeshire, UK, where she lives with her husband. In her spare moments Laura loves to lose herself in a book and has been known to read from cover to cover in a single day when the story is particularly gripping. She also loves to travel—especially to visit historical sites and far-flung shores.

Author Note

Eight years ago I stood in a museum in Sydney looking at the images depicting the first British settlers in Botany Bay and Sydney Cove. I was fascinated by the challenges these first settlers faced, and also by the lives led by the men and women who made Australia their home. There was a lot of information about the convict settlers and the dire conditions on the transport ships, and I was intrigued by the stories of the men who turned their lives around and saw the fledgling settlement in Australia as their land of opportunity.

When starting to write *Courting the Forbidden Debutante*, I wanted to create a hero who had risen above his convict beginnings and made a success of his life. To have him then return to England and into London Society with all its rules and etiquette was great fun to write, and all the time I drew my inspiration from the tales I read in that little museum in Sydney.

I hope you enjoy *Courting the Forbidden Debutante*, a Regency romance with a twist of Australian flavor!

For my boys. You fill my life with love.

Chapter One

❦

'It's scandalous who they invite to these balls.'

'I heard they were ex-convicts, recently returned from Australia.'

'Surely not. Lord Gilham would have higher standards than that.'

'A dear friend of mine told me they were fishermen, grown rich off the proceeds of smuggling,' the first lady said in an exaggerated whisper, eliciting thrilled gasps from her companions.

Sam suppressed a smile. They'd been at the ball for less than five minutes and already the gossip was rife. He was surprised at how accurate this gaggle of middle-aged women were about their country of origin, at least. Despite spending much of his young life close to the sea, he'd never tried his hand at fishing before, or smuggling.

'Enjoying yourself?' George Fitzgerald asked as he clapped Sam on the back.

Surveying the room, Sam grimaced. This was not his

world, not what he'd been born into. The cravat at his neck felt uncomfortably tight and the well-tailored jacket suddenly was too snug across the shoulders. Give him an open-necked shirt any day over the ridiculous garments the rich and powerful seemed to favour.

'It's certainly…different,' Sam said.

'Tell me about it.'

The two men stood side by side. So far no one had found the courage to come up and speak to them, despite the curious stares they were getting, but it would only be a matter of time.

'These are your people, George. Shouldn't you be off cavorting with the Lords and Ladies?'

Fitzgerald grimaced. He might have tenuous links to the aristocracy—his father was the second son of an impoverished baron—but George had spent his entire life in the wilds of Australia, raised on a farm. A very successful farm that made him one of the richest men in Australia but more at home around horses and hard work than the glamour of ballrooms and soirées.

'Any sign of him yet?' Fitzgerald asked.

Sam shook his head. The whole reason they'd secured the invitation to the Gilham ball was for Sam to start his search for the man who had ruined his life. Lord Westchester. Earl, influential member of the House of Lords and, in Sam's eyes at least, the devil incarnate.

'Boys,' a high-pitched voice pierced the air, putting the two men at the centre of everyone's attention again. 'I've been looking for you for an age.'

'Aunt Tabitha.' Fitzgerald bent forward and kissed his aunt on the cheek, Sam doing the same on her other side.

'Aren't there supposed to be three of you?' she asked.

'Although maybe it is better to unleash you into society one at a time. The wicked widows won't know which of you to seduce first.'

'Crawford is off dancing with some doe-eyed debutante,' Sam said, his eyes searching the room for their friend. Crawford had picked up the steps to the most popular dances quickly and easily and never seemed short of a partner on the dance floor. Sam was a little less of a natural, but he was agile and quick on his feet. As a result he could dance a waltz or a quadrille and fool a casual observer into thinking he'd been dancing all his life.

'A man who doesn't waste any time.' Aunt Tabitha grinned, a far more salacious smile than should appear on the face of a respectable member of the *ton*. 'Now, a little bird told me you are looking for a way to get close to Lord Westchester.'

Sam opened his mouth to protest, but was silenced by Aunt Tabitha's raised hand. He shot Fitzgerald a distrusting look.

'Now, none of that,' the older woman said. 'I'm sure I don't need to know why you need to gain an audience with the Earl, but that pretty young thing over there, the one in the blue dress, she is your ticket in.'

'A relation of the Earl?' Sam asked, his senses suddenly heightened.

'His daughter. I'm sure a catch like that will have a full dance card already. But George tells me you're a resourceful man. I'd wager my pearls you can find a way to steal her away from one of these bores for a dance or two.'

'Lady Winston, you're a gem,' Sam said, stooping down and kissing her on the cheek.

Straightening up, he took a moment to square his shoulders, stiffen his spine and focus in on his prey. He rather thought this was how a general would feel when sighting his enemy on the battlefield.

He strode across the ballroom, ignoring the curious stares that followed him. Everyone wanted to know the truth behind the three mysterious *gentlemen* who had appeared in society as if by magic, but he would not be stopped by even the most persistent of enquirers.

The Earl's daughter stood in the middle of an eager gaggle of men of varying ages, all of whom seemed desperate to see to her every need, even those she didn't know she had. Sam paused for a moment, listening to the men clamour for her attention, and the young woman's polite but uninterested replies.

'Perhaps another glass of lemonade, Lady Georgina?' a boy who couldn't have been more than twenty suggested.

'I'm perfectly fine, thank you, Mr Forrester.'

'Would you care for some fresh air, Lady Georgina?' another young man suggested.

'I think our dance will be starting soon,' a slightly older man said, eyeing the younger bucks with distaste.

The popular Lady Georgina smiled, but it didn't quite reach her eyes, and Sam knew instantly that she wouldn't object to being taken away from her many admirers.

'Excuse me,' he said, his voice deep and low, clearing a space through the crowd that surrounded her. 'Your mother asked me to find you. She has an urgent matter to discuss.'

Lady Georgina's eyes snapped up and she regarded him with a half-smile on her face for a few seconds. She knew he was lying, knew it was a ruse to get her to himself for a little while, and for a moment he wondered if she was going to call his bluff. As her eyes met his Sam felt a *fris-*

son of excitement and a sudden burst of attraction. She was pretty, with thick, dark hair and deep green eyes set in a heart-shaped face with smooth, creamy skin, but it wasn't until she looked at him that Sam understood the gaggle of suitors surrounding her. There was life in her eyes and Sam felt the pull, the unconscious urge to rush in and join her in whatever adventure she suggested.

'Oh, I do hope it's nothing serious,' she said, raising a dainty hand to her mouth and trying to effect a worried expression.

'Don't overdo it,' Sam murmured in her ear. He'd managed to manoeuvre most of the admirers out of the way and place himself firmly by her side. 'Just a family matter,' Sam said brightly. 'I'm sure you'll be back to…everyone very shortly.'

She placed the dainty hand in the crook of his arm and together they took a step forward. Through the thin material of her dress Sam could feel the heat of her skin and for an instant he wondered what it might feel like under his lips. Quickly he dismissed the thought. He'd only just met the woman and, more importantly, she was a means to get closer to his objective, not a suitable companion for a dalliance.

'I say, shouldn't I accompany you, Lady Georgina?' a man of about Sam's age said, his brow furrowed with suspicion. 'Rather than this…stranger.'

'What makes you think I'm a stranger?' Sam asked, enjoying himself for the first time this evening.

'Surely you don't want to be going off with *him*,' another man prompted. 'You must have heard the rumours?'

'Gentlemen, my mother has asked for me and Mr…'

'Robertson,' Sam supplied helpfully.

'Mr Robertson has been kind enough to deliver her message and escort me to her. I'm sure I will be back shortly.'

Without a backwards glance Sam led Lady Georgina through the crowds, noting the curious looks from the assembled guests.

'What's your plan now, Mr Robertson?' Georgina murmured in his ear.

'Perhaps we could find somewhere a little more private,' he suggested. Images of a deserted room, darkened except for the light of a few candles and Lady Georgina seductively draped across the arm of a chair popped into his mind. That wasn't what he'd meant, but it was appealing all the same.

'With the entire ballroom watching us? I have my reputation to think about.' Sam wasn't sure if he imagined the moment of hesitation, the slight blush to her cheeks as if she'd been imagining the same as him.

'They do seem unnaturally interested in our every movement,' Sam said, feeling at least twenty pairs of eyes on him at that very moment.

'I think people are worried the big bad stranger might take advantage of innocent little me.'

'Unlikely,' he said, realising that he meant it. Lady Georgina might be the pampered daughter of an earl, used to having her every need seen to by a bevy of servants, but she was no shy and retiring innocent. She'd known he was lying about the message from her mother from the very instant the words had left his mouth, yet here she was on his arm, enjoying the break from the mundane for a few moments, those exotic eyes looking up at him with anticipation.

'Perhaps the terrace?' Lady Georgina suggested. 'There will be plenty of couples taking the air, but it may be a little quieter.'

Sam led her on another loop of the ballroom and out on to the terrace. She was right, of course, there were couples dotted along the stone balustrade and strolling backwards and forward taking the air, but there were fewer eyes on them here. He realised suddenly how out of his depth he was in this world. It had never even crossed his mind that there would be a terrace for couples of withdraw to. The whole scene, the whole evening, was completely foreign to him. He felt more at home on horseback, galloping through the Australian countryside on a mission to find out why a remote well had dried up or scouting for valuable land for crops.

'You're quite the talk of the ballroom,' Lady Georgina said as they paused at one end of the terrace.

'All good things, I'm sure,' Sam murmured.

She laughed and immediately Sam knew it wasn't the laugh she reserved for her suitors. This was Lady Georgina's true laugh. It lit up her face from her eyes to that perfectly pointed chin.

'If *all* the rumours are to be believed, you're a pirate, one of those ruthless corsairs based off the coast of Africa. You're an ex-convict from the wilds of Australia. And you're a French spy, eager to find a way to restart the war that ended six years ago.'

'I am a busy man,' Sam said, feeling the easy smile spread over his lips. 'I wonder I have enough time for so many pursuits.'

'And you managed to fit in a visit to this humble little ball.'

'No doubt to further one of my nefarious goals.'

She laughed again, attracting curious glances from another couple who were strolling past slowly. Quickly she composed her face into a more serious expression, but Sam had caught a glimpse of the woman underneath.

'What are you doing here?' Lady Georgina asked.

For a moment she thought he might answer her, but instead he flashed her that dazzling smile that was a little too distracting for anyone's good and winked.

'Running errands for your mother,' he said.

'Now I know that is nonsense. My mother is tucked up in bed with an awful headache, with no plans to surface until at least midday tomorrow.'

'Ah, I see my little lie has been uncovered,' Mr Robertson said, treating her to that lazy smile again that Georgina knew had melted many hearts over the years. He was handsome with dazzling blue eyes set in an open face with the widest grin she had ever seen. He exuded charm and had that easy confidence of someone who is sure of who they are and what they want. It was difficult not to like the man on first impressions, but as Georgina's insides did a little flip she knew spending too much time with him would be dangerous—he was the sort of man young women lost their heads over.

'You still haven't answered my question,' she said, resolutely trying to avoid his eyes in case she found herself unable to look away.

'Would you believe me if I said I just wanted to make your acquaintance?'

It would be easy to take the compliment, far too easy, and even easier to let his charm and beguiling smile lull her into doing something she might regret. She'd never understood before how young ladies allowed themselves to be ruined, how they forgot everything they had been told time and time again about stepping into dark corners with men who could not be trusted, but right now she felt the fizz of anticipation deep inside her and knew it would be all too tempting to do something she might regret. Quickly she rallied and set her face into a serious expression.

'Then you should have had someone introduce you,' she said primly.

'But you forget, I'm a pirate, a French spy and an ex-convict, I have barely any connections in English society and no one to introduce me to a beautiful young woman at a ball.'

'Yet here you are,' Georgina murmured.

It was curious, how he and his two friends had just waltzed into society, rumours bouncing off them left and right, without anyone really knowing who they were. One of the more believable pieces of gossip was that one of the young men was related to Lady Winston, which would explain their easy entrance to the ball, but other than that Georgina didn't know what to believe.

'Tell me,' Mr Robertson said, leaning casually against the stone balustrade, 'Do you like all the attention from your little crowd of admirers?'

Georgina sighed. She'd been out in society for three years after making a rather late debut at the age of eighteen and ever since she'd been followed around by a persistent group of men. Every ball, every evening at the opera, she would find herself with too many glasses of lemonade, too many offers of an escort, too many eager faces ready to do her bidding at the snap of her fingers. At first she'd enjoyed the attention—what young woman wouldn't?—but after a few weeks she'd realised why they were quite so attentive.

'Sometimes I think I might marry the next man who

asks just to be rid of them,' she said, surprising herself with her honesty.

Throwing his head back, Mr Robertson laughed, drawing curious looks from the other couples on the terrace.

'It sounds terribly conceited, I know,' Georgina said quickly.

'You think they're after you for your family connections?'

'And my dowry.'

Georgina knew she was pretty enough and her mother had ensured she was tutored in all the things women were supposed to be accomplished in; she could play the piano and sing like a lark, she could organise a household with military precision and she could paint a vase full of flowers with any type of paint, but all of these things were just little bonuses. The real prize was being married to the daughter of an earl, an earl who was one of the most influential men in England.

'You've turned down marriage proposals?' Mr Robertson asked.

Nodding, Georgina felt the heat rise in her cheeks when she thought of quite how many men she'd turned down. Her father hadn't minded, not at first, but she knew soon his patience would wear out. The next well-connected, titled gentleman who asked for her hand in marriage would be pushed upon her whether she liked him or not.

'I should be getting back,' she said, taking a step towards the glass doors.

A hand on her arm stopped her instantly. It was warm and firm and made Georgina want to throw caution to the wind.

'Surely a couple more minutes couldn't hurt,' Mr Robertson suggested. 'Or will your father be looking for you?'

'My father?' Georgina asked, frowning.

'You said your mother was home in bed…'

'My father never attends these sorts of events. I came with a friend and her mother.'

There was a flash of something in Mr Robertson's eyes. For an instant it looked like disappointment, but whatever it was the look was gone quickly and replaced by the relaxed amusement Georgina was already beginning to associate with her companion.

'Then there really is no reason we shouldn't tarry a little longer.'

'You forget my reputation, Mr Robertson. If I am not back in the ballroom within the next couple of minutes, all fashion of rumours will begin to spread.'

'I find rumours are best ignored.'

'But some of us are unable to ignore them. A young woman is only worth as much as her reputation. It has been lovely talking to you, Mr Robertson, but I must return to the ball.'

With a small bow he offered her his arm and led her back towards the glass doors. As they stepped inside Georgina felt the collective stare of the guests upon her. It had been foolish allowing Mr Robertson to lead her outside in the first place, foolish to want a break from the monotony of a ball she felt as though she'd attended a thousand times. Now there would be whispers, nothing *too* malicious, she was the daughter of an earl after all, but whispers all the same.

'They're striking up for a waltz,' Mr Robertson said, his lips surprisingly close to her ear.

'I think I'm meant to be dancing with Mr Wilcox,' Georgina said, glancing around the room to see if she could spot her next companion.

'Dance with me.'

She laughed, thinking he was joking, but the expression on his face told her he wasn't. It was tempting, oh, so tempting. Just the thought of being held close by his strong arms, being smiled down upon with those lips that never seemed to stop smiling, but Georgina knew she had to have more willpower than that.

'I cannot disappoint Mr Wilcox,' she said, pulling away.

'Even though you want to?'

Before she could stop him, Mr Robertson had pulled her into his arms and manoeuvred them into a free spot on the dance floor among the other couples getting ready to dance the waltz. Out of the corner of her eye she spotted Mr Wilcox striding towards them, stopping as he saw Georgina in the arms of another man, taking her first steps as the music began.

'What do you think you're doing?' Georgina hissed.

'Dancing with the most beautiful woman in the room.'

'I told you I was engaged for this dance. With someone else.'

Mr Robertson shrugged, managing to complete the movement and continue to hold her in the correct position without missing a step.

'I wanted to dance with you, Lady Georgina, and I find not much is achieved in this world if you are content to stand back and wait your turn.' Normally she would shy away from a man with quite so much self-assurance, but it suited the man in front of her and she found herself pulled in by his easy manner and strong arms in equal measure.

He was a good dancer, certainly not a natural, but managed to twirl her round with a practised ease. She wondered how a proficiency at dancing a waltz fitted in to any of the rumours about his origins, but then as he gripped her a little tighter all thoughts of corsairs and French spies left her mind.

'You're a good dancer,' he said as he executed a turn, taking the opportunity to pull her in another inch closer.

'I'm an adequate dancer,' she corrected. It was true, she could remember the steps, seldom stomped on her partner's toes and was able to keep a conversation going throughout the less energetic dances, but she would never be one of *those* debutantes. The ones who sailed across the dance floor with barely any effort and looked as though they were skating across ice, their movements so smooth.

'You're a difficult woman to compliment,' he murmured, silencing her protest with a stern look. 'Not because it is difficult to find things to compliment you on, but you do argue back rather a lot.'

'Not normally,' Georgina said under her breath. Normally she accepted compliments with a small smile and a demure downcasting of her eyes. Her many suitors often extolled the beauty of her hair, her eyes, the curve of her mouth, and Georgina found it all rather ridiculous, but normally it was easier just to accept the compliment rather than get into a discussion about why her eyes weren't like two shimmering emeralds.

'You owe me,' Georgina said, hastily changing the subject.

'I owe you?'

'Now I will have to find a way to make it up to Mr Wilcox for missing his dance.'

'Lucky Mr Wilcox.'

Georgina ignored the provocative remark and pushed on. 'So as my reward I want to know the truth about you.'

'Whether I'm a French spy or an evil criminal?'

'Exactly. Who are you, Mr Robertson?'

He leant in closer, far too close for propriety, but Georgina couldn't bring herself to pull away. All eyes would be on them, and she knew by midday tomorrow her mother would be aware that Georgina had danced a little too closely with an unsuitable gentleman, but still she let his breath tickle her ear.

'If I tell you, that would ruin the intrigue,' he whispered, 'and then you'd have no reason to want to see me again.'

Georgina felt a shiver of anticipation run down her spine. Mr Robertson was hardly a suitable suitor, her parents might not even allow him to come to call on her, but he was refreshingly different. And different was alluring when you'd been courted by most of the eligible bachelors in London and still found them hard to distinguish from one another.

The music stopped and Mr Robertson held on to her for just a moment longer than was proper, then leaving her feeling bereft, pulled away and bowed formally.

'I think someone is trying to get your attention,' he said, indicating into the crowd of guests.

'Lady Yaxley, my chaperon for the evening.'

'No doubt to scold you on your choice of company.'

'It has been a pleasure, Mr Robertson, but now I must take my leave.'

'Until next time, Lady Georgina. I hope it will not be too long an interval.'

Chapter Two

'Georgina, you must be more careful in the company you keep,' Lady Yaxley scolded her as they took a slow walk around the ballroom. 'And running off and abandoning those nice gentlemen like that. Your poor mother would have a seizure if she knew.'

Georgina had to stifle a smile as Caroline peered over her mother's head and rolled her eyes. When Lady Yaxley got started on the subject of propriety and good manners it was best to let her scold until she ran out of steam.

'The rumours about that man, Mr Robertson, you would not believe. It is entirely inappropriate for you to ever speak to him again. Perhaps if you keep your distance now the damage will be minimised.'

'Mama…' Caroline groaned.

'You're no better, young lady. Don't think I didn't noticed you crossing nice Mr Fielding off your dance card. That is unacceptable.'

'His breath is worse than a pile of manure,' Caroline informed Georgina over her mother's head.

'This is no laughing matter. Three seasons you girls have been out and neither one of you married off.'

'Not from lack of proposals on Georgina's part,' Caroline teased.

'Yes, your father has been rather indulgent,' Lady Yaxley said disapprovingly.

Georgina had known the Yaxleys for her entire life. Born just days apart, she and Caroline had been destined to be friends. Their families lived on bordering estates and there were no other titled families for forty miles in each direction. It had been luck that meant they were perfectly suited to one another and from the age of five had been inseparable. Lady Yaxley was more like family than merely her friend's mother, but that did mean Georgina was scolded by the older woman as if she were another errant daughter.

'Mother, isn't that Lord Westcott trying to get your attention?' Caroline said, nodding to the other side of the ballroom.

Watching in amazement, Georgina smiled as her friend caught the Baron's eye and raised a hand in greeting, directing her mother's gaze just as the Baron returned the gesture, making it seem as though he was the one who initiated the contact.

'I need a trip to the retiring room,' Georgina said quickly, to save them from having to talk to Lord Westcott. 'Caroline, will you help me straighten out my dress?'

Lady Yaxley gave them a suspicious glance, but nodded for the young women to take their leave.

'Now tell me,' Caroline said, linking her arm through Georgina's. 'Tell me everything about Mr Robertson.'

They made their way through the ballroom and out of the double doors at the end, keeping up the pretence of heading for the retiring room, knowing Lady Yaxley's eyes would be on them until they were out of sight.

'There's nothing much to tell,' Georgina said with a shrug, realising it was the truth. Although she'd spent at least twenty minutes in the man's company she didn't really know any more about him than anyone else in the ballroom. 'Don't look at me like that. I'm not being coy.'

'You went outside with him,' Caroline declared. 'You never go outside with anyone.'

Paranoid about being caught in a compromising situation with a man she didn't want to marry, Georgina had a rule about not being alone with a gentleman, ever.

'We weren't alone,' she mumbled. 'There were plenty of other couples taking the air.'

'I've known you far too long, Georgina Fairfax. Don't play coy.'

'He was very forward,' Georgina said, trying her best to sound disapproving rather than impressed. She didn't want to be a stereotypical empty-headed young woman who was swept away by the first man to break with convention.

'Did he try to kiss you?'

'No.' He hadn't tried to kiss her, and Georgina realised she felt a little disappointed. He *had* looped an arm around her to pull her into the waltz and then at the end of the dance held on to her for just a few seconds longer than was strictly necessary, but Georgina wasn't sure whether that had been deliberate or just a sign that he hadn't spent much of the last few years honing his ball etiquette.

'He hasn't danced with anyone else. Just stood there with his friend, surveying the room in that brooding fashion.'

'You sound smitten,' Georgina said suspiciously.

Her friend sighed. 'I'm fed up, Georgie, fed up of the balls and the dinner parties and the operas. Fed up of boring young men pretending to want to get to know me when in reality all they want is an introduction to you.' She waved off Georgina's protests. 'If a dashing French spy or an Australian convict asked me to run away with him, then I probably would. Don't you want adventure? A little excitement?'

Caroline had made her debut at the same time as Georgina, and people had started to whisper that three years was a long time to go without even a single marriage proposal. Georgina knew her friend was more than worthy of the bachelors of the *ton* and, with a substantial dowry and her family connections, there really should have been at least one proposal. Some times Georgina wondered if Caroline deliberately discouraged any proposals to allow her to remain free and unmarried a little longer, but mostly dismissed the idea. They'd been raised to be wives and mothers—even Caroline wasn't so rebellious to actually *want* to be an old maid.

Still, Georgina could see the appeal of being left alone to live the life you wanted, with no husband to dictate what you could and couldn't do. Far too often she found herself daydreaming about a life where she got to make her own decisions, from the small things about where to reside to the bigger things such as leaving everything behind to travel the world. It was a dream that was so far-fetched Georgina knew it could never happen, but in quieter moments she still found herself thinking of a life where she was her own mistress.

'Indulge me,' Caroline said as they exited the ballroom

and started to make their way through the hall towards the retiring room. 'Tell me every last detail about him.'

'About whom?' A deep voice sounded behind them, making both young women jump.

Even before she turned Georgina knew who it would be. His voice was unmistakable, clear and sharp, but without the refined tones of the hundred other men at the ball who'd attended one of the three most prestigious schools in England.

'Mr Robertson,' Georgina said, turning slowly, 'may I introduce my dear friend Miss Yaxley.'

'A pleasure to meet you, Miss Yaxley.'

'We were just talking about you, Mr Robertson,' Caroline said, and inside Georgina groaned. She loved her friend more than anyone else in the world, but some times she wished Caroline wouldn't blurt out everything that was in her head. 'Although Georgina is being a little reserved.'

'Unlike you,' Georgina muttered under her breath, giving Caroline a dig in the ribs.

Mr Robertson gave her an amused look. 'May I escort you somewhere, ladies?' he asked. 'And perhaps on the way I can answer some of your questions.'

'I am just popping to the retiring room,' Caroline said quietly. 'But, Georgina, why don't you go with Mr Robertson and I will come join you in a moment.'

With her mouth parting in disbelief, Georgina shot a warning look at her friend.

'I'll only be a minute or two,' Caroline said cheerfully, walking away.

Left alone with Mr Robertson, Georgina turned on him suspiciously.

'Were you following me?' she asked.

'Do many men follow you?'

'Not so brazenly,' she muttered, feeling completely set up by Caroline and needing to take her annoyance out on someone.

'I find it pointless to be subtle,' Mr Robertson said, with that confident smile lighting up his face and causing Georgina to lose track of her thoughts for a moment.

'Evidently.'

'You lied to me,' he said, leaning in a little closer. Georgina felt her pulse begin to quicken as his arm brushed innocently against hers.

'No, I didn't.'

'You said a woman should never be alone with a man...' he paused '...yet here we are.'

Quickly Georgina looked around the hallway. Damn him, he was right. They *were* alone, not out of any machinations on her part, but alone all the same. If some particularly nosy matron caught them here in the hall together, then rumours would start to fly. No matter that a few minutes ago there had been more than half-a-dozen people escaping from the heat of the ballroom, milling around the spacious hallway, now it was just she and the mysterious Mr Robertson.

'You should leave,' she said, keeping one eye fixed on the door from the ballroom. 'Before anyone catches us together.'

'Tell me,' he said, not making a single move to depart. 'What would happen if we were found alone out here?'

'My reputation would be ruined and my father would marry me off quickly and quietly to any man that would have me.'

'We can't be having that,' Mr Robertson said, taking her gently but firmly by the arm and pulling her around the corner just as two elderly women exited the ballroom, discussing the musicians as they headed in the same direction Caroline had disappeared in.

Georgina found she was holding her breath, hoping they wouldn't pause and glance in the opposite direction and see her pressed into a corner with an entirely inappropriate gentleman. Only when they were safely out of sight did she realise quite how close she was standing to her companion.

'Safe?' he asked, moving to one side so he could check over her shoulder. He was close, his body barely a few inches from hers, and she could feel the heat of him emanating through the layers of his clothing. It wasn't a contrived closeness, though—in fact, he barely seemed to register her and certainly wasn't moving in to try to touch her or kiss her.

An unfamiliar disappointment started to uncurl inside Georgina. Most men would have used this situation to their advantage and, while normally that irritated her beyond belief, she realised with surprise that she wouldn't have minded Mr Robertson moving in for a kiss. Of course she would have rebuffed him, but the attempt would have been nice.

'We need to leave,' Georgina said, pulling herself together. 'Separately.'

He looked at her then, a gaze that seemed to take in every inch of her body, and she fancied she saw something change in how he was standing.

'As you command, my lady,' he said, executing a mock bow. 'But only if you grant me one favour.'

With her heart pounding in her chest Georgina nodded, wondering when she had reverted back to a giddy eighteen-year-old.

'Allow me to call on you tomorrow.'

She'd expected him to ask for a kiss and had been prepared to offer him her hand. Momentarily thrown, she found herself nodding before she'd thought through the request.

'Then I will take my leave a happy man,' he said, catching her hand in his own and planting a kiss just below her knuckles.

With a quick glance to ensure they were still alone Mr Robertson walked away, returning to the ballroom without looking back. Georgina still hadn't moved when Caroline exited the retiring room two minutes later and quickly had to find her composure before her friend guessed something had happened.

Chapter Three

'Mercenary,' Ben Crawford commented as he took a long slurp of tea from the delicate china teacup. In his hands the drinking vessel looked foreign and out of place, but Crawford didn't seem to notice.

'What's mercenary?' Sam asked, rising from his seat to help himself to another portion of smoked haddock from the serving plate on the sideboard. His normal breakfast consisted of porridge and some bread—it seemed a strange luxury to be eating fish for breakfast.

'You are.'

Raising an eyebrow, he waited for his friend to continue, tucking into his breakfast while the silence dragged out.

'I know you want to get your revenge on the old Earl, but compromising his daughter—that's dark, even for you.'

'I'm not…' Sam began to splutter, then paused, swallowed his mouthful, took another sip of tea and continued to talk. 'I'm not planning on compromising the daughter.'

'You went halfway there last night. All I heard the entire evening was how scandalous Lady Georgina was acting over a *ne'er-do-well* stranger.'

'I only danced with the girl.'

'And led her off into dark corners.'

'Hardly.'

'They have different rules here,' Crawford mused, his voice dipping. 'No dragging your intended off over one shoulder and holding a pistol to their head until they capitulate into marrying you.'

'Because that happened all the time in Australia.' Sam paused, leaning back in his chair, rocking on the back two legs in a motion that he knew irritated his friend. 'I'm not going to compromise Lady Georgina,' he said firmly. 'I merely need an acquaintance with her to gain me entry into her house and a little familiarity with the family.'

'So you're not going to punish the father by ruining the daughter?'

'No.'

The thought had briefly crossed his mind, if he was being completely honest, but Sam, despite his past conviction, thought himself as an honourable man. It was one thing to seek vengeance against the man who had ruined his life, quite another to drag an innocent into it all merely because she was his daughter.

He hadn't expected to like her. She was the daughter of the man who'd nearly destroyed him and he'd been fully prepared to have to pretend to enjoy her company to get close to her. But in reality he'd found her interesting and, in truth, perhaps a little too alluring. It was the way she'd looked at him with those intense green eyes, the heat he'd felt deep inside when his arm had looped around her waist, the overwhelming urge to kiss her he'd had to fight as they'd waited in the hall together. All in all he knew he shouldn't like her, but he did, and it made him resolve not to involve her more than was absolutely necessary in his plans for revenge.

'Did you get what you wanted?' Ben asked, reaching out and tugging on his friend's chair until all four feet were on the floor again.

'Lady Georgina agreed to me calling on her today,' Sam said, feeling inordinately pleased with himself.

When he, Ben Crawford and George Fitzgerald had decided to return to England, Sam's main motivation had been revenge. He wanted to look Lord Westchester in the eye and confront the man about how he'd treated him eighteen years previously. Lord Westchester had been solely responsible for Sam's false conviction for theft and his transportation to Australia. Now he would always be an ex-convict; that never left you. Nor did the years of back-breaking labour, the months spent in the filthiest conditions on the hulk ship or the grief of a ten-year-old boy being ripped from his home, his family and everything he held dear. The day he'd been sentenced had been the last day he'd ever seen his family. Meanwhile the Earl had been living his life of luxury and probably hadn't given a second thought to the young boy he'd handed over to the magistrate all those years ago.

'And you're hoping the Earl is at home?' Ben asked.

Nodding, Sam swung back on his chair again, balancing perfectly until he heard footfalls behind him.

'You boys are up early,' Lady Winston said as she entered the dining room.

They'd returned from the ball in the small hours of the morning, but the years of getting up before the dawn to work on the vast Australian farms meant neither Sam nor

Crawford were in the habit of sleeping past seven o'clock and even that was a rare luxury.

'Good morning, Lady Winston,' Sam said, standing as the older woman waved a hand for both men to desist with the formalities.

'Aunt Tabitha,' she insisted, not for the first time.

'Good morning Aunt Tabitha,' Crawford said, placing a kiss on her cheek before returning to his seat.

'George warned me about your charm,' Aunt Tabitha scolded and Sam had to suppress a smile. Crawford was irresistible to the ladies, whatever their age. He had that easy-going confidence that meant they just seemed to fall into his arms.

'Now, have you boys been well looked after this morning?'

Nodding in unison, Sam wondered why he felt like a young lad again rather than a successful landowner of nearly thirty. Aunt Tabitha was no relation to him or Ben, but she treated them in the same way she did George, her nephew. The three men were like brothers, despite their different starts in life, but not many people saw fit to treat them that way. George Fitzgerald was a wealthy landowner, but his father had started life as the second son of an impoverished baron. To many people that title was important and they couldn't understand why a man of good family, like Fitzgerald, would associate with two ex-convicts, however rich and successful they might be now.

Aunt Tabitha, however, accepted their adopted fraternity and treated all three men equally, albeit like errant youths.

'Did I hear you're going to call on the lovely Lady Georgina today?' Lady Winston asked.

'Yes, I thought I'd pop around after breakfast.'

'My dear boy, one does not just *pop around* and especially not after breakfast.'

Sam grimaced. Of course there would be some long-winded social convention for paying a call on a young lady. There was for everything else after all.

'Enlighten me, Aunt Tabitha.'

'First, the proper hour to pay a call is some time after eleven, but definitely before three.'

Sam glanced at the clock at one end of the room. It was a little after eight in the morning. Waiting so long seemed a waste, but he supposed not the biggest inconvenience.

'Then when you arrive at the house you must present a calling card to the butler, who will enquire as to whether the young lady is at home.'

'Of course she'll be home. She said she would,' Sam growled, finding the whole thing a little ridiculous. Out of the corner of his eye he saw Crawford suppressing a laugh and shot him a warning glare.

'Oh, she'll probably be at home, but she might not want to receive you. If that's the case, the butler will inform you that Lady Georgina is not at home to visitors.'

'She'll snub me?'

'She might have had chance to consider the merits of your acquaintance,' Aunt Tabitha said, patting him on the hand. 'If she does accept your call, you will be shown into the drawing room, or another such receiving room where Lady Georgina will be accompanied by her mother. Twenty minutes of idle chit-chat later and you will be expected to depart.'

'Sounds like a thrilling afternoon,' Crawford said, slapping him on the back.

'And her father?' Sam asked.

'Ah, yes, the Earl. You probably won't see him, although if you are an honoured guest he might make a brief appearance.'

He was going to go through all of the palaver of trying to secure an audience with Lady Georgina and might not even catch a glimpse of the Earl for his efforts. Taking a deep breath, he calmed himself. Today was only the beginning of their second week in London, he had to remind himself, and already he'd made the acquaintance of Lord Westchester's daughter. He had time to nurture the relationship, time to orchestrate a meeting with the Earl, time to initiate the first step in his plans for revenge. If he was going to get close to the Earl the first thing Sam needed to do was check the older man did not remember him. Sam knew he'd transformed from gangly child into a well-built man since the Earl last laid eyes on him, but some people surprised you with their memories. Once he was sure the Earl did not know his true identity he could start on the next step of his plan.

'Why exactly are you so interested in Lord Westchester?' Lady Winston asked, her face shrewd and her eyes narrowed.

'It's probably best you don't know,' Sam said, trying to make light of the situation with a grin.

'You're probably right,' Lady Winston said with a sigh. 'If you're up to no good, the fewer people know about it the better.'

He *was* up to no good, but with good reason. Eighteen years ago Sam's mother had been an assistant cook in the Earl's household and on occasion took Sam to work with her to help with the odd jobs around the place. He had been accused of stealing Lady Westchester's emeralds, and although there was no real evidence against him the Earl had used his influence to ensure Sam was convicted and sentenced to be transported to Australia. Soon after he'd started his sentence in one of the filthy hulk ships his mother and sisters had been struck down with a winter fever, meaning Sam not only lost his childhood and life in England, but also the chance to ever see his family again.

The Earl had become the focus of his anger over the years, especially as Sam was convinced he'd been framed by the older man, even though he wasn't entirely sure why. Now he was back in England with the express purpose of exacting revenge and enacting a plan he'd been building for the past eighteen years.

'If I have three hours before I may call on Lady Georgina, I think I will go out for a ride.'

Being newly arrived from Australia, none of the men had access to a horse and Lady Winston only kept enough to pull her ornate carriage. However, when she'd received word of their imminent arrival she'd arranged for them to hire a horse each for the couple of months they were planning on spending in London, declaring, *'No gentleman should be without a horse.'* And no doubt cackling at her loose use of the word *gentleman*.

'Don't forget to change into your finest riding garb,' Lady Winston called after him as he left the dining room.

Grumbling at the ridiculous way the English seemed to have a different outfit for each activity within the space of the day, he none the less changed into a pair of buckskin breeches, a long jacket and a pair of high riding boots. Although he had the strong urge to not conform with society, he didn't want to stand out too much before he'd achieved his aim and got close to the Earl.

As he began to climb the stairs to his grand bedroom he found himself thinking of Lady Georgina. She should be nothing more than a necessary step in his plan for revenge, a way to get close to the Earl, but numerous times in the past twelve hours he'd found his thoughts slipping to the curve of her smile, the way her eyes had glimmered in the half-light on the terrace and the beautiful curves of her body. It would be no hardship to spend more time with her, but he had to keep reminding himself to focus. Eighteen years he'd waited for this moment—he couldn't allow himself to be distracted by a woman, even if she was the first woman to hold his interest for a very long time.

With a furtive glance over her shoulder Georgina slipped out the back door and into the yard where Richards, the young groom, was waiting for her. She shouldn't be out at such an hour, especially after such a late night, but always after a ball she found it impossible to sleep. The music was still ringing in her ears, the sips of champagne still fizzing in her blood and the lights and bright flashes of opulent fabrics filled her mind every time she closed her eyes.

Her mother would no doubt scold her later for not trying to get at least get a few hours of sleep before the first of the visitors came calling. At least she'd stopped reprimanding Richards for accompanying Georgina on her early morning rides, acknowledging the young groom couldn't do anything to stop the headstrong Georgina and was only accompanying her out of concern for her safety.

With practised ease Georgina pulled herself up into the saddle, preferring to test her own strength and agility rather than rely on a boost from the groom. It was another thing her mother scolded her for, chastising her for being unladylike, but Georgina reasoned you never knew when you would be stuck out on your own somewhere with no man to give you a boost. Being able to mount a horse alone would be a very useful skill.

Secretly she dreamed of adventures where she might go riding off into the wilderness with no groom, no entourage to accompany her. It was an impossible dream, but one she still allowed herself to harbour none the less.

'Where would you like to go this morning, my lady?'

'Hyde Park, Richards. We can give the horses a little exercise that way.'

She saw the young groom suppress a groan and had to hide a smile. They would head towards Rotten Row. Normally the popular riding spot was busy with the cream of society riding out for pleasure, dressed in their finest and eager to be seen. At this time in the morning, however, there would be a few other dedicated riders, but mostly grooms exercising their masters' horses. By mid-morning there was an unwritten rule that you travelled down Rotten Row no faster than a sedate trot, but at eight in the morning no one really cared and often a more adventurous rider would be seen streaking past at a momentous gallop.

As always she took the lead, expertly guiding her horse through the streets until they reached the entrance of the park. Only once they were inside, riding over the familiar paths, did Georgina allow herself to relax. Luckily not many of her suitors had found out about her love of early morning rides through the park. If they did, no doubt she would be inundated with *chance* meetings and another of her little pleasures would be eaten into by the men who were only pretending to be interested in what she said.

'Please don't go too far ahead, my lady,' Richards called from a few feet behind her.

At the moment they were riding close together, but from experience the young groom knew it was only a matter of time before Georgina leant forward and urged Lady Penelope, her beautiful grey mare, into a gallop and left Richards faltering behind.

Nodding in greeting to the few people out and about this early in the morning, Georgina slowly loosened her grip on the reins, signalling to Lady Penelope to start picking up the pace. As they began first to trot and then to canter Georgina threw her head back and marvelled at the feeling of wind through her hair, wishing she could unfasten it and wear it streaming down her back like a medieval princess.

Rotten Row itself was only just under a mile long and to Georgina it felt like a matter of seconds before she was reining in Lady Penelope to navigate the turn at the end. Richards was a couple of hundred feet behind her and even at this distance Georgina could picture his face, screwed up with concentration and effort. Knowing she shouldn't be cruel she allowed her speed to fall to a much more sedate pace, giving the sweating groom a few minutes to catch up.

This end of Rotten Row was quieter, with some of the grooms preferring to stick to the Hyde Park Corner end, spending much of their time talking and catching up on the gossip about their masters rather than exerting the horses. However, as she turned, one lone rider was coming up past Richards.

Immediately she felt her body tense. She recognised him from his posture, the way he held himself. Of course he would be at ease on horseback; the man seemed to do everything naturally. Trying to suppress the bubble of pleasure at the thought of meeting Mr Robertson again, she wondered if he had contrived running into her while out riding. It was unlikely, she kept these early morning rides to herself, and it wasn't as though many ladies in London kept a horse in the city, let alone made a habit of being out riding at such an early hour.

'Lady Georgina,' he said, his voice deep and warm as he slowed to match her pace. Richards was just coming up behind them and she motioned for him to keep his distance, signalling everything was all right.

'Mr Robertson, what a surprise to see you here,' she said drily.

'You think I'm following you?' he asked, a smile forming on his lips, revealing surprisingly white teeth contrasting against his bronzed skin.

'It is rather a coincidence…' she said, even though she'd convinced herself this was nothing more than chance. Or fate. As she looked at him she tried to limit her admiration to the easy way he sat on his horse, his good posture and clearly excellent riding skills, but she found her eyes roaming over his body. It was hard not to notice the sculpted muscles under his riding garb and the tanned skin that spoke of his time under the blazing sun… Quickly she snapped her eyes back to his and tried to focus.

'I suppose I did follow you from the ballroom last night,' he said, 'but even I wouldn't dream of ambushing a young lady while she's out riding for pleasure.'

'And you? Are you out riding for pleasure?' Georgina asked.

Even though she knew very little about Mr Robertson she did know quite a lot about how society worked. A man newly arrived in London, with few family connections, would struggle to easily find a horse to ride. To want to hire one for the Season showed either a deep love of riding or a view that all gentlemen should have access to a mount at any time. Given what she'd seen of Mr Robertson so far it seemed far more likely to be the former than the latter.

'Indeed. Back home I'm in the saddle at least five hours a day. Riding for pleasure isn't quite the same, but it is better than the alternative of not riding at all for months at a time.'

'Back home?' Georgina asked, trying to make her question sound casual.

He regarded her for a moment, and she wondered if he would once again dodge the question about his origins. 'Australia,' he said eventually. 'The Eastern Coast.'

Where they transported convicted criminals.

Telling herself not to be foolish, Georgina found her imagination running away with her. Thoughts of brutal criminals, men in chains, toiling away under a baking sun filled her mind. She'd never even seen a picture of Australia, but in her imagination it had sands the colour of amber and harsh conditions.

She felt her mouth go dry as the unbidden image of Mr Robertson shirtless, toiling away in a chain gang, popped into her head. She'd felt the hard muscles of his chest the night before, muscles made strong by manual labour. Quickly she reached for a question, any question, to distract herself from the image.

'What's it like?' Georgina asked.

Mr Robertson laughed softly. 'Like nothing you could ever imagine.'

She didn't think he was going to say any more, but after a moment he continued.

'It's nothing like England,' he said, 'In any way whatsoever. The people are coarser, no time for these customs or manners that matter so much in London. The land is beautiful, but harsh. I've known many a man go wandering off into the wilderness never to be seen again.'

'That wouldn't happen in Surrey or Sussex,' Georgina murmured.

'But despite all the trials it throws at you there's something rather enchanting about it. I've never seen such blue sea or golden sands. Or such vast expanses of land where there's not a single sign of a settlement.' He was staring off into the distance as if remembering fondly. 'I suppose that's how you feel about your home, wherever it may be.'

'You were born there?' Georgina asked.

He looked up abruptly, his eyes narrowing slightly. 'No,' he said brusquely.

They rode in silence, side by side, for a few moments, Mr Robertson clearly still deep in thought, reminiscing about the land he seemed to both love and fear a little.

'You were born in Hampshire,' he said after a few minutes.

'You've been enquiring about me?'

Shrugging, a gesture not normally seen among the men of the *ton*, he grinned. 'I'm residing with Lady Winston. She seems to know everything about everyone.'

'That's how it is,' Georgina said, almost glumly. There was no mystery among the *ton*. Those whom her mother deemed to be suitable friends or companions for Georgina numbered very few and her social circle was small. The wealthiest members of society, those with the oldest family names and largest estates, only socialised with people of a similar position, meaning even if you didn't like someone very much you ended up spending rather a lot of time with them.

'Are you related to her?' Georgina asked as they neared Hyde Park Corner, turning their horses for another lap of Rotten Row.

'Not exactly...' He paused. 'I'm in England with two good friends, Mr Sam Crawford and Mr George Fitzgerald. Fitzgerald is Lady Winston's nephew.'

It was a strange way of putting it, *not exactly*, but she supposed some people had friendships that were as close as family ties. It might be that he considered these two men his brothers and as an extension Lady Winston as a relative as well. In a way it was only like her considering Caroline a sister.

Georgina was about to open her mouth to ask another question, when she heard a shout in the distance. She saw Mr Robertson turn his head and focus in on the cry, and followed the direction of his gaze to do the same.

Hurtling towards them, although a good few hundred feet away, was a riderless horse. The groom who had been exercising the spirited animal had been thrown to the ground and was now struggling to rise. The horse seemed petrified of something, nostrils flaring and head thrashing from side to side, and as they watched, it showed no signs of slowing.

'Stay to one side,' Mr Robertson ordered, gripping her horse's bridle and guiding her next to the fence. Here she was in very little danger, a good few feet away from the main path, but Georgina knew better than to move at all. She had a great respect for horses, knew the damage they could do by throwing a rider, or worse stampeding.

As she watched Mr Robertson narrowed his eyes as if trying to work out something, then urged his horse forward into a canter, heading away from her and the runaway beast. At first she wondered if he was fleeing, but quickly dismissed the idea. Of the little she knew of the mysterious Australian, she could tell he wasn't one to shy away from a little danger.

The runaway horse was gaining on him and Georgina watched as slowly he picked up the pace, so that by the time the riderless horse was level with him he was travelling more or less at the same speed. They were running out of path and if he didn't do something soon the horse would escape into the rest of Hyde Park where it could injure an unsuspecting person out for a morning stroll, or even worse dart onto the street, causing an accident.

Just as she thought there was no hope she saw Mr Robertson lean across and take the horse's bridle, then in one swift manoeuvre he leapt off his horse's back and onto the runaway animal's. The horse bucked, but after a few seconds seemed to settle and within half a minute was wheeling round in a gentle trot.

As Georgina watched Mr Robertson dismounted, caught his own horse and began leading both animals back up towards her and the amazed groom. She could see him muttering soothing words, all the time working to keep the animals calm.

'Thank you,' the groom said, his cheeks red with embarrassment at having to be saved in such a fashion.

'Spirited beast,' Mr Robertson said, almost admiringly, handing the reins back over.

'Where did you learn to do that?' Georgina asked when they were once again alone, although receiving curious looks from all the other grooms out exercising their master's horses.

'It's what I do,' he said with a shrug. 'I own the largest stud in Australia.' He grimaced. 'More or less the only stud in Australia.'

'You breed horses?'

'Breed them, raise them, train them and sell them.'

Not a life of crime, then. Georgina sighed—he was probably very wealthy, although she wasn't sure how the income of Australian landowners compared with English ones. Not that it would matter to her parents. They were destined to disapprove of him immediately. He was *new money*, someone who had raised themselves up and made their fortune through hard work. Although some might think it admirable working to make their legacy, her parents certainly did not agree with that opinion. To them the only people who mattered were those who had been born into money, preferably a very long line of it.

With a glance sideways she wondered if this was why she felt an irresistible pull whenever she thought about Mr Robertson. He was handsome in a rugged way, certainly had a good physique with broad shoulders and hard muscles in all the right places, but Georgina thought it was more than a physical attraction. She knew some young women flirted with and pursued the *wrong sort* of men, exactly because their parents wouldn't approve of them. She'd never thought herself to be that rebellious, or that shallow, but here she was wondering how she could spend more time with Mr Robertson, even when she knew nothing could ever happen between them.

'I should be getting home,' Georgina said, suddenly feeling a little uncomfortable. If she had any sense she would break off their connection immediately and resolve never to see this man again.

'Would you like me to escort you?'

'No,' she said quickly, far too quickly, earning herself an amused grin from Mr Robertson. 'Thank you, but, no,' she said, forcing the words to come out at a more normal speed.

'But you will allow me to call on you later, as we agreed?'

She should say no. Find some excuse, but silently she nodded.

'And you will accept my call?'

It was custom for callers to be screened before being admitted to the house and Georgina had on occasion informed their butler to tell the caller she was out. She hated doing it, though, hated to think someone had made the effort to visit and she wouldn't deign to see them.

'I will,' she said.

'Until later, Lady Georgina.'

'Goodbye, Mr Robertson.'

Chapter Four

With practised discretion Georgina stifled a yawn. The poem Mr Wilcox was reading must have been three pages long and they were still on the first page. It wasn't good and it wasn't entertaining, and really she was trying not to listen to it out of fear she might laugh. And that would be rude. Mr Wilcox was a nice enough young man, persistent in his courtship despite not receiving any signs of encouragement from Georgina, and she really didn't want to hurt his feelings, but the poem was truly terrible.

If I could liken your skin,
To the creamy plaster of a fountain.
I would liken your lips
To the red rose that grows beside it.

She wasn't even sure if fountains were made from plaster. All the ones she could think of were stone.

'Mr Robertson to see Lady Georgina,' the butler announced, directing his words towards Lady Westchester, who glanced enquiringly at Georgina.

'I made his acquaintance at the ball last night,' she said, trying not to meet her mother's eye. 'He is related to Lady Winston,' she fibbed.

'Show him in.'

Georgina studied the needlework in her hands, trying to compose herself for the minutes ahead. Her mother would immediately disapprove of Mr Robertson, that much she was sure, even without knowing about his questionable background. He was too different to the other men they socialised with for her mother not to notice.

'Lady Georgina,' Mr Robertson said, bowing in her direction as he entered the room.

'My mother, Lady Westchester.'

Another bow. 'Lady Westchester.'

'And I think you met Mr Wilcox last night.'

Mr Wilcox certainly remembered Mr Robertson—his eyes narrowed and his lips trembled a little in indignation. Too late Georgina remembered it was Mr Wilcox who'd lost out on the promised dance when Mr Robertson had whisked her on to the dance floor.

Once everyone was seated Lady Westchester fixed Mr Robertson with a piercing stare.

'I do not know you, Mr Robertson. Who are your people?'

Georgina felt like burying her head in her hands. Normally her mother waited for at least a few seconds before the inquisition began.

'My people?'

'Your family? From where do you hail?'

'I was born and raised in Hampshire, my lady.'

Georgina frowned, wondering why Sam hadn't mentioned it when they had discussed her childhood before. 'Hampshire, how delightful, that is where our primary estate is situated. Perhaps we know your family.'

'I doubt it, Lady Westchester,' Mr Robertson said. 'My parents died when I was young and I was fortunate enough to be taken in by a kind and wealthy benefactor. I have not set foot in Hampshire for many years.'

'How unfortunate.'

'Shall I continue with my poem?' Mr Wilcox asked.

Georgina had quite forgotten he was in the room. She shot a glance at Mr Robertson, who had settled back into an armchair. If he felt at all uncomfortable or out of his depth he wasn't showing it.

'Please continue,' Georgina said, forcing a smile on her face.

'Your eyes compare to the starry sky—'

'Lady Westchester, there is an urgent note from Lady Yaxley,' the butler interrupted.

Georgina watched as her mother weighed up the situation. She could hardly ignore an urgent note from her dearest friend, but equally she was responsible for Georgina's reputation. She held out her hand for the note, read it quickly, then stood.

'I shall be back within a few minutes,' she said, leaving the room quickly.

'I brought you a gift,' Mr Robertson said, rising immediately and moving to take up a position next to Georgina on the sofa.

'I say,' Mr Wilcox said, 'I was just reading Lady Georgina a poem.'

Mr Robertson raised an eyebrow, but to his credit his lips didn't even twitch into a smile.

'I find poetry to be a quite personal, intimate thing,' he said. 'Perhaps it is better saved for when it is just the two of you. I wouldn't want to kill the mood and ruin your poem.'

Mr Wilcox opened his mouth to protest, then seemed to consider what the other man had said.

'Well, I suppose you're right,' he mumbled.

'Perhaps you could even make a copy for Lady Georgina, something she can keep and look at in her own time.'

'That's a rather good idea,' Mr Wilcox said, looking down at his handwritten poem. 'I'll get to work on it this afternoon, Lady Georgina.'

'Thank you, Mr Wilcox.'

'It's only something small,' Mr Robertson said, reaching into his pocket and taking out a handkerchief. Georgina watched with mounting anticipation as he unfolded the square of material and reached inside. 'It's a flower from the tea-tree plant.'

Pressed and perfect, it had whitish-pink petals and a vibrant pink centre and was by far one of the most beautiful flowers she'd ever set eyes on.

'They're everywhere in Australia,' he said. 'All different varieties and colours.'

'You brought it all the way over here?'

'By accident,' he admitted. 'So many things are undocumented in Australia. My friend, George Fairfax, is keen on cataloguing wild plants and animals, so when I'm out and about I pick anything interesting for him to have a look at.'

'And this one found its way to England.'

'I must have left it in a pocket.'

Georgina was no stranger to gifts from her suitors. Many

of the men came armed with huge bunches of flowers, or expensive delicacies, sometimes even intimate items such as a new pair of silk gloves, but most were extravagant, aimed at showing their wealth and status. This was a much more thoughtful gift, a little insight into a world Georgina would never know.

'I love it, thank you,' she said, looking up into his eyes. They were startlingly blue, a vibrant dash of colour in his tanned face. For a moment she forgot Mr Wilcox was in the room with them, so mesmerised was she by the man in front of her. She felt a hot flush take over her body as she imagined him wrapping those strong arms around her and not for the first time she felt her eyes flicker to the crisp white of his shirt, imagining once more what his body looked like underneath.

'I'm sure your mother will be back shortly,' Mr Wilcox said, with a polite little cough. He looked pointedly at the position Georgina and Mr Robertson were in on the sofa, far too close for propriety, and hurriedly Georgina moved away. She felt hot and bothered. Mr Robertson only had to look at her and she felt her pulse quicken, and Georgina didn't like not being in control of her own body.

'I hope whatever called your mother away is nothing serious,' Mr Robertson said, not acknowledging Mr Wilcox's pointed stare. 'Is your father at home?'

It was a nonchalant enquiry, slightly too casual, and immediately it sparked Georgina's interest. Men often wanted to see her father to curry favour with one of the most influential men in England, or, on the more worrying occasions, to ask for her hand in marriage, but she hadn't expected Mr Robertson to want either of those things. Perhaps she had misjudged him, perhaps he was looking for a boost up the social ladder and was hoping an acquaintanceship with her, and by extension her family, would help him on his way.

'Father rarely comes to London these days,' Georgina said. 'He prefers to stay in the country, unless his commitments demand his presence in the city.'

She watched Mr Robertson's face intently, but could see no hint of disappointment. Either he was a talented liar, or he had only been enquiring about her father for politeness' sake.

'He remains in Hampshire?'

'Yes, for the foreseeable future at least. He will come up once the Season is properly underway I'm sure, to attend to his political commitments, but he doesn't like to arrive too prematurely.'

Lady Westchester hurried back into the room, noting Mr Robertson's new position on the sofa with a frown, but given there was a respectable distance between him and Georgina there was nothing she could say.

'What are your plans while you are in London, Mr Robertson?' Lady Westchester asked.

Georgina nearly rolled her eyes at her mother's abruptness. She might as well have asked if Mr Robertson had come to the capital to search for a wife. No doubt her mother would soon begin hinting at the perfect pedigree they expected in any suitor for Georgina's hand.

'A little business,' Mr Robertson said, seemingly unfazed by Lady Westchester. To stay calm and collected in the face of her mother's unwelcoming demeanour was not an easy feat and Georgina felt her admiration grow for the man. 'I also wish to reconnect with some people from my past. Having been out of the country for so long I find myself eager to be reacquainted with those I have been thinking about over the years.'

'Out of the country?' Lady Westchester's tone was mild, but Georgina had to suppress a groan. It was entirely the wrong thing to say. Her mother didn't trust foreigners and she included anyone who chose to spend any time away from England in that category, unless for some necessary and noble purpose in her eyes, such as fighting in a war.

'The benefactor I mentioned lived in Australia. He passed away recently, so it seemed like the right time to return to England.'

'Australia,' her mother gasped.

'Mother,' Georgina murmured, glancing at Mr Robertson, before realising that he looked more amused than offended.

'It's a beautiful country,' he said, 'You should visit one day.'

'Mama is not keen on foreign travel,' Georgina said quietly. For her part she'd always dreamed about seeing the world. It was an abstract dream for a woman of her class and upbringing. If she was lucky she might find herself honeymooning around Europe, but that would be the extent of her travels. Well brought-up young ladies did not go any farther afield than Italy. Despite that Georgina had always paused on the pages of books with pictures of exotic locations, places like Egypt and India, or the wilds of Africa.

'I understand,' Mr Robertson said. 'It isn't for everyone.'

He glanced at her then, as if seeing whether Georgina shared her mother's view on travel. She felt her heart beat a little harder in her chest and had to concentrate to stop her face betraying her emotions. It wouldn't do to let her mother even glimpse the slight fascination she had for this man. Georgina knew it was just because Mr Robertson was different and perhaps because of those dazzling blue eyes and rather captivating smile, but she couldn't help wanting to get closer to him, to learn more about him. Of course she knew that could never happen; the differences in their stations in life meant they couldn't even easily become friends. Nevertheless she hoped she would see Mr Robertson again.

'I must take my leave,' he said, standing. 'Thank you for receiving me, Lady Westchester, Lady Georgina. I do hope we see each other soon.'

He'd behaved perfectly, ensuring he did not overstay his welcome, and despite her mother's obvious reservations about the man Georgina did not think she could complain about his behaviour, just his origins.

'You mentioned the Hamiltons' music evening,' Georgina said smoothly. 'Perhaps we shall see one another there.'

It was bold, far too bold, but she wasn't quite ready to say goodbye to Mr Robertson yet. She wanted to hear more about Australia, hear more about his background, so she'd decided to drop a hint as to where she'd be later in the week and see if he took up the invitation.

Chapter Five

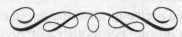

'Drowning your sorrows?' George Fitzgerald asked as he clapped Sam on the back, flopping down into the free seat beside him. 'Did the beauteous Lady Georgina turn you away?'

'Of course not.'

'Difficult types, these daughters of the nobility.'

'She didn't turn me away.'

'Why the long face then?'

'The Earl is in Hampshire and there's not much chance of him making an appearance any time soon.'

'Ah. I see.' Fitzgerald drummed his fingers on the table before motioning to one of the serving girls for two more jugs of ale. 'I take it you're not giving up.'

'No.' Giving up was the furthest thing from his mind. 'I'll have to go to Hampshire, that's all.'

He'd hoped to avoid returning to his home county. There were painful memories back in his childhood home that he didn't wish to confront. The last time he'd been there, his mother and two younger sisters had been alive. Now he had no close relatives left in Hampshire, but the memories of his childhood and all he'd lost were based there and he had planned on leaving those ghosts to sleep.

'You'll struggle to even catch a glimpse of the Earl if you just turn up. You need an invitation.'

'To go to Hampshire?'

'To infiltrate the Earl's estate.'

Sam tapped his fingers on the table and considered for a while. For years he'd sworn one day he would return to England and make Lord Westchester pay for stealing his childhood and ripping him from his family. As a young lad his fantasies of revenge were elaborate and often involved the old Earl falling to his knees, begging Sam for forgiveness. Now, older, and more worldly wise, Sam knew it was unlikely Lord Westchester would even remember the day he carelessly wrongfully accused a young boy of stealing. But he wanted the older man to at least acknowledge the wrong he had done and perhaps suffer in some small way, too.

'These wealthy types often have house parties at their country estates, don't they?' Sam asked, his mind ticking through possibilities.

'Yes,' Fitzgerald said slowly, 'I believe so, but probably not in the depths of winter.'

'Doesn't matter. I'm in no rush.'

'And you'd have to be invited.'

Sam grinned. It would be a challenge. Lady Georgina liked him, that much he was sure of, but in the way you liked a rather exotic animal in a menagerie: interesting to study for a few minutes, but certainly not someone you allowed close. Then there was Lady Georgina's mother. She'd judged him within seconds of their meeting and he knew he hadn't come out favourably. His family were not one of the select few she approved of and as such she would regard him as unsuitable for her daughter to spend any time with.

Feeling the rush of anticipation at the idea of spending more time with Lady Georgina, he quickly tried to dampen the feelings. It didn't matter she was the first woman in a long time to pique his attention, she was not the one for him. He had to focus, not allow himself to get distracted by those soulful green eyes and the sense that there was so much more to Lady Georgina than most of her suitors gave her credit for.

'They might not even host a house party,' Fitzgerald said, but nothing could dampen Sam's enthusiasm.

'I'm sure I can persuade the fair Lady Georgina it would be a splendid idea,' Sam said.

Rolling his eyes, Fitzgerald clapped Sam on the back. 'One thing you've never suffered from is a lack of self-confidence.'

'No point going through this world not believing in yourself. Not many other people will.'

Sam didn't quite believe that sentiment, despite voicing it. He'd been lucky enough to have someone believe there was more to him than his convicted criminal status. George's father, Henry Fitzgerald, had taken both him and Crawford in to his family and given them a chance to build good lives for themselves in Australia. If it wasn't for the older man they would probably both be travelling from farm to farm, selling their services as farmhands like hundreds of other ex-convicts, with no real base, no real purpose. Sam would be eternally grateful his life had taken a different turn.

'Drink up,' Fitzgerald said. 'You don't want to be spotted in such an insalubrious establishment if you want to be accepted by Lady Georgina's crowd.'

He thought it unlikely anyone even acquainted with Lady Georgina would wander into the tavern, but drained the rest of his ale all the same. It looked like he was going to be in London for the foreseeable future and he had a lot to plan if he was going to secure invitations to all the events the Earl's daughter would be attending. A little bribery of Lady Georgina's household staff might smooth the way. At least that way he would know which events the Earl's daughter would be attending.

Giving in, Georgina crossed to the window and peeked out from behind the curtains. Her bedroom looked out over the gardens of Grosvenor Square and often she would stand watching the exhausted nannies and nursemaids chasing their energetic charges along the perfectly kept paths. Today, however, she'd fancied she had seen Mr Robertson out there.

She looked for thirty seconds, peering from her hidden position, before feeling rather stupid and stepping out from behind the curtains.

Of course there was no sign of the enigmatic Mr Robertson. There was absolutely no reason for him to be in her street, especially five hours after he'd paid his call.

'Silly girl,' she murmured to herself. She refused to behave like a lovesick fool.

Forcing herself away from the window, she had just turned when the door opened and Caroline came flouncing into the room.

'What are you doing?' she asked suspiciously.

'Nothing.' Georgina felt her cheeks begin to colour at the lie.

'Then why are you blushing?'

'I was looking out the window,' Georgina said.

'For?'

'For no one. Just looking.'

For once she wished her friend was a little less astute. It was clear Caroline didn't believe her and Georgina watched as she crossed to the window and spent thirty seconds peering out.

'There's no one there,' she said eventually.

'I know. I told you, I was just looking.'

'Hmm.'

'You looked like you had news,' Georgina said, deftly changing the subject.

'I do. I've been asking around, very discreetly of course, and your Mr Robertson *is* from Australia,' Caroline said triumphantly.

'I know.' Georgina didn't correct her friend and inform her that Mr Robertson might have recently sailed from Australia, but was actually originally from Hampshire.

'How do you know? Hardly anyone knows anything about him.'

'He told me himself.'

'You've seen him again? Already?'

'Don't look so pleased,' Georgina groaned. 'He called on me today, that is all.'

She left out their meeting in Hyde Park, knowing Caroline would be utterly fascinated and demand every last detail.

'Anyway, he's not my Mr Robertson.'

Waving a dismissive hand, Caroline flopped down on the bed. 'Tell me everything,' she said dramatically.

'There's nothing to tell. He came to call, Mother was

here, as was Mr Wilcox. We sat and talked for a few minutes, then he left.'

Georgina didn't add that she'd found it hard to banish Mr Robertson from her mind ever since his visit, ever since their encounter the previous night.

'Will you see him again?' Caroline asked.

'I'm sure our paths might cross at some event or another. He is staying with Lady Winston.'

'A relative?'

'No, he's a friend of her nephew.'

'How wonderful,' Caroline said dreamily, throwing herself back on to the bed and staring up at the canopy above.

'He is just another acquaintance.'

'So why were you looking for him out your window?'

'I-I wasn't,' Georgina protested, but knew her stutter gave her away.

Chapter Six

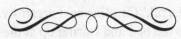

'**W**here's the third one of you?' Lady Winston asked as she elbowed her way through the crowd towards Sam and George.

'He had a prior engagement,' Sam said, although he didn't know that was the truth. Ben Crawford had been acting strangely all week, ever since the ball where they'd first made their entrance into society.

'A woman, no doubt,' Lady Winston cackled. 'He's a good-looking boy.'

'The ladies do love him,' Fitzgerald murmured.

Lady Winston didn't answer and he followed her gaze across the room to where Georgina and her mother had just entered.

'Shoo,' Lady Winston whispered to her nephew.

Suppressing a laugh at Fitzgerald's disgruntled expression, Sam raised an eyebrow at Lady Winston, silently asking her what she was doing.

'Better not to have to introduce anyone else when we get your Lady Georgina over here,' she said. 'Too much distraction.'

'So pleased to be nothing more than an unwanted distraction,' Fitzgerald murmured, but wandered off all the same.

'Lady Westchester,' Lady Winston called, much louder than was proper. A few conversations stopped as heads turned in their direction, but Sam could see her break with etiquette was not a surprise to most of the other guests.

'Lady Winston,' Georgina's mother said as they made their way through the small crowd.

'I believe you have been introduced to Mr Robertson,' Lady Winston said. 'He's a dear friend of my nephew.'

'A pleasure to see you again, Lady Westchester, Lady Georgina,' Sam said, executing a small bow. He was beginning to get to grips with the social etiquette required when out and about among the *ton*. Correct forms of address were to be adhered to at all times, the more polite you were the better and it was unseemly to talk to one person for too long.

In truth, all the bowing and titles seemed bizarre to him. He'd been brought up the son of a clerk and later, when his father had passed away and his mother had resumed her role as a cook, the son of a servant. His mother had ensured he was always polite, but titles and peerages had not been part of his world. Even less so after his conviction. First on the hulk ship, then on the transport ship and once they'd arrived in Australia there was no room for politeness. You pushed and shoved with the rest of the filthy men and women to ensure you got your rations for the day and respect for the guards was hard to summon when they ruled with whips and fists.

When he thought about it he should be much more uncouth than he was. It made him laugh when he remembered back to the dirty young lads he and Crawford had been when George Fitzgerald's father had taken them in. Slowly he'd cleaned them up and taught them not only how to survive in Australia, but also reminded them how to read and write, how to address people respectfully and how to behave like decent members of society. It had taken years, but the older man's patience had meant he and Crawford were slowly transformed from coarse convict lads to young men who could hold their own with people from any level of society.

'Come, sit with me,' Lady Winston said. 'My legs aren't as young as they used to be.'

There was no denying that Lady Winston was a sly old woman. Sam knew there was nothing wrong with her legs, it was just a ploy to help him sit with the lovely Lady Georgina. Once the two Westchester women were seated it was unlikely that they would move throughout the performance.

'I hope you are well, Mr Robertson,' Lady Georgina said as she took her seat next to him.

'Much better for seeing you.'

'Empty flattery does not suit you,' she said, but Sam could see the smile that was trying to break out on her lips. He suddenly wanted very much to see her smile again, to watch as those rosy-pink lips curved upwards and to know it was he who'd made them do so. Unbidden, images of those lips doing much more than just smiling at him began to creep into his mind and he had to use all of his resolve to push them away and focus on the conversation they were having instead.

'It's true. I'm told tonight will be an evening of musical excellence and I need your expertise to help me navigate through it.'

'I'm hardly an expert.'

'Do you play an instrument, Lady Georgina?'

'Of course. I play the piano.'

'And you sing?'

'There aren't many young ladies who don't.'

'And I'm guessing you've been to a few of these musical evenings before.'

'Ten to twenty,' she admitted with a smile.

'Then compared to me you are an expert.'

'They don't have events like this in Australia?' she asked.

Sam smiled. Of course people socialised in Australia—there were a few taverns Sam liked to frequent and he was sure some of the daughters of the wealthier landowners liked to pay visits to one another, but he couldn't imagine the hardened men and women of Australia sitting through a musical recital. It was enough to make him nearly laugh out loud.

'I've never heard of one,' he said.

'Perhaps you could introduce the idea when you return.'

'I'm not sure my reputation could withstand it.'

'Reputation?' Lady Georgina asked.

'Just as it is important here for you to maintain a certain image, it is the same for me back home. I can't imagine trying to gain the respect of any of the landowners if I suggested we sit down and listen to some classical music.'

He'd lose all credibility and be laughed out of the region.

'I can't imagine,' Lady Georgina said with a frown.

Sam had known his life in Australia would be of interest to people here in England, just as they were interested in the exotic animals brought from overseas to the menageries for the public to ogle at. Not many men made it back from Australia and certainly not any who would move in the same circles as Lady Georgina.

'The people are coarser, less refined, even those who own great swathes of land. There is much less of a class system, the divide comes between those who have been transported and are still serving a sentence and those who are free men, able to take what work they choose.' Luckily for him, he thought. In Australia there was no shame in being a self-made man—in fact, coming from a background as a convict and building yourself into a success was what most men strived for. 'Life is harder, there is no question about it, and more basic. Even the wealthiest people live in simple homes and will go out to work every day. There is no idle life.'

'You must find it very strange here,' Lady Georgina said, 'where the men spend their time playing cards and attending their gentlemen's clubs and the women play the piano and go to balls.'

'That's the beauty of visiting somewhere else,' Sam said. 'You get to experience a different life, a different way of doing things.'

Lady Georgina sighed and looked away and Sam wondered if he'd struck a sore spot. In many ways Lady Georgina had it all—wealth, a good family name, every physical comfort she could desire—but what she did not have was freedom. After being locked up and condemned to transportation, Sam knew more than a little about a lack of freedom. Now he could choose to go anywhere in the world, he was his own master. Lady Georgina would never experience that. She was destined to spend her life under the control of another, for now her father, and once she was married, her husband.

Sam started to try to convey that he understood some of that frustration, but his words were lost as a small man entered the room and their hostess for the evening clapped her hands for everyone to fall silent.

'Good evening,' Mrs Hamilton said. 'It is my pleasure to introduce to you Signor Ratavelli, master musician and kind enough to grace our humble little gathering with his presence.'

There was a smattering of polite applause as Signor Ratavelli took a bow, then sat down behind a piano at the front of the room.

With no musical inclination or training even Sam knew from the very first note this man was talented. Normally he had little interest in music—it had not played a major part in his life. There had been no music in his simple but comfortable home in Hampshire and there certainly had been no music in his life after transportation save for the occasional work songs sung by the convicts to try to keep morale up. Nevertheless he felt a little of the soft melody seeping under his skin and found that despite himself he was enjoying it.

Turning to Lady Georgina, he regarded her for a few moments. She was completely entranced, watching the small musician through the gaps in the rows of people sitting in front of them, occasionally having to crane her neck to see.

She looked beautiful like this, her lips slightly parted, her cheeks suffused with colour and her eyes sparkling with interest. Easily he could see why she was considered the catch of the Season, even without her family connections and hefty dowry.

With his head half-turned to look at her he felt eyes burning into him from somewhere behind. Discreetly he turned, trying to keep the movement as subtle as possible, to see a man of about thirty glaring at him. Puzzled, Sam nodded in greeting, unable to help himself despite knowing it would anger his unknown observer further, then turned back to face the front.

No doubt it was one of Lady Georgina's many admirers, upset that he did not get to sit with the object of his affection.

The first half of the musical recital had lasted for nearly forty minutes and Sam surprised himself by enjoying all of it. When the last note died away he clapped along with everyone else, wondering what the men he employed on his farms would say if they could see him now.

'What did you think?' Lady Georgina asked, leaning in towards him a little to be heard over the swell of conversation now the music had stopped.

'I enjoyed it,' Sam said, rising quickly as he saw Lady Georgina's mother glance at her daughter and frown, unable to extricate herself from the brilliant job Lady Winston was doing at keeping her talking. 'Would you care for a drink?'

'That would be lovely. I'll accompany you. I need to move around after forty minutes of sitting still.'

Just as he had hoped. He offered her his arm, glancing quickly back over his shoulder, expecting the man who had been staring at him throughout the performance to be bearing down on them, but finding no one there.

After collecting two glasses of wine, they moved on to the large terrace. The doors from the music room had been thrown open to combat the stuffiness in the room and, despite the cold weather, many of the guests had moved outside for a breath of air.

'You're shivering. We can go back inside,' Sam said as they reached the edge of the terrace.

'No, it's a beautiful night.'

Together they both glanced up at the sky where the night

was clear and a few stars visible along with the brilliant white of the crescent moon.

'I'm sure the skies are much different in Australia.'

Sam thought of the endless expanse of darkness, which on a clear night was lit up with hundreds of stars. When you were out in the wilderness it could feel overwhelming, but beautiful all the same. Again he noted the slightly wistful note in her voice, the dreamy way she looked as she imagined the country he now considered home. If he wasn't very much mistaken, Lady Georgina was an adventurer at heart, trapped by the suffocating conventions of society.

'I notice a difference when I'm at home in Hampshire,' Lady Georgina said. 'The skies are darker, somehow, and the stars brighter.'

She shivered again and quickly Sam shrugged off his jacket and started to place it around her shoulders.

'I couldn't...' she protested.

'You're cold. It's only a jacket.'

Looking around to see if anyone was watching, he saw her run the fabric of the jacket through her fingers as if deciding whether it would be wholly inappropriate to accept the gesture.

'Surely one of your many admirers has lent you his jacket before,' Sam said with a grin.

'I don't ever step outside with anyone,' Lady Georgina said.

Sam raised an eyebrow and eventually she corrected herself.

'I don't *normally* step outside with anyone.'

He felt an unbidden tightening deep inside him and for a second the lights and sounds from the house faded away and it was as if they were the only two left in the garden.

Quickly he regained control of himself. Lady Georgina was pretty, that was true, and she had something that intrigued him, something that made him want to get to know her better, but he had to keep reminding himself that wasn't what he was here for. His purpose was to somehow get close to her father and he had to remember Lady Georgina was part of that mission. Allowing anything more, even too much of a friendship to develop, would only serve to hurt her in the long run.

Still, he felt himself being pulled towards her, towards that captivating smile and the sense that underneath her perfectly honed public persona was a woman with hidden depths just crying to get out. He could see it in the way she asked so many questions about Australia, in the wistful, dreamy expression that filled her face when they discussed how their worlds differed. For a moment he wished he could take her there, show her the country he had come to love so much, but he knew that was impossible. Even the overwhelming desire he had to simply take her hand, to brush his fingers against hers, would be too much. Somehow he had to suppress the attraction he felt for the woman in front of him and focus his mind on the reason he'd returned to England.

'Signor Ratavelli will be starting again in a few minutes,' Lady Georgina said, a slight catch to her voice Sam hadn't heard before. 'Shall we take one more turn about the terrace?'

Offering her his arm, they walked side by side down the length of the terrace. Most of the guests had returned back inside, but a few still lingered, talking quietly in groups and enjoying the fresh, cold air.

At the end of the terrace they paused as Lady Georgina stumbled, gasped softly, then laughed.

'Sorry,' she apologized. 'I have a stone in my shoe, nothing more.'

Without thinking Sam led her a few feet off the terrace and over to an ornate bench no more than ten steps onto the grass. Pressing her to sit, he crouched in front of her and lifted the hem of her dress to reveal a completely impractical shoe. It was all fabric and decoration, with hardly any substance to it. Definitely not a shoe that would survive five minutes in Australia.

Shaking the shoe, he saw a small stone drop out and on to the grass. Before he could stop himself he had placed the shoe on the ground and ran his hand over the bottom of Lady Georgina's stocking. It was an instinctive move, something Sam would do to himself if he got a stone in his shoe, a way to check nothing more would disrupt his comfort, but as soon as his fingers touched the silky material of her stockings Sam knew it was completely inappropriate.

Lady Georgina inhaled sharply, but Sam noticed she didn't pull away. He was frozen in place, too, unable to move his hands off her foot, but also equally incapable of stopping his fingers in their slow backwards and forward motion.

'Lady Georgina,' a loud voice rang out through the crisp night air.

They jumped apart guiltily and Lady Georgina fumbled to put her own shoe back on.

'Take your hands off her.'

A wholly unnecessary command. By time the words had crossed the man's lips Sam was standing at least three feet away. The comment was designed to draw attention from the assembled guests inside the house and it had the desired effect within seconds.

'Are you harmed, Lady Georgina?' the man asked, his voice thick with concern.

'What happened?' This was from their hostess of the evening, eager to install herself in the middle of any gossip-worthy scandal.

'I found this scoundrel out here all alone with Lady Georgina, with his hands all over her.'

'It wasn't anything like that, Mr Hemmingate,' Lady Georgina said with remarkable composure.

Sam risked a glance at her and saw her cheeks suffused with colour, although whether from embarrassment or anger he could not tell.

'I was simply—' he started to say, but was cut off by a sharp jab in the ribs.

'Mr Robertson was simply escorting myself and Lady Georgina for a turn about the garden,' Lady Winston said.

Sam turned to her, trying to hide his incredulity. No one was going to believe that, Lady Winston had arrived outside along with everyone else.

'You were in the ballroom,' Mr Hemmingate said, his voice and manner indignant.

'Are you calling me a liar, Mr Hemmingate?' Lady Winston said, fixing him with a penetrating stare.

'Well, no. But you weren't—'

'Mr Robertson was kind enough to escort an old lady around the garden and we stopped to talk to Lady Georgina for a moment. Nothing scandalous. Nothing to see.'

The assembled guests murmured and glanced from the stuttering Mr Hemmingate to the confident Lady Winston.

'Now, I trust no one here will be nasty enough to spread untruths about what happened this evening,' Lady Winston said, ensuring she caught everyone's eye in turn. 'Good. Nothing I dislike more than unkind words.'

Quickly she gripped hold of Sam's arm, leaning on him more than she needed to, keeping up the pretence of him escorting a frail old woman around the garden.

'Surely no one believes you,' Sam whispered as they entered the music room. Over his shoulder he could see Lady Georgina being hustled inside by her mother. No doubt to sit as far away from Sam as possible.

'I'm a dowager countess,' Lady Winston said with a wicked smile. 'They have to believe me.'

'Thank you.'

Lady Winston turned to regard him as they sat. 'That was foolish, but I put it down to youthful exuberance. Just be careful with the girl. She doesn't have another country to retreat to once all of this is over.'

Good advice, Sam thought grimly. The more he got to know Lady Georgina, the less he wanted to hurt her. It had never been his plan to seek revenge on the father by ruining the daughter, but he hadn't given much thought to a few hurt feelings along the way. Now he was keen not to hurt Lady Georgina in any way, even by association. He would have to tread carefully from now on.

'Not that they'll let you near her again,' Lady Winston said as Signor Ratavelli re-entered the room and took up his place behind the piano.

With a bubble of panic welling up inside him, Sam glanced back over his shoulder to where Lady Georgina and her mother were sitting. Both were studiously avoiding all eye contact with him. A row farther back the interfering Mr Hemmingate was frowning as if displeased with how events had unfolded.

Chapter Seven

Dear Mr Robertson,
Please accept my apologies for the events of last night.
It was, of course, nothing more than an unfortunate
misunderstanding.
* I am sure you will understand that I cannot see*
you again.
Lady Georgina Fairfax

Georgina sat staring at the short letter in front of her for
a full five minutes before sighing with frustration. There
really was nothing more to be said. Quickly she folded the
paper, addressed the front to Mr Robertson and made her
way downstairs to find a footman to organise delivery for
her.

'Georgina,' her mother called from the drawing room
as she passed.

'One moment, Mother.'

Only once she had safely handed the letter over to Brennan, her favourite footman, did she dare enter the drawing room. Georgina had been dreading this moment. Her mother had kept quiet about the previous evening's fiasco during the carriage ride home and throughout an awkward breakfast this morning, but Georgina had known this couldn't last for ever.

'Take a seat, Georgina,' her mother said, indicating the hard sofa at right angles to her own chair. It was more ornamental than made for comfort, but Georgina was feeling too on edge to do anything more than perch anyway.

'Yes, Mother.' She waited, wondering what route her mother would take into her scolding.

'The events of last night have caused irreparable damage to your reputation.'

'Yes, Mother.' There was no point denying it. She had been caught alone with an entirely unsuitable man. With her foot in his hand no less. It was only Lady Winston's interference that had stopped her from being the subject of gossip at every breakfast table in London this morning.

'Mr Robertson is not the sort of man you should be associating with,' Lady Westchester said.

'No, Mother.'

'And you know better than to be found alone with any man in any circumstance. Be that man reputable or not.'

'Yes, Mother.'

'We are fortunate that the party was small and Lady Winston dampened down some of the speculation, but I think we would be foolish to think there is no damage to your reputation.'

'Yes, Mother.'

'Georgina,' her mother said with a sigh, 'both your father and I have been very patient with you. We love you and don't want you to be unhappy.'

Sensing an end had come to this patience, Georgina looked up sharply. She'd always known the day would come when her father's indulgence over her choice of husband would finally run out. She was twenty-one, hardly a young debutante any more, and had been out in society for three years. Suitor after suitor had asked for her hand, or expressed his interest in a less formal fashion, and one after another she had turned them down.

To her father many of them had been adequate matches. Titled men, influential men, wealthy men. Most of them had been perfectly acceptable, too, even Georgina couldn't deny it. There was the odd drunk, or man who had gambled away too much of his family's fortune, but most had nothing really *wrong* with them. And it wasn't as if Georgina was expecting to be swept off her feet. She was realistic, knew good marriages didn't often start with love, but she wanted to feel *something.* An excitement, a tightening, a sense of anticipation when she looked at her husband-to-be. And so far everyone had been rather bland and unimpressive.

She knew her father had been indulgent with her. To most he was abrupt, even unkind, but he'd always harboured a soft spot for his only daughter and she for him. Of course she knew one of the reasons he'd allowed her to turn down quite so many proposals was his own ambitions. He was closely involved in politics, championing an up-and-coming young man who her father hoped would be leader of the Whigs one day soon and Prime Minister after that. If someone truly influential offered for her hand, someone like a duke or an earl, someone who could be counted on to support her father's political ambitions, then she knew no matter what she thought of the man he would be accepted on her behalf.

'I know, Mother,' Georgina said with a sigh. And she probably wouldn't be unhappy. If she married one of her many suitors, she would probably be perfectly content.

'I am going to write to your father,' Lady Westchester said, 'and ask him to come to London. When he arrives I expect he will arrange things from there.'

It wouldn't take much for her father to persuade one of the men who had been so eager to marry her a few months ago to ask her again. A hint about an increase in her already generous dowry and a promise that this time the proposal would be accepted would be more than enough.

'I will obey your and Father's wishes,' Georgina said, feeling something shrivel inside of her.

'It won't be so bad, Georgina,' her mother said more softly, rising from her seat and coming to sit next to her daughter. 'Marriage is what we are born for.'

And marriage was what Georgina had always known her future held. You couldn't be the daughter of a titled man and not expect to be married off sooner or later. She'd known that her entire life and in truth she didn't really mind. Yes, she would rather wait for someone she could imagine spending a lifetime with, but she *did* want to get married one day.

Marriage meant a house of her own, a life of her own, children in the near future. All things she wanted. The dreams of adventure, of seeing some of the world or meeting people outside her very limited social circle, were just that, dreams, nothing more.

'Why don't you have a little think,' Lady Westchester said, patting her daughter on the arm, 'and see if there is anyone suitable we could guide your father towards?'

'I will.'

Georgina felt the tears well in her eyes unexpectedly. She didn't want to disappoint her parents, didn't want to bring scandal or disrepute to the family name. Her parents hadn't asked much of her over the last few years, just that she conduct herself with poise and decorum. Now she had jeopardised her reputation it was time to accept her father's wishes and find a husband.

'Go see Caroline,' her mother urged. 'I'm sure she will be a help with your decision.'

It was a good idea and immediately Georgina felt a little more positive. No doubt Caroline would swiftly cut through the list of suitors, dismissing the unsuitable ones in that matter-of-fact way of hers.

'I've never seen the appeal,' Caroline said as she huddled in closer to Georgina, bringing a welcome increase in body heat.

They were walking arm in arm along the path that abutted the lake, watching the dozens of people braving the freezing temperatures to ice skate on the frozen surface.

'It looks rather fun,' Georgina protested. She'd never ice skated, not even in the seclusion of their Hampshire estate. There were certain things the daughter of an Earl just did not do. It did look to be rather fun, though.

'Slipping and sliding across a thin layer of ice that could give way at any moment, plunging you into the freezing water. No, thank you.'

Georgina gazed at the couples, arm in arm, gliding across the ice. Some were confident and proficient, while others struggled to move, giggling at one another at their attempts.

'I need to get married,' Georgina said as they crossed the blue bridge.

'We all need to get married.'

'Now. Well, at least reasonably soon.'

'What's happened?' Caroline asked, pausing and waiting for Georgina to turn to face her.

Caroline's ignorance on the events of the night before was a good sign at least that the murmurings about her being found in a dubious position with Mr Robertson hadn't spread too far or too fast.

'Something happened last night, didn't it?' Caroline said, her voice full of excitement. 'Tell me everything.'

'There's nothing to tell, not really. It was all a misunderstanding.'

'With the delectable Mr Robertson?'

Georgina felt the blood rush to her cheeks and wished there was a way to stop it. She *hadn't* been doing anything wrong, not really. Perhaps it had been ill advised to step outside with Mr Robertson and no one else, but she hadn't engineered the scene on the bench. Or had any inkling of quite how peculiar she would feel when his fingers caressed the bottom of her foot. It was a foot, for heaven's sake, not anything erotic, but still she'd felt a tingling spread through her whole body.

'I had a stone in my shoe,' she said, 'and Mr Robertson merely led me to a bench so I could sort it out.' She didn't tell Caroline that they'd been found with her stockinged foot in his hands. 'It was Mr Hemmingate who noticed us and he wasn't about to be discreet.'

'Probably hoping to shame you into marrying him,' Caroline said in disgust. She shared Georgina's view on Mr

Hemmingate, who had been persistent in his suit even after Georgina had turned his proposal down a few months ago.

'Mother is writing to Father,' Georgina said, trying to keep her voice positive, 'and she has urged me to consider who I might find acceptable as a husband. Father will then make arrangements.'

'At least no one forced you to get engaged to Mr Robertson there and then,' Caroline murmured.

It was true. Had Lady Winston not stepped in, there would have been the expectation that Mr Robertson at least ask for her hand in marriage, not that he'd probably know that with his strange views on etiquette. For a moment Georgina contemplated a marriage to Mr Robertson. Of course it could never happen, their stations in life were too far apart, and Mr Robertson could not be of use to her father in any shape or form, but still it was an interesting idea.

'Lady Georgina, Miss Yaxley,' a deep voice interrupted.

Georgina's eyes widened and she took an involuntary step back.

'May I introduce my dear friend, Mr George Fitzgerald.'

With her eyes fixed on the man she was meant to be keeping a good distance from, Georgina greeted Mr Fitzgerald.

'Did you get my note, Mr Robertson?' she asked. Perhaps he had been out when it was delivered.

'Indeed. Very sensible proposition.'

She blinked, wondering how to phrase the next question. She couldn't really come out and ask if he were just ignoring her request that he kept his distance, not with Caroline and Mr Fitzgerald there; it would be too blunt, too rude.

'Unfortunately it seems London is a small city. Our paths are bound to cross at some point.'

It was true. Although she hadn't expected it to be quite so soon.

'Quite a coincidence, seeing you again so soon,' she murmured, knowing she couldn't accuse him of following her, but unable to completely ignore her suspicions.

Mr Robertson laid a hand gently on her arm and Georgina frowned as his friend, Mr Fitzgerald, smoothly offered his arm to Caroline and began to stroll away.

'We can't be seen together,' she hissed, glancing around furtively.

'Of course we can. We're properly chaperoned.' He motioned to their friends a few feet ahead of them.

'It doesn't matter.' She swallowed her next words about him already ruining her life. Georgina wasn't prone to dramatics and she wasn't going to let Mr Robertson induce them in her now. 'How did you know where I was going to be?'

'This meeting is purely coincidence,' he said calmly. Too calmly.

'I don't believe you.'

'I thought it was rude to accuse a gentleman of lying,' he said, amusement in his voice.

'It is,' she said bluntly, 'but I find my usual manners have deserted me this afternoon.'

'I wanted to apologise,' Mr Robertson said, placing his free hand over hers where it rested on his arm. Even through her thick winter gloves she could feel the heat and strength coming off him.

She made the mistake of glancing up and being caught in the gaze from his penetrating blue eyes and suddenly she forgot why she was quite so angry. It only took her seconds to recover this time and quickly she looked away. She wasn't some naïve young girl; she could withstand the suggestive gaze of an attractive man.

'Thank you,' she said stiffly.

'I never meant to put you in an awkward situation.'

That much she believed. Out of all the men of her acquaintance, there were certainly a few who would try to lure her away to some secluded spot to compromise her, but Mr Robertson wasn't one of them, she was sure. It had been a simple misunderstanding, a temporary lack of caution on her part as much as his. She shouldn't expect him to understand all the rules of their society being so newly arrived from Australia; it had been her fault as much as his.

What she was annoyed about was his appearance here, after her firm request that they not see each other again. Not for one moment did she believe it was coincidence, although how he had been aware of her movements was a complete mystery.

'My mother has asked my father to come to London,' she said quietly. 'To arrange my marriage.'

That news at least rendered the usually unflappable Mr Robertson speechless for a few seconds.

'Don't worry, not to you,' she said quickly.

'Who?'

Georgina shrugged. That was the painful part. There was no one she wanted to marry, yet in a few weeks she would be a bride. It was entirely unfair, but it was what she had been brought up to expect, to have others make her decisions for her. All her life she'd had to suppress the independent streak she had running through her, to quietly accept that her life was not her own, but sometimes it was almost too difficult. She wanted the freedom to decide whether or not she married, or whether to take a spontaneous trip to an exotic location, or even just to choose not to socialise for a month or two. In short, she wanted the freedom of a man.

'I don't think it matters too much.'

'And this is all because of last night?'

She nodded. 'Lady Winston was very kind stepping in, but the rumours will still circulate. I need a husband, a respectable match, and to be married off as quickly as possible.'

'That's ridiculous.'

Sighing, she shook her head. 'Not really. It's the rules of the society we live in. I knew the rules, I knew the consequences for breaking them.'

'You had a stone in your shoe.'

'I should have returned to the music room and sorted it out discreetly there.'

He shook his head in disbelief. 'All this for a stone.'

'All this for being caught with a man who has no intention of marrying me, on my own in the dark,' she corrected.

'I can see why you were eager to keep me away.'

'We cannot be seen together,' she said, then raised her voice slightly. 'Caroline,' she called.

Caroline and Mr Fitzgerald paused and allowed them to catch up.

'At least let me take you for a warm drink, properly chaperoned, of course. These temperatures are icy,' Mr Robertson offered. 'Then I promise to leave you alone.'

'I really should be getting home,' Georgina said. Some perverse part of her wanted to accept the offer, but enough damage had been done already.

'There's no harm in it if I'm there, too,' Caroline murmured quietly.

'I can't,' Georgina whispered back.

'That sounds like a lovely idea, Mr Robertson,' Caroline said cheerfully. 'I know of a splendid little tea room just outside the park.'

Not much in the world made him feel guilty, but sitting and watching Lady Georgina's expression as her friend recited name after name of possible marriage candidates certainly would pull on his conscience for the foreseeable future.

Who would have thought a simple stone in a shoe could cause so much trouble? He hadn't given it a second thought when he'd led her to the bench in the garden, hadn't even considered it might be inappropriate to take off her shoe and remove the offending pebble. Of course when his fingers had caressed her foot there had been a primal reaction inside him, but not one he'd ever shown outwardly.

'Lord Williamson,' Caroline suggested. 'Rich, influential, he would certainly meet with your father's approval. He is a little on the jowly side, but I'm told looks aren't that important for many.'

Jowly? How old was this man?

'He's just become engaged to Miss Prentiss,' Georgina said.

'Mr Felixstow,' Caroline continued without even taking a breath. 'He is handsome, young and rich enough. I know there are *those* rumours...'

'What rumours?' Sam asked abruptly.

'Just a little gossip,' Caroline said, "that his future wife might need to be content sharing her clothes with her husband.'

It took all sorts in the world and Sam knew many men had strange proclivities, but he couldn't imagine Georgina happy with a man who was more interested in her clothes than her. Then again, what did he know? They'd been acquainted for only a short while.

He glanced over at her, sipping her tea calmly as her friend reeled off name after name. To look at her you wouldn't know the momentous decision she was being forced to make and it was all because of him.

'Lord Rosenhall,' Caroline suggested. 'Now he's quite a catch. War hero, rather nice to look at.'

'He has an overbearing mother,' Georgina murmured, 'but I suppose that isn't a good enough reason to rule him out.'

'This is really how you're going to choose a husband?' Sam asked, incredulous.

'What do you suggest?' Lady Georgina turned to him. There was no aggression in her voice, just a calm interest.

'Surely it is better to wait for someone you actually like, someone you feel a connection with.'

'Is that what they do in Australia?'

Sam hesitated. In truth he didn't know. The past ten years he'd spent focusing on building a life for himself, but that life hadn't involved any serious relationships. Australia was a heavily male place. There were women, of course there were, but none he'd been particularly interested in. He knew in the past he had kept his distance from anyone he might feel an attachment for. Crawford had often told him it was the by-product of losing his family at such a young age and Sam supposed his friend was right. You couldn't get hurt by anyone if you didn't allow any relationships to form.

'The best we can hope for in a husband is a man who is not too demanding and benignly uninterested in our everyday lives,' Caroline said.

Sam had to suppress a smile. He liked Lady Georgina's friend. She had a sly sense of humour and didn't hold back from speaking her mind, even though he could imagine that it would often get her into trouble.

'Lord Rosenhall could be a good option,' Lady Georgina mused. 'I'll add him to the list.'

At that moment Fitzgerald returned to the table, a perplexed look on his face.

'I need your assistance,' he said jovially to Miss Yaxley. 'Apparently there are sixteen different types of tea being served and it is vital I choose one of them. I asked the serving girl just to pick any and she looked horrified.'

Rising, Miss Yaxley followed Fitzgerald to the counter, leaving Sam alone with Lady Georgina for a few moments.

'I feel terrible,' he said.

'Don't. I had to get married one day. Perhaps it is for the best.'

'Your father is coming to town to make the arrangements?' he asked.

'He'll probably arrive in a couple of weeks. I'm sure it won't take him long to organise a suitable husband. I'll likely be married within two months.'

He should feel elated that the Earl was making the trip to London. It was what he wanted, to engineer a meeting with the old man, but the nagging sense of ruining an innocent young woman's life was stopping him from celebrating the moment.

Trying to tell himself he hadn't done anything wrong, he reasoned Lady Georgina was right. It wasn't as though she would never get married, even without this little push. At the very worst he'd just expedited her nuptials.

With the guilt eating at him inside Sam tried to focus instead on his plans for revenge. Eighteen years he'd had to concoct a plan and now he was allowing himself to get distracted. All those years ago there had been rumours about the Earl getting a little too personal with the maids. On more than one occasion he'd seen his mother comforting a pretty young housemaid after one of these encounters. There had never been any hint of the Earl physically forcing himself on these women, but given his position of power it wasn't like they could refuse, which was almost as bad.

His initial plan had been to track down some of the women the Earl had wronged over the years and convince them to go public with their stories. With enough gossip about it, the Earl's reputation would be ruined. However, since returning to London Sam had discovered the Earl had political ambitions—he wanted to be the man who backed the next Prime Minister. Lord Westchester had built up his reputation as a morally upstanding family man and this was the agenda of much of his political campaign. It raised the stakes—if Sam could show the Earl to be a hypocrite as well as a letch it would ruin his political ambitions alongside his reputation.

For all this to work he needed to get close to the Earl and find a much more recent affair, preferably one still ongoing, so the Earl wouldn't be able to claim he was a reformed man.

Although ruining the Earl's reputation would be nothing compared to the life the older man had ripped away from Sam, at least he would see that his actions had consequences, even years later.

Beside him Lady Georgina shifted and with a sideward glance he tried to push away the little voice that was telling him to reach out and touch her again. She was right; they probably shouldn't even be seen in one another's company, let alone with him pawing at her, but there was an irresistible pull whenever he looked at her.

Too long without a woman, he reasoned. And too much curiosity about a woman of Lady Georgina's social class.

Reaching out under the table, he gently laid a hand on top of hers. She'd removed her gloves in the warmth of the tea shop so his fingers brushed against her bare skin. He watched as she stiffened, but noticed she did not pull away immediately.

'We can't,' she whispered, her eyes coming up to meet his. There was hope in there, alongside a hint of defiance, but mostly just regret.

'I know.' Still he didn't move, unable to pull his fingers away from their slow caress across the back of her hand. For the most part he didn't care about the rules of society. He'd dragged himself from convict boy to wealthy man without the need to conform to the conventions the *ton* seemed to place so much emphasis on. He was keen, however, not to cause Lady Georgina any more distress than he had already, so he surreptitiously looked around to check no one was watching.

Only when Fitzgerald and Miss Yaxley came bustling back over, laughing over some comment from the serving girl, did he pull away, noting Lady Georgina's heavy breathing and the beautiful flush to her cheeks.

Chapter Eight

⟨ornamental divider⟩

Today he would not be a fool. That was his aim. Well, one of his many aims, but perhaps the most important.

Mounting the horse Lady Winston had hired for his use throughout his time in London he urged it gently through the quiet streets. He was heading for Hyde Park. It was his third early morning outing this week, all of them designed to coincide with when Lady Georgina liked to ride out along Rotten Row, although so far he'd been unsuccessful in accidentally bumping into her.

As for not being a fool, he was determined that should they meet, he would remain objective. He needed to re-open their friendship, just enough to gain an introduction to her father when he arrived in London. He was certainly not in favour with Lady Westchester, so it would have to be Lady Georgina who introduced him.

After tea a few days earlier Lady Georgina had turned to him with those soulful green eyes and asked him not to try to see her again. Of course he'd agreed—at the time there was no other option—but he needed her to reconsider.

You miss her, a small voice taunted him inside his head.

That was nonsense. How could he miss a woman he barely knew? A woman he was only pursuing a friendship with to get closer to her father? Admittedly he'd expected Lady Georgina to be shallow and self-involved, whereas she'd turned out to be witty and just that little bit too alluring for comfort, but that didn't mean he missed her when they hadn't seen each other for just a few days.

Involuntarily an image of her leaning in towards him popped into his mind. Her lips were parted, her cheeks flushed, and she looked like she was just begging to be kissed. It wasn't an image from memory, Lady Georgina had never looked at him like that, but it was an image that had haunted his dreams the past few nights.

'Perhaps one kiss,' he murmured to himself as he rode through the gates into Hyde Park. One kiss couldn't be all that disastrous. Not if it were conducted when there was no chance they would ever be discovered.

Smiling ruefully, he silently chastised himself. There would be no *one kiss*, no more inappropriate thoughts. He hadn't clawed his way up from the lowest point in his life to become a wealthy Australian landowner and a success-ful, influential man by giving in to passing desires. Focus, that was what he needed now.

As he approached one end of Rotten Row he slackened his grip on the reins of his horse a little, allowing the ani-mal to stride out and quicken the pace. Before pushing it into a gallop, he cast an eye over the other riders. No sign of Lady Georgina—in fact, the whole area was particularly quiet. Especially for such a glorious morning. It was cold, bitterly so, and the frost on the grass was thick and glittering in the sunlight, but the sky was blue and there wasn't a cloud to be seen.

Coming from such warm temperatures in the Australian summer, he had been shocked at first at how the cold could bite at your fingers and whip around your ears, but memories of icy winter days from his childhood soon came flooding back.

Pushing his horse into a gallop, he bent low to minimise the sharp sting of the wind against his face and spared a thought for his horses toiling away in the soaring temperatures back home.

Only once he had done two stretches backwards and forward along Rotten Row did he slow as he saw the now familiar figure of Lady Georgina on horseback. Today she was dressed in a bright red riding habit which made her look regal in appearance, especially with the gold trim around the hem.

With difficulty he stopped himself from racing to greet her, instead allowing his horse to select its own pace towards her.

'Lady Georgina,' he greeted as he approached. 'We must stop meeting like this.'

Eyeing him suspiciously, she inclined her head in greeting. 'You contrived to meet me here,' she said bluntly.

'I did.'

This response surprised her. She'd evidently expected him to deny engineering another meeting.

'I've been thinking about what you said,' he said softly, 'and you're right.'

'What bit of it?'

'All of it. We shouldn't see each other again, not one on

one.' He held up a hand as she went to interrupt. 'What I came here today to say was that I hope we can still be civil at social events. I'm in London for the next few months at least, our paths will cross, and I don't think I could ignore you when we meet at a ball or event.'

'No, of course not, that would look strange,' Lady Georgina agreed.

'I'm sorry for the harm I have caused you and I thank you for your friendship,' he said, trying to read the expression in her eyes, but failing. 'I will not seek you out again.'

Before she could say anything he pulled on the reins and turned his horse around, bowing his head, and set off without a backward glance.

She tried not to watch him leave, but after a few moments found it impossible to resist turning round in the saddle to check he had really gone.

Shaking herself, she turned back and quickly spurred her horse forward, eager to feel the cold wind in her hair and put as much distance between herself and her thoughts about Mr Robertson.

'Lady Georgina,' a voice called as she had just reached a fast trot. For a moment she wondered if she could just ignore the call, pretend she hadn't heard it, but her pesky manners got the better of her and she slowed.

'Lady Georgina,' the voice called again and she had to work at setting her face into a serene expression despite the dread rising inside her.

'Mr Hemmingate,' she greeted him, noting his uncomfortable seating position on the horse he rode and the way his knuckles were white because he was gripping the reins so hard. Not a man who was comfortable on horseback clearly. Which suggested this meeting was entirely engineered as well. A man like Mr Hemmingate would not normally be out at such an early hour, exercising his horse in the park.

'I was hoping we might meet,' he said, awkwardly manoeuvring until his horse was walking alongside hers. 'After the terrible events at the musical soirée, I have been most eager to reassure myself all is well.'

No thanks to you, she almost blurted out.

'Quite well, thank you, Mr Hemmingate.'

'And that scoundrel of a man, Mr Robertson, hasn't been bothering you?'

'Not bothering me at all.'

'Quite remarkable how unrefined and unaware a man posing as a gentleman could be of the rules that govern our society.'

Georgina smiled weakly. She'd never liked Mr Hemmingate, not since their very first meeting when he'd taken pains to find out the names of the rest of her suitors and slipped her discreet little nuggets of information about them. None of it very complimentary. He was weaselly and underhand, and she couldn't think of anyone she would wish to further an acquaintance with less.

'I cannot believe he put you in that position, forcing you to be alone with him.'

'Mmm,' Georgina said, biting her tongue. If she could just keep her mouth shut hopefully she wouldn't say something she regretted.

'He did force you?' Mr Hemmingate looked at her earnestly.

'We were never alone,' she ground out through clenched teeth. 'Lady Winston...'

He smiled, revealing teeth that were far too pointy and slightly yellowed by the pipe he smoked with such pride.

'Of course, you have to keep up that pretence, but *we* know the truth, don't we, Lady Georgina?'

'I really must be getting...'

'I won't keep you much longer, Lady Georgina,' he said.

How rude would it be to just turn her horse around and gallop out of the park? She knew she could outpace him, knew he wouldn't dare follow her home, not at this hour in the morning. It was tempting, but like so many things in Georgina's life, not *Acceptable Behaviour for a Lady.*

'My mother is expecting me,' she said firmly.

'I wanted to tell you I really don't mind the scandal. Many men would be withdrawing their suit, but I know that despite recent events you are a woman of superb moral character, Lady Georgina.'

'Thank you,' she said, wishing for once someone didn't think of her as a woman of superb moral character. Anything to make him think twice about pursuing her.

'I shall be calling on your father when he arrives in London,' he said.

Georgina blanched, jolting forward in the saddle and almost losing her balance.

'Mr Hemmingate,' she said, trying to think quickly. If she didn't say the right thing he would be approaching her father for her hand in marriage. Who knew what her father's response would be, especially after he heard first hand of the scandalous situation Georgina had landed herself in? If she wasn't careful she could end up being engaged to Mr Hemmingate, her least favourite of all her suitors. 'I'm flattered by your interest, but are you sure we suit?'

'I've been sure of it since the day we first met, Lady Georgina.'

Feeling a little nauseous, she clutched the reins of her horse tighter. She would just have to hope there would be more acceptable gentlemen offering for her and that her father would let her have a say in whom she accepted. He'd been indulgent up until now, perhaps if she reassured him she would choose *somebody*, he would allow her to be part of the decision-making.

'I think if we just spent a little more time together you would see what a splendid match we would make,' Mr Hemmingate said, giving her an encouraging smile.

'I really—' Georgina began speaking, but quickly Mr Hemmingate interrupted her.

'Spend some time with me over the next few weeks,' he said, 'And if after that you still don't think we would suit then I will withdraw my proposal.'

The last thing Georgina wanted to do was spend the next few weeks with Mr Hemmingate, but perhaps it was the opportunity she needed to show him they would make a disastrous couple, not least because she despised him.

'What do you suggest?' she asked warily.

'Perhaps we could compare schedules,' he suggested.

'Of social events? I suppose that could work.'

She made a little mental note to find some hideous punishment for Mr Robertson next time she saw him. He deserved painful and prolonged torture for putting her in this situation. And of course, being a man, he got away without any consequences.

'Shall I send you a note with my planned engagements later today?' she asked. 'I really must be getting home, my mother will be worried if I'm much longer.'

'I could call on you,' Mr Hemmingate suggested.

Swallowing down the despair she felt, she nodded in agreement.

'Until this afternoon, Lady Georgina. I await our next meeting with great anticipation.'

Murmuring something incomprehensible Georgina gestured to her groom to start heading back. She was irritated by the entire morning. Not only did she now have to tolerate the company of a man she could not stand, she hadn't even been able to ride out properly. Lady Penelope, her beautiful and headstrong horse, would have to wait for another day to fly through the park and she would have to wait to feel the sharp whip of wind against her cheeks and the spark of exhilaration as they reached high speeds.

Chapter Nine

'We really must focus,' Georgina's mother was saying as they entered the ballroom. 'Your father will be here within a week and if we want to influence his choice of husband for you, then we need to use our remaining time wisely.'

Suitors—that was all Georgina had been allowed to think about these past two weeks. She'd been pushed by her mother to accept every invitation and couldn't keep count of the times she'd been reprimanded for not smiling sweetly enough or not filling her dance card with the most eligible of men.

'Unnecessary,' Georgina mumbled.

'What was that, dear? And make sure you enunciate when you speak. No man likes a mumbler.'

Georgina didn't dare point out at full volume that this whole fiasco was completely unnecessary. The rumours about her and Mr Robertson had been short-lived and over-shadowed by a young debutante, unmarried of course, who had mysteriously disappeared to the country after her seamstress let it slip to another customer about her rapidly expanding waistline. However, Georgina knew her mother had seized on the opportunity and now nothing would stop her from seeing her daughter married within a couple of months.

'Lord Walters is in attendance tonight,' her mother said, dropping her voice to appropriate gossiping tones. 'And Lord Rosenhall. You must make sure you dance with each twice. I have a good feeling about Lord Rosenhall.'

'Lady Westchester,' Georgina jumped in surprise as Lady Yaxley came hurtling towards them at great speed, closely followed by Caroline. 'Have you heard?'

Georgina was always fascinated by the relationship between the two women. As she supposed most young girls did, she'd always seen her mother as exactly that, her mother. To get a glimpse into Elinor Fairfax, a woman in her own right with a life outside of the family, and more specifically friends, was always intriguing.

'Heard what?' Lady Westchester's eyes sparkled in anticipation. Both women liked a little gossip.

'The Duke of Heydon is in attendance.'

Georgina's mother gasped theatrically and placed a hand over her mouth.

'Don't tease me, Sarah.'

'I wouldn't, Elinor. Not on a matter so important. And rumour has it that he's looking for a wife.'

'Rumour would put every eligible bachelor as looking for a wife,' Caroline murmured in Georgina's ear.

'He's notoriously picky about his social appearances,' Lady Westchester said. 'I can't imagine he would be out and about for much less than searching for a suitable bride.'

'Probably looks like a goat,' Caroline muttered, causing Georgina to giggle involuntarily.

'Enough, girls,' Lady Yaxley chastised them. 'You—' she stared pointedly at Georgina '—are in need of a husband. And you—' she turned her gaze on her own daughter '—well, let's just say I'd like grandchildren before I'm too old to appreciate them.'

'He'll seek you out,' Caroline said quietly, her face turning serious. 'You're the daughter of an earl and quite the most desired woman in this room.'

'Desired for my father's connections.'

'Not by all.' Georgina followed her friend's line of sight to where Mr Robertson had just entered the ballroom. She felt an involuntary squeeze in her chest as he smiled at something one of his two companions said, before offering his arm to the spritely Lady Winston.

Two weeks—that had been the length of time since she'd last seen him, riding off into the distance on horseback. To say she hadn't thought of him would be a lie, a huge lie at that. She found herself looking for him at balls, searching the crowd at the opera, seeking out his face as she strolled through the park. True to his word he had not sought her out.

Which was a good thing, she had to keep telling herself.

She'd been the one to warn him to stay away, but part of her wished he hadn't found it so easy to comply with her wishes.

'Mr Robertson does not spare me a single thought,' she said quietly. 'I'm quite sure of it.'

Not a single letter, not a single glimpse in the last two weeks, yet she'd found herself thinking about him every single day. Perhaps imagining his beautiful Australia over breakfast, or finding herself remembering the light touch of his fingers on her hand just as she was about to fall asleep.

It was ridiculous, he'd never really given her any indication that he was interested in her in anything other than a platonic fashion.

'We could move closer,' Caroline whispered, 'ensure he notices you.'

'Certainly not.' She wasn't going to parade around in front of him like some desperate society miss just to gain his attention. 'Let's find this Duke, see if he really does look like an old goat.'

'A goat?' A deep voice came from behind her shoulder. Georgina closed her eyes and counted to five before turning, trying to stop her lips from quivering. 'I've been called a lot of things in my life, but goat was not one of them.'

She had to raise her chin to look him in the eye and immediately she knew this was the elusive Duke of Heydon. Tall, slim and handsome, with an air of confidence about him that put him in the upper ranks of the nobility.

'Your Grace,' she said, bobbing into a low curtsy, nudging Caroline to do the same.

'Lady Georgina, if I am correct?' She nodded. 'And Miss Yaxley?'

'A pleasure to meet you, your Grace.' Caroline's voice had a slight wobble to it, something Georgina had never heard before. One thing she loved about her friend was her ability to treat the lowliest mister in the same manner as she might the Prince Regent. Normally titles did not faze her.

'Any particular type of goat, Lady Georgina?' the Duke asked.

She shook her head, but managed to keep her eyes locked on his.

'Shame, I've always been fond of those little mountain goats with the tufty beards.'

Surreal—that was the only way to explain the conversation they were having. Completely and utterly surreal.

'I'm told I should ask you to dance,' the Duke said, a little smile playing on his lips.

'Oh? What are your feelings on the matter?' Georgina finally found her voice. He was just a man, she reminded herself. A very powerful man who had overheard her liken him to a goat, but a man all the same.

'I would very much like it if you would save me a dance this evening, Lady Georgina. And you, too, Miss Yaxley.'

Georgina was about to answer when she heard Caroline twitter, 'Of course', in a most peculiar voice. They'd been the closest of friends for near on a decade and a half and never had she seen her act like this.

'Perhaps we could dance the first quadrille,' Georgina suggested, 'and Miss Yaxley will save you her first waltz.'

'Until later,' the Duke said with a bow.

'What are you doing, Georgie?' Caroline hissed.

'Exactly what he asked, arranging a dance.'

'You gave him my waltz.'

'Caroline, I know you better than I know myself. And you just went weak at the knees at the sight of that man.'

'I did not. Anyway, he's not interested in me.'

'How do you know if you don't give him a chance?'

'He could be the answer to your problems,' Caroline whispered. 'You could be a duchess.'

'I called him a goat. I hardly think he's considering me as a suitable wife.'

'He seemed remarkably good tempered about it,' Caroline mused.

'We can both dance with him,' Georgina said, 'and that way we see if either of us...' She trailed off, distracted by the sight of Mr Robertson with the beautiful Miss Felicity Fowler on his arm.

Focus, she told herself. Right now there was a man, an entirely suitable and respectable man, offering to dance with her. Someone her parents would certainly approve of. She should not care what Mr Robertson did, or who he did it with.

Sam could tell the plan was working. Even from this distance, out of the corner of his eye, he could see Lady Georgina was doing her very hardest not to stare at him and failing miserably.

It had been Ben Crawford's idea, of course. Crawford who was so successful with the ladies, Crawford who had never had less than three admirers at one time.

'Make her jealous,' was what he'd said.

So that was what Sam was doing. At first he hadn't thought it would work, but it seemed absence did make the heart grow fonder. Two weeks he'd left it, two weeks of avoiding all the social engagements he knew Lady Georgina would be attending. His list was exceedingly accurate, sent every few days by a maid he'd bribed in the Westchester household. Tonight, after two weeks of avoiding Lady Georgina, it was step two of his plan. To let her see him having fun.

Sam knew he was stepping on thin ice. His intention, of course, was still not to seduce the girl, he liked her far too much for that, just to prompt her into making contact again, so they could pick up their friendship and he would gain access to her father when he arrived in London.

'So are the rumours true?' the current pretty young thing on his arm asked, her voice a little breathless from the energetic dance they had been sharing.

'Which ones?' He couldn't remember her name and right now was eager to detach her steely grip from his arm, but even he knew he had to extricate himself politely.

'Everyone is saying you're from Australia.'

'That rumour is true.'

'And that you're a dangerous criminal.'

'Do you really think Mr Hardcastle would let a hardened criminal into his home?' Sam asked, gesturing at the sumptuous ballroom filled with the cream of society.

'No.' She sounded a bit disappointed.

'If you would excuse me,' Sam said, peeling her fingers from his arm. 'It has been a pleasure, the highlight of my evening. But there's someone I need to have a quick word with...'

Quickly he darted through the crowd, at first thinking to make his way to the gentlemen's retiring room, but as he saw Lady Georgina step into his path he smiled. He felt a warm rush of affection and the irresistible pull he was beginning to associate with the woman in front of him. It was undeniable—he had missed her these last two weeks, however foolish that might be.

'Good evening, Lady Georgina,' he said and bowed, as he knew was the convention, making sure to keep some distance despite his urge to reach out and run his fingers down her cheek.

She looked radiant this evening, in a gold and white gown with intricate embroidery across the bodice, drawing the eye to a rather low neckline. Quickly he looked up. That way ruination lay.

'You've been avoiding me.'

'You asked me to,' he said.

She smiled, seeming unsure of herself for the first time since they'd met.

'How's the husband hunting?' he asked.

She shook her head and there was a momentary flash of sadness in her eyes.

'Dance with me,' he said, holding out a hand. Really she should refuse, she should do one of those pretty curtsies she was so practised in and move on to someone more suitable, but he saw her hesitate, saw the war between common sense and desire in her eyes.

After a long few seconds she surprised him by taking his arm and looking up at him expectantly.

Feeling his pulse quicken, he led Lady Georgina to the dance floor, looping an arm around her waist to get her in position, and as the music began he swept her across the floor. As they danced she looked up at him, her cheeks flushed, her lips parted slightly and a glimmer of something that looked rather like desire in her eyes. Sam had the urge to throw her over his shoulder and carry her away like the barbarian he was, and it was only the dense crowd that stopped him from doing just that. It was a moment of madness, but for a few minutes Sam forgot his plans for revenge, forgot the true reason he was here and allowed himself to enjoy Lady Georgina's company.

He saw her breath quicken as his arm brushed accidently against her chest, saw her eyes glaze over slightly as she looked up at him and he knew that if he suggested they sneak off somewhere more private Lady Georgina would have as hard a time as he would resisting the desire they were both feeling.

The dance ended and once again he stood for much longer than was proper with his arm around her waist, feeling every little movement of her body.

With great effort he pulled away, executing another bow and then taking another step back to put even more distance between them. He didn't know what he would do if he stayed in such close proximity.

'Thank you for the dance,' he said.

'It was my pleasure.'

In the confines of the ballroom, with everyone else listening, their conversation was stilted. It wasn't as though Sam could tell her what he was really thinking. *That* was not appropriate for the ears of society.

'I will let you get back to your mother,' he said, seeing the petite Lady Westchester bearing down on them, no doubt to chastise her daughter on spending time with an entirely unsuitable man once again.

As she turned he slipped away, feeling more than a little unsettled. His plan had been to make her miss him with his absence, but he hadn't expected to feel such an overwhelming rush when he saw her again. He was close to losing control of himself and the situation.

Quickly he darted through the crowd, stepping out into the hallway and making his way to the gentlemen's retiring room. A couple of games of cards were going on across the hall and he had to suppress a smile as he saw Crawford lounging comfortably at one of the tables. He'd learnt long ago never to play cards with Crawford. His friend's mind was too quick, his brain too calculating. It turned a game of chance into a game of no hope. No doubt gentlemen around London would be cursing Ben Crawford's name over the breakfast table tomorrow morning.

'Mr Robertson,' a familiar voice called softly just as he placed his foot on the first step. She'd somehow evaded her mother and followed him.

'Lady Georgina. We shouldn't be seen together out here,' he said quietly, glancing over her shoulder at the noise from the ballroom. So far no one had followed her out, but it would only be a matter of time until another of the guests ventured out into the hallway.

'You're right.' Still she did not move or make any effort to bid him farewell. 'Can we…?' She trailed off.

Standing a step beneath him, looking up, she looked so forlorn, so lost that he wanted to gather her in his arms and hold her tight. He knew exactly how she was feeling; he, too, felt peculiarly unsettled by the dance they had just shared.

'Come,' he said, 'quickly before anyone sees.'

He took her by the hand and pulled her along the hallway, trying door handles until one gave way and opened into a darkened room. Grabbing a candle from a nearby recess, he ushered her inside and closed the door firmly behind him.

They had entered a small study, with a large oak desk at one end and a few armchairs in front of the fire. Definitely Mr Hardcastle's domain.

'I can't be gone long,' Lady Georgina said, glancing over her shoulder. 'Mama will miss me.'

Sam waited in silence. It hadn't been he who'd requested this meeting, although he was glad they were on speaking terms again.

'Was there something you wanted to ask me, Lady Georgina?'

She stepped closer, her chin tilted so her eyes were looking directly up at his. Careful, he cautioned himself. In private, in the soft glow of the candlelight, a man could get into grave trouble.

'I just…' She trailed off, her voice catching as she took another step forward and placed a tentative hand on his jacket. He saw the hesitation in her eyes, the mixture of desire and confusion.

Sam knew she wanted to be kissed, she just didn't know how to ask for it. He also knew that, despite every fibre of his body telling him it was a bad idea, there was no way he was going to be able to stop himself.

Savouring the moment, he bent lower and brushed his lips against hers, gently at first, and then slowly he increased the pressure of his lips against hers.

Her lips were soft on his, hesitant and unsure, but sweet all the same. Every part of his consciousness screamed at him to step away, that he couldn't do this, but instead he found himself looping an arm around her waist and pulling her in closer.

'We shouldn't,' he murmured, kissing her again, knowing that even though the kiss shouldn't be happening it felt so sublimely *right*. Gently he nipped at her lower lip, causing her to gasp in surprise, and then kissed her as if she were the only woman on earth.

Underneath his hands he could feel the heat of her body and slowly he ran his fingers down the length of her spine. Even through the fabric of her dress he could feel every contour and involuntarily an image of Lady Georgina stepping out of her pooled dress sent a sharp stab of desire through his body. Cupping her chin, he kissed her again, groaning as she brushed against his breeches accidentally.

'I'm sorry,' Lady Georgina whispered. 'I know we can't

do this.' Still she did not pull away completely, just enough to tilt her chin up and look into his eyes.

'No harm done,' Sam said, his voice thick with desire. He wanted nothing more than to lower her onto the rug, strip her naked and cover her body with his own.

'I don't know what came over me,' she said, still pressed up against his chest.

'Sometimes two people cannot ignore the desire they feel for one another,' Sam murmured into her ear, unable to resist placing a soft kiss on the delicate skin of her earlobe. 'It may be foolhardy, but it is impossible to resist.'

'Nothing more can happen.' It was phrased as much as a question as a statement.

'I suppose not,' Sam said, wondering how damned he would be if he just slipped a finger under the material of her dress and ran it around the silk detail of her neckline.

Sighing, Lady Georgina pulled away and Sam felt peculiarly bereft by her distance.

'I'm sorry,' she said, twiddling with the material of her skirt, but before she could say any more the door flew open.

Sam closed his eyes as Mr Hemmingate burst into the room. He was sure he'd locked the door, could actually feel the flick of the key in his fingers, but he must have not turned it quite far enough.

'Unhand her,' Mr Hemmingate shouted, far too dramatically for the scene that was in front of him.

Despite what had been occurring just a minute previously Lady Georgina was now standing a good three feet from him, her body turned in profile as she tried to compose herself. She looked a little flushed, but luckily not too dishevelled.

'There's nothing going on,' Sam said through gritted

teeth. No doubt Mr Hemmingate meant to draw a crowd to embarrass Lady Georgina the way he had a couple of weeks ago.

'You scoundrel, you filthy cretin. I know your type, seducing an innocent young woman who is far above your station.'

'You need to go,' Sam said, turning to Lady Georgina. The last thing he wanted was for her to be caught in another scandalous position because of him.

'Someone will see me,' she muttered. 'He's making too much noise.'

'You will regret ever laying hands on one of the sweetest, most innocent women I've ever had the honour to know,' Mr Hemmingate said, advancing on Sam.

Drawing himself up to his full height, he glared down at the man in front of him. Mr Hemmingate was not short, but lacked any real substance or muscle. Sam, on the other hand, had spent his days toiling physically under the Australian sun and as a result had a broad physique and a right hook to be proud of.

'The window,' he said, throwing the words back over his shoulder to Lady Georgina.

'You want me to climb out the window?' she hissed.

'It's either that or the door.'

She grumbled something about the situation being farcical, but headed for the window anyway. He heard rustling behind him, but already had turned his attention back to Mr Hemmingate, who had been momentarily distracted by Lady Georgina wrestling with the window sash.

'Wait,' he called, 'you don't need to run, Lady Georgina. I will protect you.'

'By causing her ruin?' Sam asked in disgust.

It was clear the man desired Lady Georgina and was trying to use the prospect of a scandal to force her to accept him as a husband.

'What's going on?' a voice asked as a gaggle of middle-aged women entered the room.

'I found this criminal cad forcing himself on Lady Georgina,' Mr Hemmingate said.

'Slander,' Sam said, not daring to turn around to see if Lady Georgina had made it out of the window in time.

'Slander?' Mr Hemmingate spluttered. 'Twice I've found you with your hands all over poor Lady Georgina.'

'Be careful what you say, Mr Hemmingate,' one of the ladies cautioned.

'Do you see Lady Georgina?' Sam asked.

'You sent her out through the window,' Mr Hemmingate spluttered.

All eyes, including Sam's, turned to the window. There was no sign of Lady Georgina and even in her haste she'd managed to push it closed behind her.

'You're starting to sound ridiculous,' Sam said, his voice low.

'He's a criminal, a foreigner,' Mr Hemmingate protested, looking for support in the ever-growing crowd of people.

'And you are trying to besmirch Lady Georgina's good name in the hope she will be forced to marry you.'

A muttering spread through the crowd and Sam could see many of the assembled guests believed his version of events.

'What's going on?' The deep voice of their host, Mr Hardcastle, cut a path through the guests.

'I found this wastrel in your study, forcing himself on Lady Georgina,' Mr Hemmingate repeated.

'Lady Georgina, she's outside. How can she be being seduced when I spoke to her not thirty seconds ago?' Mr Hardcastle asked.

Sam tried not to gawp as Lady Georgina appeared as if on cue through the crowd, arm in arm with Miss Yaxley.

'You have to stop this now, Mr Hemmingate,' she said softly.

'Stop…?' He spluttered, then, turned to the rest of the guests. 'Surely none of you believe this farce?'

Already people were beginning to leave, not wanting to see any more now it appeared there was nothing scandalous going on, just a man desperately trying to get the belle of the Season to notice him.

'I will have my satisfaction,' Mr Hemmingate demanded, turning back to Sam. 'Tomorrow morning at dawn.'

Sam stared at him blankly, not comprehending his meaning.

'A duel,' Mr Hemmingate spat. 'Hampstead Heath, tomorrow at dawn. Your choice of weapon.'

'I'm not going to fight you.'

'Too cowardly. I should have known. It's not as if you're a gentleman.'

'Fists.'

'What?'

'That's my choice of weapon. Fists. Unless you want to back out, of course.'

'That is not acceptable for a duel,' Mr Hemmingate spluttered. 'Do you know nothing?'

'Are you worried you'll lose?' Sam asked.

Mr Hemmingate paused, looking at Sam for a long moment, before saying, 'Fists it is. Bring a second.'

Mr Hemmingate turned and left the room, leaving just

Sam and Mr Hardcastle, their host for the evening. Wordlessly the older man poured two generous glasses of whisky.

'Lady Georgina, eh?' he said with a grin.

Chapter Ten

'I can't,' the young groom protested. 'Your mother will dismiss me if she finds out.'

'Please, Richards.' She knew what she was asking was too much, but she also doubted her mother would dismiss the groom if she discovered what Georgina had been up to. Lady Westchester wouldn't be so cruel as to punish Richards for Georgina's mistakes.

Mistakes—how many of those had she made in the last twenty-four hours? She wasn't sure what had come over her, it was as though an entirely different person was inhabiting her body and making all these rash decisions.

Surely one more couldn't hurt, then.

There was no reason for her to attend the duel and so many reasons for her to stay away. The biggest of which was Mr Robertson.

She'd spent the entire night tossing and turning in bed, wondering what had come over her. She'd never kissed anyone before, and had even managed to avoid the pawing attentions of the more desperate of gentlemen in a darkened hallway or terrace. It had been her first kiss and it had been wonderful.

Quickly she returned to her bedroom and pulled on the groom's clothes, tucking her hair under a flat cap. As she regarded herself in the mirror she knew she still looked like a woman, but perhaps on first glance no one would pay her too much attention. It wasn't as though she were going to get close enough for either Mr Hemmingate or Mr Robertson to see her. She just wanted to catch a glimpse of the duel, it was her fault after all, and she didn't like the idea of anyone being injured in her name.

'Let me come with you,' Richards suggested.

Georgina hesitated, wondering if she would look less conspicuous with the young groom as her companion. Thinking it might help her blend in, she agreed, sending him off to ready a horse.

They left the house before it was light, at first leading the horses through the streets and then, as they drew farther away from Grosvenor Square, mounting and riding. It was a fair way out to Hampstead Heath, and it would have been easier to take a carriage, but that wouldn't have allowed her the same anonymity.

By the time they reached the Heath, Georgina was beginning to feel exceedingly foolish. It was a large area, hilly and open, but difficult to find exactly where this duel was meant to be with only the first rays of sunlight filtering over the grass. She supposed gentlemen just knew where the duels took place, but she was having to scour the entire area and so far the place was deserted.

'We should go home,' Richards said after ten minutes of

riding. 'I've heard that bad things happen to people who come out here.'

Highwaymen were less of a problem than they had been a few years before, but Hampstead Heath had a bit of an unsavoury reputation.

'Five more minutes,' Georgina agreed, 'and if we can't find them we will head home. I give you my word.' She wished she didn't have to creep around like this, wished that she had the same freedom of the young men of her class, but knew it would never be that way. She had been born a lady and that meant conforming to certain rules, and if you broke them, like Georgina was doing now, there could be harsh consequences.

Grumbling, the groom allowed her to lead the way. The sun was almost up now, the darkness dissipating with every minute, and Georgina wondered if maybe the two men had come to their senses.

'Five more minutes,' she repeated to herself. After that she would admit the foolishness of her plan and begin the long ride home.

Sam eyed the approaching men and groaned. He'd hoped Mr Hemmingate would decide his challenge to a duel was both foolish and unnecessary and send apologies. Lady Winston had advised him the evening before that reneging on a duel was actually far more common than going through with the fight, but it seemed Mr Hemmingate was not about to have his honour come into question.

'Don't kill him,' Crawford muttered as he watched Mr Hemmingate and his second approach. 'They wouldn't just transport you for killing a gentleman, you'd get the noose.'

'Doesn't look like it would take much,' Fitzgerald added.

It was true—in the cold light of the dawn Mr Hemmingate looked scrawny and unprepared for the fight to come. He was dressed in a morning jacket and trousers, with boots unsuitable for the muddy terrain.

Although duelling etiquette dictated bringing just one second, there had been no question about both Fitzgerald and Crawford accompanying him. These men were closer than brothers to him and he valued their advice and counsel equally.

'Isn't there meant to be a doctor?' Crawford asked, as Fitzgerald broke away and strode out to meet Mr Hemmingate's second.

Sam shrugged. He never sought out a fight, but had learned to defend himself in the years he'd spent on the transport ship and working as a convicted criminal in Australia. The men they'd been transported with were a mixture of thieves and brawlers, not all violent men, but when cooped up together fights were bound to happen. Sam had learned very quickly to avoid confrontation if possible, but if that wasn't an option to strike quickly and with maximum force. He was confident he wouldn't be the one needing a doctor.

Fitzgerald returned, looking grim. 'He won't back down, doesn't want an apology, wants to follow full duelling protocol.'

'What does that mean?' Sam asked.

Shrugging, Fitzgerald grinned. 'You're mistaking me for one of these English lunatics.'

'Fight to the death?' Crawford asked.

'Surely not.'

Sam shook his head in disgust. Of all the ridiculous ways

to lose your life, duelling over a woman who could never be either of theirs seemed particularly foolish.

'They're just waiting for the doctor,' Fitzgerald said.

A minute later a figure was seen hurrying over the grass, carrying the bulky black bag that signified his profession.

With a grimace Sam shrugged off his jacket and began rolling up his shirtsleeves. He'd dressed for the occasion, choosing simple trousers and a shirt. The whole outfit did not give the impression of a gentleman, but was what he felt much more comfortable in than the frills and fancy designs he'd been forced to wear to appear in society these last few weeks.

'What's the weapon?' the doctor asked with no preamble as he arrived, a little out of breath from the walk over the boggy grass.

'Fists.'

A raised eyebrow was the only indication this was not the norm.

'I don't want any dead bodies today, gentlemen,' the doctor said.

'Fine by me,' Sam said.

'We fight until I have my satisfaction,' Mr Hemmingate said, although his voice lacked conviction. Sam wondered if he knew he was going to lose, but just couldn't find it in himself to back down.

'First blood?' Mr Hemmingate's second suggested. He looked uncomfortable to be there and Sam noted a slight similarity in appearance and wondered if this was a relative roped in to fulfil the role of second, a cousin, perhaps, or a brother.

Mr Hemmingate shed his jacket and approached slowly.

'You don't have to do this,' Sam said quietly so only his opponent could hear. 'We can just walk away, no harm done.'

'After everything you've done? It's a matter of honour.'

'And being beaten in a duel is honourable?'

'You assume you'll beat me.'

Sam shrugged. He knew he would beat him. 'Last chance,' he said. 'Once we begin I will not hold my punches.'

'Neither will I.'

They circled one another, warming their muscles and trying to get an idea of their opponent. Sam waited for Mr Hemmingate to strike; he wasn't going to deliver the first blow, but what he'd said a moment ago was true: once the fight had begun he would not hold back. It would be quicker and cleaner just to throw a couple of hard, accurate punches, draw blood from a split lip or eyebrow, and finish the duel within a minute or two. No point prancing around trying to save Mr Hemmingate some bruises.

Mr Hemmingate punched with his right, a well-formed right hook that lacked much strength. It pointed to a history of sparring matches and being taught to box at some posh school, but not to any experience in a proper fight. Sam dodged it easily and quickly went on the offensive, catching Mr Hemmingate under the chin with a forceful uppercut and then battering his head from the other side with a left hook to the cheek.

There was blood, a trickle from the split skin on Mr Hemmingate's cheek and Sam immediately dropped his fists and took a step back, waiting to see if this would be enough for Mr Hemmingate.

The other man touched the trickle of blood with his fingers, then looked at the crimson stain on his fingertips. Sam could see the moment Mr Hemmingate's eyes narrowed and his temper flared. The man began to lash out, forcing Sam to take a couple of steps back before he could mount a proper defence. A punch glanced off his chin, snapping his head back, but not causing any real damage. Quickly Sam rallied, landing a succession of punches, each harder than the last. Only when he saw Mr Hemmingate stagger back did he pull away, watching carefully to see if the other man would recover.

He tottered, his eyes rolling in his head, and then promptly fell backwards on to the grass.

No one moved for a moment. The doctor recovered first, stepping up and feeling for a pulse. Sam felt his heart hammering in his chest. He knew he'd given the other man every chance to back away, but he hadn't ever wanted to hurt him. And he definitely did not want to have a man's death on his conscience.

'He's alive,' the doctor said after an agonising ten seconds. He pulled open Mr Hemmingate's eyelids and inspected the pupils. 'Hopefully no lasting damage, but who can tell at this stage.'

Sam shook his hands, flexing his fingers and ignoring the throbbing pain. Punching someone was extremely painful—not at the time, when the exhilaration of the moment seemed to mask the damage being done to the tissues, but later, when the rush and heat of the fight had worn off and all you were left with were bruised fingers and a sense of regret.

'Sloppy,' Crawford said, grinning as he clapped Sam on the back. 'You let him get a punch in.'

Sam had first met Crawford on the transport ship to Australia. Sam had been twelve, Crawford fourteen years old, frightened and out of their depth cooped up on a ship full of hardened criminals. They'd bonded immediately and from that day on had weathered many ups and downs together. It was Crawford who had stepped in when Sam was being shaken down for his measly rations every morning and night by a gang of much older men. And it was Crawford who had stood with him when a particularly cruel guard had taken a dislike to Sam and wrongfully wanted to punish him with ten lashes. It had cost them both twenty lashes, but it was worth it to know there was someone always to rely on.

Out of everyone he knew Crawford was the one he trusted most to tell him the truth, no matter what.

'I think he's coming round,' Fitzgerald said, taking a step towards the supine Mr Hemmingate. 'Did you bring a carriage?' This was directed to the man's second.

'We left it at the bottom of the hill.' He gestured behind them.

'Good. Do you want to get him home? If that's acceptable, Doctor?' Fitzgerald asked.

'No point in him lying on the cold, wet grass. I can see to him at home,' the doctor replied.

'How will we get him to the carriage?' Mr Hemmingate's second asked.

Sam suppressed a grin as Fitzgerald sighed, bent and hefted the unconscious man over his shoulder, lifting him easily as if he was nothing more than a bag of corn. George Fitzgerald might be loosely considered a gentleman, the only son of a second son of a baron, but he had earned his muscular physique just like the rest of them, with hard labour under a hot sun.

They followed Fitzgerald down the hill, watched him unceremoniously dump Mr Hemmingate in the carriage and waited for him to return.

'Regards, gentlemen,' Mr Hemmingate's second said, as he stepped up next to the unconscious man. 'I hope we do not have cause to meet again.'

Together they watched as the carriage disappeared. Sam was just about to suggest an early breakfast when a movement caught his eye about thirty feet away. Turning, he watched a small copse of trees for a few seconds, then heard himself growl. Without an explanation to the others he strode off quickly in the direction of the movement.

'Don't even think about it,' he called, watching the lithe figure vaulting up on to the back of the horse with practised ease. He didn't think many women would be able to mount so easily without someone to aid them and for an instant he could picture her in Australia touring his land or helping out at the stud. It was ridiculous, but he could imagine her fitting right in.

She glanced back over her shoulder, as if torn as to what to do, then sighed and relaxed her grip on the reins. He waited until she slipped back down to the ground and turned to face him before speaking.

'Lady Georgina,' Sam said through clenched teeth.

'Mr Robertson.'

'Please enlighten me as to why you're out here in one of the most dangerous spots in London with no suitable escort.' His tone was harsh and clipped, but really it was a miracle he wasn't raising his voice.

'I have Richards.' She gestured to a scrawny-looking groom who was studiously avoiding his eye.

'*Not* a suitable escort.' Sam regarded the man for a moment. 'Could you give us a moment?' he asked.

The groom looked at Lady Georgina, who nodded her

head quickly. Sam watched as the young man stepped away just out of earshot, turning his back and shuffling his feet.

'I haven't come to any harm,' Lady Georgina said defiantly, although Sam could see a flicker of uncertainty in her eyes. She knew she had been foolish, but was too stubborn to admit it.

He tried to rein in the feelings of panic that had seized him when he'd first spotted Lady Georgina. She wasn't his to worry about...despite that kiss...despite how he had an overwhelming urge to gather her in his arms and hold her close to his body.

'You forget, Lady Georgina, I know all about the bad people in this world.' He held up a hand to stop her from interrupting. 'Thieves, highwaymen, murderers, rapists. Men with no morals, men with no compunction. They do not care that you are the daughter of an earl.'

'How?' she whispered.

'How what?'

'How do you know all about the bad people in this world?'

'That doesn't matter,' he said quickly, remembering that she didn't know the truth about his background. 'What matters is the unnecessary danger you've put yourself in.'

'I wanted to see what happened. It was my fault.'

He gripped her by both arms, aware of the groom standing a few feet away, but drawing her closer even still. 'It was not your fault. That man, that fool of a man, had every opportunity to walk away.'

'He did catch us in a compromising position.'

Momentarily Sam was taken back to the moment of their kiss. His eyes flicked to Lady Georgina's lips, so full, so rosy and oh, so inviting.

'And then we lied and made him out to be the dishonourable one,' Lady Georgina continued, oblivious to the fact that she'd lost Sam a few moments ago.

Her cheeks were flushed, her hair scraped back under an ugly cap and she was wearing men's clothes, probably something the groom had lent her. Not the poised and groomed Lady Georgina that society knew and loved, but there was something rather alluring about this version of her.

'Will he recover?' Lady Georgina said.

'What? Who?' Sam tried to focus, but found his eyes wandering again.

'Mr Hemmingate. It looked like he went down quite hard.'

'He'll be fine,' Sam said dismissively. He didn't want to think about Mr Hemmingate right now.

'But…'

'Hush,' he said, placing a finger on her lips. He needed her to stop talking so he could concentrate.

'But…'

He kissed her. Pulled her bodily towards him and kissed her and didn't stop until he was struggling for air.

Slowly he pulled away and traced a finger down her perfectly smooth cheek. She was lovely, far too lovely for the likes of him.

'But…'

He kissed her again, deep and passionate, as if it were the last time he would ever kiss anyone. Running his hands down her back, he felt the flowing contours of her body beneath the oversized clothes and for a moment forgot where they were, wondering how quickly he could undress her.

From somewhere to their left, he heard the groom move a little farther away, rustling the undergrowth as he did so. He was happy to ignore it, but under his hands he felt Lady

Georgina stiffen and then pull away. She looked at him with a mixture of raw desire and confusion, before glancing guiltily at the back of the groom who was meant to be keeping her from danger.

'Mr Robertson,' Lady Georgina said quietly.

'Sam.'

'Sam,' she conceded, 'we can't be doing this.'

'I know.'

They had very different reasons, but the conclusion was the same: a dalliance between them was set to end in disaster. Lady Georgina could not afford to be caught in his arms, it would ruin her marriage prospects and see her wed to some less-than-satisfactory husband, someone like Mr Hemmingate.

And he—well, he was still set on revenge. Not even the allure of the beautiful and charming Lady Georgina was enough to wipe the memory of the pain and suffering her father had caused him. Ruining the Earl's reputation and ending his political aspirations was nothing compared to what the old man had done to him, but Sam thought it would allow him to finally move on, to feel like some measure of justice had been served.

His problem came with needing to keep her close, close enough to gain access to her father, without letting his desire get the better of him. Normally he was more in control of himself.

Part of the reason for his success at self-control was how hard he'd worked to keep his heart shuttered, to not allow any relationships to form just in case he lost the person he cared about. It had been this way for a long time, probably ever since losing his family. Crawford and Fitzgerald had managed to penetrate his affections, but he'd never allowed a woman to get close enough to do so. It was alarming how easily Lady Georgina could slip under his defences. If he was honest, he cared too much about her already.

'I shall escort you home, Lady Georgina,' he said.

'Georgina,' she whispered, 'if I'm to call you Sam. And we shouldn't be seen together. Not at this hour of the morning. I shall be safe with Richards.'

Sam heard the low growl that came from his throat before he realised he'd uttered it.

'Just as he kept you safe by allowing you to come out here?'

'I didn't give him a choice. It was either escort me or I'd come alone.'

'Don't ever do anything like this again,' Sam said firmly. He wasn't normally particularly chivalrous. Of course, if a woman was in danger he would instinctively step in, but in day-to-day situations he didn't consider himself to be gentlemanly. His experience on the transport ships and the early years in Australia had taught him to look after himself before anyone else, or you could end up with a sharp knife in between your ribs, but there was some deeply buried instinct that surfaced when he was faced with the prospect of any harm coming to the woman in front of him.

This need to protect oneself was something common among the men who had suffered so much aboard the transport ships, but Sam knew for him the instinct ran deeper. It wasn't just his physical well-being he guarded closely, but his emotions as well. What he found unsettling was how quickly Georgina had penetrated the walls he'd built around his heart.

'I will escort you as far as Primrose Hill,' he said. 'No

one will recognise us there and you should be safe completing your journey home with Richards after that.'

He saw her open her mouth to argue and gave her his best glare, a look that cowed even the hardest of criminals.

'That would be most kind of you,' she said instead.

'My horse is with my friends,' he said. 'We shall collect it on the way past. Do you need help mounting?'

He knew she didn't, had seen her, lithe as a cat, vault onto the back of her horse unaided, but was perversely pleased when she allowed him to help her up. His fingers brushed against a slender calf and once again he felt the overwhelming need to feel the warm softness of her skin.

Before he could do something they would both regret he stepped away, called to the groom and began making his way out of the little copse of trees.

They rode in silence until they had made their way off the Heath, but Sam was acutely aware of Georgina's presence beside him. Every delicate movement she made he caught out of the corner of his eye. She was an excellent rider, confident and assured, and for a moment he pictured her riding through the wilds of Australia with him, her thick brown hair flowing over her shoulders in the breeze and her eyes lit up with pleasure. Sometimes he saw glimpses of wistfulness in her when he spoke about his home and he thought deep down, buried underneath all the things that made her a lady, was a woman who craved excitement and adventure. No wonder she'd done something foolish like venture out to the Heath alone when she didn't have a sensible outlet for her adventurous spirit.

'Tell me,' he said, slowing a little to draw out their journey even longer, 'have you ever left England?'

She glanced over at him before answering, 'No. My

mother does not like to travel—even the journey from Hampshire to London she finds tedious.'

'And you are confined by your mother's wishes?'

For so many years Sam had known only rules and restrictions, having to obey the guards first on the transport ships and then when they arrived in Australia, but that was a long time ago. He'd been his own master, able to make his own decisions for so long now, but he pitied anyone who had that basic freedom taken from them.

'Yes. My mother and father now and my husband when I am married. Perhaps I will be fortunate and my husband will enjoy travelling, or maybe even take me on a honeymoon to Europe.'

'Don't you want more than that?' he asked quietly.

Regarding him with those eyes that seemed to reach deep inside him to his soul, she smiled sadly. 'Of course I do. I read the books in my father's study, look at the pictures of India, of Egypt, even of the Americas, and I dream. I imagine myself taking a cruise on a felucca down the Nile, marvelling at the magnificent temples near Madras or riding with the wild horses on the American plains.' She sighed, her shoulder drooping forward slightly. 'But that is all they are—dreams. My life is on a different course and I must learn to appreciate what I have instead.'

'Anything is possible if you want it enough,' Sam said quietly. He'd gone from son of a servant and convicted criminal to one of the most successful men in Australia. He owned more land than the five wealthiest landowners in England put together and never had to answer to another man as his superior again. Anything was possible.

'Not for me,' Georgina said. 'I can't just drop everything and run away. It isn't how the world works. I would probably be refused passage on a ship anywhere as a woman travelling alone and escorted back to my father.'

'No,' Sam said, shaking his head, 'you wouldn't. And surely that risk is better than being married off to someone you don't know and probably won't like. Surely it is worth at least attempting to do something you dream of.'

'You're a man,' Georgina said quietly. 'It's a different world for you.'

'That is true, but it doesn't mean you can't realise any of your dreams. There is always a way.'

'Do you think I haven't fantasised about it?' Georgina asked, a sadness on her face that Sam hated to see. 'But I have no money of my own, no connections in the real world. I probably wouldn't even get as far as the London docks.'

'Then enlist someone to help.'

'Who?'

He was about to say him, but at the last moment was able to bite his tongue. As much as he might want to, it wasn't his place to whisk Georgina off from her unsatisfactory life and show her the wonders of the world. His whole reason for being in England was to seek revenge, to finally be able to move on from the wrong the Earl had done to him all those years ago.

'It is just a dream,' Georgina said. 'And that is all right.'

They continued to ride in silence with Sam wishing he could reach out and pluck Georgina from her horse and gallop off into the distance, ready to show her the world.

Chapter Eleven

'I hear a decision needs to be made,' Lord Westchester said from his position behind his large desk.

Georgina was standing, as she often did in the presence of her father. He wasn't an affectionate man, to many he was abrupt and even rude, but he did have a soft spot for his only daughter. She could see it in the way he'd been so indulgent to this point with her marriage proposals. Not all fathers would allow their daughters to decline quite so many perfectly decent gentlemen. For her part she knew he could be cold and cruel to others, and was rude to the servants and staff on the estate, but he was still her father and she loved him.

'Yes, Father.'

'Your mother assures me your reputation is still intact, although more through luck than anything else,' he said sternly.

'Yes, Father.'

'Nevertheless, it is time to choose a husband. I have been more than patient and I now wish to have the matter settled.'

'I understand, Father.'

'Your mother has suggested a few suitable gentlemen. She has proposed that we host a small gathering in Hampshire to encourage these gentlemen. It is inconvenient and a little unusual to have such a party in the middle of the Season, but I defer to your mother's expertise in this matter.'

Georgina nodded, silently thanking her mother for giving her this chance. Although the sensible part of her had accepted she would be married within a month or two, she still couldn't quite believe it. There was no single gentleman she could picture herself wed to. No single *suitable* gentleman, she corrected herself.

Now was not the time to be thinking about Sam Robertson. He was not suitable, not in the slightest. Her father would never approve of someone with so undistinguished a family lineage and certainly not a farmer from Australia, however rich and successful he might be. Not that Sam had ever suggested anything like marriage. The only man she had ever kissed and the only one who hadn't immediately rushed to her father to ask for her hand.

'She has proposed a date in two weeks' time. I expect she will consult you as to the identities of the guests. But do not misunderstand me, Georgina—you will be engaged a few days after the house party and a wedding will follow shortly after.'

'Yes, Father, I understand.'

'Good. That is all for now. I'm sure I don't have to remind you about our engagement tonight. It is important for both you and your mother to be there alongside me.'

Her father was a vocal supporter of the Whigs and the

main reasons he came to London was to drum up support for his proposed candidate for the next Prime Minister. Mr Moorcroft was an animated man who seemed to appeal to the voting men from different social classes and Georgina knew from various sources that he might well be chosen as the Whig candidate for the next election. The public meeting tonight was one to discuss how to combat the slipping moral standards of the country, something her father often spoke animatedly on, and a point they were basing Mr Moorcroft's candidacy bid on.

Without anything further he returned to the papers on his desk, leaving Georgina standing in front of him for a few seconds. She knew she'd been dismissed, but hesitated, needing her father's reassurance on one small matter.

'Father,' she said, noting his impatient smile when he realised she was still there, 'a gentleman by the name of Mr Hemmingate has been pursuing me.'

He frowned. 'Insubstantial man, a little grovelling,' he said, showing he did take an interest in the men who came to ask for Georgina's hand. 'You don't want to accept him?'

'No,' she said. 'Quite the opposite. He's been making a bit of a nuisance of himself.'

'Tell the staff not to admit him,' her father said simply.

'Yes, Father,' Georgina said, realising that was all she was going to get from him on the matter. At least she was reassured her father did not like Mr Hemmingate as a possible future husband for her. Not that he'd sent any further tokens of his regard since the duel. Georgina had enquired discreetly and discovered he had woken up a few hours after Sam had knocked him out. Perhaps that little humiliation would see the end to his suit.

Trying to focus on more important things, she set her mind on the house party they would be hosting in two weeks. Two weeks. Two weeks to forget Sam Robertson, forget the way her whole body tingled whenever he touched her, and to find a suitable husband.

'The things I do for you boys,' Lady Winston grumbled, choosing a seat near the back of the room and dropping down onto it.

'You have my eternal gratitude,' Sam said, sitting down next to her while he surveyed the room.

'Bunch of interfering do-gooders,' Lady Winston murmured, scowling at anyone who tried to approach.

'I thought it was a political meeting?'

He had persuaded Lady Winston to attend the meeting tonight where one of the potential Whig candidates for Prime Minister was going to be speaking about their poor country's descent into immoral ways. He'd discovered Lord Westchester was Mr Moorcroft's most vocal supporter and no doubt would be here at the meeting tonight. Rumour had it that the Earl might actually introduce the political candidate himself, which had caused a stir among the audience. Sam had to question their life decisions if this was what caused a thrill.

'Utter nonsense,' Lady Winston said. 'The whole campaign is built on shaming those who should be helped instead. Did you know they're proposing harsher laws for prostitutes?'

'What I don't understand is why a man like Lord Westchester would get so involved. His title makes him influential enough already, surely?' Sam asked.

'There will be some benefit for him. Imagine being able

to pull the strings of the man in charge of the whole country,' Lady Winston said sceptically.

With Lady Winston by his side he hadn't had any trouble gaining entry into the meeting. Slowly he settled back into his seat, glad that they'd chosen a spot towards the back of the room so he would be able to observe Lord Westchester surreptitiously without attracting any attention from the old man himself. He felt nervous, he realised, as if he had been building up to this day his entire life, and part of him felt frustrated that even after so long he allowed the Earl to be so important to him.

Over the years Crawford and Fitzgerald had both urged him to try to forget the Earl and what he'd done, insisting that keeping it in the forefront of his mind all the time was more damaging to him than Lord Westchester. Sam had been unable to forget, and unable to forgive, and as such his entire life since being sentenced to transportation had been building to this moment.

'Good evening, ladies and gentlemen.' A small, squirrely man rapped the side of a lectern to get the assembled crowd to be quiet. 'It is my pleasure to welcome you to this meeting, thank you for all coming out in support of Mr Moorcroft. Before we hear from the man himself, we have the privilege of hearing from one of our most generous and influential supporters this evening, Lord Westchester.'

A smattering of polite applause followed as a tall man stepped up to the front. He was accompanied by his wife and daughter and for a long moment Sam couldn't tear his eyes away from Georgina. She was dressed conservatively, with a high-necked, plain dress in a dull shade of grey. Still she looked beautiful—she could be dressed in a sack and look beautiful. Her hair was pulled back into a simple style and her eyes remained cast down towards her hands. She was the very picture of demure womanhood and certainly an asset to a father who liked to portray himself as a man dedicated to bringing good morals to all levels of society. Sam almost snorted out loud at the thought. He was sure that the Earl had been terrorising the maids in his employ for decades and as such he was hardly an upstanding role model. The whole campaign was hypocritical and one day soon Sam would expose the Earl for the scoundrel that he was.

With a racing heart Sam slowly turned his attention to the Earl. He looked much as he remembered, although of course older. His once-dark hair was now smattered with grey and his face was etched with lines, but the years had been kind to the Earl and he was still recognisable as the man who had condemned Sam to six years' hard labour.

'I come in front of you tonight to speak of a terrible...' the Earl said, but Sam wasn't really listening. He couldn't tear his eyes away from the older man's face. In the first few years of his sentence, while he'd been kept as a prisoner on one of the filthy hulk ships moored on the Thames, he'd seen the Earl's face every night in his dreams. Sometimes the old man was pleading with a magistrate, confessing he'd made a mistake and an innocent young boy was being wrongfully punished. Sometimes Sam was confronting Lord Westchester, hatching an ingenious plan for revenge. After arriving in Australia the years passed, and especially after Fitzgerald's father had taken him and Crawford in and treated them like his own sons, thoughts of the Earl had become less invasive, but they'd never gone away completely.

'Pompous old man,' Lady Winston muttered under her breath, making Sam turn his attention back to the speech.

The Earl was sermonising on moral virtues, his face

turning red with the force of delivery of his words. The assembled crowd were enthralled, all listening intently. All except Lady Georgina.

He saw her eyes wandering out over the sea of faces. Her body was completely still, her posture perfect and her expression serene and demure, but her eyes flitted backwards and forward. For a moment he wondered if she were searching for him, but quickly dismissed the thought. Lady Georgina would have no reason to think he would be in attendance. He'd never portrayed himself as a supporter of the Whig party, or of being particularly interested in politics.

After a couple of minutes he saw her move her head in his direction, taking in the faces in his row, and he knew the moment she noticed him in the crowd. Their eyes met and hers widened. Although her expression and demeanour did not change he saw a slight tinge of colour in her cheeks. She was pleased to see him, despite knowing she shouldn't be.

For his part Sam knew he needed to suppress the surge of pleasure he felt whenever Lady Georgina was near. Even if his main aim in coming to England wasn't to expose and confront her father, there was no way they could ever have anything more than a passing friendship. He liked to think he wasn't the sort of man to ruin a young woman, especially one he liked as much as Lady Georgina.

One kiss had been foolish, two unforgivable. To admit that he had been dreaming of a third went against his notion of himself as a respectable man.

Glancing up, he saw Lady Georgina trying her very hardest not to look at him.

'She's smitten,' Lady Winston whispered from her position beside him.

Sam mumbled a response, something that sounded negative, but was incomprehensible. Lady Georgina was a little smitten, he could see that. For all her desire to be level-headed and sensible, it was as if her hard practised sense of reason flew away when she looked at him.

Finally the Earl finished and was rewarded with a standing ovation, before stepping off to one side to allow Mr Moorcroft to speak. Sam barely heard a word the man said, but was still thankful when he finally left the stage.

'Now we mingle,' Lady Winston told him. 'Although who I'd want to speak to here is another matter entirely. You go do whatever it is you need to with that horrible Lord Westchester.'

She glided off, tapping her ornate cane on the floor as she went, clearing a path in the indomitable way of hers. Sam watched her go affectionately. She might not be his aunt, but the older woman had treated them as family ever since their arrival. He owed her so much.

Focusing, he stood, stretched and steeled himself for the encounter ahead. He knew exactly what needed to be done, but a part of him was nervous that he might fall at this first hurdle.

It would be the first time he'd spoken to the Earl in eighteen years and even all that time ago all he'd managed to utter were the frantic pleadings of a scared young boy. Now, he had to swallow his hatred and put on a façade of earnest interest. Somehow he needed to persuade the Earl to see him as a worthy contemporary.

'Lord Westchester,' he said, weaving his way through the crowd of the Earl's admirers. There were at least a dozen men and women clustered around him, congratulating him on a speech well delivered.

The Earl turned his gaze on Sam and momentarily he felt

all the hatred and years of suffering bubble to the surface. Quickly he worked to suppress the emotions and instead adopt a more welcoming expression. This was the moment he'd planned for so long, the first step of his scheme: testing to see if the old man remembered the boy he'd condemned to transportation all those years ago.

'Please excuse me for interrupting,' he said with a bow. 'I know we have not been introduced, but I was so eager to make your acquaintance.' Sam extended a hand. 'I am Mr Samuel Robertson and it is truly an honour to meet you, Lord Westchester.'

The Earl gave him a perfunctory look over, but there wasn't even a flicker of recognition in his eyes and quickly he moved to turn back to his other companions.

'I know it is irregular, but I am part of a small team looking to combat the corruption in the governing of Australia and we are looking to set up a political system,' Sam said. Now he was sure the old man hadn't recognised him it was time for the second step of the plan—to insert himself into Lord Westchester's life so he could get as much ammunition for ruining his reputation as possible.

He could tell this piqued the Earl's interest so pushed on quickly. 'I'm sure you can imagine the whole country is rife with criminals and others of low virtues, but we are eager to set up a fair and equitable system for its government. We feel we have a unique opportunity, a clean slate.'

'What did you say your name was?' the Earl asked.

'Mr Samuel Robertson,' Sam repeated.

Lord Westchester took his proffered hand this time and shook it.

'Tell me more about your organisation,' he instructed, taking Sam by the elbow and guiding him a few steps away from the rest of the guests. Sam had to suppress a smile—the opportunity to get involved in the evolution of a new system of government was too much for Lord Westchester to resist.

'At present we are only a small outfit,' Sam said, 'but we are calling for an end to the corrupt ways the Governors run things and looking at setting up a fairer system.'

'You are funded by donations?' Lord Westchester said.

Sam nodded. 'Mostly from the god-fearing wealthy landowners in Australia itself—they are keen to see their country run fairly by someone who understands the particular needs of a fledgling country—but also one or two benefactors here in England.'

'We must talk more,' the Earl said. 'You would like some advice?'

'I would.'

'I have commitments here, people I must talk to, but why don't you join me for a drink at my club later this evening. Perhaps ten o'clock?'

'I would be honoured,' Sam said, trying not to show his glee. It was clear Lord Westchester was flattered by Sam approaching him.

Lord Westchester moved away and Sam let out a loud exhalation of air. His hands were shaking and his clothes felt uncomfortably tight, but he'd done it. He'd survived his first conversation with the Earl without punching the man or vomiting on his shoes.

'What are you doing?' Lady Georgina whispered from behind him.

'Talking to your father,' he said as he turned around.

'What about?'

'Politics, what else?' Sam said with a smile.

'You're interested in politics?'

'You sound disbelieving.'

She opened her mouth to reply, but promptly closed it again as she caught sight of something over his shoulder.

'Mother,' she murmured and quickly grasped his arm, pulling him through the crowd. He allowed himself to be led, ignoring the curious glances from a few of the other attendees, until they were in a quiet corner.

'Why are you really here?' Georgina asked, glancing around almost furtively as if she expected her mother to jump out from behind one of the potted plants.

For a moment he had the urge to confess, to tell her everything that had happened to him at the hands of her father, but quickly he suppressed the idea. Telling Georgina she had been used by him to get close to the Earl would not end well and, although Sam knew nothing lasting could develop between them, he was reluctant to jeopardise his chance to spend even a few more hours in her company. One day in the not-too-distant future she would hate him for what he'd done to her father, but for now he would keep quiet.

'I couldn't keep away,' he murmured and realised it was the truth.

'You need to try harder then. It's not as though we can spend any time together anyway.'

'It has been worth it just to see you,' he said, taking her hand and placing a kiss just below the knuckles so quickly Georgina didn't have time to protest, then he was off through the crowd, distancing himself from the woman he really shouldn't care so much about.

Chapter Twelve

'Georgina, Georgina,' her mother called, her voice high with excitement. 'Georgina, where are you?'

Smoothing down her dress, Georgina rose from her favourite spot in the small library of their town house and went to find her mother.

'The Duke has accepted,' her mother said triumphantly, brandishing a letter in one hand. It was a short note confirming the Duke of Heydon would travel to Hampshire for the house party next week.

'Wonderful.' Georgina smiled, trying to summon up some excitement for her mother. After all, the Duke had seemed perfectly pleasant.

'You shall need new dresses, only the finest material, if you are to impress the Duke,' her mother gushed. 'We'll take a trip to the modiste today. Just imagine, if we do everything properly you could be a duchess.'

She knew the idea of being a duchess should excite her, but in truth Georgina didn't feel anything but mild panic.

It was only a week until their house party in Hampshire. In three days they would be travelling back to the country to ensure everything was prepared for the arrival of their guests, and in just over a week Georgina would be engaged.

It was ridiculous, knowing you were to be engaged, but not knowing to whom. Nevertheless, her father had made it clear that she would end the weekend with the decision to become betrothed to some suitable gentleman and out of the proposed guests he didn't much mind which.

'Three new evening gowns,' her mother was saying. 'And at least three new day dresses, perhaps more if we are to schedule different activities through the day.'

'Won't it look a little ridiculous if I change between each activity?' Georgina asked.

Her mother looked at her admonishingly. 'Georgina Fair-fax, you will not be the only young woman at the party. Everyone will be trying to impress the Duke. You need to stand out.'

'Yes, Mother,' she said meekly, knowing there was no point in arguing.

'I've got an addition to this little party of yours,' Lord Westchester said as he emerged from his study.

'An addition?' Georgina's mother asked, a hint of panic in her voice. Georgina knew her mother had spent hours tweaking the guest list before invitations had been sent, trying to entice the most eligible gentlemen down to Hampshire and balance the party with debutantes less well connected and less attractive than her own daughter. It had been like a military operation and Georgina could see the fear in her mother's eyes that her father would ruin everything with his next words.

'A young man interested in politics, looking to set up a new political system in Australia.'

'Is he a potential suitor?' Lady Westchester asked mildly.

Georgina's father laughed, 'No, no, nothing like that. But if I'm going to be stuck at home surrounded by these society bores I might as well have someone to have a sensible discussion with.'

Society bores—a very pleasant way to think of her future husband.

'Yes, dear,' Lady Westchester said resignedly. 'The man's name? Then I can organise an invitation.'

From her mother's face she knew it wouldn't be as simple as organising one invitation. To balance the numbers they would now need to find another young lady to attend the party, a young lady who might draw one of the suitors' focus away from Georgina. But there was no way Lady Westchester could argue with her husband; they didn't have that sort of relationship.

'Mr Robertson,' Lord Westchester said. 'Staying with Lady Winston, I believe. He's happy to bring a friend if you need to balance your numbers.'

Trying not to react, Georgina slowly let her eyes rise up and meet her mother's, wondering if she would say anything. Her father had not connected Mr Robertson with the man who had caused the scandal that was forcing the issue of her marriage and Georgina didn't know if her mother would try to dissuade the addition to the house party by informing him.

'I'll arrange it,' Lady Westchester said after a few seconds' pause.

Chapter Thirteen

'Two old convicts on their way to an earl's house party,' Ben Crawford said as they turned in through the ornate gates of the Westchester estate.

Sam grimaced. The journey through Hampshire hadn't taken them past his old village, but there were plenty of familiar sights that had brought back painful memories. Memories of a time when he'd been happy living at home with his mother and sisters, before he'd been wrenched away from all of that and thrown into a dank jail cell.

The two men were on horseback, opting to brave the winter winds in favour of being cooped up in the carriage Lady Winston had loaned them for the weekend trip away. The carriage was somewhere behind them, transporting their luggage as well as a valet neither man needed but Lady Winston had insisted on to make them look a little less like savages.

'Probably not the best way to introduce ourselves,' Sam

said. 'The Earl thinks I'm of outstanding moral character and trying to change the way Australia is governed.'

'You always were a good liar, but that is far-fetched even for you.'

'As long as he believes it,' Sam said. He wanted to get to know the Earl's household and see if the old man was continuing his immoral behaviour with the maids as he had been prone to all those years ago. There would be at least one disgruntled servant willing to talk, surely. Sam was hoping to find someone who would stand up to the old man and go public with his behaviour. With the Earl's focus on promoting good moral values for his political candidate, Mr Moorcroft, he could publicly shame him—men had been ruined in politics for far less.

'At least he doesn't recognise you,' Crawford said.

There hadn't been much chance of that. Sam doubted Lord Westchester spared a second thought for the boy he'd condemned to years of imprisonment and hard labour. Or the family he'd been cruelly separated from never to see again.

'I wasn't important enough to make a lasting impression,' Sam said. It had been a tense few seconds when Sam had stood in front of the Earl a couple of weeks earlier to see if the old man recognised him, but there hadn't been even a flicker of recognition in the old man's eyes.

They rode on along the drive. It was so long there was no sign of the house even though it was a good few minutes since they'd entered the grounds of the estate. Sam had been here before, as a child, but his memories of that time were a little vague and he certainly hadn't been paying attention to the landscaping. Now he looked over the grounds with a landowner's eye. Much of the surrounding farmland, filled with both crops and livestock, would belong to the Earl, productive and practical, but here in the grounds of Westchester Place it was all about appearance. Manicured lawns stretched to either side and the drive itself was lined with well-established oak trees. Farther ahead Sam could see the gardens started in earnest—neat flowerbeds waiting for the spring weather to be planted with all manner of flowers.

'Bit different to back home,' Ben murmured as he, too, took in the view.

At this time of year in Australia everything was sun-scorched yellows and browns with the vibrant blue backdrop of the sea and the sky. Here in England the colours of winter were much more muted—hazy greens and greys as well as a lot of muddy browns.

The house came into view, an impressive stone structure with a central square building and two curving wings to either side. It was large, but not excessively so for a man of the Earl's status and wealth.

Sam felt a shudder of anticipation as he saw Lady Georgina standing beside her mother greeting a guest who had just arrived. She was covered head to toe in a thick cloak to combat the near-freezing temperatures. It was maroon in colour, lined with white fur, and made her look like a wintery princess. As they drew nearer he could see her cheeks were flushed with colour and the tip of her nose was pink from the cold. Her dark hair was tucked inside the hood of the cloak, but a few loose tendrils fell over her shoulder seductively. Grimacing, he realised she would have to be making an effort to impress the gaggle of suitors descending on Westchester Place, all weighing up if Lady Georgina would make them a suitable bride.

'Mr Robertson,' Lady Westchester greeted him coolly as he dismounted and bowed his head first in her direction and then in Lady Georgina's.

'It is my pleasure to introduce Mr Crawford,' Sam said.

Sam's invitation had come with the option to bring another gentleman along with him. He'd been puzzled at first until Georgina had sent a brief note explaining his last-minute addition to the party had meant her mother having to try to balance the numbers of male and female guests. She'd had to settle on two pretty but penniless sisters and could not have invited one without the other. Hence Crawford's invitation to the house party to even up the numbers once again.

For his part Crawford had been eager to get out of London for a few days, although tight-lipped as to the reason. Sam suspected it was something to do with a woman—with Crawford it often was—and had given up trying to pry. A few days in the country would do his friend good and hopefully give whatever young woman Crawford had been dallying with time to get over her infatuation.

'A footman will show you to your rooms,' Lady Westchester said. Her eyes were cold and unblinking and Sam had no doubt as to her feelings on his presence at this gathering. He wondered why she hadn't informed her husband he was the reason they were having to rush Georgina's marriage, but for now was just pleased that she hadn't.

As they entered Sam felt a heavy sensation in his chest as he recognised the entrance hall from his visits eighteen years ago. The circumstances then were completely different—he'd entered through the back door, of course, but once or twice had peeked upstairs from his spot in the servants' quarters. His mother had been newly employed as an assistant cook, her recently widowed status making it necessary for her to find work again. On a few occasions she'd brought Sam with her to Westchester Place, where he'd happily fetched and carried and done a few odd jobs. He'd been almost invisible, not even a real servant, just the son of one.

Now he might not be the most welcome of guests, but he was a guest all the same. What a difference nearly two decades could make.

Pushing aside the memory of his mother's pale, worried face when he'd last been in the grand house, he followed the footman up the sweeping staircase to the first floor. He'd never ventured up here before, despite the Earl's allegations all those years ago that he'd stolen Lady Westchester's priceless emeralds from her jewellery box in her bedroom.

Their two rooms were at the end of a long hallway, and although he doubted they were the finest guest rooms the house had to offer they were still pretty impressive. Each was furnished with a four-poster bed, complete with canopy and heavy curtains. The wallpaper was fresh and the furniture polished to a gleam. And his room had a spectacular view across the formal gardens directly to the rear of the house to the lawns beyond. Despite it being only mid-afternoon already the wintery sunlight was fading and long shadows were beginning to form, but still he could see it was a garden maintained to the highest standard, as he was coming to realise the Earl seemed to insist on in all aspects of his life.

'Drinks will be served at seven in the drawing room, and dinner is at eight. If there is anything you need, please do not hesitate to ring. I shall show your valet where everything is kept,' the footman said before departing.

Crawford turned to Sam, his eyes wide with amazement.

'Bit much,' he said, grinning.

Although they'd been in plenty of grand houses in London since their return to England, nothing was quite as impressive as this. The town houses were elegant and beautifully presented, but on a much smaller scale than the country estates, and Westchester Place was no doubt among the finer of the ancestral homes in England.

'Four hours until drinks,' Sam said. 'Should be just enough time to work out how to tie your cravat.'

Georgina dawdled, fidgeting with her dress and hair even though everything had been declared *perfect* by her mother fifteen minutes before. She didn't want to go downstairs, didn't want to face all of her suitors together for the first time. It made the realisation that she was going to have to marry one of them all the more immediate.

'Cheer up,' Caroline said, bursting in through the door to Georgina's bedroom. 'I had a peek in before I came up to get you and they're not too bad a bunch.'

It was true, her mother had been very selective in the gentlemen she'd invited to this house party. Most of the men were perfectly nice, perfectly normal with no heinous vices. If Georgina was being sensible, she would admit that she could have a contented life with many of them. She'd been raised to believe that a good marriage was not built on love or friendship, it was built on a foundation of two people of the same social status working towards the same things. Namely producing a family and furthering the good name of that family.

It had worked for her parents, it worked for so many couples. True, there were many unhappy marriages, rumours of affairs and mistresses, but Georgina suspected that was the same whatever the reason a couple first became linked.

A marriage arranged by and approved of by her parents was what she'd always been raised to expect, but now it was her reality she still couldn't help but doubt whether she would ever truly be happy married to a man she barely knew.

In truth, she wasn't sure if she would be happy being married at all. Of course she wanted a house of her own and children, but marriage meant giving up on her hidden dreams. No longer would she be able to hope for a life of adventure, of sailing off into the sunset, of a life where she got to make all the decisions. Once she was married she would have to honour and obey her husband for the rest of her life and Georgina found the idea more than a little suffocating.

'The Duke is here,' Caroline said, 'looking rather dashing dressed all in black.'

'Mmm,' Georgina murmured as she fiddled with her hair again.

'And I saw Mr Robertson with that handsome friend of his.'

Georgina tried not to react. She'd been surprised when her father had insisted Sam Robertson join their little party. Of course, her father had not been suggesting him as a potential suitor, but had said something about wanting to discuss Mr Robertson's interest in politics in Australia. Georgina had even penned Mr Robertson a note asking him what he was doing, but in the end thought better of it and had thrown it away before it was sent. After their kiss in the study and then again on Hampstead Heath a couple of weeks ago she knew she had to try to forget about him, even if the memories were seared into her brain and she could see Sam's face in her mind every time she closed her eyes.

'He's here as Father's guest,' Georgina said, trying to keep any emotion from her voice. Despite confiding almost everything in Caroline normally, she hadn't told her about the kiss in the study or her foolish trip to the site of the duel the next morning. Her friend would probably urge her to live a little, to follow her heart while she still could, and Georgina knew she didn't need any encouragement on that front. Her duty was to her parents, to behave like a respectable daughter of an earl, and that meant staying well away from Mr Robertson.

'Your mother sent me to fetch you,' Caroline said, briefly checking her own appearance in the mirror. 'We shouldn't keep her waiting too long.'

They walked downstairs arm in arm, Georgina glad of the steadfast support of her closest friend. Inside her chest her heart was hammering and she had to pause before she stepped into the drawing room. One of the men inside would be her husband in a matter of weeks.

'Let's play a game,' Caroline whispered. 'Let's pretend the first man you set eyes on will be your future husband. Whisper his name to me when we're inside.'

Georgina smiled, some of her tension already seeping away. It was hard to stay so agitated with Caroline around.

They stepped into the room and for a long moment Georgina found herself looking at her shoes, unable to bring herself to raise her eyes. Her heart was hammering in her chest and her mouth felt dry despite the glass of water she'd had just a few minutes previously.

Taking a deep breath, she raised her gaze, squeezing Caroline's arm as she did so. Letting out a short laugh of relief, she felt her breathing settle and her heart slow.

'Who was it?' Caroline asked.

'My father,' Georgina whispered.

'Well, you can't marry him. Look again.'

She did, but it was impossible to tell who she'd seen first. Her treacherous gaze was drawn to Mr Robertson who was standing slightly to one side with his friend Mr Crawford. But it could have been the Duke she'd seen first, or Lord Rosenhall, it was hard to tell.

'Georgina,' her mother called, gliding through the crowd and gripping her daughter by the arm. 'Give the Duke your attention tonight,' she added in a whisper.

'Yes, Mother.' Really she had no choice. She had no doubt she would be seated next to him at dinner and, as the most eligible bachelor in the room, he would expect her mother to thrust them together on every occasion.

Out of the corner of her eye she saw Mr Robertson grin at her in that cavalier way of his and had to stop herself moving towards him. Normally so in control, Georgina found it difficult to resist the primal pull she felt towards him. She'd never experienced anything like it before and wasn't entirely sure how to deal with it.

'Unfair,' she muttered to herself. Why couldn't she feel this way towards someone suitable? The Duke, or at least a man who could trace his family origins back a century or two.

'Go,' her mother hissed, thrusting her into the centre of the room in the direction of the Duke.

Smiling serenely, Georgina pulled herself up straight and glided through the assembled guests. She could do this. Twenty-one years she'd been preparing for exactly this sort of situation, all she had to do now was remember everything she'd been taught.

As she made her way towards the Duke she couldn't help but notice Mr Robertson moving as if to intercept her. She tried to ignore him, but found herself disappointed when he changed course and veered off slightly ahead of her.

'Sly…' she murmured as she watched him strike up a conversation with the Duke. Now she had no way of avoiding him.

'Lady Georgina,' the Duke greeted her, 'and Miss Yaxley. You both look lovely this evening.'

'Your Grace.' Georgina sank into a low curtsy as was appropriate and felt Caroline do the same beside her.

'A pleasure to see you both again,' Mr Robertson said.

Slowly Georgina lifted her eyes to meet his. It would be rude not to greet him formally, but right now she didn't trust herself entirely.

'Mr Robertson was just telling me about life in Australia,' the Duke said. 'Fascinating place.'

'I understand you are involved in politics,' Georgina said, a little sharper than she intended to.

Mr Robertson threw his head back and laughed, a hearty chuckle that drew stares from around the room. Georgina could see her mother frowning out of the corner of her eye, but at the moment didn't make a move to come over.

'Aren't we all?' Mr Robertson asked, a twinkle in his eye that Georgina was trying not to notice. 'As a landowner one has to decide how much living in a decent place matters to you. If it does matter, then surely it is our responsibility to put something back into that society, to help to shape and nurture it.'

'An admirable sentiment,' the Duke said. 'We are all

responsible for the country we live in. No man can say he isn't interested in politics. It is the cornerstone of how we live, everything we do.'

'We owe it to those less fortunate to care,' Mr Robertson said quietly. 'Those who do not have a voice or a vote.'

'Women?' Georgina asked sharply. There were a few fantasists among her circle who thought one day women might be allowed into the world of politics. Georgina did not believe it. In a world where a few rich and influential men held all the power, they weren't going to share it without a fight.

'Women, children, convicts, those men who do not have the *right* to a say in their own country,' Mr Robertson said.

'You would like to introduce a government to Australia?' the Duke asked.

'Perhaps one day,' Sam said, 'but we're a long way off from that. The first step would be somehow trying to unite the colonies.'

'Surely the Governor of each colony does a decent enough job?' Georgina asked.

'One man can be corrupted, paid to make a decision or to rule in a certain way,' Sam said.

'That's why the House of Commons was created,' the Duke said. 'To wrest the power away from just the very rich few and share it among the many.'

'Do you object?' Georgina asked, turning to the Duke. He was one of the richest and most powerful men in England.

He laughed. 'Goodness gracious, no. I wouldn't want the responsibility for running this country on my shoulders. It is enough trying to keep my own tenants happy.'

'But some of the lords would rather the power was in their own hands,' Sam said, 'and some have embraced the new wave of politics and are busy making connections with the top politicians in the House of Commons so they still control as much as possible.'

'Like my father with Mr Moorcroft,' Georgina said. She knew that was why her father was such an avid supporter of the Whigs. By supporting Mr Moorcroft now he was hoping to have the man in his debt should he become Prime Minister one day.

'Exactly,' Sam said.

She should feel offended at his low regard for her father's motives and character, but seeing as it was the truth it was difficult to be annoyed.

'It's interesting,' the Duke said. 'In a way Australia is a clean slate. You have an opportunity to build a system that really works there. Have you gained much support while you've been visiting London?'

Sam grimaced. 'I find it best not to say too much about where I'm from—not everyone is welcoming when they hear you live in untamed Australia.'

'How did you end up there?' the Duke asked. His expression was curious and Georgina could see there was no malice in the question.

'Convict ship,' Mr Robertson said.

There was a pause, four long seconds and then five, before the Duke let out a hearty laugh and slapped Mr Robertson on the back.

'You nearly had me believing you,' the Duke said. 'Remind me never to play cards against you.'

Georgina glanced at Mr Robertson for a moment. She didn't know him well—despite the intimacies they'd shared she'd probably spent less than half a day in his company in total—but she'd have wagered her most precious jewels he'd been telling the truth. Shaking her head, she tried to rid herself of the notion. Of course he couldn't be an ex-convict, he was too refined, too suave and confident among the *ton*. And he was staying with Lady Winston, who might be a little unconventional, but she wouldn't accept a common criminal into her home.

'Please excuse me,' he said with a bow. 'I see my good friend Mr Crawford is trying to get my attention.'

As he stepped away, Caroline leaned in and whispered so quietly only Georgina could hear, 'He can't keep his eyes off you.'

Chapter Fourteen

Dinner had been uneventful. Sat at the very bottom of the table, next to a pleasant-looking but empty-headed young debutante, Sam had conversed about the weather, the decor of the room and the food, and by the end of the meal would have gladly given his right hand to escape the twittering attentions of Miss Lovett.

He'd steadfastly tried to ignore Georgina. She'd been seated near the head of the table next to the Duke, of course, with another eligible gentleman flanking her other side. Once or twice he'd caught her staring pensively in his direction, not trying to catch his eye exactly, but looking him over as if trying to figure something out.

He knew exactly what. His comment about the convict ship had, of course, been meant to be viewed as a joke, but now he could see it had been a dangerous comment to make. As soon as the words had left his mouth he'd seen Lady Georgina's eyes narrow as if she were probing for any truth. Now she might not entirely believe he was an ex-convict, but the seed had been planted, which wasn't what he'd planned at all.

The Earl, the man he should be focusing his attention on, was seated at the very head of the table, far too far away to hear what he'd been conversing about. As he watched the older man Sam felt his resolve hardening even more. Eighteen years ago this man had ripped him from his family and condemned him to a life of hard labour and harsh conditions. Then he'd gone back to his normal life and most likely completely forgotten the boy he'd been so cruel to. Even just destroying his reputation, and the chance of succeeding in his political aspirations, didn't seem harsh enough punishment, but at least it would be a good start.

'Come for a drink,' Lord Westchester said, clapping him on the back as they rose from dinner, the ladies making their way out of the dining room first. The gentlemen were split, with a couple following the Earl to his private study and a few staying in the dining room where cigars and whisky had already been provided.

They were seated around the roaring fire, built up with thick logs to keep out the winter chill, but even in the comfortable armchairs with a fine whisky in his hand Sam found it hard to relax. He was conscious he was in the enemy's lair and felt as though he would be exposed any moment, but so far no one had called him out as an imposter.

'Confounded dinner parties,' the Earl said with a scowl as he flopped into the free armchair closest to the fire. 'Lady Westchester insisted on the whole weekend. Waste of time if you ask me.'

'I thought the idea was for Lady Georgina to find a husband,' Sam said mildly.

'Girl has been dragging her feet for far too long,' Lord

Westchester said. 'I'm determined the matter will be settled by Monday. But there would have been less *invasive*
ways to go about it.'

Sam glanced at the Duke and Lord Rosenhall, the two
other gentlemen invited into the Earl's private study. They
didn't seem perturbed by the conversation and Sam wondered not for the first time at how unemotional everyone
seemed to be around the subject of marriage. To the men
in this room, and even to Lady Georgina, it was a business
transaction. There was no consideration of love or compat-
ibility, not really. It was all about who would make the best
ally to the family.

Thinking back to when he was young he remembered his
parents' marriage. They'd never been rich, but had always
had enough to survive on, and more importantly they'd truly
cared for one another. They'd been happy and in love and
that love had filtered down to Sam and his sisters, giving
them a happy home to grow up in.

He'd never thought much about marriage. For so long his
existence had been bleak that even now, after years of being
a successful and free man, sometimes he doubted his good
fortune could continue. He knew he had also always shuttered his heart, wary of getting too close to anyone after
losing his family at such a young age.

Until now.

Shaking his head ruefully, he dismissed the image of
Lady Georgina, lips parted, eyes closed, just inviting him
in. Not only was the whole idea of this weekend to find
her a suitable husband, once she found out about his history with her father he doubted she would want anything
to do with him.

Still, a man was allowed to dream. And his dreams had

been particularly vivid and particularly uncomfortable these past few weeks.

'My wife has organised a hunt for tomorrow,' Lord Westchester said, turning his attention to Sam. 'I understand the ladies will be occupied with some other activity. After will be a good time to discuss your propositions in more detail.'

'Of course, my lord,' Sam said.

'I had thought to discuss it tonight, but the travelling has exhausted me,' the Earl said. 'I will not be able to give you my full attention and the benefit of my years of experience working with the Whig party.'

'I'm just grateful for your guidance,' Sam said, even managing a smile. 'You have been a most generous host already. I think I will retire myself so as to be fresh for the morning.'

He stood, inclined his head to the other men, and left the room, heading back upstairs to his bedroom. Sam felt Lord Rosenhall's eyes on him as he departed. The Viscount, like many of the other guests, had watched him and Ben Crawford warily throughout dinner. With his sideways glances and none-too-subtle sneers he'd made it clear what he thought of two untitled, unknown men socialising within their circle. Sam had made a point of clapping him on the back on a few occasions just to make the man more uncomfortable. He didn't have time for people who were so shallow as to only judge a man for their ancestry.

Two hours later and the house had finally fallen quiet, the guests settled in their bedrooms after the dinner and drinks that followed. Sam sat on the windowsill, looking out over the gardens, wondering how best to approach the servants and enact the next step of his plan. He wanted to gather his evidence as quickly as possible—the house party only lasted three days and he didn't want to hang around too much afterwards. Being back in Hampshire was just dredging up old and painful memories.

As he looked out over the frosty gardens he saw a flash of colour, even in the darkness. The moon was out illuminating the sky and as he peered down he saw the figure of a woman walking slowly over the grass. Immediately he knew it was Lady Georgina. The way she walked, the way she held herself—over the last few weeks it was as if he'd memorised every little characteristic and could identify her now from the shortest glimpse.

Before he could think through the consequences of what he was about to do, he found himself halfway across the room, picking up his coat on the way.

Outside he had to hunch his shoulders against the cold and quickly strode across the grass, following the direction he'd seen Lady Georgina disappear off into. He saw her a couple of minutes later, sat on a small, decorative bench staring up at the sky.

'Beautiful, isn't it?' he said quietly, trying not to alarm her.

Slowly she turned to him and he saw the tears on her cheeks glistening in the moonlight.

'Georgina,' he said, taking a step forward before hesitating. She motioned for him to come and sit at her side.

They were far enough away from the house so that anyone looking out the windows wouldn't see them, so he took a seat next to her, feeling the warmth of her body despite the many layers she'd wrapped herself in.

'You shouldn't be here,' she said softly.

'Nor should you. You should be tucked up in bed.'

'No, I mean you shouldn't be here in Hampshire. It makes everything harder.'

He knew exactly what she meant. 'I'm sorry. When your father invited me, I couldn't find it in myself to say no.'

'I have to choose one of these men to marry.'

'I know.'

'And all I keep seeing is you.'

'I'm sorry.'

She turned to face him again and the despair he saw in her eyes was heartbreaking.

'I've never minded,' Georgina said after a long pause, 'the idea of marrying someone I barely know. It's what I've been brought up to expect and my father has allowed me to turn down quite a few proposals.'

'But now it's actually happening you feel hemmed in?' Sam asked.

'I wouldn't have…' She trailed off miserably. He knew their closeness over the past few weeks was making the inevitable harder for her. The whole situation was a mess. He wanted her badly, wanted to kiss her and comfort her and make her his own, but he needed to focus. For eighteen years he'd dreamed about getting revenge on the Earl, he couldn't allow himself to become distracted by Georgina. Although if he were honest he was already distracted.

He wanted to wipe away the tears on her cheeks and pull her into his arms, but he knew that would only make things worse. Already he was the reason she was so reluctant to choose one of her perfectly decent suitors as a husband. He couldn't ever give her anything more than heartbreak, but still he wanted to kiss her.

'I'd never kissed anyone before you,' she said quietly.

'I'm no good for you,' Sam said quietly. 'I'm not of your world, not the kind of man the daughter of an earl can be with.'

'I know.'

Leaning forward, he raised a hand and gently wiped the tears from her cheeks, feeling the velvety-soft skin under his fingertips. Even once the tears were gone he lingered, unable to pull his hand away, instead cupping her cheek.

'Tell me something that will make this easier,' she said quietly.

'The rumours are true.' Sam felt the words slip out before he could think through what he was saying.

'The rumours?'

'About my origins.'

'You're a convict? I don't believe you.'

'It's true. A very long time ago I was sent to Australia as a convicted criminal. I served the first two years of my sentence on a ship on the Thames and the rest in Australia where I was lucky enough to be taken in by a kind man and his family. He showed me there was still some good in the world and gave me the tools to become the man I am today.'

'And who is that man?'

'As I told you before, I'm a wealthy landowner, I own and run the largest stud in Australia and I'm well respected among both the freedmen and the settlers. All of that was true.'

'What did you do?' Georgina asked quietly.

'Would you believe me if I said nothing?'

She studied him for a moment, her eyes searching his face. 'Nothing?'

'I was accused of stealing.'

'And that was enough to have you transported?'

'It was a very wealthy and influential man who did the accusing. I was nothing, a nobody. Even though there was no hard evidence against me, this man's word was enough.'

'He believed you did it?'

Sam hesitated. He wasn't entirely sure of the answer to the question. It was something that had been niggling away in his subconscious for more years than he cared to remember.

'I don't know. I've always wondered...' He shook his head. It was more than just wondering. In the first few weeks after his conviction Sam had believed it was a genuine mistake. The Earl had seen the jewellery was missing and honed in on a boy he didn't know and didn't trust. But as time went on Sam had begun to doubt this version of events. Lord Westchester had been so firm in his accusation, so damning, that Sam had wondered if he had chosen a young boy with no connections and no one to stand up for him as a scapegoat. That was when his true desire for retribution had reared its head. A mistake was one thing, but to deliberately condemn a young boy of ten was just evil.

As time went on he'd begun to believe more and more that it had been a deliberate set-up. Oh, no doubt the jewellery had been stolen, but he believed the Earl had deliberately protected the real thief by accusing Sam. He remembered the calculating looks Lord Westchester had given him, the dismissive attitude when Sam had begged him to look for the true thief. Over the years he'd wondered if Lord Westchester had accused him to protect one of the maids he'd had a dalliance with, perhaps one who thought she deserved some kind of payment for the service she'd provided. He had absolutely no way of knowing if this was the case, but it was the only thing that made sense in his mind.

'And you were convicted on just his word?' Georgina asked.

'Indeed. I had no one to stand up for me. My father had passed away, my mother was a mere servant. His word was good enough for the magistrate.'

'How old were you?'

'Ten.'

Georgina gasped and a hand flew to her mouth in shock. 'You were a child.'

'Not for long,' Sam said grimly.

Up until the conviction he had been protected from some of the harsher realities of day-to-day life by his mother, but as soon as he was arrested he'd been entirely alone. He'd grown up fast out of necessity.

'What sentence did you get?'

'Six years for stealing. Initially I thought it would be served here in England and I was able to fool myself that six years wasn't the end of the world. I'd be free by the age of sixteen, I could return to my family, perhaps build a life for myself.'

'But they transported you?'

'I didn't even realise what was happening, I didn't understand the sentence. It was only when they placed me on one of the hulk ships that my fate truly sunk in.'

'And your family?'

Shaking his head, Sam took a moment before replying. 'My mother and two sisters contracted a fever before my ship left for Australia. After I was arrested I never saw them again.'

Georgina slipped her hand into his and squeezed it tightly.

'That's awful. Truly awful. I'm surprised you ever wanted to return to England.'

Rallying, Sam turned to her and gave a small smile. 'Sometimes you have to put old ghosts to rest before you can move on with your life. I found myself ruminating about the past far too often—the only solution was to see if I could lay it to rest.'

'And that's why you returned here?'

He wasn't about to admit his main motivation was revenge.

'I wanted to see my childhood home again, visit my parents' and sisters' graves. Try to remember the happier times instead of letting everything be overshadowed by what came next.'

'Then you'll return to Australia?' Her voice was flat as she asked the question.

'Yes.' There was no point in lying. He didn't have anything keeping him in England, only a woman he could never have and bitter memories.

'And I'll be married.'

They sat in silence for a long time until Sam realised she was shivering beside him. Without thinking he wrapped an arm around her shoulders and pulled her in closer to his body. She resisted, but only for a fraction of a second, and then her chest was pressed against his, her cheek nestled in the hollow of his neck.

'The Duke seems a good man,' Sam said quietly.

'Don't.'

He nodded. It wasn't his place.

Suddenly Georgina sat up, her eyes searching for his. 'You were born in Hampshire,' she said. 'That's why you're here, isn't it?'

Not trusting himself to answer, he allowed her to continue.

'I thought it was strange, tricking my father into inviting you down here, but it is so you could have an excuse to visit the area, isn't it? To see your old home.'

'Yes.' It was easier her thinking that than the truth: he was trying to ruin her father, to show the world what an immoral old hypocrite the Earl truly was.

'Your home is close to here?'

'I grew up in a village called Little Abington.'

'I know it. It's only four miles away.'

'That close?' Sam knew exactly how close it was. It had taken him and his mother a little over an hour to walk the distance between their humble home and the Westchester estate.

'We could...' Georgina trailed off. 'I don't want to intrude, but I could accompany you if you would like to visit.'

'I'm not sure your mother would approve.'

The mischievous smile on her face made her look like a naughty little imp and Sam had to hold himself back to stop the almost overwhelming urge he had to kiss her.

'I've been sneaking out of the house under Mother's nose for more years than I care to remember,' Georgina said. 'I'm sure a little trip could be arranged.'

'With all your suitors here?'

She waved a dismissive hand. 'As you said, the Duke seems perfectly decent. And if he doesn't offer for me I can always fall back on Lord Rosenhall.'

'With the meddling mother?' Sam asked, remembering Georgina's comments about her suitors from a few weeks earlier.

'I've already got one meddling mother, I'm sure I can cope with a second.'

Chapter Fifteen

'**M**ount up, gentlemen,' the Earl called, already astride a huge horse that was stomping a hoof with impatience.

Sam looked around at his fellow guests, none of them looking too keen to be out at such an hour in the freezing temperatures. It was not yet ten, but the Earl had insisted on an early start time and, being their host, no one had dared to suggest to him he might like to make it later. Overnight a thin sprinkling of snow had fallen, not enough to cover the landscape entirely, but the ground was hard and unforgiving, and potential dangerous ruts in the earth were concealed, making the ride more dangerous.

For Sam the whipping, icy wind took him back to his childhood and he tried to work out how many years it had been since he'd seen snow.

'My daughter the intrepid rider,' the Earl called as Georgina rounded the corner on her beautiful grey horse, although all eyes were drawn to the majestic figure she cut in her royal-red riding habit. Sam had no doubt Lady Westchester had agreed to the hunt solely in order that the assembled suitors would see what a fine rider Georgina was and because she looked so damn attractive in a riding habit.

Only two other young women had decided to join them: Georgina's friend Miss Yaxley, who was fidgeting astride a frisky bay mare, and a Miss Farley, a young woman who had an unfortunately large nose on an otherwise pretty face and who Sam had been informed did not have the dowry to make up for this small shortcoming.

'Tell me,' Crawford said, manoeuvring his horse so he could be heard only by Sam, 'is the whole point of this actually to chase a fox?'

'Apparently so.'

'Seems a bit barbaric.'

'Chasing a poor defenceless animal and then watching it get torn apart by dogs?' Miss Yaxley said, inserting herself into their conversation. 'That's why I always root for the fox.'

'I can't really see the sport in it,' Sam murmured.

'One of the reasons I always insist on riding out,' Miss Yaxley confided quietly. 'I find my *inferior female* riding skills sometimes slows down the pace of the hunt, meaning it can give the fox chance to make his escape.'

'Commendable,' Crawford said.

'And how about you, Lady Georgina?' Sam asked as Georgina came to join them. 'What are your views on the hunt?'

'Horrible,' she said decisively. 'But Father will not be discouraged.'

As they spoke the barking of the dogs got louder and more frantic as if they sensed the hunt was about to begin. With a great flourish Lord Westchester called the assembled guests to attention before the horn was blown and the hunt underway. There was a hint of bloodlust in some of the men's eyes as they raced off after the dogs, the thundering of hooves and wild barking just seeming to rile them up further.

Sam glanced at Crawford, shrugged and spurred his horse on, following the rest of the men out of the courtyard and on to the estate. They'd only ridden perhaps less than half a mile when the first horse stumbled. It was being ridden by Lord Rosenhall, one of the men Georgina seemed to be seriously considering as a future husband, despite his overbearing mother. The horses had followed the dogs into a dense patch of wood and Lord Rosenhall had misjudged the width of a stream. The water had frozen solid in the freezing temperatures and the horse's hooves had scrabbled for purchase, but ultimately the animal had slipped and fallen.

Lord Rosenhall had been about halfway back from the front of the hunt and all the riders ahead of him had carried on oblivious to the slip, too intent on following the frenzied dogs who had caught the scent of a fox a few minutes previously.

Sam vaulted down from his horse and flung the reins to Crawford. They'd ridden together so many times he didn't even need to look back to know his friend had caught them before he slowly approached the frozen stream and the distressed animal.

Lord Rosenhall had been thrown, but unfortunately not far enough to be clear of the horse, and one leg was trapped under the animal's flank. He was groaning in pain as the horse repeatedly tried to stand on the slippery surface and each time slid a bit farther backwards.

'Hush,' Sam said, edging his way on to the frozen surface, cautiously stepping towards the fear-stricken man and animal. Gently he laid a hand on the horse's nose and began muttering soothing sounds. In the course of his work he often had to calm scared or wild horses, and he found a firm but gentle approach the best. 'Let's see if we can get you out of here,' he said.

Lord Rosenhall had fallen quiet and Sam spared him a glance to check the man was still alive. His face was screwed up in pain and deathly white, but the man seemed to be trying to follow Sam's lead and keep quiet so he didn't spook the horse any further.

Quickly Sam looked around, trying to find a safe path for the animal. A little to their left the stream turned a corner and there was a slightly shallower bank. The ice was still slippery, but it was worth a try.

'You take the horse, I'll take the man,' Crawford said from over his shoulder. Sam nodded and gently began to coax the horse upright again, guiding it towards the shallower bank. He heard a loud groan as Lord Rosenhall was freed, but didn't look back, trusting Crawford had everything under control.

After thirty seconds the horse was up the bank, stomping and snorting, but with no obvious injuries. Only then did Sam turn back to see what damage Lord Rosenhall had sustained.

Sam had been thrown from horseback more times than he cared to remember. It was a hazard of the job when you ran a stud. Once he'd broken his arm, an agonising injury that had kept him from riding for near on six weeks. On the other occasions he'd been lucky, knowing when to fall and roll and when to grimly cling on and try to make for softer ground. He knew how dangerous horses could be; they outweighed their riders several times over and could kill instantly if a hoof met with the wrong part of a man's body.

Lord Rosenhall was pale and drawn, unable to support himself entirely and clinging on to Crawford grimly, his face drawn with pain.

'I'll take him back,' Crawford called. 'You see to the horse?'

Sam watched as Crawford, Miss Yaxley and Miss Farley, who had also been at the rear of the hunt, prepared to return to Westchester Place. Georgina hesitated, hanging back as Lord Rosenhall was boosted on to the front of Crawford's horse and the party retraced their steps.

'I probably should inform my father of what happened,' she said, her eyes wide as she approached him.

'No,' he said, catching her hand. 'You're not riding anywhere on your own with the conditions like they are.'

'I've ridden in the snow plenty of times.'

'Then more fool you. Icy surfaces and uneven terrain can unseat even the most proficient rider.'

He felt a pang of panic at the idea of Georgina being the one thrown from her horse, stuck under the beast as it panicked and kicked.

'You think I'm a proficient rider,' she said, a faint smile on her lips.

'You have some talent,' he said.

'A compliment indeed coming from the only horseman in Australia.'

'Do you need help to mount, Lady Georgina?'

'A few weeks ago you called me Georgina.'

'A few weeks ago you kissed me,' Sam said.

Her cheeks pinkened at the memory and he wondered

how bad the consequences would be if he just gave in and kissed her again.

'Is that the price?' she asked. 'A kiss and in return you'll call me by my name.'

'A fair trade.'

If she'd leaned in then, he would have been powerless to stop himself, but she stood exactly where she was, biting her lip and looking like the most beautiful woman in the world. It was beyond foolish, this notion that anything could happen between them, but right now Sam wasn't thinking about the future. He wasn't thinking about his plans to seek revenge on her father or her impending nuptials with some yet undecided *suitable* gentleman. All he was thinking about was her lips, her body, the way her skin felt under his fingertips.

'Georgina,' he murmured, stepping forward. She smiled at him and not for the first time he wondered if he should just give up the idea of avenging his younger self and find a way to make her his. Not just for a day or a week, but for ever. It was a tempting thought, but unrealistic.

Every morning since their kiss a couple of weeks ago Georgina had woken with the image of Sam in her mind. He'd haunted her dreams with his confident grin and his teasing words, but mostly she'd woken feeling hot with thoughts of him kissing her, running his lips over her skin and making her his.

They were not thoughts a well brought-up young lady should have. Ever. Even about her husband, if much of society had their way. And certainly not about a convicted criminal who she barely knew while she was supposed to be searching for a reputable husband.

Despite trying to put him from her thoughts, vowing every night she would wake up and think of nothing more than spring flowers and newborn lambs, every morning there he was, haunting her.

And now here they were. Alone again, unchaperoned and able to do whatever they pleased with hardly any chance of being found out. The rest of the hunting party had moved on and Sam's friend would be almost back at the house by now with Lord Rosenhall.

Georgina swallowed, feeling her feet move towards him before her conscious mind acknowledged her decision.

'Kiss me one more time,' she murmured. Knowing that whatever she said she didn't want it to be the last time.

His lips were on hers instantly, gently at first, but within seconds his hands were tangled in her hair and he was pulling her even closer. Georgina looped her arms around his body, feeling the taut muscles of his chest and back.

Momentarily he pulled away and Georgina groaned as his lips found her neck, trailing kisses across the sensitive skin just below her earlobe and making her shiver with anticipation.

'I know we shouldn't…but I can't seem to keep away from you,' she whispered as his mouth sank lower, brushing up against the high neck of her riding habit.

'We shouldn't,' Sam agreed, his lips barely leaving her skin.

He pulled her closer again and through the thick layers of both their clothes she could feel his hardness. A primal longing somewhere deep inside her started to well up and it was all she could do to resist tearing at his clothes and begging him to make her his.

She gasped as he slid a finger beneath the thick material

of her riding habit and deftly undid the fastening that held the neck together. Only a small patch of skin was exposed, but immediately his lips found it and once again Georgina's body responded instantly.

'Wait,' he said, pulling away, and to her embarrassment she actually groaned as his lips left her skin.

This should have been the moment they came to their senses, Georgina knew that, but instead she watched impatiently as he tied the horses' reins to an overhanging tree branch and then turned back to her, a hungry and almost possessive look in his eyes.

Quickly he led her over to a fallen tree trunk, gently pushing her down on to it and then sinking down next to her. His fingers pushed back the riding habit from her shoulders. Only the skin of her neck was exposed, Georgina had worn multiple layers to combat the cold and Sam let out a groan of frustration.

'Damn weather,' he murmured, tracing a finger along her bare skin. Then he kissed her again, taking her breath away, and for a long time Georgina could think of nothing but his lips on hers.

When he pulled away, Georgina had no sense of how long they had been sitting there, only the icy chill in her feet indicating it was probably much longer than they should.

'We have to get back,' she said, a sudden panic washing over her. The party might have been split, but their absence would be noted eventually. Even though all she wanted to do was stay in the woods with Sam, it couldn't happen. Already she'd been beyond reckless, kissing him again, allowing the totally unrealistic fantasies to build in her mind.

She glanced at him, half of her hoping he would protest, wrap his arms around her, and refuse to let her go. A stab of disappointment ran through her as he nodded curtly and stood, turning back to take her hand and pull her from the fallen tree trunk. She had to keep telling herself that to him she was nothing more than a dalliance. And he should be nothing more than a temptation to be overcome in these few weeks before her wedding.

Allowing him to help her mount, she didn't wait for Sam to vault onto his horse's back and take the reins of Lord Rosenhall's mount before setting off through the forest. She didn't want him to see the tears in her eyes.

'He's never promised you anything,' she whispered to herself over and over again. And it was true. He'd never talked of a future together, never given her false hope. It wasn't hard to see that he genuinely liked her, that the kisses they'd shared weren't calculated to boost some deeper, hidden agenda. They were spontaneous and, just as she couldn't seem to keep away from him, she could see he fought the same struggle with her.

Despite all this Georgina still felt disappointed. He hadn't promised her anything, but that didn't mean she didn't want anything. Time and again she'd found herself daydreaming about riding through the wilds of Australia with Sam by her side as her husband. It was a life of freedom, a life of choices, the exact opposite of what she had now.

'Georgina,' Sam called from somewhere behind her, but they were out in the open now and she had the advantage of not needing to lead another horse back to the stables.

Pretending not to hear him, she pushed on, opening up the distance between them.

'Lady Georgina,' another deep voice called from somewhere to her left.

Quickly she turned, spotting the Duke making straight

for her, and with a grimace slowed her pace. *This* was the man she ought to be thinking about, not wasting her time on someone who was completely unsuitable.

'Your Grace,' she said, summoning her sunniest smile. 'I noticed your absence at the hunt—is anything amiss?'

'Lord Rosenhall took a tumble,' Georgina said, trying to ignore the sound of Sam riding up behind them. 'Mr Crawford has ridden on ahead and taken him back to the house, but the rest of the party, those who witnessed the fall, thought it best to return as well.'

Georgina saw the Duke's eyes flicker to where Sam was approaching.

'Miss Yaxley and Miss Farley, myself and Mr Robertson have returned. The rest of the hunting party didn't notice, I don't think,' Georgina said, trying to make out she hadn't been alone with Mr Robertson.

'No, I only noticed a few minutes ago and thought I would ensure nothing had happened,' the Duke said grimly. 'I apologise for my lack of observation.'

'There is no need to apologise, your Grace.'

'Shall we return to the house and check on Lord Rosenhall? If need be, I can always ride out to alert the rest of the hunting party and your father when we have more information.'

Together they turned their horses towards the house and set out at a comfortable pace. Georgina was aware of Sam hanging back, allowing her to arrive at Westchester Place with the Duke and not him. She should have been pleased with his consideration, but inside she felt as though her heart was bruised.

'Did you enjoy the hunt?' Georgina asked, knowing she

needed to make more of an effort with the man who might well end up being her future husband.

Glancing at him from the corner of her eye, she wondered what it would be like to spend the rest of her life as his wife. He was attractive enough, although in completely different ways to Sam. The Duke was tall and lean with dark hair and fair skin—a look that hinted at a life spent mainly indoors. Sam was the complete opposite, with a firm physique and taut muscles that could only be acquired through physical work and tanned skin that hadn't lost its glow despite him spending the past month in England in winter.

Stop comparing them, she told herself silently.

The Duke seemed kind and easy to talk to and so far she hadn't spotted any repulsive habits, but despite this she just couldn't imagine waking up as his wife every day for the rest of her life.

Chapter Sixteen

The house was in disarray, with half the male guests still out hunting with Lord Westchester and everyone else gossiping about what had happened to poor Lord Rosenhall. Georgina ensured she had paid the injured man a short visit, accompanied by her mother, just as the doctor was leaving. Lord Rosenhall had probably broken some ribs, but luckily his legs had escaped any fractures and were just bruised and sprained. He would recover and until then the doctor had given him a hefty dose of laudanum to ease some of the discomfort he was feeling.

With her duty done, Georgina informed her mother that she was suffering with a headache and was going to lie down for the rest of the afternoon. Normally her mother would have protested at Georgina abandoning her guests like this, but it was evidence of how much the accident had shaken Lady Westchester that she just murmured her agreement and said she would see Georgina at dinner.

Sitting at her writing desk, Georgina fiddled with the

ink pot, wondering what she should put in the note she was trying to write on the blank piece of paper in front of her. Last night she'd promised to accompany Sam to the village where he'd spent his childhood.

What she *should* put in the note was an apology and excuse for backing out of their plans, but somehow her fingers wouldn't obey the rational part of her brain. She needed space from him, time to try to understand what the roiling emotions deep inside her actually meant. The last thing she needed was to spend an illicit afternoon in his company.

Although…she *had* promised.

Dipping her pen in the ink, she wrote quickly before she had a chance to change her mind again.

Dear Sam,
I will meet you at the estate gates at three.
Georgina

Peeking out of her bedroom door, Georgina waited for a passing maid and quietly asked her to deliver the note to Mr Robertson. No doubt there would be a little gossip in the servants' quarters, but it was safer than Georgina being caught in the guest wing with an incriminating message.

Sam didn't carry a pocket watch—there wasn't much need for it when he was back home, timings were determined by the brightness of the sun and the heat of the day, and his social calendar hadn't exactly been full. He'd left the house at half past two, saddled up his horse, declining the offer of help from the grooms, and taken a leisurely ride down the long drive to the front gates. Now he was waiting.

Part of him wondered if Georgina would change her mind. It would be the sensible thing to do after their kiss in the woods, it was what he should be encouraging, but instead he found himself hoping to see her appearing around the curve in the driveway.

'Keep your distance,' he cautioned himself, knowing that he wouldn't take his own advice. Even though he knew one day soon Georgina would probably hate him for what he would do to her father, he still couldn't seem to keep her from his thoughts.

'Good afternoon.' The voice came from behind him, causing Sam to wheel around quickly. Georgina was approaching along the lane leading to the main gates of the estate. 'I thought it best to leave the grounds through one of the smaller gates,' Georgina explained, 'just in case anyone noted our movements.'

'Very sensible,' Sam murmured. He was too distracted to say any more, his mind remembering their kiss just a little too vividly and his body responding to that memory. He wanted to lean across the gap between them, pull Georgina from her horse and settle her in his lap.

'I probably shouldn't have come,' Georgina said as they set out at a sedate pace down the lane.

'Probably not,' Sam agreed.

'Normally I'm very sensible,' Georgina murmured. 'It's just these last few weeks…'

She glanced at him and he grinned at her.

'It's my irresistible Australian charm.'

'I think I'm losing my mind. I should be back at the house trying to get the Duke to propose to me.'

'Do you want the Duke to propose to you?'

He found it hurt more than it should when she shrugged. 'It would keep my parents happy.'

'What about your happiness?'

'That doesn't come into it,' she said.

Sam could understand the notion of not having any choices in life. For years he had been treated as less than human, not allowed to even decide what clothes he wore or when he rose from bed in the morning. When he had served out his sentence, during those first few heady weeks of being a free man, he had felt a little overwhelmed by the multitude of decisions he had to make throughout the day. Even then, he would never have wanted to go back to not being able to decide the little things like what to have for breakfast or the big things such as what to do with his life. Everyone deserved that freedom.

'Enough about me,' Georgina said brightly, as if trying to push away a horrible thought with a breezy tone. 'This afternoon is about you. We've spent enough time dwelling on my inevitable marriage.'

In truth, Sam would like to dwell on it a little more, until Georgina saw she shouldn't have to go through with a union that might make her unhappy for the rest of her life. Instead he nodded in agreement. After all, it wasn't as though he could offer her an appealing alternative future.

'Would it be too painful to tell me about your childhood?' Georgina asked.

He shook his head. His childhood contained mainly happy memories. Although his father had died when he was young, Sam's mother had strived to provide a happy and safe home for her children. They might not have had much money, but Sam had always felt loved. That he was grateful for.

'My father died when I was young,' Sam said, 'so my mother raised all of us children by herself. She was a strong woman and I can't ever remember wanting for anything despite the loss of our father.'

'Did she work?'

Sam nodded, remembering the day she'd started work at Westchester Place. All the family had harboured high hopes of the future. After a bleak spell following Sam's father's death the job at Westchester Place had seemed like a godsend, a fresh start for the bereaved family. His mother's fears that she would not be able to provide for her children had subsided with her new source of income and her optimism had rubbed off on her children.

'She was a cook,' he said, trying to keep his answers as vague as possible. There were only a handful of families in the area with a house anywhere near as grand as Westchester Place and Georgina would be familiar with all of them. 'She enjoyed her work,' he added. Both his parents had believed that if you worked hard and lived a good and honest life then you would be rewarded in kind. Their philosophy had rubbed off on Sam as a child and it had made being arrested for a crime he hadn't committed that much harder to accept.

'And you said you had sisters?'

'Two younger. Anne was eight when I was sentenced and Betty was six.' Two beautiful little girls with the same golden blond hair as him. They'd looked perpetually angelic, with wide smiles and perfect dimples, although they had been cheeky and full of life. It had been a while since he'd thought of his two sweet little sisters, always finding the memories too hard, too painful. When he thought of the lives they could be living now a lump formed in his throat.

'I'm sorry,' Georgina said and he could see she truly felt for him. Not that he supposed she could imagine losing her freedom and entire family within the space of a few months. 'You said it was a winter fever?'

He grimaced. That was the simple explanation. His mother and sisters had contracted one of the deadly fevers that spread through the villages every winter and that year they had succumbed, but Sam knew there was more to it than that.

'After I was arrested, my mother lost her job and from what I could gather found it hard to gain another position,' he said, trying to keep the bitterness out of his voice. 'Without my father around, or any other close family, they would have struggled to buy food. When the fever hit they would have been malnourished and vulnerable.'

He'd seen it time and time again as a child. It was always the weakest, those who had not had a proper meal for weeks, that were the most susceptible, succumbing to the illnesses and diseases that would claim their lives.

Georgina shook her head. 'Sometimes you don't realise the far-reaching consequences of a single action. One false accusation and it doesn't just ruin the life of the accused, but those around him as well,' she said quietly.

It was something he'd often pondered, whether his family would still have been alive if the Earl hadn't accused him of theft. Sam knew in reality it was impossible to say one way or another, but in his heart he believed they would be.

They rode in silence for a few minutes, bending their heads against the icy winds and flexing their fingers against the chill.

'Have you ever thought about confronting the person who accused you?' Georgina asked as they rounded a bend in the road. Up ahead in the distance Sam could just about make out the steeple of Little Abington's church. It was a sight that conjured up all manner of memories, always the first sight to be seen on any journey home.

'The E...' Sam quickly trailed off. He'd nearly let slip it was an earl who'd condemned him to six years of hard labour and been instrumental in the deaths of his family. Georgina's father was the only Earl for miles and miles, it would be rather obvious who he meant. 'The evil old bastard that ruined my life?' he corrected himself quickly.

Georgina nodded, not commenting on his language.

'I've fantasised about it for years.'

'It might help you to move on,' she said softly, 'if you could look him in the eye and tell him what he did to you.'

'He'd probably laugh in my face, but maybe that would be worth it to make him pay for what he did.'

Georgina shook her head. 'He might have dismissed a ten-year-old boy, but you're a man of influence now, it would be much harder to dismiss you.' She paused, throwing him a sideways glance as if trying to assess his reaction. 'You said he was an influential man—I'm guessing he was at least a member of the gentry. I do know most of those families, as well as the titled ones, of course. Perhaps I could arrange a meeting.'

'No,' Sam said quickly and a little too abruptly. He needed to change the subject before Georgina found out the truth. She might act meek and mild for her suitors, but Sam knew she was shrewd and intelligent. He'd have to tread carefully or she would find out their whole acquaintance had been orchestrated to allow him to get close to her father.

Grimacing, he pictured her reaction. It wasn't pretty. However he imagined it she was hurt and betrayed by his deception and irate that she'd been used in such a way.

For now he pushed these thoughts from his mind. One

day soon Georgina would find out about his lies and the idea of losing her was almost too much to bear. But he was so close, so near to achieving his aim. For eighteen long years he'd fantasised about the moment he got to confront the Earl and in some small way have his own revenge. He couldn't give up now, not even for the woman riding beside him.

'Today I don't want to think of him,' he said quickly. 'I don't want him to intrude on the memories of my mother and sisters.'

Next to him he saw Georgina nod and then, coaxing her horse closer to his, she reached across and placed her gloved hand over his.

Chapter Seventeen

Watching him closely, Georgina saw the host of emotions flitting across Sam's face. Little Abington must have changed considerably in eighteen years, but she could tell Sam was seeing it how it used to be rather than how it was now. He looked past the new houses on the edge of the village, making his way directly to the church that stood proudly in the very centre.

They paused just outside the graveyard, looking over the low stone wall before dismounting.

'Would you like me to come in?' she asked. He shook his head, handed her the reins of his horse and pushed open the gate. He only took a couple of steps before stopping. She could see he hadn't reached any graves yet, instead he looked frozen in place as if unable to continue. Georgina had never lost anyone she was really close to—of course her grandparents had passed away many years earlier and a distant aunt when Georgina was no more than a child—but she'd never had to deal with the loss of a parent or sibling.

Looking at Sam's face, she couldn't begin to imagine how difficult it must be to lose your entire family.

The seconds ticked by and still he didn't move. Georgina quietly dismounted, tied both reins to an overhanging branch and stepped into the graveyard. Only once she was by Sam's side did he look up and notice her.

Throughout their acquaintance Georgina had never known Sam to hesitate, he'd always done exactly what he wanted when he wanted, but right now she could see through the confident public persona to the man underneath.

Gently she slipped her hand into his and felt his fingers curl around her palm. He looked down at her then and she wished she could wash away all the years of hurt and suffering that she could read on his face.

'Come on,' she said softly, 'let's go together.'

He stepped forward, weaving through the graveyard until he stopped in front of a simple stone with four names engraved on it. *Thomas Robertson, Marianne Robertson, Anne Robertson, Betty Robertson.* Georgina felt the tears spring to her eyes as she watched Sam crouch down in front of it and place a hand on the top of the gravestone.

For a moment she had to look away, feeling uncontrollably sad for the little boy who had lost his freedom and his entire family within the space of a year. She doubted he'd had much chance to grieve in the early days. If the stories about the hulk ships and the conditions convicted criminals were transported under were to be believed, he would have needed his entire focus to be on surviving.

Wishing she'd brought some flowers to place on the graves, she glanced at the hedgerows, but it was the middle of winter and there were no wildflowers blooming. In a couple of weeks she would return with something cut from the garden.

After a few minutes Sam stood, his face unnaturally stony, but Georgina could see the tears in his eyes.

'You loved them very much, didn't you?' she asked.

'I did.'

Silently she wrapped her arms around him, feeling his head droop and rest on her shoulder. They stood together for a long time, neither moving, neither saying anything, but Georgina could feel the beating of his heart and rise and fall of his chest which was peculiarly reassuring.

'Shall we return?' he asked eventually.

'Is there anywhere else you'd like to visit?'

He shook his head and Georgina got the impression the memories the visit was raking up were a little too painful. They walked back through the graveyard hand in hand and, before they remounted their horses, Sam turned to her, brushing a stray strand of hair back behind her ear.

'Thank you,' he said, his voice low and grave. 'I don't think I could have done that without you.'

Not many men of Georgina's acquaintance would admit such a thing. Without another word he took the reins from her and vaulted up onto the back of his horse.

As they rode Georgina kept stealing little glances at Sam. He was deep in thought, a frown etched on his forehead and his mouth set into a hard line. She could tell he was thinking of the man he thought responsible for ruining his childhood and ultimately causing the deaths of his mother and sisters.

An unfamiliar sensation started to creep over Georgina. She suddenly felt protective of Sam, wanted to take away some of his pain. A part of her wanted to confront the man who had done this to him, to fight for some sort of peace to be restored inside Sam's mind.

You're falling for him, the little voice in her head whispered. Georgina tried to banish it. She wouldn't deny she found him physically attractive and, when he turned to her with those sparkling blue eyes and that beguiling smile, she wanted to throw herself into his arms, but that was physical. On an emotional level they were friends, nothing more. It might be an entirely inappropriate and ill-considered friendship, but a friendship was what it was.

You want him, the voice taunted. Georgina shook her head, trying to get the image of Sam as her husband out of her mind. It was an impossible dream; she had to marry someone respectable, someone rich, someone titled. Someone her parents would approve of. If she didn't, if she did something foolish and ran off with Sam, then she had no doubt they would disown her. They might love her, but she was under no illusion that she would be cut from her parents' lives instantly and entirely. Everything she'd ever had, everyone she had ever known, would be wiped away in an instant.

But what if it was worth it? No, she couldn't think like that. She had to believe that an arranged marriage to a suitable man she did not love that allowed her to keep her friends and family, her position in society, would be better than throwing all that away for one man. Even if she did feel a warmth deep inside her whenever he looked at her.

They arrived back at the main gates and Sam quickly dismounted and took her hand.

'Thank you,' he said, squeezing her hand. They both wore thick gloves to protect them from the cold, but Georgina fancied she could still feel his warmth through the layers.

As he looked up into her eyes Georgina felt her heart begin to pound in her chest and she knew, in that instant, that if he asked her to run away with him she would.

Instead he raised her gloved hand to his lips, turned it over, and placed a kiss on the bare skin of her wrist, where the material of her riding habit didn't quite meet her glove. Before she'd had chance to recover he'd let go of her hand, mounted his horse, and disappeared through the gates and down the winding drive, leaving her to enter the estate from a different direction.

'Fancy a game?' Crawford asked, holding up a pack of cards in his hand.

As a rule Sam didn't ever play cards against Crawford if money was involved; his friend had an unbelievable talent when it came to most card games that left his opponents heavily out of pocket. However, a game where there was no money at stake would be a good way to take his mind off the events of the afternoon.

They were sitting at the little table in Sam's room, dressed and ready for dinner, but neither of them too keen to rush downstairs to start socialising with their hosts or the rest of the guests.

'How was it?' Crawford asked quietly.

'Pretty damn terrible.'

'You glad you went?'

Sam shrugged, unable to put into words how it was cathartic to finally see his mother's and sisters' resting place, but how it had also been like a dagger to the heart. When he'd first stepped into the graveyard he had frozen and, without Georgina's intervention, without her reassuring presence by his side, he doubted he would have been able to continue.

Crawford leaned over, clasped him on the shoulder, and squeezed. Over the years the two men had gone through so much together and often, like right now, no words were needed between the two men; it was enough to know that he was there.

'How much did you tell the lovely Lady Georgina?' Crawford asked after a few minutes of playing cards in silence.

'I told her what happened all those years ago, nearly everything except the name of the man who accused me. She suggested she facilitate a meeting with the man who was responsible for everything.'

'I take it she doesn't know that was her father.'

Sam shook his head grimly.

'Sam,' Crawford said, his voice filled with concern, 'you know I wouldn't normally meddle...'

It was true, they were all grown men, all perfectly capable of making their own decisions and their own mistakes. They made it a habit not to interfere in each other's life decisions, only to be there to support and help if needed.

'But I'm worried about you. I'm worried about all of this.'

'It's just bad memories,' Sam said.

Crawford shook his head. 'You're falling for that girl,' he said bluntly.

Sam looked up in surprise. He'd expected his friend to start talking about how revenge wasn't the answer to his problems, how it wouldn't really change anything, wouldn't give him the peace he was looking for. All things that Sam had thought himself on the journey over here and the time they'd been in England. Over and over he'd questioned whether it was really worth pursuing the Earl, whether it would solve anything. Deep down he knew even after he confronted the old man nothing would change, not really, but Sam had to do this for himself. For the scared little boy who'd been torn from his family at the age of ten and the mother and sisters he never saw again.

'Georgina?' he asked, trying to buy himself some time.

'You're falling for her,' Crawford repeated.

'I'm not.'

'Trust me, I know the signs.' It was true that his friend was rarely without a woman or two as a willing companion, but Sam didn't think Ben had ever been in love. Surely he would know about it. 'You can't stop thinking about her, she invades your dreams, she influences everything you do.'

All those things were true. But it didn't mean he was in love.

'What's going to happen when Lady Georgina finds out you only befriended her to get close to her father?'

Sam stared at the cards in his hand. He'd pondered the same thing over and over again and the answer was simple: she'd never forgive him.

'Or when you humiliate her father, expose him for the man he is?'

'She won't ever speak to me again,' Sam said quietly.

'And you're willing to sacrifice what you have with her for a revenge that won't even make you feel much better?'

'I don't have anything with her,' Sam murmured. 'She has to marry someone influential, someone with an impressive title, not a convicted criminal from Australia.'

'Nonsense,' Crawford said with a dismissive wave of the hand. 'She doesn't *have* to do anything. You could elope, you could whisk her back to Australia and live a full and happy life with her.'

It was a tempting idea, but one that could never be.

'I couldn't ask her to give up everything, to leave everyone she's ever known behind.'

'And that, my friend, is love,' Crawford said quietly.

Closing his eyes, Sam tried to banish the dangerously appealing idea of whisking Georgina away from his mind. He couldn't do it to her. She'd been born into a life of luxury and privilege. Raised to be a countess or even a duchess, he couldn't ask her to give that all up to be the wife of an ex-convict in the wilds of Australia.

'Think about it,' Crawford said, rising from his seat and placing a hand on Sam's shoulder for a second. 'No point you both being unhappy. And once you've revealed who you really are and why you're here, there will be no going back.'

Sam had stayed sitting in the same place for at least twenty minutes after his friend had left the room, contemplating his words. Crawford was an idealist, despite everything that had happened to him in his life. He sailed through the world, approaching everything with optimism that generally meant he got what he wanted. If this was his dilemma, Sam knew that his friend would abandon all thoughts of revenge and work on ensuring that they would live happily ever after.

Enough, he told himself. Nothing had changed. To think he, a servant's son who'd been transported for stealing, had a chance with the most eligible young lady in England was laughable. He would do better to stick to his original plan and try to get some closure on the old wounds her father had inflicted on him.

* * *

'Perhaps you'd care to step outside for some air,' the Duke said, offering Georgina his arm.

She smiled sweetly, almost politely declining straight away. Up until very recently her policy had been to never step outside alone with a gentleman. She'd only broken the rule twice and that had landed her in this situation where she was being pushed to marry to save her reputation. Then she caught her mother's expression out of the corner of her eye and remembered that she was meant to be trying to get the Duke to propose.

'That would be lovely,' she said.

It was bitterly cold out and Georgina paused before stepping through the glass doors to motion to one of the footmen to fetch her warmest cloak. Only once she was securely wrapped up did she take the Duke's arm and step out on to the terrace.

'How are you enjoying the party, your Grace?' Georgina asked.

'It is diverting, although a shame about what happened to poor Lord Rosenhall.'

'Indeed.' Georgina realised guiltily that she hadn't spared a thought for the injured lord since visiting him earlier in the afternoon.

'It's cold, Lady Georgina,' the Duke said, turning to face her, 'so I will get straight to the matter in hand.'

Georgina's heart plummeted. She'd received enough marriage proposals to know when a man was about to ask for her hand.

'I find myself approaching forty and my life is not what I expected it to be. I have my estates, my political commitments, and, of course, the title, but I had always imagined having a family by now. A wife to share my life with and children to carry on the family name.'

This was exactly what she should want. To be the wife of a duke was an honour and she knew almost every other single young woman of her acquaintance would be jumping with joy at the direction of this conversation. Instead she found herself wanting to run away before he could say any more.

'We do not know each other well, of course, but over our last few meetings I have got the impression that we would suit one another…' He paused, searching her face as if looking for confirmation. 'That is, as long as you do not have your eye on someone else.'

She glanced up sharply, wondering if he had heard the rumours about her and Sam.

'I like you, Lady Georgina, and I'm sure I could give you a happy life, a contented life.' He picked up her hand and kissed her lightly across the knuckles. Georgina smiled weakly. He was right, he probably could give her a contented life. With his fortune and title she would want for nothing and her first-born son would be the next Duke.

'Take a day or two, consider my proposal,' he said with an indulgent smile. 'I want you to be sure in your decision. If you agree, we can approach your father at the end of the weekend.'

Unable to trust her own voice, Georgina nodded. If her mother were here she'd be pushing Georgina to accept immediately—he was a duke, after all. And she probably would accept him, but she needed a little time first, time to come to terms with the fact that she would be marrying a man she did not love when there was a man she was starting to fall for staying in the same house. She would be choosing wealth and status over love and she needed at least a couple more days to fully accept that.

Chapter Eighteen

Throughout dinner he'd found himself staring at Georgina time and time again. It was ill advised, he knew that, and the direction of his attention had earned him some black looks from Lady Westchester, who'd spent most of the meal staring at him.

He'd planned to make a speedy exit and retire to his room straight after the meal, but Lord Westchester had gripped him by the arm and guided him towards the older man's study. Two hours Sam had listened to him sermonising on the immorality of the poor, two hours of clenching his teeth and biting his tongue. Throughout his mind kept wandering, kept trying to escape the toxic opinions, but the Earl didn't seem to notice. He had his captive audience and that was all he cared about. On more than one occasion Sam had been sorely tempted to ask about the poor maids the Earl had pushed himself upon, whether they would agree that Lord Westchester had an upstanding and moral character.

'I lead by example, of course,' the Earl was saying as Sam

rose from his chair after suggesting it was probably time to call it a night. 'Make sure my wife and my daughter are well turned out at the society meetings, that sort of thing.'

'They're a credit to you,' Sam murmured.

'This year I will see the fruition of all my work, with Mr Moorcroft as Prime Minister, all being well. Then I can really begin to influence some of the policies of this country.'

As soon as he could he bade the older man goodnight, wondering if there was anything he'd heard in the last two hours that might help with his confrontation with the Earl, but he couldn't find anything of use. Sighing he climbed the stairs, turning into the guest corridor to find Miss Yaxley, Georgina's friend, hovering outside his door.

'Good,' she said in a theatrical whisper. 'I thought I may have missed you and you'd retired already.'

'Should you be here, Miss Yaxley?' Sam asked.

Waving a dismissive hand, Miss Yaxley then motioned at the bundle at her feet. Sam peered at it, but couldn't make out what it was.

'I've been friends with Georgie for longer than I can remember,' she said softly. 'She's good and kind and loyal, and she deserves at least one night of happiness if she's going to be pushed into a marriage she doesn't want.'

Sam's eyes widened at the idea of 'one night of happiness'. Images of Georgina writhing beneath him, her back arching, her hips coming to meet his own, came unbidden into his mind. Surely that wasn't what Miss Yaxley meant.

'Georgie likes you,' Miss Yaxley said, 'and we all know nothing can come of it, but I've seen the way you look at her, too.'

Like he wanted to devour every inch of her and then spend the rest of time with her in his arms.

'I sent her a note telling her to meet you by the pond at midnight. Perhaps you could show her what it is like to be wooed by a man who cares about her and not her title or her dowry, just for one night.'

Deftly she picked up the bundle at her feet and passed it to him. It was heavy and by the time he'd unwrapped it Miss Yaxley had disappeared down the corridor.

Inside there were two pairs of old ice skates. They were dusty and looked as though they hadn't seen daylight in at least a decade, but from what he could see they looked functional. One pair was much larger than the other, but both had laces to help adjust the size. He wondered where Miss Yaxley had found the old skates—by the looks of them they'd been hidden away in an attic room or at the back of a cupboard for a very long time.

He debated. What he should do was put aside the skates and retire to his bedroom. Alone.

It would be beyond foolish to seek out Georgina at the pond, but, he reasoned, it wouldn't be gentlemanly to leave her there waiting for him if he didn't show.

Before the sensible part of him could object he went into his room, gathered a selection of his warmest clothes and made his way downstairs, slipping out a side door so as not to draw too much attention to himself.

She was already waiting for him, her figure silhouetted in the light of the moon. As he drew closer he saw she, too, had come prepared, dressed in a thick cloak, the hood lined with fur. Immediately he started to undress her in his mind, imagining peeling off layer upon layer until he reached the creamy softness of her skin. It was a tantalising thought and one he would not be able to put from his mind.

'I wasn't sure you'd come,' Georgina said softly as he stopped beside her. 'Caroline and her grand schemes.'

'You knew what she'd planned?'

Georgina looked at him with a small smile. 'She thinks I deserve to have one night of happiness before I resign myself to a loveless marriage.'

Sam swallowed. It was a lot of responsibility, the expectation he could give her that night of happiness, but he was damn well going to try. He watched her unconsciously sway towards him and knew he wouldn't be able to keep his hands from touching her. Every time he saw her he felt a fire deep inside and soon it felt as though it would consume him.

'And what would make you happy, my lady?'

In the moonlight he saw her tongue flick out between her lips nervously and he knew then that she wanted all manner of things she could never put into words. She was the daughter of an earl, a respectable young woman. It would be too hard for her to come out and tell him exactly what she wanted him to do to her.

'Perhaps a kiss?' he suggested.

Wordlessly she nodded and his lips were on hers in an instant. She tasted sweet and Sam felt his whole body tighten in anticipation. If he were a gentleman, he would walk away right now before Georgina did something she would come to regret. But he wasn't a gentleman, he was a country boy made good, an ex-convict, a man who didn't have to conform to society's rules. So instead of walking away he pulled Georgina closer and tangled his hands in her hair.

At last he pulled away, aware that if he kissed her for a moment longer he might lose control completely and ravish her on the hard, cold ground.

'Miss Yaxley gave me a present,' Sam said, brandishing

the bundle. With Georgina's eyes on him he unwrapped it, pulling out the two pairs of skates.

'Ice skating?' Georgina asked, her voice incredulous, 'Only Caroline could think of these things.'

'Would you like to...?'

'I've never skated before. Father has always said it is an activity the upper echelons of society should not engage in.'

'Your father has some strange ideas.'

'Have you skated before?'

Sam thought back to the cold winters of his youth, of his father taking him out on the frozen pond in the village for the first time, and then later occasions with friends. They didn't have ice skates, of course, but that hadn't stopped them.

'Not for many years,' he said, taking her hand and leading Georgina to a tree stump a few feet away from the edge of the pond. 'But I'm sure it is something that comes back quickly.'

Deftly he unlaced her boots, pulling them off before pausing. He looked up into her eyes, both of them remembering the shoe-related incident that had put Georgina on the path to marriage. Unable to stop himself, he ran his fingers over the sole of her foot, feeling her tense as he did so.

'One night of happiness...' he murmured to himself. He wondered if that meant the same to Georgina as it did to him. He hoped so—for so long he had been keeping his desires under tight control, but tonight they threatened to overflow.

Taking his time, he fitted the skates on her feet, allowing his hands to linger on her slender calves, his fingers caressing just a little higher than was strictly needed. As he touched the soft skin just beneath her knees he heard

Georgina inhale sharply and when he glanced up he saw her face was flushed, but she wasn't giving him any indication she wanted him to stop.

He heard her groan ever so quietly as he pulled away to fit his own boots. This wasn't a good idea, at least it wasn't a sensible idea, but Georgina wanted one night of happiness and he was damned if he would do the sensible thing and walk away. He wanted Georgina, and, for a long time, Sam had ensured he got what he wanted.

'Come on,' he said, pulling her up onto her feet once his own skates were fitted. His boots were a little tight, probably a size or two too small, but it was worth the discomfort when he saw the smile light up Georgina's face as they tentatively stepped on to the surface of the pond.

'Is it safe?' she asked as she gripped his arm.

'The pond is small and frozen solid,' Sam reassured her. 'It's safe.'

After a few minutes he had found his rhythm and, with Georgina on his arm, began to move a little faster. The quiet shrieks of delight that came from her as they glided across the ice made him grin and as he felt her body pressing against his he knew the unspoken desire between them was unlikely to be kept under control for much longer.

'Would you like to try on your own?' he asked.

She looked up at him and shook her head, clinging tighter on to his arm. Slowly he spun her round, encircling her with his free arm as he did so, and in the middle of the frozen pond he kissed her again.

'You're shivering,' he said, reaching up a hand, pulling off a glove and touching her cheek. It was icy cold. 'We need to get you inside.'

'I don't want this moment to end,' Georgina said quietly.

'Me neither.'

They stood there for a few seconds longer, looking into each other's eyes, and Sam had images of what it would be like to have Georgina in his life for ever. Pictures of them riding out through the Australian wilderness, collapsing into bed together at the end of the day and enjoying long, lazy mornings with just one another for company. It was a dream, nothing more, but in that moment Sam could imagine it so clearly.

'Come here,' he said, pulling her into his arms. He kissed her, feeling the chill of her skin contrasting with the warmth of her mouth, and knew tonight she would be his, even if only for a few hours. 'Shall we go somewhere a little warmer?'

'Perhaps...' Georgina started to say, then trailed off.

Sam knew this was the moment where she decided whether to throw away her virtue, to sacrifice it for one night of pleasure, or whether to keep it for the first night of a loveless marriage.

'Perhaps we could go to the old gatehouse,' she suggested after a long pause. 'The old couple who lived there recently moved out and Father hasn't found any new tenants. All the furniture is still there...'

He kissed her again before she could change her mind and whisked her off the ice. It took a couple of minutes to change from the ice skates back into their boots, but then they were half walking, half running across the grass towards the gatehouse at the entrance to the estate.

Sam held Georgina's hand tightly, ensuring she didn't stumble in the darkness, and felt the anticipation build inside him. It felt as though they'd been building to this moment for so long. He was determined just to enjoy it, to enjoy *her*, bring her pleasure, and to put out of his mind the fact that this was their one and only night together before they both had to go their separate ways.

'It's locked,' Georgina said, her face falling as they tried the door.

'You forget,' Sam said with a grin, 'you're in the company of a convicted criminal.'

'You know how to break into a locked house?' Georgina asked, her eyes wide.

'Well…' Sam shrugged and then pointed up to a window on the first floor that was the very slightest bit ajar.

Georgina giggled before turning serious. 'But how will you get up there?'

The old gatehouse was built of stone, with enough handholds that Sam might have been able to scale the side of the building and manoeuvre himself through the open window. It would take a lot of effort, though, and if he wasn't careful he might end up falling from the height of a good few feet.

Glancing at Georgina, he knew that risk was worth it, but anything to lessen the climb would be helpful.

'Give me a hand,' he said, moving over to where there were a couple of old crates pushed up against a wall. Together they moved them to the spot under the open window and with a loud groan Sam hoisted one on top of the other. Now it would only be a short climb to the open window.

Deftly he pulled himself up on top of the crates and then, testing the stone handholds, quickly covered the rest of the distance to the window. Within seconds he was through the gap, tumbling onto the floor of the dark room on the other side. He took a moment to catch his breath and then headed through the dark house to the front door, opening it to let Georgina in.

'You told me you weren't guilty of the crime you were accused of,' Georgina said as she watched him throw a couple more logs on the fire. 'And then I find you're a master at breaking into locked houses.'

He grinned at her, that confident, charming grin that made her heart pound in her chest.

'You've rumbled me,' he said. 'I'm the most wanted man in Australia.'

Poking the fire with an iron poker they'd found in the living room, Sam waited until he was satisfied the logs were burning before sitting down on the end of the bed beside her. The gatehouse came furnished and they'd managed to find some bedsheets and a thick blanket in a chest in the corner of the room. Everything was ready for them to sink below the covers and, as he turned to Georgina, he knew there was no turning back now.

Now the fire was burning brightly Georgina could feel that the chill of an uninhabited house had been banished and started to pull her gloves off. They were both still clad in all their layers, but as she met Sam's gaze she knew this wouldn't be the state of affairs for long.

Nervously she swallowed, realising that now there was no going back. She'd made her decision, a decision that most would think foolish. A duke had asked for her hand in marriage, but here she was giving her virtue to a man who had never promised her anything, a man who would be hounded from society if people knew the truth about his origins.

Still, it *was* her decision. Georgina didn't get to control many things in her life, but this was something that was entirely her decision.

'Are you sure you want to do this with an old criminal like me?' Sam asked.

She nodded, unable to say the words. Reaching out, Sam deftly unfastened her thick cloak, pulling it from her shoulders. As it fell behind her on to the bed she shivered, but not with the cold. She saw his eyes devouring her, flitting over her body, and then his hands followed, fingers trailing across the material of her dress, working her up into a frenzy.

'Tell me, Lady Georgina,' he said with a mischievous glint in his eye, 'what would you like me to do to you?'

She felt the blood flood to her cheeks as she stammered, 'I don't know.' She did know, had been fantasising about it for many weeks now, but putting it into words seemed far too difficult, far too embarrassing.

'Don't lie,' he reprimanded softly. 'You know exactly what you want.'

He paused and then when she didn't say anything he began trailing kisses across the skin of her neck, stopping every few seconds to speak. 'Perhaps you'd like it if I kissed you here?' he asked. 'Or maybe you'd prefer it if I touched you here?' He dipped a finger beneath the neckline of her dress, lingering for a moment before pulling away. 'Or maybe you'd like something different entirely?'

'Yes,' she managed to stutter.

'Yes to what?'

'Yes to everything.'

She saw the fire flare in his eyes and immediately his hands were on her, unfastening her dress as if he'd done it a thousand times. He pushed down the thick material, allowing it to pool at her hips before she wriggled free. Underneath she wore a long petticoat and a cotton chemise, all layers to keep the cold out. Here in the deserted gatehouse the air was still chilly, despite the warmth the fire was giving off. Georgina felt her body tremble and saw the frown form on Sam's face.

'I'm being selfish,' he murmured. 'I've wanted to see you like this for so long.'

Quickly he ushered her under the covers on the bed, only pausing to shed his topmost layers before climbing in beside her. His hands were warm on her skin and she tentatively placed her palms on his chest, feeling the hard muscle through the cotton of his shirt.

'May I?' he asked, gripping the hem of her chemise. Wordlessly she nodded, her mouth too dry for her to form a coherent answer. With a little wriggling, and a fit of giggles when the chemise got tangled in her hair, they managed to lift it off and suddenly Georgina felt very naked. Never before had a man seen her like this and she'd always assumed it would only be her husband who did.

'You're having doubts,' Sam said, his hand falling still on her shoulder.

'No,' she said, repeating 'no' even more earnestly.

This might go against everything she had been raised to believe, but in this moment it felt good, it felt right.

To show him she meant it she gripped his shirt, pulling it over his head, and then, feeling a little brazen, slipped her fingers into the waistband of his trousers and insistently pushed them downwards. He groaned as her hand brushed against him and Georgina felt some primal satisfaction at the thought that she could do this to a man, her man.

Then his lips were on hers, his body above her, his hands caressing and making her writhe with pleasure. He dipped his head under the covers and slowly, teasing all the time, he took one of her nipples into his mouth and Georgina had to hold a hand to her lips to stop herself from screaming with pent-up desire.

She ran her hands over his back, feeling the smooth contours of the muscles, raking her fingers over his buttocks, and then pausing before taking his manhood into her hands. He looked her in the eyes, kissed her hard on the lips, and then began to push inside her.

The sensation was like nothing Georgina had ever felt before, but just as she thought it might be too uncomfortable Sam paused, stroked her hair, and kissed her long and hard. Slowly he began moving again, thrusting his hips backwards and forward gently at first, building with each passing minute. Georgina felt her own hips raise instinctively to meet his as deep inside a warmth was staring to build.

'Sam,' she murmured, with that one word begging him not to stop.

He looked down at her, his eyes intense, but that same familiar smile on his face. Faster and faster they moved, until Georgina felt the pressure inside build to such a level she knew it was going to explode. All at once her muscles contracted and wave after wave of pleasure spread through her body. Above her Sam groaned and tensed, and they stayed pressed together for a long minute while they both came back to earth.

He kissed her before rolling to one side and gathering her in his arms. Georgina knew she should feel shame or guilt, but right now all she felt was warmth and happiness. She was being held in the arms of a man she thought she might well be falling in love with. It couldn't last, but right now in this moment she was happy.

* * *

It was dark outside and quiet, but Sam could feel Georgina's chest moving up and down under his arms and hear her steady breathing.

'Are you awake?' she asked, shifting in his arms slightly.

'Yes.'

'I don't want to fall asleep as I know when I wake up this will be over.'

'Don't think about that.'

'Tell me about your life in Australia,' she said. 'Distract me.'

'What do you want to know?'

'Tell me how you went from a young boy transported for stealing to the man who owns the only stud in Australia.' She said it lightly, but he could tell it was a question she'd been wanting to ask for a while.

'An old man's generosity,' he said quietly.

'This was your friend Mr Fitzgerald's father?'

'It was. After we'd been in Australia for a couple of years, Crawford and I were assigned to Mr Fitzgerald's farm to work. I was fourteen at the time and had two years of my sentence left to serve.' He paused and for a moment he was back under the baking sun. 'We were working in the fields one day, not far from the house. Mr Fitzgerald's son was out working, too. I think it was harvest time and every pair of hands was needed.'

As he spoke Georgina turned to face him and he could just make out the glint of her eyes in the darkness.

'It was getting dark. Crawford and I were working side by side with George, Mr Fitzgerald's son. We both saw a movement through the crop at the same time, a flash of colour so bright we immediately knew it to be a threat.'

He heard Georgina take a sharp inhale of breath as if caught up in the moment and waiting to hear what happened.

'It was a snake. Both Crawford and I pounced simultaneously, just as the snake launched itself at Fitzgerald. We tackled it before it could get its fangs in to his skin.'

'It was poisonous?' she asked.

'Deadly.'

'Fitzgerld told his father what had happened and the old man was convinced we'd saved his son's life. From that day on he didn't treat us like convict workers, although we still had two more years of our sentence to serve.'

'He wanted to reward you for saving his son.'

'He gave us an education, taught us all he knew about running a farm in Australia, treated us as though we were family.'

For Sam, being treated as a human again, someone with feelings and emotions and needs, had been what he appreciated the most. All those years he'd been nothing more than a number, a boy to be worked until he was past weary and half-starved in the process. Mr Fitzgerald had given him a home, a future, and restored his belief in mankind.

'He sounds like an exceptional man.'

'He was. For a young boy who'd lost his father he was the perfect role model. I won't pretend I wasn't bitter for a long time, bitter about the loss of my family and the loss of my life as I knew it, but he taught me to see past all of that, to focus on the future.'

'And that's how you became so successful?'

Sam grinned at a memory. 'When we turned eighteen Mr Fitzgerald gave us all a parcel of land, not much, just enough to grow some crops or have a small number of livestock. He wanted us to prove to ourselves we could be a success.'

'And it worked?'

'It worked. Between us we own nearly half of New South Wales, and have land in some of the other territories as well.'

'It sounds like an awful start, but you've got to where you want to be now,' Georgina said and Sam could hear the wistfulness in her voice.

'And what about your dreams?' he asked. He knew she had them, knew she wished to travel the world, to be free to make her own decisions and not be tied by the expectations of society.

'Mine are unrealistic,' she said softly.

'Sixteen years ago, when I first arrived in Australia a scared young boy with nothing and no one I would never have believed I would end up where I am today,' he said, tracing a pattern across her shoulder with his fingers. 'Anything is possible. Tell me about your dreams.'

Georgina was quiet for a little while as if collecting her thoughts, but eventually she spoke. 'I suppose I want freedom. The freedom to choose whether I ever get married or not, the freedom to come and go as I please, to travel without having to have a man by my side. I want to be my own mistress, to make my own decisions.'

'What's stopping you?'

'The world I live in.'

'Then change that world.'

'I don't know how,' Georgina said softly. 'I don't know how to break free from the expectations everyone has of me. I don't want to hurt anyone or disappoint anyone. I just want to have the same freedom a man of my class would have.'

'I suppose you have to decide what is more important

to you: not upsetting the people around you or leading the life you want.'

Georgina fell quiet in his arms and Sam wondered if he had pushed her too far. He knew how difficult it would be for her to buck convention and make her own path in life, but she was a free spirit and he hated the thought of a husband crushing her dreams every day for the rest of her life. Silently he kissed her in the darkness, then wrapped his arms around her. They lay like that for a long time and Sam knew Georgina would be mulling over everything he'd said. He hoped she would decide to fight for her freedom, to choose how her life turned out, but he'd said all he could for now. Eventually he felt her breathing deepen and her body relax, and as the sky began to lighten a little outside the window he drifted off to sleep, too.

Chapter Nineteen

The first rays of sunlight filtering through the uncurtained windows woke Sam and for a moment he felt disorientated, unsure of where he was. It was only when he felt Georgina's warm body in his arms that the events of the night before came back to him and he remembered they were in the old gatehouse.

The fire had burned down, but there were still a few glowing embers in the grate so the room wasn't completely freezing in temperature and Georgina's body was warm and soft beside his.

'Good morning,' she murmured as she opened her eyes.

'Good morning, beautiful.'

Many women in her situation would have sat up and panicked, knowing they had given away their virtue to a man they could not marry and were still lying beside him in the morning, but Georgina just smiled and snuggled in closer to him.

'We should be getting back soon,' he said gently. The

last thing he wanted was for her to think he was trying to get away, to move on from their intimacy without any repercussions. What he was concerned about was someone going into Georgina's bedroom, perhaps a maid to light the early morning fire or to bring her that first cup of tea, and finding the bed empty and not slept in.

'Five more minutes,' she said, arching her neck and kissing him softly on the lips.

Immediately he felt himself harden and knew it wouldn't just be five more minutes.

This time they made love frantically, as if they both knew it would be the very last time. Sam wanted to absorb every detail of Georgina's body, from how her back curved into her buttocks to the smooth skin of her thighs that he couldn't help kissing. He knew a man like him should never have got to know the intimate details of a woman like Georgina's body and he wanted to be able to remember every inch of her. One day soon she would be married and he would be on his way back to Australia.

As they lay there afterwards, both breathing heavily, he saw the moment Georgina forced herself back to reality—it was as if a dark veil had come down over her face.

'The Duke has asked me to marry him,' she whispered into Sam's chest.

He hadn't expected the stab of pain to his heart at her words. It wasn't as though he'd ever expected anything more than this.

'And what have you said?' he asked, trying to keep any hint of emotion from his voice.

'He gave me a few days to consider my answer.'

'Is he a kind man?' He couldn't bear to think of her with

someone cruel. In truth, he couldn't bear to think of her with anyone else.

'I think so...' she shrugged '... I've spoken to him only a handful of times.'

'Will he make you happy?'

'No.' She said this sadly and looked up at him from her position cradled on his chest. 'But perhaps happiness is too much to expect.'

'Is it?'

'Isn't it?' she shot back.

'Come away with me,' he said before he could stop himself.

'You don't mean that.'

He didn't answer. He wanted her, wanted to take her back to his home and show her all the delights of Australia, wanted to wake up next to her every morning and build a future with her.

Georgina looked deep into his eyes and sighed. 'It can't be,' she said. 'Our worlds are too different.'

'What if you're pregnant?' he asked. The idea had crossed his mind the night before, the possibility of a pregnancy, but he'd quickly forgotten in the heat of the moment.

'I'm to be married soon,' Georgina said, a hint of sadness in her voice.

'I will not let another man bring up my child,' he said. That was unthinkable.

'Let's not worry about it now,' she said. 'It's unlikely to be the case anyway.'

Nodding, he knew he had to leave it there. He might be developing feelings for Georgina, feelings he suspected might even be love. But it wasn't he who would have to give up everything and everyone he knew for them to be together. The one thing he would have to give up on—his deep-seated need to confront Georgina's father about the past—he couldn't do. So it was unfair to ask Georgina to give up so much more.

Sadly she smiled at him before getting up off the bed, quickly pulling her chemise on over her head to cover her modesty. He watched her, marvelling at how she dealt with all the intricate fastenings of her dress apart from the bits at the very back. Before she could ask him to help he was on his feet, allowing his fingers to trail over the skin of her neck as he finished helping her get dressed. It was only when she turned to look at him, her eyes wide, that he remembered he was completely naked.

'You should leave first,' he said as he pulled his trousers on. 'There will be more concern if you are not where you should be when the household wakes up.'

'You're right,' Georgina said, pulling on her thick cloak and giving him a wistful look. He wondered if she wanted him to beg her to stay, beg her to refuse the Duke and run off with him instead. Silently he counted to ten to suppress the urge to do just that. It might be what she *thought* she wanted in this moment, but the reality would be very different to the fantasy she had in her mind. Sam knew exactly what it was like to leave your entire family, your entire world, behind and he could never ask anyone to do that for him.

At the door she paused for a second, turning back to him and lifting herself up on her tiptoes so she could kiss him on the lips.

'Stay just for a minute longer,' Sam whispered. Even though it had been he who had urged her to return so no nosy maid would find her bed empty and unslept in, he couldn't quite bring himself to part from Georgina just yet.

'Just a minute,' she murmured, tilting her chin as he trailed kisses along the angle of her jaw. Beneath his hands she felt soft and warm and for a moment he wished they could just tumble back into bed. He'd hoped their night of passion might slake the desire he felt for her, but it had just increased it tenfold. Every inch of his body wanted to possess her again and as her hips swayed forward into his he heard himself groan involuntarily.

'I have to go,' she said eventually, pulling away. Sam caught her hand and kissed her fingertips, watching as she closed her eyes to steady herself.

He knew this had to be the end, but he just couldn't seem to let go of her. In a few minutes she would once again be the untouchable Lady Georgina and he would be the man who could never legitimately have her.

'Enough now,' she said, more to herself than him. 'Goodbye, Sam.'

Then she was gone, casting a long, desire-filled glance back over her shoulder before disappearing around the corner of the gatehouse.

'You did it,' Caroline stated as she linked her arm through Georgina's and pulled her away from the rest of the group.

Feigning confusion Georgina frowned. 'Ice skating?' she asked. 'Yes, Mr Robertson was kind enough to accompany me on the ice.'

'Stop it,' Caroline said, her face earnest. 'You know exactly what I mean. Tell me everything. Was it wonderful?'

'I can't believe you set it all up,' Georgina said, glancing at her friend. She was incredibly grateful Caroline had arranged for her and Sam to spend some time alone, but she couldn't quite believe her friend had had the audacity to set them up.

'In a month's time you're going to be married to some old bore,' Caroline whispered, lowering her voice as she received an enquiring glance from her mother. 'Surely every young woman deserves to be swept off her feet by a rugged foreigner before settling in to the monotony of marriage.'

Georgina turned to her friend. 'What about you?' she asked. 'Have you been swept off your feet by someone?'

Caroline blushed, something Georgina had only seen a handful of times.

'No, and the way my mother is nagging me I'll be engaged to some old decrepit lord by the end of the year... but all that means is you have to tell me every last detail. I shall have to live vicariously through you.'

'Georgina, come here, dear,' Lady Westchester called, motioning for her daughter to quicken her pace.

'Don't think you're getting away with not telling me,' Caroline whispered after her.

Georgina quickly caught up with her mother, filling the place that had recently been vacated by Mr White, one of the untitled but obscenely rich young gentlemen her mother had invited for this little house party.

'You looked flushed, dear,' her mother said, regarding her critically. 'Are you feeling unwell?'

It was tempting to claim she was coming down with something so she could retire to her room and wallow in her feelings, but her mother would probably insist on calling a doctor who would give her some hideous infusion to drink.

'Just the cold weather, Mother,' she said, summoning a smile.

'Good…' Her mother paused, waiting for the rest of their party to draw away a little. It was frosty in the gardens and a little more snow had fallen overnight, but many of the guests had opted for a mid-morning stroll around the grounds to get some fresh air after the copious amount of wine that had been served at dinner the night before. 'The Duke is not with us,' her mother continued when they were alone.

'No,' Georgina said, ensuring her voice didn't give away any emotion.

'Did I notice him looking at you fondly over breakfast?'

Of course Georgina had not told her mother of the Duke's offer of marriage. Lady Westchester would accept immediately on her daughter's behalf and the wedding would be arranged before the day was out. Georgina knew she had to accept, but she just wanted a few more hours.

'I didn't notice anything, Mother.'

She wasn't sure why she wanted a few more hours, perhaps to fantasise about running away with Sam, perhaps to remember their wonderful night together without a black cloud overshadowing the moment.

'I'm sure he's going to propose,' her mother whispered. 'He is notoriously picky about his social engagements and I doubt he would have accepted this invitation if he hadn't decided you were the one for him.'

'Why hasn't he married before, Mother?' Georgina asked, trying to distract her mother from the topic of proposals at least a little.

'Oh, the normal reasons, I should imagine,' Lady Westchester said with a dismissive wave of her hand. 'Many men like to live their lives unencumbered by a wife or a family. Then when they reach a certain age they start to think about their mortality, the continuation of their family line, and they decide the time is right to get a wife.'

It confirmed what Georgina had thought. There were no ugly skeletons, no succession of murdered fiancées or debts so large they could sink a small country. The Duke might not ever love her, probably wouldn't ever care for her more than he did his favourite horse or valet, but there was no reason to think he wouldn't make a decent enough husband.

And if she wanted more than that…well, it was her own fault for letting Sam in, for allowing him to seduce her with his charm and his oh-so-tempting stories about his world, a world she would never get to experience.

Chapter Twenty

'It's far too cold to go outside,' Lady Westchester said, 'even for a stroll into the village. Such a shame we've been besieged by such weather.'

Sam followed her gaze out the window at the blizzard-like conditions swirling around the garden and had to agree with their hostess. It *was* far too cold to venture outside. The English winter was not something that he missed about his old homeland—give him a mild Australian day over this weather on any occasion.

Allowing his eyes to rove around the room, he found it hard not to linger on Georgina. Only a few hours earlier she had been naked in his arms, willing to give him every piece of herself. Now he couldn't stop himself remembering how she looked when he kissed her in a particular way, how she moaned when he touched her.

'You're a fool, Samuel Robertson,' a low voice said next to his ear.

'Aren't we all fools?'

'None as much as you,' Crawford said. 'If I had a woman like Lady Georgina willing to give everything up for me, I would whisk her away before she could change her mind.'

'She's not...'

Crawford raised an eyebrow to silence his friend.

'If I'm not very much mistaken, she's given you the most valuable thing she possesses,' Crawford said quietly. 'Of course she'd be willing to give you anything else.'

Deep down Sam knew it was true. He only had to ask, only had to offer.

'It wouldn't be fair. She would have to give up everything.'

Crawford shrugged. 'True. But I suppose only she can decide whether it would be worth it.'

Sam turned back to the rest of the room, catching Georgina staring at him before she blushed slightly and turned away.

'She could marry a duke.'

'But does she want to?' Crawford asked.

He knew the answer to that one; Georgina most definitely did not want to marry the Duke, or anyone else her mother had carefully selected to be at this house party as a potential suitor.

'The real question you have to ask yourself, is why haven't you asked her?'

Sam spun around, but already his friend had moved on, crossing over to the ornate sideboard, and pouring himself another cup of tea.

He hadn't asked her because...well, because if he asked her to give up her family, her friends, her whole life, then he would have to give up his plans for revenge on the Earl.

Sam would do almost anything for Lady Georgina, but he didn't think he could do that. For so long it had been his main motivation, his whole reason for returning to England—he couldn't just give up on it now he was so close, could he?

'She'd never forgive me,' Sam murmured to himself, trying to reason that even if he did give up on the idea of revenge one day Georgina would find out the truth about why he had sought her out in the first place and that would ruin their relationship.

No, it was best to leave things as they were, to have this interlude as a time of happy memories but nothing more. It was best for Georgina and best for him.

'That's agreed, then. We'll remain inside and anyone who wants to can join in the games,' Lady Westchester was saying. 'Our first game will involve hiding and searching. Georgina will be given five minutes to hide somewhere in one of the downstairs rooms. We then all split up and attempt to find her. Once you've found her, instead of announcing her whereabouts, you hide with her. This continues until everyone has found the hiding place.'

A group of ten remained, six ladies and four gentlemen, the rest filtering away to amuse themselves in some other way. Sam almost slipped away, too, but a pleading look from Georgina made him stay.

Mr White agreed to record the five minutes, lifting a gold pocketwatch from his jacket for the job. With a slightly beleaguered smile Georgina swept through the door, closing it behind her, and the only sound was her receding footfalls.

'Five minutes,' Mr White declared when the time was up. Everyone trickled out of the room, turning in different directions. At first Sam moved slowly, not overly thrilled to be spending his afternoon playing games such as this, but suddenly he realised if he found Georgina first they would be alone together in a confined space. With a very good reason to be there.

Trying to think like Georgina, he checked room after room, pausing in the library. Miss Lovett had just left this room, but after being sat next to her on more than one occasion for dinner he didn't rate her powers of observation. Quietly he entered the room, closing the door softly behind him. Before he took any more steps he took a few moments to listen and fancied he could hear the faint sound of someone breathing in the room somewhere. With a grin he moved forward, casually kneeling on a comfortable sofa and peering over the back. Georgina stifled a giggle as she looked up from her crouched position.

Sam took her extended hand, but was taken by surprise when she tugged hard and he toppled over the back of the sofa, landing almost entirely on top of her.

'Lady Georgina, I must ask you to behave with the appropriate amount of decorum...' he said, trying to resist the urge to slip a hand under her dress.

'Always, Mr Robertson,' she whispered.

He gave her a long, hard stare and she had to clap a hand over her mouth to stop herself from giggling.

'We might have a minute to ourselves or an hour,' he said, placing a hand on her cheek. It was almost the only bare skin he could find. To combat the cold weather Georgina was wearing a high-necked dress with sleeves down to her wrists. It was made of the most beautiful dark blue silk and no doubt had cost a small fortune, but all Sam could think about was ripping it off her.

'What do you propose we do with that time?' Georgina asked.

'I can think of one or two worthwhile pursuits.'

Taking care not to crinkle her dress or muss her hair, he kissed her, stiffening as the door to the library opened again. They inched apart as the footfalls moved closer and by the time Mr White's face appeared over the back of the sofa they were a decorous foot apart.

'Jolly good,' Mr White exclaimed, moving around the back of the sofa and inserting himself on the other side of Georgina. She shuffled a little closer to Sam on the pretence of making room, but he felt a little thrill as her hand slipped in to his. 'What fun this is,' Mr White commented and Georgina turned towards their new companion, bestowing one of her dazzling smiles on the richest of her suitors.

As he listened to the whispered conversation between Georgina and Mr White he felt Georgina's backside wriggle backwards almost imperceptibly. Her skirts had billowed and pooled around her and Sam felt his fingers inching towards the hem of the material. He had to suppress a grin as she stiffened when his fingers brushed against her leg, but to Georgina's credit she did not otherwise react. Slowly he traced a pattern on the silky skin of her calves, moving higher inch by inch as she tried to continue her conversation with the man in front of her. Only when the door to the library opened again and Miss Halsham let out a squeal of delight at finding their hiding place did Georgina get a chance to turn to him and flash him a look filled with desire and reprimand all at the same time.

The game was over quickly then, with the remaining participants all finding the hiding spot in the library within the next few minutes as the spot behind the sofa became cramped. As the last person, a baron by the name of Lord Foxton, discovered the rest of the participants everyone edged out from around the sofa. Only Georgina lingered for a moment, long enough for Sam to lean in and whisper in her ear.

'Run away with me,' he said. 'I mean it, run away with me.' At first he thought it was an impulsive suggestion, shocking himself with the request as much as Georgina, but then as he considered it more he realised the last couple of days had been leading up to this moment.

Sam felt himself reeling as he suddenly realised he really *did* mean it. He wanted her to run away with him and he was willing to do anything to make it happen. For eighteen years he'd planned his revenge on the Earl and now even that seemed insignificant compared to the chance of having Georgina by his side for the rest of his life.

For a second she studied his face, but before she could answer Miss Yaxley pulled on Georgina's arm and the connection between them was lost.

'Who found you first, Georgie?' Caroline asked.

'I think it was Mr Robertson,' Georgina said quietly, turning to him for confirmation.

'It was.'

'Then you must hide first this time.'

'I shall time your five minutes,' Mr White said.

Sam almost declined, almost made some excuse to retire to his room and think about the ridiculous suggestion he'd just made to Georgina. He knew there was hardly any possibility of her saying yes, but he'd asked all the same.

'Hurry, Mr Robertson,' Georgina said, her eyes filled with something Sam could not quite interpret. 'We shall be along to find you in five minutes.'

The small possibility that Georgina would find him first was enough for Sam to incline his head in agreement and saunter out the door. He knew exactly where he was going to hide and it wouldn't need five minutes.

Crossing the grand hallway, he moved quickly to the morning room and the wide double doors that led out to an ornate glasshouse. In here Lord Westchester tasked his gardener with growing some more exotic plants that would not normally thrive in English temperatures.

The cold hit him as soon as he entered and closed the door quietly behind him. There was no sun today to beam through the glass panels and warm the room and as such it was only a few degrees warmer than it was outside. Nevertheless he moved forward, determined to find a hidden spot to wait in and hope it was Georgina who found him first.

He'd only taken three steps when he realised he was not alone in the glasshouse. From somewhere towards the end of the freezing room came faint noises, the sound of someone breathing and, as Sam listened, a soft moan.

From the months he'd spent on the convict ship he was familiar with the sound of a couple illicitly copulating and instantly he stiffened, not wanting to embarrass anyone unnecessarily. He was almost back out the door before he paused. The unmistakable voice of Lord Westchester, the man who liked to portray himself as a moral and upstanding man, cut through the air.

'Yes, like that,' the Earl commanded.

Sam turned around. He doubted Lady Westchester was the one receiving Lord Westchester's attentions. A countess was unlikely to allow herself to be cornered in the glasshouse, although it was possible, of course. You never knew what really went on behind a closed bedroom door.

No, it was much more likely Lord Westchester was doing

exactly what he preached against in his political campaigning and engaging in extra-marital relations.

Moving closer, Sam peered through the thick foliage, seeing first Lord Westchester's pale backside, with his breeches around his ankles. Not wanting to focus on this unpleasant sight for too long, Sam shifted to get a better view of the woman underneath him. She was laid back on a workbench of convenient height, her dark skirts hitched up around her waist. Catching a glimpse of her face, Sam recognised one of the maids. She was young, certainly no more than nineteen or twenty, slender, but with a plain, unremarkable face.

He'd seen enough. Enough of the copulating couple and enough to know he'd been right all along. Lord Westchester did still cavort with the maids as he had all those years ago when Sam had been a boy. The man who touted himself as a moral leader was taking advantage of his own maids. Politically it would not go down well; it would ruin his upcoming campaign and probably put an end to his political aspirations.

Sam had to think quickly. His original plan had been to encourage some of the maids Lord Westchester had taken advantage of over the years to speak out and he'd got as far as procuring a list of the maids who'd left or been dismissed from the household over the last five year, but now he wondered if it would be more effective if the Earl was caught in the act. Preferably by somebody with the propensity to gossip.

Stepping away so he was hidden among the leaves, he waited. If he was lucky all he would have to do was let the game run its course.

For a moment he hesitated. Something didn't feel quite right. An image of Georgina's face flashed into his mind, the look of hurt and mistrust when she found out he'd been working on his plan for revenge this whole time. It would ruin her. There was no doubt she would refuse to come away with him when she found out the truth, but then her father's public disgrace might mean other marriage proposals dried up as well.

Stepping back, he shook his head in confusion. For so long this had been all he'd wanted: the chance to confront the Earl and hurt him a fraction of the amount the old man had hurt him. It had been the whole reason for coming to England, the whole reason for gaining entry into society and weaving his way into Georgina's life. Now he had the chance to fulfil his aim and here he was hesitating.

He didn't want to hurt Georgina, he'd never wanted to hurt her, but he had fooled himself that he would be able to find a way to damage her father without impacting her.

Thinking back to the moment the request for her to run away with him had slipped from his lips, he closed his eyes and breathed deeply. Probably she would refuse. It would be the sensible thing to do, but if there was even the slightest chance she agreed, he didn't want to jeopardise that.

He needed time, time to decide exactly what to do, and he needed to talk to Georgina.

The door opened and the sound was enough to make the Earl pause. The heavy footsteps as someone came deeper into the glasshouse soon galvanised both the older man and the young maid into action. Sam watched as the Earl quickly pulled up his trousers before roughly hauling the maid from the workbench. Behind him he saw a lady's shoes come into view and heard an excited giggle. If he wasn't mistaken it was Miss Lovett, the airheaded young thing with a pretty face but a poor dowry. Sam needed to distract her attention and allow the Earl and his maid to escape through the door into the garden.

He shifted, drawing Miss Lovett's attention towards him and away from the end of the glasshouse. The Earl spun and through the foliage his eyes met Sam's. With a look of a cornered animal he shot Sam a warning glance, before ushering the maid forward.

Ensuring he rustled the leaves of the tree he was standing next to a little more, he saw Miss Lovett turn towards him and he summoned a smile as she hurried over. From somewhere behind him he heard the door into the garden closing quietly.

'Am I the first to find you?' she asked.

'Yes,' he said, unable to concentrate enough to initiate any further conversation. He'd just missed the opportunity to expose the Earl as a hypocrite and perhaps ruin the reputation he was relying on to further his political aims.

'How exciting. So do we just hide here until someone else finds us?'

'I believe so,' he ground out.

'Hasn't it been a fun weekend?' Miss Lovett twittered.

'I believe the idea is to stay as quiet as possible so it takes longer for everyone to find us,' Sam said, trying to keep the exasperation from his voice and failing completely.

'Oh, of course.' She fell silent and a few seconds later the door to the glasshouse opened again.

'Lady Georgina,' Sam greeted her almost guiltily. She looked disappointedly at Miss Lovett, but summoned a sunny smile after a couple of seconds.

He searched her face, trying to find some clue as to whether she was even considering running away with him. The chance of her agreeing was miniscule, but he knew he would have regretted it for ever had he not asked. She looked serene, too serene to be thinking about leaving all her friends and family behind. Probably she had already worked out how to break it to him gently, how to tell him she'd enjoyed their time together, but she would not jeopardise her whole future for him. For a moment Sam thought about withdrawing the offer, about protecting his own heart, but he managed to stop himself. He knew that was just a reaction to the thought she might refuse, his way of protecting himself from the emotional pain a refusal would cause, after all these years with barriers around his heart. If there was any chance at all of Georgina accepting, he couldn't jeopardise that.

'I'm sorry,' he murmured before he could stop himself. Both women gave him a puzzled look, but were prevented from asking any questions when the door to the glasshouse opened again and someone else stepped inside. He shouldn't have asked her, it was selfish, but he hadn't been able to help himself.

Georgina shifted, moving slightly closer to Sam and slipping her hand into his.

'Meet me before dinner,' she whispered into his ear.

Sam nodded, unable to refuse. There was just a glimmer of hope and he clung on to it firmly. Now all he had to do was decide what to do about the Earl.

Chapter Twenty-One

Nervously Georgina ran her fingers over the selection of dresses in her wardrobe. They were all expensive, made with the finest materials, some with hand-embroidered detail, some with beautiful French lace or panels of velvet.

All of them had been bought with her father's money, of course, all of them designed to display her in the best light to attract the most desirable husband. And here she was wondering which to choose to take with her when she ran away with an entirely unsuitable man. Likely they would have to travel light so the choice was important. Of course they hadn't made definite plans yet, but Georgina wanted to be prepared. If they were going to do this it would have to be soon, probably within the next couple of days.

A giggle that sounded just a touch hysterical burst from her lips. She was really going to do this. All her life she'd been a good girl, she'd attended her lessons, never put a foot wrong in society and dutifully obeyed her parents. Now she was planning on running away with a man who had spent much of his life working as a convict labourer in Australia. Not that she thought him a criminal—Georgina had believed him from the very start when he'd confided that he had been convicted for a crime he had not committed. Sam was a good man, that she was sure of, and it softened the fact that she was about to betray her parents and leave them behind.

'You're going to run away with him,' Caroline hissed as she burst into Georgina's room.

She hadn't seen her friend since making the decision so she didn't know how Caroline had worked this out.

'Quiet,' Georgina instructed, moving over to the open door and peering out in to the corridor to check it was deserted before closing it.

Caroline's mouth fell open. 'You actually are going to run away with him?' she asked in disbelief.

Nervously Georgina nodded her head. It mattered to her what Caroline thought, nearly as much as it mattered what her parents reaction would be.

Caroline sat down on the bed, her skirts billowing out underneath her, and stared at her friend, shaking her head every few seconds as if she couldn't quite digest what Georgina was saying.

'Do you love him?' she asked eventually.

'I do.' Georgina had realised it some time while they were making love in the old gatehouse. She wouldn't have given herself to anyone but the man she loved and she had loved Sam for quite a while.

'Does he love you?'

'I think so.' He'd never said the words, never declared anything for her, but she believed he did. Sam was an honourable man, he wouldn't have asked her to run away with him for anything less than true love. She knew it was she making all the sacrifices, which was why she suspected he hadn't asked her earlier, but Sam loved her, she was sure of it.

'Then I suppose there is nothing else to be done,' Caroline said, standing and crossing the room to Georgina. She wrapped her arms around her and hugged her tight. 'It's not like your parents will approve of you marrying him here.'

Georgina nodded sadly. That would be the ideal solution, to be allowed to marry the man she loved and stay close to her family, but it was never going to happen. Even without Sam's history as a convict they would never approve of her marriage to someone from such lowly origins, no matter how rich and successful he was now.

'Will you…?' Caroline started asking, but had to pause as her voice broke a little. 'Will you be returning to Australia with him?'

Georgina nodded. At least she expected that would be the plan. Once her family had disowned her there would be no reason to stay here and Sam had his business to take care of.

'I'll miss you,' Caroline said quietly.

'I'll miss you, too. Promise me you'll come and visit?'

'I promise.'

They both knew it was a promise she probably wouldn't be able to keep. Australia was so far and not part of the civilised world. Caroline would not be allowed to travel there alone and Georgina very much doubted any future husband would consent to taking his wife to the other side of the world to visit an old friend.

Suddenly the enormity of what she was about to do hit Georgina. She was giving up her entire life, everyone she knew and loved, all for a man she'd only known a couple of months.

Forcing herself to take a couple of deep breaths, she pictured Sam's face. She loved him, that was why this was worth it. Instead of a lifetime of marriage to a man she merely tolerated, she would have a lifetime of passion and love. That was worth anything.

'Be brave,' Caroline whispered in her ear, sensing her momentary uncertainty. 'You're taking your future into your own hands, you won't regret it.'

Georgina felt the tears trickle down her cheeks as she realised this might be one of the last times she saw the friend who had been more like a sister to her.

'Hush now,' Caroline said. 'Let us focus on the practical considerations. You will need enough clothes to last you your journey. Nothing too fine, it would be better to choose warm and hardy materials.'

In unison they both looked at Georgina's wardrobe. None of the dresses had been designed to be practical. They were all pretty, carefully crafted to show off Georgina as an attractive young woman to a potential husband, not withstand the extreme weather conditions aboard a ship to Australia.

'Well, I'm sure Mr Robertson can purchase you a few pieces before you set off,' Caroline said. 'When will you leave?'

'I'm unsure, but Father is expecting me to be engaged by early next week, so I suppose we will have to leave before then.' It seemed so soon, but she wasn't prepared to promise herself to another man, not when she knew she would never go through with the marriage.

She wasn't sure Sam had made any firm plans. His request for her to run away with him had been spontaneous,

Georgina knew that—it was as if he couldn't help himself. Most likely he hadn't thought through the practicalities, but Georgina was sure he would not change his mind. He loved her.

'Promise me you won't go without saying goodbye,' Caroline said, hugging Georgina one last time.

'I promise.'

With a sad smile on her face Caroline left the room and Georgina turned back to her wardrobe and began selecting a few of her more practical dresses, folding them as best she could and placing them in her trunk.

'Mr Robertson,' Georgina said, trying to keep the tremor from her voice. Their efforts to meet clandestinely before dinner had been thwarted by her mother first wanting to discuss the next day's events and then insisting Georgina look in on the invalided Lord Rosenhall.

'Lady Georgina.' He bowed his head, not risking anything more intimate.

'We should…' she began to say, but stopped as her mother stepped closer.

'Georgina,' her mother practically hissed at her, 'the Duke is all on his own.'

Georgina glanced over to the window and saw her mother was correct. It was rare for a man of the Duke's status and fortune to be left alone at any social event. Either the young ladies would be trying to snare him, or the gentlemen, both young and old, would be trying to make a lasting connection with a man who wielded more power than the rest of them put together. Despite this the Duke was standing by himself by the window.

'Mother!' Georgina exclaimed, inclining her head towards Sam. Her mother might not approve of his presence here, but it would be inexcusably rude to just abandon him in the middle of a conversation, even to go and talk to the Duke.

'I shall keep Mr Robertson company. I would like to have a private word.'

That sounded ominous, but try as she might Georgina could not think of a reason not to obey her mother's request. She threw a quick glance at Sam, but he looked distracted this evening. Perhaps planning on how to execute their escape.

With an apologetic smile Georgina stepped away, glancing back nervously over her shoulder to try to glean the topic of conversation between her mother and Sam.

'You look radiant tonight,' the Duke said as she approached.

Georgina looked down at the deep red evening gown she'd chosen for dinner. It was low cut at the front with a delicate gold-thread embroidery around the hem and the sleeves.

'Thank you,' she said.

'May I have a moment in private with you?' he asked with no further pleasantries.

Her eyes wide, Georgina nodded, allowing the Duke to escort her to an unoccupied corner of the room. Here no one else would be able to overhear their conversation provided they spoke in hushed tones.

'Please let me assure you, Lady Georgina, my purpose tonight is not to rush your decision on my offer. I said you must consider my proposal until the end of the weekend and I stand by that.'

Nodding gratefully, Georgina tried to adopt a serene but

interested expression. It wouldn't do to let on to anybody that she was thinking of turning down every suitor her parents had carefully chosen to be here this weekend in favour of eloping with a man who would never be part of their world.

'I think we would make a fine match, Lady Georgina,' the Duke said quietly, 'and, although we would of course share certain activities, I am a man used to the life of a bachelor. I can promise you a union where you would be free to continue with your pastimes and pleasures.'

Georgina knew he was looking to reassure her that he would not take over her life, but his idea of a good marriage saddened her a little. In his mind, as was the case for most of the people she socialised with, a good marriage was one where both parties were happy spending most of their time apart, perhaps only meeting for the odd meal or social occasion, and of course to beget the heirs.

'However, I do not wish to stand in the way of something more.'

She looked up sharply.

'We barely know one another and I would be lying if I told you I feel anything more towards you than a mild affection. Of course more might come in time, but if we married I think we can both agree that it would not be a love match.'

Not knowing how to react or where this conversation was going, Georgina nodded her head, holding her breath as she waited for him to continue.

'As I said, I do not wish to stand in the way of something more. While I have never experienced love, I have seen friends marry entirely unsuitable women because they loved them and they have found happiness.' He paused and fixed her with his gaze before continuing. 'If there is someone you feel this way towards, I would not want to jeopardise what you may have with him.'

No words would form on her lips. How did he know? They'd been careful, especially since Sam had arrived for the house party. And more pressingly, if the Duke had guessed what was going on between her and Sam, who else suspected?

Unable to stop herself, she glanced over his shoulder to where Sam was still cornered by her mother. He looked calm, while she could see her mother getting more and more agitated.

'How...?' She trailed off, wondering if she should deny it. 'I...'

The Duke smiled. 'I like to watch people, Lady Georgina. I find it the most interesting of pastimes.'

Looking around, she saw her father begin to move in their direction.

'Never fear,' the Duke said, 'my lips are sealed. I am assuming you have a difficult decision ahead of you.'

She couldn't believe he was being so relaxed about the possible feelings the woman he'd proposed to harboured for another man.

'I shall await your decision tomorrow.'

'You are not withdrawing your proposal?' she asked, her voice hushed.

'No. It is your decision.'

She nodded as he took her hand in his and kissed it. Georgina knew it was a passionless kiss, but all the same she glanced guiltily in Sam's direction before catching herself. Perhaps she was easier to read than she had hoped.

The Duke moved away and she tried to plaster her sunniest smile on her face as she turned back to face the room.

Her mother had finished whatever discussion she'd been having with Sam and now he was off in one corner, his head bent as he and his friend, Mr Crawford, talked about what looked like a serious matter.

'Mr Robertson, would you oblige me by stepping outside for a moment?' Lord Westchester asked calmly as the ladies began to withdraw from the dining room. Sam had been expecting this summons—the Earl had seen him in the glasshouse and no doubt he wanted to ensure he could rely on Sam's silence.

It was still icy outside, with fresh flurries of snow arriving every couple of hours, certainly not the most comfortable place for their discussion, but Sam supposed the Earl wanted to ensure no one would overhear what they were about to talk about.

'Of course,' he said, waiting while the Earl instructed a footman to bring their coats.

Georgina was the last of the ladies to leave the dining room and Sam caught her eye as she glanced back over her shoulder. They had things to discuss, right after he'd decided how to best deal with her father.

'How are you enjoying the weekend?' the Earl asked conversationally. His tone was friendly, overly so, and he clapped Sam on the arm as if they were co-conspirators in some grand scheme.

'It has been a very diverting weekend,' Sam replied. The memory of Georgina's naked body underneath his flashed into his mind and he had to quickly distract himself before Lord Westchester guessed something was wrong.

'I am pleased to have been able to include you in our party,' the Earl said, subtly reminding Sam normally he would have not got an invitation. He coughed, cleared his throat, and coughed again. Sam knew the request to keep quiet about what he'd seen in the glasshouse was coming next. 'I wanted to talk to you, man to man, about what happened earlier today.'

Sam nodded, keeping his face neutral.

'I think you might have witnessed…er…a moment of weakness I am a little ashamed of,' he said, glancing at Sam. 'I am of course grateful for you keeping quiet at the time and wanted to ensure you would continue to do so. For the sake of my family, of course.'

'Of course,' Sam murmured. There was no *of course* about it. The Earl's request was purely selfish. He didn't want society knowing he engaged in the same immoral behaviour he'd built his entire political campaign on with Mr Moorcroft. He wasn't thinking of his daughter and he most certainly wasn't thinking about his wife.

It was difficult for Sam to keep the anger from his voice, so he pressed his lips together and said no more. No doubt the Earl had been taking advantage of the maids in his household for at least two decades and it made Sam feel sick to think of all the young women he'd forced himself on.

'I knew I could rely on you, upstanding chap, that's what I told Lord Rosenhall the other day.'

The Earl made to turn back towards the house but Sam stopped him with a light hand on his arm. As soon as the Earl paused Sam withdrew it, not wanting to touch the man for any longer than was strictly necessary.

'There is something I would like to discuss, Lord Westchester,' Sam said, trying to keep the tremor from his voice. Every time he looked at the older man he felt a deep-seated revulsion and wave upon wave of anger at how he'd so casually ruined Sam's life all those years ago. The Earl looked momentarily irritated, but covered it well as he remembered he needed Sam's goodwill.

'Of course, would you like to retire to my study? The night is cold.'

Sam could see no harm in having this discussion in the warm, so allowed the older man to lead the way back inside the house.

Georgina edged away from the other young women, catching Caroline's eye, but certain no one else had noted her departure. Her mother had retired early this evening, exhausted after three long days of playing hostess and matchmaker at the same time. This meant Georgina was free to do the same, or at least pretend to be making her way to her bedroom. She knew her father had accosted Sam for some reason, probably to discuss his politics further with someone willing to listen, and she was eager to catch him on the way out.

The best place for her to wait was the library. Her father's study had a door into the hall, but also a set of sliding doors into the library. Normally these were kept securely fastened, but she should still be able to hear when Sam left the next room from there.

She was just about to enter the library when she noticed with a frown that the door to her father's study was wide open. Entering, it was clear the room was empty and clear that it hadn't been used all evening—the fire had died down in the grate and the room had a slight chill to it. Puzzled, she was just about to leave when she heard Sam's voice, approaching from the corridor, and her father's shortly after.

'Thank you for your time, Lord Westchester, I am most eager to discuss this matter with you.'

'I'll pour us a brandy each and we can get down to business.'

Georgina should have left, or at least stayed, but made herself known to the two approaching men. She'd never before spied on her father, never listened at a keyhole or below an open window, but as she stood frozen in the dark study she felt a sliver of indecision. The proper thing to do would be to slip out, but then she would never know what Sam had to discuss with her father. Panic seized her as she wondered if he would be foolish enough to actually ask for her hand in marriage. If he did, their plans to run away together would be ruined. Her father would lock her up, accept a proposal from the Duke on her behalf and only let her out again to go to the church on her wedding day.

Before she could properly think through her actions she crossed to the door adjoining the library, unlocked it, and slipped through into the darkened room. She pulled the doors back together again, but didn't close them completely, allowing a small chink to let the voices drift through.

Sam settled back in the comfortable armchair, trying to get the revulsion and years of pent-up anger for the man in front of him under control. The Earl had summoned a maid to bring candles and rebuild the fire and already the room was feeling warmer. This was the moment he had been waiting for all those years and suddenly he just wanted the Earl to sit so he could get it over with.

How did you confront the man who had ruined your life?

'What can I do for you?' Lord Westchester asked as the maid left, closing the door behind her.

'I wanted to ask you about a matter that occurred some years ago,' Sam said, his voice strong and his manner confident. He was no longer the small, scared boy he'd been years ago when he'd stood in front of the Earl accused of stealing Lady Westchester's emeralds. 'Do you remember a crime that happened in this house? A young boy accused of stealing some jewellery?'

The Earl nodded slowly, his eyes narrowing. 'The cook's son, I think.'

Sam didn't correct him. The servants would be interchangeable to a man of Lord Westchester's station.

'Why do you bring it up?'

'Do you remember what happened to the boy?'

'The thief,' the Earl corrected. 'I'm not sure. Probably went to prison, that's what normally happens to thieves.'

'And the emeralds? Were they found in the boy's possession?'

'I can't remember, this all must have been twenty years ago. Why do you bring it up now?'

'Why were you so sure the boy was guilty?' Sam pressed on, ignoring the Earl's question.

'As I said it was a long time ago and a matter for the magistrates, not me. I didn't determine the child's guilt or innocence and I didn't sentence the boy.'

The Earl was being just a little too dismissive. The disappearance of expensive jewellery was not a matter easily forgotten, even eighteen years on.

'But you did. It was your insistence that condemned him. Your influence that meant his sentence was particularly harsh.'

'What's your interest in the boy?' Lord Westchester asked, his voice much less friendly than it had been a few minutes earlier. 'What does it matter to you what happened to some little ragamuffin twenty years ago.'

'Eighteen years, four months, eight days,' Sam corrected quietly.

Lord Westchester frowned in confusion.

'That's how long ago you falsely accused me of stealing your wife's emeralds, gave an untrue statement to the magistrate, and lobbied for me to be transported for the crime.'

Sam studied the other man's face, seeing first disbelief, then anger and then a cold, calculating look. This was the true character of Lord Westchester coming through.

'Get out,' the Earl hissed. 'Get out of my house.'

Sam sat completely still as Lord Westchester levered himself from his chair and towered over him. It might have been a move that intimidated him eighteen years ago, but now he saw the Earl for what he really was: a cruel and immoral bully. Raising an eyebrow, he stared the older man down. Now he was going to get answers.

'I'm not going anywhere,' Sam said calmly. 'Sit down and answer my questions.'

'If you think...'

'You forget what I saw you up to this afternoon. If that gets out your political campaign will be over and Mr Moorcroft will fall with you. Your influence, your chance to have the ear of the next Prime Minister, will be over.'

'No one will believe you, a criminal from a family of servants.'

Sam smiled, beginning to enjoy himself. 'Perhaps, perhaps not. But you know the power of rumour in politics.'

'I will not be blackmailed.'

'Sit down,' Sam commanded again, this time his voice ultimately authoritative. 'All I want is answers. And if you don't give me what I want I have a lot of free time to dedicate to ruining your reputation as a moral and upstanding family man. I will find all the maids you've ever pawed and subjected to your sweaty attentions and I will persuade them to come forward and tell the world what you expect of a pretty young thing working in your house.'

'You wouldn't.'

'I would. I will, unless you tell me the truth. And I have all the time and plenty of money to dedicate to ruining the reputation that is so important in politics.' Sam paused, checking he had got his point across. Slowly the Earl sat down in his chair, a look of defeat momentarily on his face. Sam knew it wouldn't last. Men of Lord Westchester's status could not be kept down for long. Their self-confidence had been bred into them and reinforced by decades of knowing they were at the very top of the food chain.

'What do you want to know?'

'You set me up,' Sam stated. 'I didn't steal your wife's emeralds and you knew it at the time. Why did you blame me?'

The Earl shrugged, refusing to look contrite even as he was confessing to ruining Sam's young life. 'It was convenient,' he said simply.

'Convenient?'

'I was foolish enough to get caught up with one of the young housemaids. She found herself in some difficulty and when I refused to give her the money she desired to start afresh, she made off with Lady Westchester's emeralds. My wife discovered the theft before I had time to replace the necklace, so I had to find a plausible scapegoat.'

'You ruined my life because you were too mean to pay off the woman who was pregnant with your child?'

'I didn't like being threatened,' the Earl said pointedly. 'If she'd just asked for the money…but she demanded it, said she would tell my wife if not.'

'I could have been hanged.'

'Unlikely. A young boy and a first offence.'

Unlikely but not impossible.

'Did you feel any remorse?'

The Earl sighed. 'If you want the complete truth, I never gave you another thought once you were in the hands of the magistrate.'

Sam felt slightly sick. His life had meant nothing to the Earl. He'd been chosen to be a scapegoat so Lord Westchester could keep another one of his tawdry affairs secret from his wife and then, once out of the way, he'd been promptly forgotten about.

'Now is there anything else?'

All in all their conversation had lasted less than five minutes. This had been the moment Sam had been building up to for so long and now it seemed like a complete anti-climax. For years he'd fantasised about confronting the Earl, about dragging a confession, and perhaps even some remorse, out of him and now it was over. Sam had expected to feel different, for the confrontation to have changed his life somehow, but he was still the same man with the same history.

None of it mattered, he realised, not any more. Yes, the Earl had ruined his life, ripped him away from his family all those years ago, a family he would never see again. That mattered, of course, but getting this selfish oaf of a man to feel any remorse, that didn't matter. Nor did his idea of revenge. Sam had flourished since finishing his sentence; he was a successful man running a successful business surrounded by good friends. And he'd been obsessing about the past instead of focusing on what he was blessed with in the present.

'Nothing else,' Sam said, standing. Suddenly he didn't want to be in the same country, let alone the same room as this man any longer.

'And you will keep quiet about my little indiscretion?' the Earl asked. 'It was a gentleman's agreement after all.' Sam would give up on his plan to reveal the Earl as a womanising cheater and ruin his political aspirations, but it wasn't because of any agreement—it was purely for Georgina. The woman he loved. Eighteen years he'd spent plotting the Earl's public shaming and now it didn't seem important any longer. He had the chance at true happiness and that meant letting go of all the bitterness and focusing on the woman who'd made him see there were some things more important than old grudges.

'You forget, Lord Westchester, I'm no gentleman.'

Striding out of the room before the Earl could say another word, Sam found himself smiling. It was time to put the past behind him and focus on the future. And that future included Lady Georgina.

Chapter Twenty-Two

Feeling the tears streaming down her cheeks, Georgina stifled a sob. She covered her mouth with her hand, trying to claw the noise back in, all the time conscious that her father sat in his study a few feet away with the adjoining door open half an inch. As well as she could hear everything that had gone on between Sam and her father, he would be able to hear her if she made too much noise.

She couldn't bear to face her father after everything she'd heard. It was almost inconceivable he'd behaved in the way he had, accusing an innocent young boy just to protect his own reputation. And taking advantage of the maids, young women who would find it hard to say no, that was downright disgusting. It was as if she didn't know her father at all.

As if in a trance Georgina stood and crept out of the library, all the time wondering if she would make it to the privacy of her bedroom before collapsing. Her heart was breaking, she had a ripping pain in her chest and her head was swimming.

And Sam had used her. The man she had been about to give everything up for had used her. That first night a few months ago when he'd sought her out in the ballroom he'd been planning this all along, she realised. She'd merely been a way to get close to her father, nothing more, and she'd convinced herself he loved her.

Georgina made it to her bedroom before collapsing onto the bed. She squeezed her eyes tightly together and tried to slow her breathing. Wave after wave of nausea washed over her body as a new thought spiralled out of control in her mind. Was she Sam's way of getting revenge on her father?

Her father—the man she'd loved unconditionally despite his often abrupt manner and temper that could be quick to anger. She couldn't believe everything she'd heard about him, couldn't believe that he had done something as terrible as he'd just confessed. Without any remorse he'd ruined a young boy's life, all so his sordid little affair wouldn't become public. She wondered if her mother knew about her father's dalliances with the maids. The thought made her sick.

Burying her face in her pillow, she couldn't stop thinking about Sam—she raked over every look, every touch, every kiss. Surely it hadn't all been a lie. He was a smooth and charming man, but she'd really believed the smouldering looks and the honeyed words had come straight from his heart. Never had she imagined she was nothing more than a way to get revenge on her father. She didn't know if he'd set out to ruin her, to make her fall in love with him and give up her virtue before exposing her and humiliating her father at the same time, or if she'd just made it too hard for him to resist when she offered herself so wantonly.

She looked up as there was a soft knock on the door.

Swallowing back some of the tears, she stayed completely silent. She didn't want a visitor, no matter who it was.

'Georgina,' Sam's voice whispered through the thick wood.

Slowly she saw the door handle turn and she fought to remember if she had clicked the lock when she'd first entered the room. As the door opened a crack she felt her heart sink. She didn't want to see Sam now, she didn't want to see him ever again.

'Go away,' she hissed as he stepped quietly into the room.

He stiffened, obviously surprised to see her there at all when she hadn't answered his knock.

'Go away,' she repeated, hearing the venom in her voice.

'Georgina. What's happened?' Sam asked, closing the door softly behind him and crossing the room in a few long strides.

'Leave me alone. You've done enough.'

He shook his head and moved closer still, sitting on the edge of her bed and placing an arm around her shoulder. Quickly she shrugged him off and shifted away.

'What's wrong, talk to me?'

Suddenly she felt all the humiliation and anger bubbling up inside her and fighting to get free.

'What's wrong?' she asked, hearing the hysterical tone to her voice. 'I loved you, Sam. I actually loved you. What a fool I am.'

She saw the confusion on his face and saw him open his mouth, but realised she didn't want him to explain. Her heart couldn't be trusted; she'd fallen for him once and she was determined not to let herself succumb again.

'I know everything,' she said. 'I heard you and my father.'

As the look of panic crossed his features she realised

she'd still been hoping she had somehow got it all wrong. The guilt on Sam's face told her she did not.

'You don't understand…' Sam said.

Georgina felt herself harden. 'What don't I understand? That you only pursued an acquaintance with me to get close to my father, that every word that came out of your mouth was a lie? That I gave every part of myself to you and none of it was real?'

'Don't say that.'

She looked at him and felt herself soften momentarily at the pained look on his face. She knew he had suffered terribly all because of her father and in some ways could understand his desire for revenge, but she couldn't forgive the fact that he'd used her to get closer to that goal. She reminded herself this was a man practised in deceit, he'd fooled her for two months, but she couldn't let him fool her again.

'It was real,' Sam said quietly. 'Every touch, every kiss. Every whispered word.'

'I don't believe you. I *heard* what you said to my father.'

Sam reached out to touch her, but she shrugged him off.

'I admit I did seek you out initially to find out more about your father,' Sam said, his fingers resting just a fraction of an inch from hers. 'He ruined my life, Georgina. I was convinced I needed to confront him, to make him suffer, to punish him for what he did to me.'

Angrily she wiped the tears from her cheeks again. She would not cry any more for this man.

'So you thought you would seduce his daughter, ruin me and humiliate him in the process?'

'No,' he said vehemently. Firmly he gripped her by the shoulders and turned her to face him. Georgina had no option but to look him in the eye. 'No,' he repeated, quieter this time, 'that was never my plan, never my intention.'

But he'd done it all the same.

'I just wanted to get close to him, find an opportunity to confront him.'

'Well, you've had it so you can go now.'

'I can't.'

She looked up again and felt the tears start rolling down her cheeks again. 'You're still looking for a way to humiliate him.'

'No. I couldn't care less about your father or what he did to me all those years ago...' He paused. 'All I care about is you.'

For a moment she felt her heart soar before she pulled it back to reality. She couldn't trust a word that was coming out of Sam's mouth. She didn't know him, not the real him, and she couldn't let herself be deceived again.

'I don't believe you,' she said, her voice hard and her expression unwavering.

'I love you, Georgina.'

She'd been wanting to hear those words for days and now they meant nothing.

'I love you, Georgina.'

'I don't believe you.'

He took her face in his hands and she felt the irresistible pull she always felt when she was around him.

'I love you.'

'Stop saying that.'

'Never.'

'Leave me alone, Sam.'

'Never.'

He caught her hand in his own and held it tight, refusing

to let her pull away. Only once she looked up into those irresistible blue eyes did he let their hands drop.

'I wanted to get close to your father,' he said, 'but that
was before I got to know you. The last few weeks, all that
we've shared, that's been real.'

Georgina found herself believing him. You couldn't fake
the way he looked at her, couldn't fake how his eyes lit up
when she entered a room.

'It doesn't matter, Sam,' she said more softly. 'I can't
trust you. And I can't give up my whole life for a man I
don't trust.'

He held her gaze for well over a minute and in that time
Georgina felt her heart breaking all over again. Even though
she was beyond angry with him she couldn't help feeling
sad, too. This was probably the last time she would ever
see him, the last time she would ever set eyes on the only
man she would ever love.

'Goodbye, Sam,' she said when she could bear it no longer.

Turning so he wouldn't see her break down completely,
she wondered if he would protest further, but ten seconds
later she heard the door close quietly behind him.

Georgina collapsed on the bed, burying her face in her
pillows and letting all the pain and hurt flood out of her.

Thirty minutes later, when there were no more tears left
to cry, she crossed to the small writing desk in the corner
of the room and took out a sheet of paper. Now probably
wasn't the wisest time to make such a momentous decision,
but she needed to draw a line under the episode in her life
with Sam Robertson.

Your Grace,
I would like to accept your offer of marriage. Please
let me know when would be convenient to talk to my
father.
Yours,
Lady Georgina

Chapter Twenty-Three

'I've never seen him like this before.'

'He's barely eaten in a week.'

'He's like a man possessed.'

Sam raised his head from the table where it had been resting in his hands and growled, 'I can hear you. I'm hungover, not deaf.'

It had been two weeks since he'd returned from the Westchester estate down in Hampshire. Two weeks since he'd last set eyes on Georgina, two weeks since she'd sent him away for ever.

'Here,' Fitzgerald said, handing him a glass of water. Crawford wasn't far behind with a plate of warm, buttery toast.

Mumbling his thanks, Sam tucked in gingerly, unsure if his roiling stomach would be able to keep even just the water down, but after a few bites he was feeling better already.

'Do you remember that thug, Walter Ristwald?' Crawford asked quietly as he took a seat next to Sam.

'Warthog Walter?' Sam said through a mouthful of toast. It really was good.

'The very same.'

Warthog Walter had been an unfortunate-looking man who'd presided over a gang of thugs on the transport ship he and Crawford had travelled to Australia on. Whereas most of the criminals transported were thieves or pickpockets, Walter boasted of more violent crimes. If he was to be believed, he'd raped and murdered his way through half of London. This was unlikely, seeing as he'd escaped the death penalty, but you never knew if a judge had been bribed or cajoled into a lighter sentence.

'And you remember Annie?'

How could he forget Annie? A sickly little thing, eighteen or nineteen years old, but with the intellect of someone much younger. They'd never found out what crime had resulted in her being on the filthy transport ship, but someone somewhere should have been losing sleep over sending such a poorly equipped girl out into the world to fend for herself.

Warthog Walter had set his sights on Annie and, instead of rolling over and complying as many of the women did to gain the protection of one of the stronger men, she had protested loudly. She'd screamed and screamed until Walter had hit her so hard she hadn't woken up for two days.

'You never gave up on her,' Crawford said. 'That was one of the things I most admired about you.'

Sam had seen the unfortunate woman resist Walter again and again, each time getting a punch or kick for her troubles while the criminal still took what he wanted. He hadn't been able to stand by and let her endure it on her own, so the next time Walter had come for her he'd stood in the way and taken the beating. He'd been twelve and half the size of the man punching him, but he hadn't stepped aside. Three times it happened before a few of the other prisoners had stepped up to Sam's side, objecting to the way Walter was hurting a woman who could not defend herself. On cold days Sam could still feel the ache of his lowest rib that had probably been broken by one of the beatings, but despite the pain he'd felt at the time he'd never given up. It wasn't in his nature.

'The sensible thing would have been to let Annie fend for herself,' Crawford said quietly. 'But you knew what you wanted, for Walter to stop hurting her, and you made it happen.'

Sam nodded. It had been years since he'd last thought of Annie. She'd died soon after they'd landed in Australia. Struck down by the fever that claimed so many of the convicts.

'So what do you want now?' Fitzgerald asked from the other side of him.

'Georgina.'

'How are you going to get her?' Crawford asked.

He shook his head. His friends were wrong in assuming that he'd given up. Far from it, he'd spent the last two weeks plotting and planning, trying to find some way to make Georgina see that they should be together. All the time and energy he'd spent up until two weeks ago planning his revenge on the Earl was now focused solely on getting Georgina back. The problem was every time he came up with even half a plan he would see her hurt face, the tears trickling over her velvety-soft cheeks, and question whether he was good enough for her. He'd become distracted and as such hadn't managed to find a way to persuade Georgina she still wanted to abandon her family and friends for a man who'd lied quite spectacularly to her.

'I don't know,' he said, holding up a hand to halt the next question. 'But I will.'

He saw his two friends grin at one another.

'What can we do to help?'

'I can get her away from here,' Sam said quietly, realising it would help to discuss his dilemma with his friends, even if it was painful to talk about. 'I've got ten different routes planned to whisk her out of the country. What I'm struggling with is how I persuade her to trust me again.'

'She was ready to run away with you before she found out about your past with her father?'

San nodded morosely. That was the worst part; he'd succeeded in persuading Georgina to give up everything she knew, to take a chance on him. And then he'd lost it all.

'Have you told her you love her?' Crawford asked.

Again Sam nodded. 'And now she's returning my letters unopened.'

Crawford was just about to open his mouth when Lady Winston sailed into the room.

'Bad news,' she said without preamble. 'The wedding is in one week.'

She slapped the gossip sheet down in front of Sam and pointed to the part that announced the rather rapid marriage between Lady Georgina and the Duke of Heydon. The author of the column speculated about the speed of the nuptials, but Sam's name did not appear anywhere.

'A week,' he said, feeling the hot flush of panic.

'Plenty of time,' Crawford said cheerfully, slapping him on the back. 'A whole week to persuade her to follow her heart.'

Lady Winston snorted and sat down at the head of the

table. 'You're going to need something quite spectacular,' she said in that no-nonsense way of hers that Sam had come to love. 'No girl wants to find out they've only been courted out of revenge.'

He didn't bother correcting her; it was what Georgina believed. It didn't matter that it had never been his intention to seduce her, ruin her, and bring shame and scandal on her father at the same time.

'Have you given up all thoughts of revenge?' Lady Winston asked.

'Yes.' It was the truth. He had hardly thought of the Earl these last few weeks. The idea of revenge seemed petty and insignificant now he had potentially lost the love of his life. He couldn't quite remember why confronting the Earl had been so important to him, it was the past, an unhappy bit of his life. Now he knew he should have been concentrating on the present and the future the whole time. Dwelling on the wrongs done to him so many years ago certainly had not brought him happiness.

'Then tell her that. Get down on your knees and beg her forgiveness if that's what it takes.'

'I would, but she's not accepting my visits when I call on her,' Sam said. He'd tried multiple times in the past week, but Georgina had never been *at home*.

'I happened to overhear her mother talking at the Yaxleys' dinner party last night,' Lady Winston said, a little smile dancing on her lips. 'Lady Georgina has a dress fitting at two o'clock this afternoon at Madame De Revere's shop. And unfortunately her mother is otherwise engaged. Lady Georgina will be there alone.'

Sam jumped from his seat and kissed Lady Winston enthusiastically on the cheek.

'Settle down, dear boy, I've just given you a location. The rest is up to you.'

'Thank you.'

Without another word he left the room, taking the stairs two at a time. His hangover was forgotten, as was the need he'd felt for oblivion the night before. Today would be the day he persuaded Georgina not to give up on him. Today would be the day she agreed to marry him.

It was cold in the dressmaker's shop, but as Georgina felt the thick material of her wedding dress being pulled over her head she was glad for the chilly temperature. She hated being clammy and overheated when being fussed over by the modiste.

'Beautiful,' Madame De Revere said, clapping her hands with satisfaction. Georgina peered at herself in the full-length mirror. She felt strangely detached, as if she was looking at someone else. The dress certainly was beautiful, ivory and gold in colour with intricate embroidery in gold thread and thousands upon thousands of little beads sewn into the material. She dreaded to think what it was costing, but her mother had insisted she have only the best.

She was marrying a duke and when someone of that status got married, the wedding was a very public affair. Her mother was adamant Georgina would look every inch the Duchess even before she'd said her vows.

'A little pinch here,' Madame De Revere was saying, pulling at the material around her waist. 'You're getting thin, Lady Georgina.'

Looking down, Georgina supposed she had lost a bit of weight. Her appetite had been poor and her interest in food almost non-existent. If she was truthful, her interest in everything had waned to a low level. Every night she found herself crying into her pillow and hating herself for it. Sam had used her, seduced her, and broken her heart—he didn't deserve her tears and her anguish.

'Don't lose any more before the wedding,' the dressmaker commanded.

One week, that was all she had before she became a wife and a duchess. She felt peculiarly isolated from the idea. The Duke had continued to be the perfect gentleman, attentive but not overly so, and had allowed her to decide on the small details surrounding the wedding. He was not affectionate towards her—apart from the odd kiss on the hand he'd barely touched her—and Georgina was glad. Theirs wasn't going to be a marriage built on love or physical attraction, but he seemed genuine and kind which was all she could ask for.

Love was for fools. She'd fallen for its allure and look where it had got her.

She mourned the loss of Sam and she mourned the loss of her innocence. She couldn't look at her father without feeling a stab of revulsion and every time she saw her mother she felt particularly sad. Georgina also knew she was mourning the loss of her chance at a different life. The opportunity to run away with Sam, to travel the world and be her own mistress. Now she was condemned to follow the rules of society for the rest of her life.

'Perhaps have an extra portion of dessert.' Madame De Revere was still talking about Georgina's slimmer figure. 'Some men like the thin look, but most I know prefer a woman to have curves.'

Georgina nodded, relieved when Madame De Revere had tweaked and adjusted the dress to her satisfaction and left one of the younger girls who worked in the shop to pin it into place.

Forcing herself to look at the reflection in the mirror, Georgina knew she would have to practise her smile before the wedding. No one liked a morose bride and she owed it to the Duke to look at least a little happy. And happy was so far from what she was feeling right now the smile would have to be forced.

'Good afternoon.'

Georgina stiffened at the sound of the deep voice at the front of the shop. For a moment she'd thought it had sounded like Sam, even though the thought of him here in the modiste's was ridiculous. Despite her best efforts she was imagining him everywhere, thinking she'd seen his shock of blond hair or heard his smooth voice.

Trying to ignore the inaudible conversation that was occurring on the other side of the curtain, she turned back to the mirror. She needed to forget Sam Robertson and focus her energies on her upcoming marriage and her husband-to-be.

'I'm sorry, I cannot allow it. My reputation...and the young lady's,' Madame De Revere was saying.

Intrigued, Georgina moved towards the curtain, twitching it aside so she could see who the normally unflappable modiste was talking to.

'I don't think you understand, *madame*, I am coming in to see Lady Georgina whether you approve or not. I'm giving you the chance to close up the shop, take my money, and nip around the corner for a well-earned cup of tea while I talk to Lady Georgina. If not, I'm afraid I will have to make a big fuss and *that* will not be good for business.'

'*Sam,*' Georgina whispered to herself as she peered

through the small gap. Here he was as confident and self-assured as ever, sending the formidable modiste out of her own shop.

'I don't think *you* understand, sir.' Madame De Revere had drawn herself up to her full height, just shy of five foot, and puffed out her chest. 'You will have to carry me out screaming before I let you harass one of my customers.'

Seeing that Sam was considering doing just that, Georgina hastily stepped out from behind the curtain.

'Perhaps, Madame De Revere, you could give me a couple of minutes with Mr Robertson?'

Madame De Revere spent at least thirty seconds eyeing Sam up as if deciding if he could be trusted with one of her best customers, then sidled over to Georgina.

'I will be upstairs. If he tries anything unsavoury, just shout and I'll be down with my broom to chase him out,' she murmured.

Trying to suppress a smile at the idea of Sam being chased out of the shop by the small Frenchwoman with a broom, Georgina nodded gravely.

'Come, girls,' Madame De Revere commanded the two pretty shop girls she employed, ushering them upstairs after quickly flicking the lock on the front door so no walk-in customers could enter to find Georgina and Sam alone.

They stood in silence for a minute, Sam's eyes raking over her, taking in the expensive wedding dress and ending up at her face.

'Beautiful,' he said. 'You look like a duchess.' There was no bitterness in his voice and Georgina wondered if he had accepted that this was how things had to be. Perhaps he'd come to say goodbye, to inform her that he had booked a passage on a boat back to Australia and was leaving for ever.

The idea made her panic a little, although her head tried to tell her it would be for the best. If he was half a world away, then she couldn't end up doing something stupid.

'Thank you,' she said, trying to keep her tone crisp and curt.

'It is a shame you will never get to wear it.'

She almost smiled at his confidence, it felt so familiar, so desired, but quickly she schooled her face into a disapproving frown.

'My wedding is a week from today.'

Sam sighed. 'Please, Georgina, don't make this mistake. You'll regret it for ever.'

'I—'

Quickly he interrupted her. 'Forget for a moment that I lied to you, take me out of the equation altogether. Think of how you felt when we were together, think of that happiness, that sense of fulfilment, knowing that you were waking up feeling love and being loved.'

For a few short days her world had been filled with sunshine and contentment, but then he'd dashed everything.

'I want you to be happy, completely happy. And I know you won't be with the Duke.'

'He's a good man,' Georgina said.

'I know. And he will make you a satisfactory husband, Georgina, but he doesn't love you and you don't love him.'

'Perhaps that's a good thing.'

'It isn't,' Sam said with certainty. 'What you would be settling for is a half-life, an existence that is just good enough rather than what you deserve: to be showered with love every day.'

'Perhaps I'd prefer the security of a man who respects me, who doesn't lie to me.'

'You're angry with me, that's completely understandable,' Sam said. 'I deceived you and I hurt you and I will regret that for ever, but don't throw away your entire lifetime of happiness just because you're annoyed with me.'

'I will be happy with the Duke,' Georgina said, trying to inject some steely determination into her voice. The problem was Sam had hit a sore spot with his words. She knew she was settling for a life without love by marrying the Duke. Perhaps over the years something might grow between them, but then again it might not. It was likely that she would never feel that heady rush of love again, she wouldn't feel that hammering of her heart and the complete contentment of being held in the arms of the man she loved.

Then again, if she didn't risk her heart it couldn't be broken.

Sam stepped closer and took her hand. She didn't resist, feeling the familiar rasp of his skin against hers where his callused fingers met her smooth palm. It would be so easy to close her eyes and forget everything, to let him envelop her and fall back into the easy relationship they had shared a few weeks ago.

'Don't throw your life away because I was a fool,' Sam said, looking deep into her eyes. 'I know I may have jeopardised our future, and I will have to live with that for ever, but I could not bear to think I'd pushed you into an unhappy marriage. You're built for love, Georgina, giving it and receiving it. That's what you deserve. Love and a life filled with adventure, not taking tea every afternoon with the same group of ladies until you expire from the boredom.'

Until she'd met Sam she had scoffed at the idea of love in a marriage. No one she knew had married for love; all of her contemporaries had made matches for the sake of a title or a fortune, but never for love.

'As for us...' he gave her a slow lingering look that stoked the fire that burned deep inside her '... I love you and I always will. I know you don't believe me, but everything we shared was real, every last kiss, every last touch. You bewitched me on our first dance and I couldn't keep away.'

It seemed so long ago that he'd whisked her away from her group of suitors with his honeyed words and that cheeky glint in his eyes. Georgina had known right then he was dangerous, but she realised she wouldn't erase the time they'd spent together. He was right that she would never love the Duke, Sam was the man she loved and she couldn't trust him, but she was pleased to have experienced the most wonderful of emotions even for just a short time.

'I admit those first few weeks I was looking for a way to get close to your father, to find some way to confront him about what he'd done to me all those years ago, but you were always there, pulling my focus. I couldn't help but want to spend time with you rather than pursuing the reason I came to England.' He smiled at her sadly. 'I should have realised sooner that nothing was worth risking you over. Not even the revenge I'd fantasised about ever since I realised I would never see my family again.'

Despite her resolve to remain steely and aloof Georgina felt a bubble of sympathy. It was hard not to. Her father *had* treated him appallingly and, even worse, didn't seem to feel any sort of remorse about it. It was difficult to know how she would have felt in Sam's situation, but she could imagine a young boy who'd been ripped from everything he knew wanting revenge on the man who'd done the ripping.

That didn't mean she forgave him, though. He'd had a

thousand opportunities to come clean to her, to confess his true identity and ask her understanding. If she hadn't overheard the conversation between him and her father, she still wouldn't know the extent of his deception.

'I promise you my aim was never to seduce you for the purposes of revenge. And as soon as I got to know you I wanted to protect you from any consequences of the actions I took.'

'But you still lied to me, schemed and tricked your way into my home and held back the most important parts of you even when I gave you everything.'

'I know,' he said sincerely, 'and I'm sorry. I was wrong. I didn't realise until it was too late that you were the only thing that mattered, not what happened eighteen years ago, not the revenge I'd spent so long thinking about.'

Stepping closer, he reached out and placed the palm of his hand against her cheek. It took all her strength not to melt into his body, not to close her eyes and pretend the last few weeks hadn't happened.

'I will always love you,' Sam said, his fingers moving backwards and forward against her skin, 'but only you can decide if you can forgive me. I've booked a passage home to Australia—the ship leaves one week today.'

She felt her heart skip a beat at the idea of the man she loved being so far away, so unreachable.

'The cabin is for two people, there's a ticket in your name. Only you can decide whether you want to stay here and marry the Duke, or take a chance on the man who loves you.'

He slipped her a piece of paper, folding her fingers around it.

'The details of the ship,' he said. 'I'll be waiting for you.'

'I don't…' Georgina said, but Sam placed a finger over her lips to silence her.

'Don't answer me now. You have a week until the wedding and a week until my ship leaves. Have a long, hard think and decide what you want from your future.'

He leaned in, looping one arm around her waist and pulling her towards him in a rustle of silks. As his lips met her own she felt the familiar contentment and a spark of desire. Quickly she began to pull away, but realised this might be the last time she was ever kissed by the man she loved, so allowed her body to relax and her lips to soften. Her body responded as it always did to Sam's touch, with heat and desire, and she knew it would be a hard decision to make. If she listened to her head she would stay and become a duchess, but if she listened to the pull of her body and the overwhelming ache in her heart, she would find a way to be on the ship to Australia with the man she loved.

Chapter Twenty-Four

With a heavy heart Georgina regarded the trunk sitting on the floor in front of her. She was meant to be supervising her maid packing, but whether that was for her new life as a duchess or for a voyage to Australia she still didn't know. Minute by minute her decision changed. One moment she was adamant she would do her duty and marry the Duke as everyone would expect of her. The next moment she was dreaming of distant shores and spending the days enveloped in Sam's arms.

'How is the packing going?' Caroline asked as she burst into Georgina's bedroom, a whirlwind of energy as usual.

Georgina motioned to the empty chest and grimaced. Of course she wasn't expected to do the actual packing herself, but she'd sent her lady's maid on an errand when it had become clear Georgina was dithering about what to actually pack in her trunk.

'Hmm,' Caroline said, frowning as she peered into the trunk. 'You're going to have to pack something at some point.'

'I know,' Georgina said wearily. It was three days until her wedding, three days until Sam left for Australia for ever, and she didn't know how she was meant to make the hardest decision of her life.

'I would run off with the muscular criminal,' Caroline said with a huge grin. 'But I suppose you're not asking me.'

'Would you, though?' Georgina pressed her friend. 'Honestly? If it meant hurting your family, leaving all your friends and loved ones behind?'

'For true love?' Caroline asked. 'In a heartbeat.'

Really that wasn't the decision Georgina had to make. She'd already decided once she would leave everything she knew behind for a life with Sam. The decision she had to make now was whether to forgive him or not, whether she could trust him again or not.

'You can't blame the man for an agenda he had before he met you,' Caroline said, rifling through Georgina's substantial wardrobe.

'I don't,' Georgina said honestly. She could understand his desire to confront her father, the man who'd so casually condemned him to a life of hard labour and transportation and his need for revenge on the man who'd been the reason he had never seen his family again. What she was struggling with was his failure to confess his true identity and agenda even when they had become so close.

'And everyone makes mistakes.'

'If I didn't know you better, Caroline Yaxley, I'd think you were trying to get rid of me.'

'You've caught me,' Caroline said with a smile. 'I want you out of the way so I've got my pick of the eligible bachelors who are always hovering around you.'

'Any of them would be lucky to have you,' Georgina said.

'I love you, Georgie, and I want you to be happy. You positively shone during the time you were with Mr Robertson. Imagine a life of happiness like that.'

'But what if that is all a lie? What if I give up everything and he doesn't turn out to be the man I hoped he was?'

'Surely it's worth the risk.'

'What is worth the risk?' Lady Westchester said, marching into Georgina's room. 'Oh, Georgina, nothing is packed. Where is Fanny? She should have taken care of this.'

'I sent her on some errands.'

'She's meant to be packing your clothes. The wedding is in three days, Georgina.'

'I know.'

Her mother looked at her shrewdly and Georgina felt a little bubble of panic. These past few years her mother hadn't interfered much with her life or enquired much about what Georgina was thinking or feeling, but right now it was as if she was looking into her soul.

'Would you give us a moment in private, Caroline?' Lady Westchester asked.

'Of course.' Caroline squeezed Georgina's hand and then gave her a quick kiss on the cheek.

Lady Westchester waited until the door closed and then sat down on the bed besides Georgina. They'd never been close, not in the way some mothers and daughters seemed to be, and Georgina couldn't remember the last time her mother had taken the time to give her advice on life.

'You're nervous,' her mother said. 'Of course you are. It's completely natural. I was petrified the day of my wedding.'

Nodding, Georgina knew that her feelings of disquiet were nothing to do with her changing role in life.

'But just remember, Georgina, this is everything we've

worked for. This is the fruition of all those hours learning to dance, learning to play the piano. You've landed the best prize—a duke.'

'I barely know him, Mother.'

'That doesn't matter,' her mother said with authority. 'I barely knew your father when we met. You'll be a duchess, mistress of your own household. And over time I'm sure you and the Duke will find the best way to live with one another.'

'Is that how it was for you?' Georgina asked.

Her mother had never seemed particularly unhappy—perhaps there was something to be said for affection that grew in a marriage over time.

'Exactly.'

'And you're happy?'

There was a slight hesitation before her mother answered that made Georgina wonder if her mother was aware of her father's indiscretions with the maids. The thought made her feel slightly nauseous. She didn't know what would be worse: her mother knowing her father liked to corner the household maids or spending all twenty-five years of their marriage ignorant of her husband's pursuits.

'Of course, Georgina.'

'And Father…' She trailed off, unsure how to best phrase her next question. 'He treats you well?'

'The Duke is a good man,' her mother said with authority, avoiding Georgina's clumsy enquiries completely. 'He will not hurt you.'

Lady Westchester regarded her daughter for a few seconds before continuing. 'It is our duty as daughters of the aristocracy to marry, to be good wives and mothers, to run the household and make our husbands' lives easier. We remain at all times dutiful, respectful, and faithful.'

'Even if our husbands do not hold themselves to the same standards?' The question slipped out before Georgina could stop it.

There was a momentary flicker of pain in her mother's eyes that told Georgina that she was aware of every indiscretion the Earl had committed. For the first time Georgina saw her mother as just a woman, like the thousands of others in the world, having to put up with her husband pursuing the maids because she had no rights. No rights in her marriage, no right to protest.

'Pack your trunk, Georgina,' her mother said softly, 'and stop worrying about things you cannot change.'

Chapter Twenty-Five

The room was a hive of activity, maids bustling backwards and forward with flowers and pieces of jewellery while Madame De Revere fussed over the dress, making last-minute alterations and checking it looked absolutely perfect. Even her father had popped his head through the door to check everything was going to plan. Georgina tried to believe his appearance was due to fatherly affection, but she had a suspicion he was just checking nothing would derail the union with a duke. Still she couldn't look him in the eye in case her expression revealed the disgust that she felt for him.

'Stand up straight, Georgina,' her mother instructed, 'and please *try* to smile. This is a happy day.'

It didn't feel like it. It felt as though someone was dying and Georgina had a sneaking suspicion it might be her happiness.

'Still not too late,' Caroline whispered in her ear after seeing her expression. 'Two hours until his ship leaves.'

Two hours until Sam started his voyage back to Australia, taking him for ever out of her reach. The past week had been an agony of indecision and only last night she'd resolved to slip away and join the man she loved, but the nagging doubt had remained and Georgina had convinced herself she couldn't risk her entire future on a man she wasn't sure she trusted.

Now she wasn't convinced she'd made the right choice.

'I can't leave the Duke at the altar.'

'Georgina Fairfax, don't make the biggest mistake of your life just because you don't want to be impolite,' Caroline hissed.

'Caroline,' Lady Westchester said sharply. 'Why don't you go and get changed yourself?'

'Of course, Lady Westchester,' Caroline said, flicking Georgina an apologetic look.

Watching as her friend left the room, Georgina tried to avoid her mother's penetrating gaze.

'Everyone out,' Lady Westchester ordered a minute later. 'I need to talk to my daughter alone.'

'Is anything the matter, Mother?' Georgina asked, trying to keep her expression neutral.

'This is about Mr Robertson, isn't it?'

Georgina had always thought her mother wasn't the most observant person in the world, but right now it felt as though her eyes were boring into her and seeking out Georgina's innermost thoughts and desires.

'I don't know...' Georgina said.

'Don't lie to me. You're still thinking about him, aren't you?'

'I liked him, Mother,' Georgina confessed. 'Very much.'

'And I am fond of our housekeeper, but that does not mean I would throw away a good life for her.'

There was no way her mother could know what she was considering, but Georgina felt like a naughty child all the same.

'Remember, duty, duty, duty. Your father is relying on your marriage to the Duke to boost his political support. It isn't every man whose future grandson will inherit a dukedom.'

'But what about me, Mother?' Georgina asked in a small voice. 'What about my happiness?'

'You will be happy,' her mother said with a dismissive wave of the hand. 'You'll have a grand title, more money than you could imagine, and one day children.'

'And did that make you happy?'

Her mother's silence told Georgina all she needed to know. Her mother had performed her duty in marrying the Earl, but, despite all the trappings and the fine life, it had never made her happy.

'Forget that man, Georgina. In a couple of hours you will be a duchess.'

Finally alone Georgina glanced at the clock. An hour and a half until the ship left. An hour and a half until she was meant to be walking down the aisle in front of half of London and marrying the Duke.

Suddenly she knew what she had to do. Sam had lied to her, he'd deceived her about who he was and manipulated her into a closer acquaintance. One day she would have to work on forgiving him for that, but she also believed he loved her. The kisses, the touches, every last sweet word he'd whispered in her ear, that had all been real. And there was no denying her feelings for him.

If she married the Duke, she was condemning herself

to a lifetime without love, perhaps without true happiness, just like her mother. If she took a chance on Sam it might all go wrong, but equally she might get to live her life by the side of the man she loved.

Eyeing the window, she wondered if she was too late. There was no way to escape downstairs without being noticed. Her best chance would be to climb through the window and hope to hail a passing hackney carriage.

Quickly she looked down at her dress and then back to the window. It would be almost impossible to escape with what felt like hundreds of layers of petticoats swishing round her ankles. She could try to take it off, but it had taken over half an hour to get her into it and Georgina didn't fancy her chances on her own.

'Ready?' Caroline asked as she slipped through the bedroom door.

'For what?'

'Your grand escape?'

'How…?'

'I know you better than you know yourself, Georgie,' Caroline said, hugging her friend. 'We don't have much time.'

Georgina felt a bubble of panic welling up inside her. Now she'd finally made her decision it might be too late. She might arrive at the docks to find the ship had already sailed.

'Fanny is distracting your mother with questions about last-minute packing,' Caroline said, 'so we can smuggle you down the back stairs.'

Quickly they raced down the hallway and started to descend the servants' stairs. As they reached the bottom, Harrison, one of the footmen Georgina had always liked, opened the back door for them with a grin.

'Good luck,' he said. 'There's a carriage waiting for you just outside.'

'How long have you been planning this?' Georgina asked as they crept through the small garden to the side gate.

'This entire week. I hoped you would come to your senses.'

'I love you, Caroline. I'm going to miss you terribly.'

'Write to me every week,' Caroline said. 'And one day perhaps I will come on an adventure to visit you.'

They hugged, using up precious seconds, and Georgina felt the tears begin to roll down her cheeks as she bundled herself into the carriage and Caroline shut the door behind her. Unable to stop herself, she poked her head out of the window as the carriage pulled away, taking one last look at the home she would probably never see again and her best friend's tear-stained face.

'Can we make a stop first?' Georgina called out to the driver, knowing it would waste precious minutes, but refusing to let the Duke be humiliated at the altar. She would at least give him a short amount of time to compose some story to explain the abandoned wedding.

Feeling nervous as they pulled up in front of the Duke's impressively large town house, Georgina hopped out.

'I'll be two minutes, then we can go to the docks,' she told the driver. He nodded good naturedly and Georgina wondered how much Caroline had paid him to make this mad dash across London.

The look on the butler's face as he opened the door was one of complete shock and Georgina nearly offered the elderly man her arm until he composed himself. Luckily the Duke strode from his study at just that moment, looking perplexed at Georgina's presence in the house when she should be preparing for her wedding.

'You can't marry me,' the Duke said without preamble.

Georgina was shocked by his directness, but felt her head begin to nod.

'I'm sorry,' she said as he led her into his study.

'Sit,' he instructed.

Aware of the minutes ticking by, Georgina knew she owed this man some sort of explanation, even if she wished she were racing through London to meet Sam right now.

'I'm sorry,' she repeated.

He nodded, sitting in the chair opposite her. She was about to launch into a lengthy explanation when she saw he didn't look terribly upset. Or surprised.

'It is Mr Robertson, I take it?' the Duke asked.

Wordlessly Georgina nodded.

'You love him?'

'I do.'

The Duke grimaced. 'Then I cannot reasonably object.'

'Of course you can. I made you a promise.'

He paused for a long moment and Georgina found herself holding her breath. 'I release you from that promise,' he said eventually.

'Really? Why?' She'd expected anger, hurt, betrayal, not calm acceptance.

'Did you know my mother was a governess before she married my father?' the Duke asked. 'From governess to duchess, rather a leap in social status.'

'They were in love?' Georgina asked, understanding dawning.

'Completely. They loved each other with all their hearts until the day they died. And they were happy. If I...' He trailed off, but then seemed to rally. 'People always ask why I left it so late to marry. It is because I was hoping for even just a slice of what they had, but, alas, it has evaded me.'

'So why did you start looking for a wife?'

'At some point duty, the need to provide an heir, has to come first,' he said with a shrug. 'But that doesn't mean we both have to be unhappy.'

'You forgive me?'

He stood and Georgina did the same.

'I forgive you. I'm sure my bruised ego will recover and I can always make up some salacious tale about what happened. The debutantes will be swarming around me again in no time.'

'Wait a little longer,' Georgina urged as she stepped towards the door. 'Just another few months. Maybe you'll find the person you're meant to be with.'

'Maybe,' he said with a smile.

She stood on tiptoes and kissed him on the cheek, feeling affection for the man who could have made this so difficult, but instead had responded so calmly.

'Good luck,' he said, opening the front door for her himself.

Georgina raced back to the carriage. By the time she was seated, all thoughts of the Duke had left her mind and all she could think about was the man she loved waiting for her aboard the ship. As the coachman urged the horses forward, she prayed for empty streets, otherwise she might not get her happy ending after all.

Chapter Twenty-Six

Sam stood tapping his fingers against the rail, his eyes moving backwards and forward as he regarded the horizon. Ten minutes, that was how much time there was left until the ship set sail. Behind him he could hear the sailors making their final preparations while the last of the cargo was being hauled up a ramp on to the deck.

'Come on, Georgina,' he murmured. Although he'd given her space and the time to make her own choice, until now he'd never really doubted that she would choose him. Of course she would, they were in love, and he might have made some mistakes, handled the later part of their relationship badly, but they still were meant to be together. Surely she wouldn't choose a life of monotony with a man she didn't care for over a life of adventure with him.

'Ten minutes,' the Captain said as he joined Sam by the rail. 'I can't hold her any longer or we'll miss the tide.'

'I understand,' Sam said, trying to keep the panic from his voice. He'd never considered he might be going back to Australia on his own. The whole reason he'd booked the passage was so they could escape from any pressure Georgina might be under to do the right thing.

Suddenly he felt completely alone. He'd said his goodbyes to Crawford and Fitzgerald back at Lady Winston's house, but now he wished he'd taken them up on their offer to accompany him to the docks to see him off. Perhaps he wouldn't have felt quite so nervous with them at his side. He'd never expected to return to Australia before his friends, but Crawford had some mysterious woman he was pursuing, someone he wanted to stay a little longer in England for, and Fitzgerald had promised his aunt he would stay at least until the end of the Season and Lady Winston was not one for broken promises. So here he was alone, waiting for Georgina.

Thinking back to the last time he'd seen Georgina just a week ago as she was having her final fitting of her wedding dress. She'd still been angry with him, still was dwelling on the mistakes he'd made, but she hadn't completely shut herself off from him. When he'd taken her hand he'd felt her relax into him and when they'd kissed her lips had welcomed him in. She still loved him, despite everything he'd done; he just had to hope that was enough.

Again and again over these past few weeks he'd cursed himself for not seeing what was important before it was too late. He had been so caught up in the past he hadn't realised it was the present and the future that really mattered, and he'd allowed his obsession for revenge to jeopardise it all.

'I'm sorry,' the Captain said as he approached Sam again, 'we really can't wait any longer.'

Morosely Sam nodded, feeling the ripping pain in his

chest as he realised this was it, this was the moment he left England behind for ever and Georgina with it.

'I'll be in my cabin,' he said, turning away from the rail. He couldn't face the pity on the Captain's face or the knowledge that now he would have to make this entire journey alone. He'd been convinced it would be a voyage of adventure, the weeks flying past as he and Georgina got to know one another intimately and he prepared her for life in Australia. The life they would share together.

'I'll have some refreshments sent down to you,' the Captain said kindly.

Sam almost refused the offer, he wouldn't be able to eat anything, but perhaps the Captain might find a bottle of something intoxicating to help ease Sam's pain. Preferably more than one bottle. He wanted to be oblivious to his heartache at least until they reached Spain.

'Thank you,' he said, stepping towards the steep stairs that led to the area below decks.

As he made his way across the deck he heard the sailors drawing up the wooden gangplank and shouting to the men below as the complicated process of casting off began. In the background he heard the distinctive sound of thundering hooves and rattling carriage wheels and momentarily he wondered if just maybe...

Shaking his head, he told himself not to be absurd. If Georgina had chosen him she'd had a week to plan her escape, it would be ridiculous to think she would have left her dash across London to the last minute. Still he hesitated, his foot hovering above the top step.

Steeling himself for disappointment he turned, taking a couple of long strides back towards the rail. He had to raise a hand to shield his eyes from the low winter sun, but after a second or two he was able to focus in on the carriage that had come to a halt in front of the ship.

His heart skipped a beat as the door was flung open and the first flash of gold came billowing out. It was Georgina, dressed for her wedding, but racing to be with him.

'Wait,' he called frantically to the sailors who were bustling about on deck. 'We need to get her on board.'

Sam watched as the men pulled on the ropes that a few minutes ago had anchored the ship to the dockside, their muscles straining, but still the ship was pulling away from the docks. For an awful moment he had a vision of the ship leaving and Georgina being left behind to be dragged back by her father to marry the Duke.

'I won't leave you,' he shouted, seeing Georgina's worried expression. Even if it meant diving into the murky waters of the Thames and swimming back to the dockside he wouldn't leave without her.

'The gangplank,' the Captain shouted, motioning for the piece of wood to be lowered, even though it was clear it would not reach the dock. 'I hope your girl isn't the nervous type,' he said over his shoulder to Sam. 'Get the lady aboard, boys,' he shouted to the men on the docks below.

With only a moment's hesitation Georgina allowed herself to be quickly guided a little further along the dock, then with wide eyes fixed on Sam she took a few steps back, waited while two of the filthy dockworkers took her arms and then, half jumping, half propelled through the air, she was sailing towards the lowered gangplank that was two feet away from the edge of the dock now. She landed on it, teetered alarmingly, but with a few rotations of her arms managed to regain her balance and clamber up the gangplank, her resplendent skirts trailing behind her.

At the top she flung herself into Sam's arms to the cheers of both the sailors on the ship and the dockworkers down below.

As he pressed her to his chest he could feel her heart fluttering. Wordlessly he folded her in his arms and buried his face in her hair.

'I thought you weren't coming,' he whispered eventually. Never before had he let anyone see him so vulnerable. There was naked fear in his voice and he knew the depth of his pain showed on his face.

'I almost didn't,' she admitted. 'Then I realised the person I would be punishing the most was myself.'

He shook his head. He wouldn't have ever got over the heartbreak if Georgina had chosen the Duke and a life of a society wife over him.

'I am sorry, Georgina,' he said, pulling away slightly so he could look her in the eye as he spoke. 'I will spend our entire lives earning your trust again.'

'I know,' she said.

'Did you...?' He trailed off, deciding it wouldn't be prudent to enquire how she had left things with her family.

'I informed the Duke on my way here.' She gave a little shrug. 'I'm sure Caroline will tell my parents when they notice my disappearance.'

'I know you've left everything for me,' Sam said, taking her hand in his own, 'but I promise I will never let you regret your decision, not even for one day.'

She smiled up at him, the smile that had first captured his heart a few months earlier, and Sam knew he was the luckiest man alive. Lucky that she'd decided he was worth taking a chance on, lucky that she had a loving and forgiving heart. Never would he hurt her again as he had a few weeks earlier, that would be his life's mission.

Slowly he kissed her, his lips just brushing against hers at first, savouring the sweet taste of her mouth under his own. He felt her body sway towards his and her mouth press more insistently against his and before he knew what was happening he had entwined his fingers in her hair and was kissing her like this was their last moment on earth.

He felt Georgina's body stiffen as a couple of the sailors whooped and cheered them and slowly he pulled away, never letting go of her completely.

'Shall we continue this in our cabin?' he asked, motioning to the steps that led below deck.

'Please,' Georgina said, her cheeks flushed.

'Come with me.'

He led her down the steep staircase to the narrow passageway below.

'I left in such a hurry I don't have any luggage, any clothes,' Georgina said, looking down at the elaborate wedding dress she was still wearing. It wasn't the most practical garment to make a sea crossing in.

'Don't worry,' he said, trying to keep a straight face, 'I think I can put up with you wearing very little these next few weeks.'

'And when we go up for dinner?'

'You'll look very fetching in a pair of my breeches and a shirt.'

He opened the door to their cabin and motioned for Georgina to enter, unable to keep the wide grin from his face. Today was the first day of his life with the woman he loved and he was determined to treasure every second.

Epilogue

'Sam Robertson, we'll be late.' Georgina giggled as he looped his arms around her waist and started to kiss her neck. She shifted slightly, allowing him to rest his hands on her heavily pregnant belly.

'It's our wedding,' he murmured in her ear. 'It's not like they can start without us.'

She had to concede his point. The vicar in the little chapel twenty minutes' ride away was ancient and probably wouldn't even remember he was supposed to be conducting the wedding ceremony today. Their witnesses were a couple of their neighbours, people who lived their lives by the sun's position and not the clocks, so it was dubious whether anyone would even be at the chapel.

'You look beautiful,' he said.

Glancing down, she had to smile. The dress she was wearing was completely the opposite of the one she had donned almost a year ago in preparation for her wedding to the Duke. Simple, cool, and practical, that was the main requirement of her clothes now. Much of the time she spent in breeches and a shirt when she was out and about on the land with Sam, but whenever she went into town or received visitors she would be clad in a dress. Or for a special occasion like today.

Her wedding dress was pale blue, made of cotton, and had a simple cut to flow over the large bump that dominated the front of her body.

'I look large.' She grimaced. She'd loved her blooming pregnancy body, but in the past few weeks the temperatures had begun to soar and now she was suffering from the extra weight she was carrying.

'Not long now, my love,' Sam said, running his hands over the front of her dress lovingly.

They weren't quite sure when the baby was due. After much consideration they thought it had probably been conceived in those heady weeks of the voyage to Australia. Weeks where they had barely left their cabin. Georgina had put the nausea she'd felt as they approached the coast of Australia to seasickness, only realising a few weeks later what was really happening once they were on dry land.

If she'd gone through a pregnancy in England she would have been surrounded by doctors, all there to ensure the heir she was giving birth to had the best possible chance of surviving. Here things were a little more lax. Sam assured her there was a doctor, but he lived an hour's ride away so it wasn't so useful in an emergency. Instead Sam had informed her he'd birthed many foals during the course of his work. Georgina wasn't sure if he was joking, but kept telling herself childbirth was natural. Women had been doing it for thousands of years without the help of a doctor, surely she could manage the same.

'Any regrets?' Sam asked as she checked her reflection one last time in the mirror that hung in the hallway.

'None,' she said with a smile.

The time had flown by. They'd spent six months on the *Liberty Hope*, their sturdy vessel that had taken them all the way from London to Australia with a few stops in between. Sam had been eager to bring her back to his home, to show her where he'd built a life for himself and where they would start theirs as a couple together. For three months they'd toured his property, checking up on the farms and the various outposts of his main business—the stud. With every passing day Georgina had been unable to believe the scale of what he owned—he easily had fifty times more land than her father possessed back home, perhaps more. All this he'd built himself, saving his profits and expanding whenever there was an opportunity. Every time she thought about it she felt proud of the man she was about to marry.

Of course she missed her family and friends. She'd written a couple of times to her mother, long letters that detailed her new life, and a few weeks ago had received one in return. Georgina couldn't bring herself to make contact with her father yet, she still felt so disgusted with how he'd treated Sam and the horrible way he'd carried on with the maids. Maybe one day she would be able to forgive him, but not yet. Most of all she wished she could have Caroline by her side today, but Georgina had to content herself with the letters that arrived sporadically, written in Caroline's humorous style.

Despite the pang she sometimes felt for her mother or her best friend, Georgina did not regret a single day since she'd left England. She'd risked everything for love and through that risk she'd found happiness.

'Come on,' Sam said, pulling her gently by the hand towards the door. 'Unless you want this baby out of wedlock.'

Georgina laughed. Once she would have been scandalised by the idea, but now it didn't seem that significant. As long as their child was born to two loving parents then it didn't much matter if they were married or not.

Gently he helped her up on to her horse. Although Georgina missed Lady Penelope, the beautiful grey mare she'd owned in England, Sam had helped her choose the best from his extensive stock. Her mare had a soft bay coat and was headstrong and fast, just as Georgina would wish, but with patience and gentle coaxing she was eminently trainable.

When he was sure she was comfortable he vaulted up onto the back of his horse, adjusted the wide brim of his hat on his head to keep the sun from his eyes, and led the way out of the dusty yard.

'Are you sure you want to tie yourself legally to an ex-convict?' Sam asked as they started the ride at a sedate pace towards the small town nearby where the chapel was situated.

'It's a little late now to back out,' Georgina said, glancing down at her belly.

The wedding was just a formality. Georgina had realised the rules that governed society in Australia were different to back home. If a man and woman lived together, produced children, shared a life and a home, then they were considered bound together with or without the marriage ceremony. Sam had introduced her to lots of couples who'd never had a wedding but still called themselves husband and wife. However, Georgina had come to realise that although she was embracing a more free, less constrained life, that didn't mean she had to rebel against everything. She loved Sam and he loved her, and one way to show that love for one another was to get married, so when he'd proposed for the third time she'd finally accepted.

It was early in the morning, the ceremony time chosen to avoid the worst of the heat, but by the time they had reached the chapel Georgina still felt the perspiration on her brow. The small town was dusty, the last rainfall having been at least a couple of weeks ago, and the fields they had ridden through that had been green not long ago were now turning brown. Despite the dry and dusty land Georgina looked at it lovingly. This was her homeland now. One day in the distant future they might brave the voyage to England again, but never again would it be home. Her home was here, with the man she loved, the man she was about to marry, and soon with their child, too.

Carefully Sam helped her dismount, lifting her bodily off the horse so she did not overbalance now she was more clumsy with the weight she was carrying around her middle.

'Lady Georgina,' he said, a familiar twinkle in his eye, 'are you ready to become Mrs Robertson?'

'I've been ready for longer than you can imagine,' she said, reaching up and kissing him on the lips.

Taking the arm he offered, she walked inside the cool chapel, taking the first step down the aisle to marry the man she loved.

* * * * *

Reunited With His
Long-Lost Cinderella

Laura Martin writes historical romances with an adventurous undercurrent. When not writing, she spends her time working as a doctor in Cambridgeshire, UK, where she lives with her husband. In her spare moments Laura loves to lose herself in a book and has been known to read from cover to cover in a single day when the story is particularly gripping. She also loves to travel—especially to visit historical sites and far-flung shores.

Books by Laura Martin

Harlequin Historical

The Pirate Hunter
Secrets Behind Locked Doors
Under a Desert Moon
A Ring for the Pregnant Debutante
An Unlikely Debutante
An Earl to Save Her Reputation
The Viscount's Runaway Wife

Scandalous Australian Bachelors

Courting the Forbidden Debutante
Reunited with His Long-Lost Cinderella

The Governess Tales

Governess to the Sheikh

The Eastway Cousins

An Earl in Want of a Wife
Heiress on the Run

Visit the Author Profile page at
millsandboon.com.au.

Author Note

When I first started writing *Reunited with His Long-Lost Cinderella* I had a very definite idea of the sort of man Ben Crawford would be. Wrenched from his family at a very young age, convicted for a crime he did not commit and sent to a country on the other side of the world, Ben would have to be a survivor to make it through all of that and come out fighting on the other side.

One of the things I found most interesting when researching for this book was the human element of crime and punishment in the late Regency period. Transportation was the sentence given for a wide-ranging number of offenses, and the effect was devastating to those sent to a penal colony. What surprised me most was the relatively minor crimes that could bring about being transported to Australia as a convict worker. Stealing livestock or food could be enough!

The ages of the convicts transported was also fascinating, with many young people among those sent on the ships to Australia to serve out their sentence. There are even records of children as young as nine being sentenced to transportation.

Reunited with His Long-Lost Cinderella is set in Regency London, but I hope Ben brings the flavor of Australia to the prim and proper ballrooms and dinner parties. His journey, and his character, is inspired by all those who were wrenched from their families at a young age and sent to a strange new world.

For Sophie.
Your friendship is one of the greatest gifts.

Chapter One

Surveying the ballroom, Ben found himself unable to believe he was actually there. Dressed in the finest evening wear, cravat tight around his neck and jacket tailored to precision across his broad shoulders, the son of a land steward was attending one of the most exclusive balls in London.

'I'm not sure these masks conceal our identities,' George Fitzgerald said from his position beside him.

Ben shrugged. 'I'm not sure they're meant to.'

They were standing at the perimeter of the Scotsworths' ballroom for what Ben had been informed was an annual masquerade ball. The women were dressed in flamboyant outfits and their masks were nearly all elaborately decorated. Many of the men had gone for a more subtle and less time-consuming approach of wearing their normal evening jackets and adding simple black or single-coloured masks that covered their eyes. Ben's was black, but did have a rather annoying feather protruding from one edge that every so often would flop in his face and tickle his forehead.

'Why are we here?' Fitzgerald asked shrewdly.

Since arriving in London three weeks ago they'd attended a number of balls and soirées, even once braving the unknown world of the opera, but tonight was the first night Ben had actually insisted they accept an invitation.

'To enjoy the magic of a masquerade ball,' Ben said with a straight face.

Fitzgerald laughed, clapped his friend on the shoulders and shook his head. 'Keep your secrets for now, Crawford—one day I'll find out what you've been up to these last few weeks.'

Ben grinned, but it was almost entirely forced. He hoped no one would find out quite how pathetic he'd been in the weeks since their arrival in London. When Sam Robertson, the third member of their little group, had suggested the trip back to their homeland from Australia, Ben had quickly agreed. He had told his friends that he wanted to see his family again, at least what was left of it. Eighteen years ago, he'd left his father and younger brother behind in a sleepy Essex village. For four years he hadn't heard a word from them—the post never arrived for prisoners held on the hulk ships on the Thames or during the eight-month voyage to Australia. Only once he was working as a convict worker for the late Mr Fitzgerald the elder did he receive a tattered and torn envelope.

His father had written every month and must have paid considerable sums of money to ensure his communications were loaded on to the ships heading for Australia. Ben had no doubt most of these letters had never left England and could be found disintegrating at the bottom of the Thames. But one had got through—one conscientious and kind pensioner guard had taken Ben's father's money and promised to do his best to place the letter in Ben's hand and, nearly a year later, he did just that.

Ever since Ben had kept in contact with his father from the other side of the world. Of course, he was keen to return to Essex and see the old man again and would do so as soon as his father returned from his poorly timed trip to Yorkshire. His father was an estate manager and as such at the whim of the Earl he worked for, but soon he would be back home in Essex and Ben would see him for the first time since the age of twelve. However, the other reason for his agreeing to the trip to England he wasn't even sure would appear tonight. For three weeks, he'd haunted the ballrooms of London, hoping to catch a glimpse of the girl he'd left behind all those years ago.

Francesca. She was a woman now, of course. A woman who'd probably hadn't thought of him much at all these last eighteen years. When he'd landed in England he'd made some discreet enquiries and found she'd been married and recently widowed. He was beginning to understand those in mourning didn't socialise as much as the rest of the lords and ladies and had started to despair of ever setting eyes on her, but tonight he'd heard a rumour Francesca would be in attendance to chaperon her younger sister.

So here he was, waiting eagerly for a glimpse of the woman who probably didn't even remember him.

He surveyed the ballroom again and for an instant it felt as though his heart stopped in his chest. There she was, unmistakable despite the mask and the eighteen years since he'd last seen her. Dressed in muted greys and violets, colours he was informed signalled the period of half-mourning, Lady Francesca Somersham still cut a striking figure. She was older than most of the debutantes, but having been married and widowed in the years since Ben had last seen her that was hardly surprising. Despite being almost thirty she still turned heads and Ben saw two gentlemen start in her direction as soon as they noticed her entrance into the ballroom.

This was what he'd been waiting for the past three weeks, but now she was here in the same room as him he was unsure of what he wanted next.

'Enough,' he murmured to himself. He wasn't the lowly son of a steward any more. Over the years since he'd finished his sentence Ben had worked hard and taken risks, most of which had paid off, meaning he was now a very successful Australian landowner. There was no need to skulk about watching from a distance. Today he would talk to the woman he had been dreaming about for the past eighteen years despite his best efforts to forget her.

Quickly, he weaved through the crowds, ignoring the appraising looks from the masked debutantes. Fitzgerald was correct, these flimsy masks didn't do much to conceal the face, but he was largely unknown and as such was a man of interest.

'Mr Crawford,' a pretty young woman murmured in his ear as he moved past her. 'We really must find some time to spend together.'

Ben grimaced, but quickly turned it into a smile. Since arriving in London he had made the acquaintance of a number of women, mostly widows or those with husbands happy to turn a blind eye. He'd danced with them, talked to them, but never anything more despite their sometimes quite obvious offering of themselves. Ben might have a reputation as a man the ladies could not resist, but nothing was going to jeopardise his getting close to Lady Somersham, especially not a meaningless fling.

'I await that moment with anticipation,' he said, planting a fleeting kiss on the young lady's hand, but moving on quickly, using the press of people to his advantage and weaving a path away from Mrs Templeton's inviting eyes.

Suddenly she was in front of him and for a moment Ben felt the breath being sucked out of his lungs. She was beautiful. Gone was the gangly-legged, freckle-nosed girl he'd played with throughout his childhood and in her place was a woman of poise and grace. Ben took a moment to study her hair, sleek and tamed into a complicated bun at the back of her head. When they were children Francesca's hair had always been an uncontrollable mess, frizzy and wild and more often than not flying behind her as she did something dangerous at great speed. He felt a sharp stab of desire deep inside him and fought to keep himself under control.

'Lady Somersham,' Ben said, pausing a couple of feet in front of her and bowing formally. He might have been brought up the son of a steward, but he was a great imitator and just a couple of days in London society had led to him being able to replicate the gestures and customs perfectly.

Francesca turned to him and, even though nearly every other part of her had changed, she fixed the same mischievous blue eyes on him that he remembered from childhood.

'You have me at a disadvantage,' she said after studying him for a few seconds.

'Isn't that the point of masquerade balls?' Ben asked. 'To conjure an atmosphere of mystery and allow you to creep into dark corners with an unknown admirer.'

'Perhaps to conjure an atmosphere of mystery...' Lady

Somersham conceded. 'But I'm sure my mother always told me to keep away from strange men and dark corners.'

'And do you always take your mother's advice?'

There was that smile, just a hint of the impish grin he remembered from childhood.

'She likes to think I do.'

'Lady Somersham,' a deep voice boomed, causing heads to turn in their direction even half a ballroom away. This was the overweight, red-faced man who was destined to be Francesca's next husband if rumours were to be believed.

'You're not meant to tell anyone who I am, Lord Huntley,' Francesca said, turning to face the man. She smiled at him, too, but Ben could tell this was forced, a mere up-turning of the corners of her mouth with no glimmer of pleasure in her eyes.

'Nonsense. Everyone knows who everyone else is. Damn ridiculous idea if you ask me, all this prancing around in masks.'

Ben noted Lord Huntley had not deigned to don a mask of his own, leaving his red-rimmed and wrinkled eyes unadorned. Surely a mask would be of benefit to this man, even if it were purely to draw one's eyes away from his generous jowls.

'I think it is rather fun,' Lady Somersham said and Ben had to wonder if she was just saying it to be perverse. Lord Huntley made him want to run in the opposite direction and he never had the awful prospect of having to one day be intimate with the man hanging over him.

'Where's your father?' Lord Huntley barked, looking around as if Lord Pottersdown might be hiding behind a pot plant or marble statue.

'I'm not sure,' Francesca said, her eyes involuntarily

flicking towards the doors that led into the ballroom. The gaming tables, no doubt. These past few weeks Ben had learned a lot about Francesca's life just by listening to gossip. The ballrooms and dinner parties were rife with it and, although there was a lot of exaggeration and a few things that were clearly completely fabricated, you could glean some very interesting things if you filtered the dross out.

'Losing more of the family fortune,' Lord Huntley snorted derisively. He'd come to the same conclusion, it would seem.

Ben saw Francesca's cheeks redden under the delicate rim of the mask and for an instant got the urge to manhandle Lord Huntley outside and send him on his way for embarrassing her. Then he remembered that he wasn't her protector, he wasn't anything to her, just a man who had once been a boy she'd known. A man she might not even remember.

'Wait here,' Lord Huntley commanded. 'I'll go fetch him. We need to pin down the agreement for this marriage.'

'I'm still in mourning...' Francesca said, but Lord Huntley had already departed, heading through the ballroom with his rotund belly leading the way. Not once had he even acknowledged Ben's presence.

'I'm sorry,' Francesca said, trying to fight the tears that were building in her eyes. 'That was incredibly rude, you shouldn't have had to see that.'

Really she was apologising for Lord Huntley, the oaf of a man who would one day soon be her husband. The thought made her feel peculiarly queasy.

Trying to focus on the man in front of her, she couldn't help but notice how he was the opposite of Lord Huntley, being tall and broad shouldered. She could tell there wasn't a single ounce of fat on him even through the thick material of his jacket. His skin didn't have that sickly grey tone to it, instead there was an unusual but healthy tan on his cheeks as if he spent a large portion of his day outdoors.

'The best way to avoid discussing your marriage to him tonight is to not be here when he returns with your father,' the masked stranger said nonchalantly. Feeling her eyes widen, Francesca tried not to splutter. Most people would politely ignore the exchange they had just witnessed, but it seemed the man in front of her wasn't about to do that. 'Come on,' he said, a gleam in his eye that Francesca found vaguely familiar.

Offering her his arm, he flashed her a rather seductive smile as she hesitated. What she should do was wait here for her father and the man who was angling to become her future husband and listen while they discussed her like a horse for sale. Not that she had any illusions that her presence would make any difference to the outcome. She had absolutely no say in whom she married or when, both her father and Lord Huntley had made that perfectly clear.

Feeling rebellious, she took the man's arm and allowed him to lead her through the ballroom away from the direction Lord Huntley had disappeared in.

'You must tell me your name,' she said, peeking up at him from under a carefully curled ringlet that framed her face. Her hair was difficult to tame, but her current maid was an expert at fighting the curly locks into submission and making her look presentable. As long as she didn't go out in the rain.

'Ben,' he offered.

'I can't call you Ben.'

He shrugged, smiled at her and said, 'That's all you're getting. This is a night of mystery after all.'

'Well, Ben,' she said, leaning in so no one would over-hear her being quite so familiar with a stranger, 'now you've removed me from having to discuss my future with Lord Huntley, what do you propose?' She felt reckless, giddy. Francesca knew it was because she was near to hysteria, her emotions running high at the thought of having her whole future decided for her and a marriage to another man she did not like.

'We could go somewhere a little more private,' he sug-gested, that glint in his eyes again. Francesca trawled back through her memory, trying to place the man. They must have been introduced before, otherwise why was she finding him quite so peculiarly familiar? It was a sensation rather than anything else, a feeling rooted deep inside that she knew the man escorting her around the ballroom.

'I don't think that's wise,' she said. Years earlier she might have been tempted. He was a good-looking man and she was desperate for a dash of romance, of adventure. But she wasn't a giddy debutante any longer, far from it. She was a widow in her late twenties, and that meant she'd had plenty of time to realise that liaisons with strange men in dark corners never ended well for anyone, no matter how tempting it might be.

She glanced at the man beside her and saw he wasn't sur-prised by her answer. Francesca knew many widows had a looser sense of what was acceptable behaviour and what wasn't, with many of them engaging in discreet affairs, but she wasn't one of them. Her father had made it clear when she'd been forced to go back and live with her parents that she would keep her reputation pristine and pure so no po-tential suitors would be put off. It had worked, she thought glumly, she wasn't even out of her mourning period for her first husband, Lord Somersham, and she was practically betrothed to Lord Huntley.

'Then dance with me,' he said, pausing before changing direction to the dance floor.

'I'm not meant to dance,' she said, gesturing to her half-mourning clothes.

'Surely this world is more fun if you do one or two things you're not supposed to.'

She felt herself hesitate. She would love to dance, especially with this man by her side. He was strong and young and had a vitality about him that neither her late husband or Lord Huntley had ever exuded. Imagining what it would be like to be swept around the ballroom in his strong arms, she felt herself nodding.

Trying to close her mind off to all the whispers and disapproval that would be coming her way, she allowed her companion to lead her into position. Francesca loved to dance, she'd loved to dance since she was small and had often roped in anyone and everyone to be her dance partner. Governesses, maids, the grouchy old butler, even Ben Crawford, the skinny little son of the estate manager she'd spent her summers playing with.

Ben. She looked up quickly, but the idea was absurd. This man, this charming and confident and attractive man in front of her, was not Ben Crawford. The son of an estate manager wouldn't be so self-assured in a room full of lord and ladies, and of course he couldn't be here, he'd been transported to Australia all those years ago. Francesca suppressed the feelings of sadness that always threatened to overtake her when she thought about her childhood friend. Now wasn't the time.

She glanced at her companion again. He *did* have something about him though, the same cheeky smile and the same mischief in his eyes. Perhaps that was why she thought the man looked familiar. He reminded her of the friend she had lost all those years ago.

The music started and Francesca felt the pleasure diffuse through her body. She felt as though she was walking on the clouds whenever she danced, loving the instinctive way her body would move to the music. Her partner was both well practised and a natural dancer, twirling her round effortlessly and all the time managing to keep those lively eyes fixed on her and a smile on his lips.

For a second Francesca wondered what it would be like to have a man like this slip into her bed every night, to feel his hard body on top of hers and his soft lips on her skin. Instinctively she knew he would not be selfish in taking his pleasure and a blush spread across her cheeks as she imagined an unending night of passion with him.

'Now you must tell me what has put such a beautiful blush on your cheeks,' he murmured, leaning in close so his breath tickled her ear.

Francesca was unable to speak, knowing her voice would come out as a muted squeak if she opened her mouth.

'Perhaps you're thinking of moving in just a little closer,' he whispered, pressing his hand ever so slightly harder into the small of her back. Against her better judgement Francesca allowed her body to press closer in to his, feeling the delightful swish of his legs against hers as they danced. 'Or perhaps you're imagining how it might feel if I kissed you here,' he said, raising a finger and oh-so-briefly trailing it across the skin of her neck.

Now she was imagining that.

'Or here.' His fingers had dropped to her collarbone.

Guiltily Francesca glanced around the ballroom to see if anyone had seen the entirely inappropriate touch she'd just allowed. No doubt the gossips were already judging her for dancing when she was still in half-mourning. Even though this was a masquerade ball she was under no illusion that no one knew who she was.

Thankfully the music stopped and she felt the spell break. Her companion stepped away and bowed formally, only the sparkling of his eyes hinting at the inappropriate way he'd acted during their dance.

'I hear the private terrace is a beautifully secluded spot,' he murmured in her ear as he escorted her back to the perimeter of the ballroom. 'If you go out of the ballroom, through the third door on the left and into the library, there are glass doors leading on to the private terrace there.'

He bowed again, then placed a kiss on her gloved hand before disappearing off into the crowd.

Francesca watched him go. There was no way she could join him on this private terrace, no matter how much her body wanted her to. Sighing, she turned back to look for her father and Lord Huntley. It had been a wonderful interlude with her mysterious gentlemen, but nothing more. She had to focus on coming to terms with marrying yet another man she did not particularly like.

Chapter Two

Ben watched her from a distance. It was strange seeing the girl he'd once known so well gliding across the ballroom, turning heads as she went. When Ben had been sentenced to transportation at the age of twelve, Francesca had only been ten. Of course she'd been pretty, but in a wild and un-fettered sort of way. Now she was elegant and there was no hint of the girl who used to race him across the fields on horseback or dare him to boost her to the top of a hay bale.

It was unsettling, talking to her again. For eighteen years he'd been unable to rid his thoughts of her. They'd only been children when he'd been arrested for stealing jewellery from her father, children who had spent every moment they could together. He'd loved her then, in the pure and innocent way one child could love another, and he knew she had felt the same way. Even when her father had cajoled and threatened her, trying to stop her from speaking up in Ben's defence, she'd spoken out, she'd protested his innocence. It hadn't changed the outcome—no one had been willing to listen to a ten-year-old girl when her father—a viscount, no less—had told a different story, but she'd defied her father all the same. All for him.

He'd thought about her a lot over the last eighteen years, wondering how her life had turned out, wondering if she would still be living in luxury as he toiled away under the heat of the Australian sun. Once he'd finished his sentence and little by little bought up parcels of land, turning them into one of the largest farms in Australia, he thought he might move on, but still he couldn't forget about her.

Ben wasn't so naïve to think she even remembered him from all those years ago. She'd probably never thought of the young boy who she had played so closely with, but he hadn't been able to forget her. So when his friend Sam Robertson voiced his plan to come to England Ben had been eager to accompany him. He wanted to look her in the eye, to see if she was the same girl he'd known all those years ago or if she had been irretrievably changed by almost a lifetime of socialising and living by the rules of the *ton*.

Never had he expected to feel quite so unsettled at seeing her again, though. She was beautiful, but Ben had known a lot of beautiful women throughout his life and none of them seemed to have this power, this pull. Throughout their dance all he could think of was sweeping her away from the ballroom, finding some deserted room and depositing her on something soft so he could spend the night exploring her body.

That was why he'd had to leave her, to give himself time to dampen down the entirely inappropriate desire he was feeling. Of course he knew she wouldn't take him up on the offer to meet him on the private terrace, but he'd been unable to resist making the suggestion, just in case she decided to surprise him.

He didn't know what he wanted from Francesca now. All his thoughts had been on seeing her again, looking into the eyes of the girl he'd once cared for so much—he hadn't thought past that initial meeting.

Liar, the little voice in his head called out. He knew exactly what he wanted from her. He wanted to gather her in his arms and sweep her away somewhere private. Somewhere he could spend the whole night becoming acquainted with the most beautiful woman in the ballroom.

'Who was that?' George Fitzgerald asked as he found his friend at the edge of the ballroom.

'A very pretty lady,' Ben said with a grin. 'Can you do me a favour?'

'Of course.'

'She's finding it a little difficult to slip away from her companions. Could you go tell her that her father is a little worse for wear and is recovering in the library, show her the way—it's the third door on the left out of the ballroom. Do it discreetly, but not too discreetly.'

'You have a trick for everything, don't you?' Fitzgerald said, clapping his friend on the shoulder and making his way through the crowd.

Ben watched for a moment then slipped away, wanting to get to the library before Francesca. It would be private and, if they were caught alone together, no doubt a scandal would ensue, but it was unlikely that would happen. Everyone was too caught up in the revelry of the masquerade ball to notice their absence. He just wanted a few minutes alone with her, a few minutes to find out what her life had been like in the years he'd been away. If he could just hear she was happy, then maybe that would be enough for him. Maybe.

'Lady Somersham,' a deep voice said quietly in her ear, 'I'm sorry to interrupt.'

It was another gentleman she did not know, with a simple black mask and a serious expression. She turned to him, smiling apologetically at the two older ladies she had been conversing with.

'Your father is a little indisposed. He has been asking for you.' The message was delivered quietly, discreetly, but Francesca knew her two companions had heard every word. Feeling her heart sink, she summoned a breezy smile.

'Please excuse me, ladies,' she said.

'He is in the library. Shall I escort you?'

Francesca shook her head. As much as she would like someone to share the burden of her father with, a stranger at a ball was not the right person. Not for the first time she wished her mother could be persuaded to go out in public, but she hadn't attended a ball or event since Francesca's debut ten years earlier.

'Thank you, it is a kind offer, but I should see to my father on my own,' she said, feeling a ball of dread in the pit of her stomach. Over the past few months, during the time she'd been only in half-mourning and allowed again at social events, her father had been *indisposed* four times. On one particularly cringeworthy occasion she'd had to enlist the help of a very kind footman to carry him out to their waiting carriage.

The messenger let go of her arm as they exited the ballroom and motioned to one of the doors on the left. 'He's in there,' he said, before bowing, then disappearing back into the ballroom.

Francesca took a moment to compose herself before she reached for the handle. Sometimes her father was a violent drunk, but most of the time he was emotional and down-cast when he'd imbibed too much. In some respects this was worse than when he lashed out. Seeing the man who had been the backbone of her family throughout her childhood break down and cry was hard to bear.

'Father,' she said, adopting a sunny smile as she entered the room. Everything was quiet and dark, not even a soli-tary candle flickered. Francesca paused, listening for some sign that her father was in the room, conscious or not. There wasn't even the hint of heavy breathing.

'You came.' A deep voice startled her from the direc-tion of the glass doors on the other side of the room. As she peered through the darkness she could see they were open and a man was silhouetted in them.

'What are you doing here?'

'This is where we agreed to meet,' he said.

Remembering the offer of a quiet liaison on the private terrace, Francesca frowned.

'I'm looking for my father.'

'There's no one else here.'

She swallowed, feeling her mouth go dry as she realised what a precarious position she was in. If she was sensible, she should feel scared, being alone with an unknown man. If she was sensible, she would turn around and head out of the door and back to the ball.

Against every ounce of common sense she possessed, she stepped further into the room.

'You tricked me,' she said, trying to catch a glimpse of

the man's face. She should know everyone who was invited to this ball. Her social circle was surprisingly small, with the same hundred or so people being invited to each ball or social event. It was irritating her that she couldn't place him, not even when she felt as though she knew him.

'I gave you the freedom from your own conscience to come and meet me.'

'You tricked me.'

She saw him grin in the darkness, a flash of white teeth, and heard a low chuckle.

'Maybe a little,' he conceded. 'But you wanted to come. It was just the consequences of being found here with me you wanted to avoid.' The confidence emanated from every bit of him—he was certainly a man who knew what he wanted.

'Goodnight,' she said firmly. Part of her *had* wanted to come, to be wooed by a mysterious stranger and feel that giddy freedom of being irresponsible for one evening, but she wouldn't ever tell him that.

He crossed the room quickly, moving from the glass doors to her side in six steps, placing his hand over hers as she reached for the door handle.

'Five minutes,' he said. 'Give me five minutes and I promise you won't regret it.'

'I know I would regret it,' Francesca murmured, feeling the heat of his hand through her glove. He was standing close and she could sense the power of his body, but she didn't feel scared at all. If she'd been cornered by anyone else she would be panicking, wondering if they would allow her to leave with her virtue unscathed, but she felt peculiarly at ease with the man standing next to her, as if she'd known him her whole life.

'Who are you?' she asked.

'Spend five minutes with me and I'll tell you,' he said, his voice no more than a whisper in her ear.

Indecisively she glanced down at where her hand still rested on the door handle. What she should do was walk out of the room and never think of this man ever again. She should seek out her future husband and ensure he agreed the details of their marriage with her father and saved her family from financial ruin.

Slowly she turned around so she was standing chest to chest with the mysterious man.

'Five minutes?' she asked.

'Five minutes.'

'Then you'll remove the mask.'

'You have my word.'

Francesca stepped to the side and around her companion, leading the way to the glass doors and the terrace beyond.

The terrace was lit by the flickering light of a few lanterns, placed at strategic intervals along the stone balustrade. It was cold, icily so, but the air was crisp and dry and the sky clear. All in all, quite a romantic spot her mysterious companion had chosen.

'Why am I here?' she asked as he came to join her, resting his arms on the stone balustrade and looking out over the garden.

'Only you can answer that question,' he said.

Thoughts of her impending marriage to a man she could not stand, of wanting to escape, to have one night, even one moment of freedom, of adventure, flashed through her mind.

'Why did you ask me here?' she corrected herself.

'I wanted to be with you. Alone. Away from the other guests.'

'Why?' she asked, her mouth feeling peculiarly dry and the question coming out as a little breathless rush.

He looked at her with a half-smile on his lips and she felt all the air being sucked from her body.

'Can a man not want to get to know a woman away from the prying eyes of society?'

Francesca laughed. 'No.'

He shrugged. It seems a foolish rule that two people can never be alone together. How do you ever truly get to know someone?'

'You don't.'

'How do you know if you want to further an acquaintance then?' he asked.

'You don't,' she said, knowing that she was standing too close when she could feel the warmth of his body next to hers, but was unable to step away. Never was she this reckless, but there was something both charismatic and comforting about the man standing next to her. He made her feel like she wanted to fall into his arms, feel his lips on hers *and* spill her deepest secrets.

Francesca felt a wave of sadness wash over her. This would never be her life. She was moving straight from one unhappy marriage to another which promised to be even worse. There was no room for a reckless liaison, no room for this sort of scandalous behaviour. Normally that didn't bother her, but tonight she wanted more than she could ever have.

'How then am I supposed to find out what's caused the sadness in your eyes?' he asked.

Glancing up at him in surprise, she wondered if she were that transparent that he could read her every emotion. 'I am in mourning,' she said, wondering if he would accept that as an explanation.

'Did you love your late husband very much?'

She thought of his indifference to her, his belittling. His downright contempt as the years went on and she didn't produce the heir he was so eager for.

'No,' she said.

'Then why the sadness?'

Looking up again, she wondered why she felt so easy in his company. He was a stranger, a man too confident and self-assured for his own good, a man she should feel wary around, but she didn't. Instead she felt as though she wanted to spill her deepest, darkest secrets.

'Surely a woman like you has everything?' he pressed. 'Wealth, family, servants to do your every bidding.'

'Appearances can be deceptive,' Francesca said. It had been a long time since either her late husband or her family had been wealthy. All the money had been squandered in failed investments and business ventures years ago. Living back at her parents' house had been depressing after being mistress of her own household, but it was made even worse when she'd explored the empty rooms which had once been filled with luxurious items of furniture, when she'd seen all the servants except the cook and two maids had been dismissed.

'So you're sad because your family is not as wealthy as it once was?' he asked.

Francesca laughed. If only it were that simple. She wouldn't mind the lack of money, not if she had some say in her life to come. Seven years she'd endured her first marriage. It had been loveless and, although Lord Somersham had never been violent towards her over the years, his resentment had grown as she failed month after month to get pregnant. He'd belittled her, bullied her, made her hate him more with each passing day. She doubted her next marriage would be any better.

'I don't want money,' she said quietly, 'I don't care about fine dresses or jewels. I don't even need a lady's maid to dress my hair and press my clothes.'

'What do you want?' he asked the question quietly, turning his masked face towards hers.

'I want to be happy. To not be forced into another awful marriage, to have the freedom to choose who I spend my time with and how.'

'You're a widow, surely you have some degree of choice in the matter.'

'No.' She didn't, not if she wanted to save her family from complete ruin. She didn't want to spill all the sordid family secrets, no one needed to know that her father owed various lenders debts the size of a small country.

The man next to her looked pensive, as if some great debate was raging inside him.

'I should be getting back,' she said.

'No.' He caught her hand, holding it softly. 'I'm sorry, I should not have pried.'

'Will you remove your mask?' she asked, peering up at him.

'I don't think you really want me to.'

'Of course I do, I feel as though I know you...'

'Wouldn't it be better to have this one mystery, this one little bit of magic?' He looked down at her with dark eyes and she had the overwhelming urge to ask him to hold her. She thought there might be something rather comforting about having those strong arms wrapped around her.

He was still holding her hand, she realised, and his thumb was tracing lazy circles across the satin of her glove. She wondered if he could feel the places the material had thinned and almost frayed—it had been a very long time since she'd had money to spend on new clothes.

'Can you hear the music?' he asked.

With her head tilted a little to one side she listened. Coming from the open doors of the ballroom on the other side of the house were the first soft notes of a waltz.

'Lady Somersham, will you grant me this dance?'

Placing her hand in his, she felt her body tremble as he pulled her in closer and began to dance. He was a natural, guiding her expertly around the small space with just the pressure of his hand in the small of her back. As the music swelled Francesca felt her worries begin to melt away until it was just her, her mysterious companion and the waltz.

After a minute she glanced up at him and found him gazing down at her. Again she felt that bubble of recognition, this time deeper inside. She felt at ease with this man, she realised, as if they had been lifelong friends.

'I feel as though I know you, Ben,' she said, seeing the easy way he smiled and wondering if she was being foolish. Surely there was no way he could be the Ben of her childhood, the boy she had loved and lost all those years ago. He'd been transported to Australia, all because of her father's actions, and he probably hadn't even survived, let alone made his way back here eighteen years later.

He spun her, pulling her in closer at the same time, and for a moment they were chest to chest. She could feel his heart beating through his jacket. And then the music moved on, he relaxed his grip and they were a more decorous few inches apart again.

'Perhaps you do,' he said. 'Or perhaps I just remind you of someone.'

'Ben…' she said quietly, all the time looking up into his eyes for some sort of confirmation.

He smiled at her, but his expression gave nothing else away and she sighed. She was probably just being fanciful. For so many years she'd longed to see her friend again, longed to hear that he'd survived, that he'd thrived despite what her father had done to him.

As the music slowed Francesca wished this moment could last for ever. While she was dancing there was no Lord Huntley pushing for marriage, no debts, no family falling apart under the strain. It was just her, the strong arms around her waist and the music. Soon it would be back to reality, back to everything she wished to escape.

'Thank you, Lady Somersham,' her companion said, bowing and placing a kiss on her gloved hand. 'It has been a pleasure to make your acquaintance tonight.'

It was over. The fantasy was shattering and soon it would be as if this moment had been nothing but a dream.

'Your mask?' she asked, already knowing he would refuse.

He hesitated and she saw the internal debate raging as a flicker of uncertainty in his eyes. 'Best not. Best to have one little mystery in life,' he said.

She didn't protest. Maybe he was right. Maybe it was better not knowing who he was, that way she could make up her own story.

He raised his hand as if he was going to stroke her cheek, but his fingers paused less than an inch from her face. Instead he smiled sadly.

'Goodbye, Frannie,' he said and then he was gone.

Francesca felt the air being sucked from her lungs as

her whole world tilted. *Frannie*—only one person had ever called her that.

'Ben,' she called out, but already he had gone. Disappeared into the darkness like a phantom.

Chapter Three

'Why the long face?' Sam Robertson asked as he came and sat down in one of the comfortable armchairs in Lady Winston's drawing room alongside Ben and George Fitzgerald. Lady Winston was Fitzgerald's aunt and their hostess for their time in London. She'd been kind to them, accepting Ben and Sam as if they were her relatives alongside Fitzgerald.

Up until recently Ben had been staying at her town house alongside his two friends, but he'd craved a little privacy to conduct his affairs and had rented a set of rooms nearby. He did, however, drop in most days for at least one meal, or to partake in the particularly delicious mid-afternoon snack Lady Winston insisted on serving. The platter of cakes, scones and biscuits was enough to keep ten men going for an entire day, but between the three of them they often devoured it completely.

'Do you remember when we were on the transport ship together,' Ben said after loading his plate up with biscuits and cakes, 'I told you about the girl I used to be friends with? The one whose father falsely accused me of stealing the family jewellery.'

'Of course. Francesca, wasn't it?'

He nodded. 'I saw her last night. I talked to her.'

'Did she remember who you were?' Robertson asked.

'It was at the masquerade. I was wearing a mask.'

'The lady in violet,' Fitzgerald said, understanding dawning in his eyes, 'The one you asked me to escort to the library.'

'Did you want her to remember you?' Robertson asked.

Ben shrugged, trying to act nonchalant. Of course he'd wanted her to remember him. For so long she'd haunted his dreams and, if he was completely honest, she was one of the main reasons prompting his return to England. He had needed to see she was happy, that her father hadn't completely ruined her life as well.

Now he had set eyes on her again, his feelings were even more complicated. As they'd danced on the terrace the night before he had seen the recognition slowly dawning in Francesca's eyes and he'd been all ready to reveal his identity to her, but then an unfamiliar stab of uncertainty had stopped him. She was a lady, the daughter of a viscount. He might be a wealthy landowner now, but his origins still meant he was an imposter in society. What if she shunned him? He'd taken the easy way out, the coward's way, and had slipped away before she confronted him about his identity.

'Did you tell her who you were?' Fitzgerald asked.

He shook his head. 'I planned to...'

'So what happened?'

Ben shrugged. 'She probably doesn't even remember me anyway.'

'Unlikely,' Robertson said. 'Surely she'd remember the man her father had falsely arrested?'

At the end of that last summer before Ben had been arrested there was a robbery at Elmington Manor, Francesca's childhood home. A large amount of jewellery was stolen, along with some cash and other small valuables. The hue and cry was raised and the magistrate along with other upstanding men in the community began their search.

After a week a small locket had been found in Ben's possession. It had Francesca's initials on it and immediately Ben had been arrested. He'd begged his accusers to just go and ask Francesca, to confirm that she'd given him the locket as a gift, as a token of their friendship.

The magistrate refused, no doubt eager to stay in favour with Lord Pottersdown, but one day a week into his incarceration Francesca had turned up anyway. She told anyone who would listen that Ben was speaking the truth—she had given him the locket. Over and over she told the magistrate that her father had set the whole thing up, that he had framed Ben in a desperate attempt to cover his own debts. Of course, no one had listened. She was just a girl, a ten-year-old who was obviously infatuated with a common thief.

Eventually her father had arrived and dragged her away. Ben would never forget the moment the door of the county gaol closed behind her; in that moment, his heart had broken. Three months later he was sent to the hulk ships that lined the Thames and a year after that he was aboard a transportation ship to Australia.

In the eight years of his sentence and the ten years since he'd acquired his freedom he hadn't ever been able to forget his childhood friend. He'd dreamed of coming back for her, to rescue her from her cruel father. As he'd grown older he'd let go of any thoughts of rescue, knowing that by now Francesca would be living her own life, but he'd never given up the hope that one day he might see her again.

What he hadn't expected was the attraction he'd felt for her. When he'd last seen her they'd both been children. He had loved her, there was no denying that, but in a way one friend loves another. Now he felt something much more primal, much more pressing. He desired her. Francesca was beautiful now, sleek and elegant and graceful. When they'd danced, he'd felt raw desire for the woman in his arms and it had taken all his self-control not to kiss her there and then on the terrace. Even though once they had been very close he knew it was unlikely a woman of Francesca's status would allow herself to be seduced by him.

'So you're just going to leave it?' Robertson asked, his voice a touch incredulous.

Ben shook his head. He couldn't leave it like that. He had just needed to regroup, that was all, decide what he actually wanted from Francesca before he saw her again.

'She was very pretty,' Fitzgerald said quietly. Probably the most perceptive of the three friends, George Fitzgerald had a way of seeing past the façade and getting to the heart of a problem.

'She's changed a lot,' Ben said carefully.

'And she's a widow...'

'Not that kind,' Ben said quickly. She was a respectable woman, he knew that much, and he also knew how reputation mattered to the ladies and gentlemen of society.

'Fair enough. Isn't she engaged, though?' Fitzgerald asked.

'Not yet,' he said, thinking of the boorish man he'd met fleetingly the night before. He couldn't imagine the girl he'd once known married to such an oaf and likely that was the source of sadness in her eyes. She'd said as much, with her desire for a little freedom in her choice, in her life.

'Then you have a window of opportunity, surely?' Robertson said.

'I do,' he said quietly. First he needed to work out what he wanted from Francesca—only then would he seek her out again.

Taking a deep breath, Francesca looked up at the building in front of her. It was in a desirable part of London, the street lined with trees and well-dressed men and women strolling along the pavements arm in arm. Really, she shouldn't be nervous.

Telling herself not to be so silly, she crossed the road and climbed the five steps that led to the front door. There she hesitated, not knowing what the correct etiquette was when visiting a gentleman's rooms.

Francesca had been an unmarried debutante for two years, unhappily married for seven, and then a widow for almost a year now. That made ten years of adulthood in which she had never visited a gentleman's rooms. Many of her contemporaries would whisper and giggle about their affairs, taking pleasure in sneaking off behind their husbands' backs to meet their lovers, but she had never done anything like that. So she lifted the knocker and let it drop a couple of times, all the while feeling completely out of her depth.

'Good morning, miss,' a pretty young girl said as she answered the door. She was dressed in a French maid's uniform that had been popular for a certain set of the *ton* to instruct their maids to wear a couple of years earlier.

'I'm here to see Mr Crawford,' Francesca said quietly, hoping no one would overhear.

'I'll see if he's in, miss, if you'd like to wait here.'

The maid indicated a spot in the hallway where a couple of chairs had been set out for waiting visitors. Francesca perched, ready to flee at the slightest sign of anyone recognising her.

Two minutes later the maid returned, almost skipping down the stairs.

'Mr Crawford will see you,' she said. 'Follow me.'

Feeling increasingly nervous with every step, she followed the young maid up two flights of stairs to the top floor of the building. There, lounging against the door frame of an open door, was Ben. Without the mask it was unmistakably him, the boy she'd called her closest friend throughout their childhood. He gave her a half-smile, full of charm, and despite her nerves Francesca felt her heart flip inside her chest.

'Lady Somersham,' he said, his voice low, 'What a pleasant surprise.' He didn't look surprised to see her, he didn't look as if anything in the world could ruffle him, especially not the mere reappearance of an old childhood friend.

'Mr Crawford,' she greeted him formally, her upbringing taking over as her mind went completely blank. She wanted to reach out, to touch his face, trace the lines with her fingers and convince herself he was really there and not just a figment of her imagination.

'I think you can call me Ben, Frannie,' he said with that roguishly charming smile. 'It's not as though we're strangers.'

He was right. They were far from strangers, but the boy she'd known had grown up into a man she didn't much recognise. A man her body was reacting to in a most inappropriate way.

'What brings you to this part of town?' he asked, still leaning against the doorframe.

With her eyes narrowing, Francesca took in his appearance. He was wearing a shirt and trousers only, no jacket and no necktie or cravat. His shirt was half-untucked and opened at the neck, revealing a hint of the bronzed skin of his chest underneath.

A moment of realisation dawned and her hand rose involuntarily to her mouth. It was the middle of the day, but that didn't mean to say he didn't have company.

'It's a bad time...' she began to say, starting to back away. How could she be so foolish? He was a grown man, a man who wasn't tied by the expectations of society like she was. She felt unexpected jealousy and quickly tried to tamper it down before it could show on her face.

'Not for me.' Ben caught her by the hand, then stepped back, motioning for her to enter his rooms first.

They were sparsely furnished with just the essentials. A small sitting room with a couple of chairs alongside a writing table and then a bedroom leading off the sitting room with a bed and wardrobe. It didn't look as though Ben had brought much of his own to personalise the space, but if the rumours were to be believed he had only recently arrived from Australia and as such probably wouldn't have much more than his clothes and a few of his dearest possessions with him.

'Would you like me to call for something to drink?' he asked, motioning for her to take one of the chairs. He perched on the windowsill, leaning casually back against the glass.

Now she was here, Francesca didn't know what to say. At the ball three nights ago when she'd realised who the mysterious man in the mask really was she'd barely been able to believe it. *Ben*, the boy she'd loved ever since she could remember. The one she'd carried in her heart all these years, never daring to hope she might see him again. And now he was here, in the flesh. All six foot of him, and he was grinning at her like they were twelve again.

'You're looking well, Frannie,' he said softly.

His words and his tone unnerved her. His voice was low and gravelly and it cut through her body and penetrated her soul. There was something about the way he looked at her that made her want to throw herself into his arms and find out just how strong the taut muscles were. Ben had aged well and barely looked his thirty years; only the faint few lines around his eyes gave away the life he'd lived already.

Self-consciously she touched her hair. Ten years ago she'd been considered a diamond of the Season. That was after hours of her maid taming and curling her hair and strapping her into beautiful dresses, but Francesca had still felt like a fraud. Then she'd been more at home in breeches and a shirt with her hair loose and streaming out behind her.

Now she was twenty-eight. Many of her friends had children the same age as she'd been when Ben was sent away. She was no longer young, no longer so smooth and polished. Years of living with a man who gradually resented her more and more had caused her to age a little. Ben, with his handsome tanned face and muscular physique, was probably used to pretty young things throwing themselves at him.

'So are you,' she said.

It was true. The boy she remembered had been all arms and legs. Tall for his age but skinny, with a cheeky grin that had been too big for his face. He'd been tanned then, too, a consequence of spending every waking hour running through the countryside.

The man in front of her bore a passing resemblance to that boy, but the changes were innumerable. He was taller now, with long legs and a broad body, no longer skinny, but a frame filled with hard muscle. His hair was still the same dark brown and his eyes a dark, deep green, but his face had changed over the years. The smile was still there, but layered behind the cheekiness was years of experience and Francesca knew instinctively it had charmed hundreds of women.

'You left the masquerade without saying anything,' she said, not knowing how to start. She could hardly come out and tell him she'd thought about him every day for the last eighteen years.

'I didn't want to embarrass you,' he said quietly.

Francesca nodded slowly, feeling the pain at the instant reminder in their difference in circumstances. It had always haunted them, always kept them apart even as children. Again and again her father had threatened to have Ben whipped if he caught her running wild around the estate with him again. He wasn't deemed suitable company for the daughter of a viscount. Now was no different, not really. Francesca was expected to marry well again and keep herself scandal-free until then. Socialising with an ex-convict would hardly be keeping a low profile.

Lord Huntley. She'd almost forgotten about him in the heat of the moment. The man she was destined to marry as soon as her mourning period was over. He would be livid if he knew she was here. He might even call off the marriage.

Even though she despised the man she *had* to marry him. Yet still she could not bring herself to leave.

'Sit down, Frannie,' he said, motioning to one of the chairs. She obeyed, glad to sink into the soft fabric. This whole encounter had drained her already and a seat was welcome while she worked out what she had wanted when she came to see Ben.

'How are you here?' she asked. There were so many things she wanted to know, so many questions she barely knew where to start.

'I took a ship from Australia,' Ben said, grinning as she rolled her eyes at him. Already she was beginning to feel more at ease.

'You know that's not what I mean.'

'I think my life story might be a little too long for you to listen to.'

'I don't need your life story,' Francesca said, leaning forward in her chair, 'Not all of it at least. Just what you've been doing for the past eighteen years.'

'This and that,' he said. 'I'm more interested in you.'

'This and that isn't a proper answer.'

'I served my sentence,' he said and Francesca noted the subtle flash of pain in his eyes as he remembered the years he must have spent toiling under the hot Australian sun. 'Then I was lucky enough to be taken in by a kind man who mentored me and showed me how to thrive in a hostile land. I had good friends and I built a life for myself out there. A good life.'

What he wasn't saying was the pain he must have felt at everything he'd left behind. His father and siblings, people who cared for him, people who loved him.

'How about you?' he asked.

'I was married,' Francesca said, wondering how to condense the last unhappy decade and a half into a few sentences. 'And now I'm a widow.' It was depressing when she said it like that. Eighteen years Ben had been gone and all she had to show for it was a dead husband she hadn't much liked and now the prospect of another marriage she was being forced into.

'My Frannie,' Ben said, slipping from his chair and kneeling in front of her. With callused fingers he reached up and stroked her cheek, and Francesca instinctively closed her eyes and sank into the caress. She didn't know this man, not how he was now, but everything about him seemed right. Her body and her heart were telling her to fall into his arms even though she'd barely exchanged a hundred words with him. 'Such sadness,' he said, 'What can I do to make you smile again?' The words were almost a whisper and conjured up thoughts of all sorts of inappropriate actions. She could almost feel his lips on her skin, his hands on her body, his legs entwined with hers. Unconsciously she leaned forward ever so slightly, catching herself at the last moment and recoiling sharply.

'I need to go,' she said, the words catching in her throat. Thoughts of Lord Huntley flooded into her mind and she had to blink away the tears. He was her future, not the man in front of her.

Lord Huntley with his wobbling jowls and mottled skin. What a contrast to Ben who was the embodiment of vigour and health. At the masquerade his eyes had seemed to penetrate to her very soul and today she felt as though his lips were teasing her, inviting her in.

'I'm sorry,' she said and stepped towards the door.

Her hand was on the doorknob when she felt a soft touch

on her arm. He must have moved as quickly and silently as one of the big cats that she'd seen the previous year at an exhibition. The black panther had stalked around the tiny cage as if constantly on the lookout for prey.

'Wait,' he said. His fingers burned through the material of her dress and she felt the heat of his skin on hers. Taking a deep breath to compose herself, she turned and found Ben standing directly behind her. They were close, far too close for propriety, but she'd thrown all notions of good behaviour away when she'd knocked on a bachelor's door. Slowly she raised her chin so she was looking into his eyes.

It was a mistake. The moment her eyes met his she knew it was futile to resist. It might not be today or this week, but one day she would succumb to those eyes, to the man behind them.

'I missed you, Frannie,' he said, raising a hand and tucking a stray strand of hair behind her ear. His fingers lingered, caressing her neck like the most intimate of lovers, and it took all her self-control not to sigh with contentment.

'I missed you, too,' she found herself admitting. She needed to get out of his rooms, needed to escape before she did something she would regret. Something that would put her whole future, the future of her entire family, in jeopardy. 'But I can't see you again.'

'Lord Huntley?' Ben asked, an amused look in his eyes.

'He wouldn't approve.'

Ben leaned in, his breath tickling her ear. 'Sometimes it feels good to be just a little bit bad, doesn't it?'

Francesca swallowed, knowing if she tried to speak her voice would come out as a series of squeaks instead of words.

'I should go,' was all she managed to repeat eventually.

Ben smiled and leaned forward, kissing her cheek with a gentle brush of his lips. Francesca was mortified by the small sigh that managed to escape from her throat and knew she was turning pink.

'If you wish,' he said, his eyes never leaving hers.

Nervously she groped for the doorknob again, her fingers slipping in her anxiety to get away. After two more attempts she had it gripped in her hand and twisted, almost falling out into the corridor. She'd hoped the spell he seemed to hold over her might break if she put a little distance between them, but it didn't seem to make any difference. With a hurried little curtsy that made her feel completely ridiculous, she scurried off down the hall, feeling his eyes on her back the entire way.

Chapter Four

Ben pummelled the punchbag, feeling the wonderful burn in his arms as the seconds ticked by. He was at the Smith-Hickory Boxing Club, a rundown boxing gymnasium close to Charing Cross. It was owned by a rugged middle-aged man called Kit Hickory, who looked as though he'd taken one too many punches in the face as a young man with a crooked nose and a marked asymmetry. It wasn't a gentleman's boxing club—Ben had been in one of those when he first arrived in London and had left after a few minutes. That sort of boxing was more prancing and pontificating than actual punching and defending.

Here he felt at home, among the working-class men, the men eager to take their frustrations out on the punchbags and their fellow patrons. Ben didn't feel uncomfortable when he attended the events of the *ton*, but it wasn't his world. This was more where he belonged.

'Lighter on your feet,' Kit Hickory called as he walked around the gym. 'Punch, punch, duck. Guard up. *Guard up!*'

The older man was shouting at the two youths fighting in a roped-off boxing ring. They were good, made better by Hickory's coaching, both destined to be local fight champions one day soon.

Turning back to his own punchbag, Ben began to punch again, feeling the tension seep from his shoulders and neck as he hit the bag over and over. He was annoyed at himself. Francesca's visit had unbalanced him and he hated to be unbalanced. These past ten years since finishing his sentence he'd strived to always be in control, to always be the one calling the shots. Frannie had challenged that.

Although he had expected to be affected by seeing his childhood friend again, he had never thought she would cause such a reaction inside him. Every waking moment he thought of her, of the graceful way she glided into the room, the way her cheeks pinkened when she was thinking something inappropriate. He had always prided himself on being in control of his emotions, on never letting anyone too close. It was a lesson he'd learned on the convict ships, to look after yourself before anyone else, and the only people he normally made exceptions for were the men who were more like brothers than friends: George Fitzgerald and Sam Robertson. Now all he could think about was making her his. Every time he looked at her he felt his body react to her. These past few nights he'd woken in a hot sweat after very erotic dreams where she'd done unspeakable things. Dreams that meant he'd had to douse himself in cold water as soon as he woke.

It wouldn't be easy, Francesca had been raised to be a dutiful wife and daughter, free from even the faintest hint of scandal. She might desire him—he'd seen that raging in her eyes during both their meetings—but she wouldn't allow that to jeopardise her duty.

Throwing a particularly hard punch, he let out a deep growl. Duty be damned. After everything they'd been through surely they deserved at least a few weeks of happiness.

'Women troubles?' Hickory asked quietly behind him.

Ben grunted. He didn't particularly want to share his deepest thoughts with the reprobate that ran the boxing club. They would likely be halfway round London within a day.

'Loosen up your shoulders,' Hickory said. 'It'll give you more power behind your punch.'

The older man moved on and Ben took a few deep breaths, trying to let the tension ease from his shoulders. He tried a few softer, experimental punches and immediately his thoughts wandered back to Francesca. The way her entire face lit up when she smiled, the light smattering of freckles over her nose that she'd had as a child and still had now, no doubt to her dismay. The soft curves of her body and the hair that he wanted to pull from its immaculate style and run his hands through as he kissed her into submission.

Then there was the sadness in her eyes, the sense that the intervening years had not been easy for her either. He found himself drawn to her, wanting to know her body and soul.

Closing his eyes, he stepped back. 'Enough,' he murmured, unwinding the strapping from his hands. This needed to stop. Somehow he needed to exorcise these thoughts, whether by fulfilling his fantasies or finding a way to move on from the woman who had haunted him for so long.

* * *

Francesca peered out from behind the curtain that covered the window of her carriage. It was hired, their family carriage having been sold many years ago, but her father had insisted on hiring one and a set of horses for the duration of the Season. *For appearances*, he'd said. Just like almost everything else they did. Their house was furnished *for appearances*. She had fine clothes *for appearances*. And they threw lavish dinner parties *for appearances*. All of it just served to make their money problems worse and Francesca was under no illusion that people didn't know quite how in debt they were.

Slouching back, she felt the despair she always had when she thought about money. Their family had once been one of the richest in England, but years of gambling, poor investments and poor judgement on her father's part had landed them in the position they were in now. Her marriage to Lord Somersham had been arranged with the idea that his wealth would trickle through to her family, but he'd ended up being just as poor a custodian for the family money as her father. The last few years of her marriage had been a familiar cycle of borrowing and the calling in of debt. When her husband had died the title had passed to some distant relative, but there had been no bequests, no tidy little allowance for his widow, meaning that once again she'd had to return home to her parents, once again a pawn in her father's quest for more money.

Sometimes she thought about refusing, thought about withdrawing from society, perhaps taking up a position as a governess or companion. She didn't want fine things, didn't particularly enjoy the continuous cycles of balls and dinner parties and nights at the opera. Then she thought of her sister, twenty-year-old Felicity, the lively, kind girl who saw everything with those huge brown eyes. She deserved a chance. And the only way she would get that chance was if Francesca married Lord Huntley.

She wasn't sure what arrangement Lord Huntley had made with her father, but she had extracted the promise from him that he would provide a decent dowry for her sister, allowing Felicity a modicum of choice about her future husband.

Trying to push the thought of another unhappy marriage from her mind, she glanced out of the window again, straightening as she saw Ben emerge from the darkened doorway. Already everything about him seemed familiar to her, his gait, his stature, even the way he turned the collar of his coat up to combat the icy temperatures.

She wasn't quite sure why she was here. It mortified her when she thought of how she'd fled from his rooms in Gower Street, her imagination filled with images of him embracing her, kissing her, doing all the things a widowed lady shouldn't. She should have left it at that, but she found herself drawn to him, unable to leave him behind entirely, but not able to trust herself to see him face to face again.

As he passed the carriage, head bent against the cold wind, she sunk back against the seat. She'd just needed to see him again, to convince herself that it hadn't been a dream. For eighteen long years she'd agonised over his fate, imagining him a broken man, worn down by years of hard labour and then the difficult life of an ex-convict. Never had she imagined the confident and seemingly successful man that he'd turned out to be.

A few steps down the road he paused, turned quickly and in a couple of paces was back by the side of the carriage.

Before Francesca had a chance to react he'd swung open the door and hopped inside.

'Lady Somersham,' he said, settling back on to the seat opposite her. 'What brings you to this part of town?'

She'd preferred it when he'd called her Frannie.

'I...' she started to say, but couldn't think of any lie convincing enough.

'It would appear that you are following me,' he said, fixing his eyes on hers and making her squirm under the intensity.

'No,' she said quickly, although that was an outright lie. She had been following him and right now she couldn't think of any other excuse as to why she might be in this part of town, peering out of her carriage just as he left whatever establishment he'd just been in.

'Boxing club,' he supplied helpfully.

'What?'

'You were wondering where I've just been.'

Feeling completely flummoxed, Francesca took a deep breath and composed herself. She was a lady, the widow of a viscount, the daughter of a viscount. Probably the future wife of an earl. All her life she'd been coached to stay calm and serene whatever the world threw at her. Surely she could do that when faced with Ben Crawford.

'I was following you,' she said slowly, giving him a half-smile as if they were conversing about something as dull as the weather.

'Couldn't keep away?' he asked.

Francesca felt her stomach drop away from her as she realised it was the truth. She hadn't been able to keep away from him. Whatever she told herself, whatever lies she concocted to cover this embarrassing little episode, she'd just wanted to see Ben one more time.

'I wanted to apologise,' she said.

'You have nothing to apologise for, Frannie.'

'For my father. What he did to you...'

'That's his sin to bear the burden of, not yours.'

'I tried everything I could,' she said quietly.

When she'd heard Ben had been arrested for theft she'd confronted her father, who had promptly slapped her so hard she'd been knocked senseless for a few seconds, then he'd bundled her into her room. For days she hadn't been allowed out, but eventually one of the maids had taken pity on her and unlocked the door. Francesca had headed straight for the county gaol and there had told anyone who would listen that Ben was innocent.

He had been accused of stealing jewellery from her family. None of it had been found in his possession, except one small locket. *Her* locket, the locket she'd given to him as a token of their friendship earlier that summer. The magistrate hadn't listened when she had tried to explain and within half an hour her father arrived to drag her off home. The last time she'd seen Ben had been through the bars of a cell.

For eighteen years she'd agonised about her part in his conviction, wondering if she'd just shouted a little louder, begged a little harder, if things would have turned out differently.

'I know, Frannie. I've never blamed you. You were just a child.'

'So were you,' she said, her eyes coming up to meet his.

As their eyes connected she felt her body react to his gaze and was reminded neither of them were children now.

Francesca had images of Ben slowly undressing her, of their bodies coming together and his lips on her skin.

'Perhaps…' Ben said, but trailed off.

'Yes?'

'I know our time together is limited,' he said slowly. 'I know you have to marry Lord Huntley.'

She nodded, not wanting to be reminded of it, but knowing there was no getting away from her fate.

'Perhaps we could find a way to make the most of the weeks we have left,' he said.

'What do you propose?' she asked, hearing the slight wobble to her voice and trying to stop herself from imagining a whole host of wonderful, but not entirely respectable, pastimes.

He smiled, holding out for a long few seconds before answering. 'Eight days for eight years,' he said.

Frowning with confusion, she waited for him to explain.

'You give me eight days of your life, one for every year of my sentence.'

'And what do we do with these eight days?'

There was a mischievous glimmer in his eyes as he shrugged. 'Whatever we want.'

It sounded wonderful. Eight days to be free, to do whatever she wanted. After that she would have to accept her fate, but for just a little while she could pretend her life was on a different track. He held out his hand to seal the bargain and tentatively Francesca placed her fingers in his.

'When do we start?' she asked, trying to ignore the warmth of his hand on hers. Neither of them was wearing gloves despite the icy temperatures and it was the first time she'd felt his skin against hers. His fingers were a little rough, probably from the years of physical work, and his hand engulfed hers completely.

'Tomorrow.'

Tomorrow was as good a day as any. She had to remember she only had a few more weeks of freedom anyway. In six weeks her year of mourning finished and then she didn't doubt her father would waste any time in arranging her marriage. She would likely be Lady Huntley within three months with no opportunity to go running after her childhood friend.

'Tomorrow,' she agreed.

Only then did he release her hand, placing it softly back in her lap. He was a man of contradictions. Physically powerful but gentle in his touch. Gone through so much suffering, but outwardly charming and jovial. And an ex-convict who could blend in at society events. He was a confusing man to be around.

'Until tomorrow,' he said, leaning over. For a moment she thought he was going to kiss her. She felt her lips part in anticipation and her heart begin hammering in her chest, but then he reached for the catch on the door, threw it open and hopped down.

'How did you know it was me in here?' she asked as he went to shut the door. 'When you came out of the boxing club?'

She didn't think he'd caught sight of her in the darkness of the interior.

'Who else would be following me?' he asked. 'I barely know anyone else in London.'

With a smile and a wink he spun on his heel, striding off down the street. As she watched him go Francesca thought she even heard him whistling a jaunty tune. Trying not to think too much about what she'd just agreed to, she leaned out and instructed the coachman to take her home. Really she should be feeling dread and regret at her agreement to his proposal—no respectable lady would agree to it—but as she searched her emotions she could only find excited anticipation.

Chapter Five

Sitting at the small writing desk in his room, Ben tried to concentrate on the letter he was supposed to be writing to the man he'd left in charge of his farms while he was away in England. He'd left detailed instructions, so detailed the stack of paper was the size of a medium-length book, with Andrew Phillips, his very capable second in command. The man was trustworthy, sensible and good-natured, but still Ben didn't feel easy about leaving him for so long. Every week he wrote the man a letter with further instructions and since being in London had received a few updates sent months before from Australia. He'd always found it difficult to trust anyone but himself, but so far it would appear Mr Phillips was doing a good job.

It was almost eleven and, unless she had changed her mind, Francesca would likely be making an appearance soon. He'd spent half the morning trying to pretend to himself he was indifferent to her and the other half wondering what had possessed him to make the silly suggestion the day before. Eight days. Eight days spent in her company. Already he could barely keep his thoughts from the gutter when his mind wandered to her—spending more time with her wasn't likely to help matters. He knew he would find it difficult to keep his hands to himself for eight days and Francesca wasn't the sort of woman who would give up her virtue to a man she would soon have to say goodbye to.

'Remember, you're in control,' he muttered to himself. That was a lie. He found her so attractive he had struggled to stop himself from kissing her the last time they'd been together. What he was worrying about was getting to know her more and then not wanting to leave. She'd made it clear soon she would be marrying Lord Huntley so he was under no illusion that they would ride off into the sunset together. Perhaps during these eight days she would irritate him and then his attraction towards her would fade. He'd never had a problem moving on from women before. His relationships were always short and fun, ending before either party had the chance to develop a lasting affection for the other. Although none of them were Francesca...

Quickly he finished the letter he was writing and tidied the desk. His rooms were always meticulously clean and tidy—probably from the years spent living on top of scores of other men. He'd got used to hiding away anything precious to him and keeping his limited living space clean despite the less-than-sanitary conditions.

Crossing over to the window, he peered out, catching a glimpse of the muted grey skirt of one of Francesca's mourning dresses. It seemed a strange tradition to him, wearing dull colours to signify your distress at the death of a loved one. Or in Francesca's case the death of a husband it would appear she didn't like very much at all.

He waited, listening as the maid answered the door downstairs. Already he'd instructed her to allow Francesca up and after a few seconds he heard quiet footfalls on the stairs.

There was a pause, as if she were hesitating, wondering if this was really such a good idea after all, then a knock on his door.

'Good morning,' he said, summoning his sunniest smile. She looked nervous.

'Good morning,' she said, her voice much more composed than her expression.

'Come in, sit down. Would you like a drink?'

'Yes, please,' she said, exhaling, some of the tension seeping from her at the normality of the offer. Perhaps she'd imagined him ravishing her as soon as she walked through the door. The thought had crossed his mind, but he wasn't that immoral. He might want to lead her to the bedroom and strip off her ugly grey dress to see the woman underneath, but he knew that couldn't happen and he would be foolish to spend too much time torturing himself.

'I'll go fetch some tea.'

He left her standing nervously looking around for somewhere to sit. As he descended the stairs he took his time, trying to figure out what he wanted from the woman upstairs in his rooms. They had been so close as children, the best of friends, and Ben had known every last thing about Francesca. Now he knew hardly anything about her. He wanted to get an insight into her life, to see the woman she'd become. Of course, he wanted more than that. He'd wanted more from the moment he'd set eyes on her again, but he would have to tread carefully. Francesca was a lady, and a woman with a strong sense of right and wrong to boot. He might want to strip her off and join her on the bed, but he had to be wary of where their relationship might lead them. In a few weeks she would be engaged to be married again and he was under no illusion that at that time he would have to fade into the background.

Quickly he tasked the maid with making some tea, asking for it to be brought up when it was ready. His rooms were part of a small establishment, there were only three other residents. They all shared the services of Hetty, the quiet but efficient maid who cleaned twice a week, showed in visitors and kept the place running smoothly. It was ideal for him, peaceful and discreet with no rules about who could visit. Some of the places he'd looked at had a strictly men-only policy which seemed absurd to him—the freedom to have whichever visitors he chose was one of the reasons he'd moved out from Lady Winston's house.

Taking the stairs two at a time, he made his way back to his rooms, wondering what exactly he was going to do with Lady Somersham for the eight days he'd asked of her.

Running her fingers nervously across the back of one of the chairs, Francesca watched the door close behind Ben. Tea would be wonderfully fortifying, and perhaps if she just sat down her legs might stop shaking.

She was under no illusion as to why she was so nervous. Ben hadn't come out and said the words as such, but she had made discreet enquiries and knew a little about his reputation, and she suspected he had certain ideas about them becoming reacquainted. The idea that their friendship might not be just an emotional one had both thrilled and petrified her. The only man she'd ever been intimate with was her husband. There had been no affairs, no lovers, and towards the end of her marriage—thankfully—hardly any intimacy

even with Lord Somersham. Not that she was complaining,
her husband had been all about duty. He'd taken his pleasure
without a single thought for the woman underneath him.

For her part, she couldn't believe she was considering
having an affair with this man she barely knew—but she
was. The past few days, Ben had invaded her every thought
and she knew that for once she was going to be reckless.
Soon her life would be about duty and responsibility again,
but for a few short weeks she was going to enjoy getting to
know Ben again. Even if the thought gave her butterflies
in her stomach.

Nervously she moved around the room. She felt unsure
of herself and a little inadequate. Ben was probably used to
women who knew what they were doing in the bedroom,
women who knew how to please a man of the world. She
knew nothing of the sort; each and every one of her encounters with her late husband had been disappointing, and she
knew she was in no position to compete with the women
Ben would normally spend his time.

Perhaps she should just show him she understood what
they wanted from one another. Of course, she wanted to get
to know the man Ben had become, but perhaps she should
show him she was ready to become an active participant in
a more physical relationship as well?

The idea thrilled her and Francesca felt herself blushing.
She wasn't supposed to be so scandalous, so reckless, but
she was beginning to understand the excitement in the eyes
of her friends who had conducted affairs over the years.
With her mind made up she stepped through to the bedroom.

Quickly she unfastened her dress, pleased she'd chosen
a simple grey sack-like thing to wear for ease of undress-

ing. Underneath she wore a chemise and petticoats and a fine pair of stockings to try to combat the icy temperatures. The petticoats she took off, folding everything neatly and placing them on a chair, then she slipped in between the sheets and waited.

Apprehension mixed with excitement. Never before had she done anything so scandalous, anything so ill advised. She'd always been a good girl, doing everything her family had asked of her, everything her husband had commanded her to. Now she was nervous, but making this decision herself felt freeing.

The door opened and from her position she could just see Ben re-enter. At first he didn't see her, glancing around the sitting room with a frown on his face.

'Tea will just be…' He trailed off as he caught sight of her. His eyes widened and immediately Francesca knew she had made a mistake. 'What are you doing in my bed, Frannie?' he asked, his voice low. She noticed he hadn't taken a single step towards her and was holding on to the back of one of the chairs so firmly his knuckles were turning white.

The blush seemed to start at her toes and work its way up her entire body until the skin of her cheeks were burning.

'I thought…' she said, trailing off as she realised she couldn't actually voice what she'd thought.

Slowly, trying not to draw attention to the movement, she pulled the bedsheets a little further up so they touched her chin.

The seconds seemed to stretch into hours as neither of them moved. Then she felt a thrill of excitement and nerves as he moved towards her. Gently he sat down on the bed, making no move to touch her, and for the first time she wondered if she had read the situation wrong. Perhaps he didn't desire her, perhaps he still thought of her as the ten-year-old girl he'd known all those years ago. Perhaps the gossips had it wrong and he was happily married and faithful to his wife.

'Frannie,' he said, his voice strained, 'you have no idea how much I want to get into that bed with you.'

She waited, wanting to hear exactly what it was that was stopping him.

'But if I do, then it might jeopardise our chance to get to know one another again.'

'When you said...' she started speaking, but couldn't finish the sentence.

His eyes raked over her and she watched as he swallowed and gripped the sheets as if having to hold himself back. A thrill of excitement travelled through her body as she realised she did this to him.

'I want you,' he said, his voice like crushed rock. 'But I don't just want your body.'

'I'm practically engaged...' Francesca said, wondering if she had led him to believe there could be anything long-term between them.

'I know that,' he said, 'And I will respect your engagement. *When* it happens. But I don't just want to tumble into bed with you and then go our separate ways.'

'What *do* you want?' she asked, her fingers edging closer to his. It was hard to resist this man whom she felt she knew so well, but knew was largely a stranger.

'I want to know you, Frannie. Find out what you've been doing these years. See what makes you smile, what makes you cry.'

'Why?' she asked, almost afraid to hear the answer.

'I've missed you. Eighteen years I tried to forget about

you and I couldn't. When I return to Australia in a few months I would like to have some new memories to take with me.'

The mention of his return to Australia pulled Francesca back from indulging in some romantic but ridiculous fantasy of them riding off into the horizon together. They had eight days—eight days to become reacquainted and make the most of each other before he returned to his life and she moved on to the next stage of hers.

'I need to get dressed,' she said, unable to meet his eye.

'Go ahead.' He gestured to her clothes on the chair, but did not turn around or make any move to give her some privacy for at least thirty seconds. Then he growled something under his breath and moved out of the bedroom.

Closing her eyes to compose herself, she sat up in bed, letting the bedclothes drop from her chin and feeling her skin prickle under her chemise as the cool air of the room chilled her. She felt a little disappointed that her first foray into the scandalous world of affairs had ended so sedately, but she had to concede Ben was right. It would be good to get to know him, to find out all the things she'd had spent the past eighteen years wondering about. And if she read the look in his eyes correctly, it wouldn't be long before they had another opportunity to enjoy one another in a more intimate fashion in any case...

Resting his head against the cool plaster of the wall outside his rooms, Ben took a deep breath to steady himself. Never before had he walked away from a beautiful woman in his bed. Then again, never before had his heart pounded every time he looked at a woman.

Be careful, he cautioned himself. He hardly knew the

woman, but he knew himself. This wasn't how he reacted to a woman, however attractive. He'd never had trouble resisting someone before, never found it hard to move on. It had only been a couple of days since Francesca had waltzed back into his life, but already he was finding it hard to imagine her married to another man while he returned to Australia.

'You should have kissed her,' he growled to himself. When he had first seen her in his bed he had wanted nothing more than to tumble her back between the sheets and spend days getting to know her intimately. It had taken all his willpower to resist and even now he was regretting it a little.

Despite the desire that still raged through his body, he knew he'd made the right decision. Ben was under no illusion that in a couple of weeks they would have to go their separate ways and he didn't want to jeopardise any of that time by causing Francesca to feel rushed into a physical relationship. In a week or two things would be different and they would be ready to enjoy each other's company in every way possible. But today he'd seen the apprehension in her eyes, the nerves. *When* they tumbled into bed together there would be no uncertainty, no doubt in her mind that it was the right thing.

Closing his eyes, he saw the image of her sitting up in bed, clothed only in a simple cotton chemise. That would certainly haunt his dreams in the weeks to come. Of course he shouldn't have looked. He should have been a gentleman and turned away. But it had been hard enough walking out through the door—he wasn't going to torture himself over one look.

'I should go,' Francesca said, slipping out of his rooms and passing him quickly.

Instinctively he reached out and caught her by the arm, feeling her stiffen under his touch.

'Where are you going, Frannie?' he asked.

For a moment he thought she might flee without answering him.

'I just thought…'

'Come back inside and drink your tea,' he said, gripping her hand in his and caressing the skin on her palm with his thumb. 'We have a lot to talk about.'

'Surely you can't want me to stay after…' She gestured in the direction of his rooms, her cheeks turning that delightful shade of pink again. She blushed at the slightest embarrassment and it was something he was finding rather attractive.

'Come back inside,' he said.

She hesitated.

'You can even take your clothes off if it makes you more comfortable.'

He saw the flash of panic in her eyes before she realised he was joking. The old Frannie, the one he'd known all those years ago, would have come back with a witty quip of her own, but it seemed that years of socialising with the richest and most powerful people in the country had stolen her sense of humour.

'Tea?' Hetty asked, coming up the stairs with a tray and breaking the tension between them at just the right moment. Francesca exhaled, glanced at him and nodded once before turning and making her way back into his rooms. Trying not to notice the enticing sway of her hips, he followed her inside. It was going to be a long few weeks and he only had himself to blame.

Chapter Six

~~~~~~~~~~~~

Francesca sipped her tea in silence, feeling her own awkwardness overshadow the entire situation. Ben had been gentle as he'd turned her down and ejected her from her bed, but it had still been a rejection and it was still embarrassing to think she'd offered herself to this man and he'd said no.

'Shall I pour?' she asked, grasping for something normal to focus on.

'Go ahead.'

Out of the corner of her eye she saw him sit back, stretching his legs out in front of him and placing his arms behind his head. He looked like a cat stretching out by a warm fire and she felt a pang of nostalgia. This was how he'd always sat, even as a child. She could remember him flopping down into a fireside chair and relaxing completely.

'How do you take your tea?' she asked.

'Just a little milk,' he said, reaching out for one of the biscuits the maid had placed on the tray beside the teapot.

Once the tea was made she handed over the cup, trying to

ignore the rush of heat she felt as his fingers brushed against hers. She doubted Ben even noticed, he seemed calm and unperturbed, watching her from under his long eyelashes.

'What exactly did you have in mind?' she asked when it became apparent that Ben wasn't about to start a conversation. 'When you proposed we spend time together?'

He shrugged, reaching for another biscuit. They did look good. Francesca resisted—she might have been able to get away with a biscuit with her tea when she was a young debutante, but now she was a little older she had to watch what she ate to maintain her figure. She eyed Ben and tried not to snort. He didn't seem to be plagued by the realities of ageing. In fact, she'd wager he looked better today than he had a decade ago. Some men had all the luck.

'What do you normally do with gentlemen of your acquaintance?' he asked. 'Apart from testing out their beds, of course.'

She looked up sharply, but Ben was studiously admiring his cup of tea, just the hint of a smile on his lips. He'd always teased her when they were children. It was one of the things she'd liked best about him. Most of the other local children were too cautious to make friends with the daughter of the nobility and, if they did happen to run into her, they were polite but not really friendly. Ben had been different, he'd always treated her like just another village child, teasing her or challenging her as he would anyone else.

'I don't socialise with gentlemen,' she said. 'I'm a widow, certain standards are expected.'

'From whom?'

'From my family, society, everyone really.'

'From your husband-to-be?'

'Lord Huntley?' she asked. 'Nothing has been confirmed

yet.' There was the slimmest chance that she might escape that horrible fate, although she wasn't overly hopeful. 'But, yes, he does expect me to behave in a particular way.'

'And if you didn't, the wedding would be off?'

She nodded.

'Are you tempted to be a little scandalous?' he asked.

Once or twice the thought had crossed her mind. It would be easy to engineer a situation to look like she'd been caught in a compromising position. Lord Huntley wouldn't tolerate too much in the way of public disgrace and she would be free from the proposed marriage. Oh, it would be wonderful not to have to worry about what her married life would be like with the ageing, pompous, overbearing man, but she knew that the alternative was worse. Without Lord Huntley's money her family would be completely ruined. They would lose their house and her sister, her beautiful, sweet little sister, would lose the dowry Lord Huntley had promised to provide. So she had to accept her fate and try to make the best of it.

'If only...' she said. 'But no. Once I'm out of mourning I expect everything will be arranged.'

They fell silent for a moment, but despite everything that had happened between them it wasn't an awkward silence.

'What *did* you mean when you proposed I give you eight days for the eight years of your sentence?' she asked, looking at him directly for the first time since he'd convinced her to return to his rooms.

For a long moment he looked at her, his eyes so intense she felt a shiver despite the roaring fire only a few feet away.

'Honestly?' he said. 'I've no idea.'

She wondered if he felt it, too, the irresistible pull between them—and, looking into his eyes, she was almost certain he did.

'You don't have to go through with it if you don't want to,' he said. 'You have enough in your life making you unhappy—the last thing I want to do is add to that.'

'No. I want to do it.' And she realised she did. She wanted to get to know the man she hadn't been able to forget all the eighteen years he'd been away. 'But perhaps we can postpone our first rendezvous until tonight,' she suggested.

'Am I going to come back from dinner to find you in my bed again?' he asked.

'No.' She held his gaze this time.

'Shame,' he murmured, but she knew he only said it to provoke her.

Quickly she stood, bade him farewell and moved towards the door. Before she could open it Ben had darted across the room, placing his hand on the doorknob and opening the door for her. Momentarily she wondered how he'd gone from convict to gentleman, where he'd learned to blend in with the cream of society so well, but now wasn't the time to ask.

'Until tonight,' he said and Francesca felt his eyes follow her down the stairs until she was out of sight.

'Do you know what you're doing?' George Fitzgerald asked as he lounged back in one of Ben's chairs, warming his feet by the fire. It was still icy out and the month of February was looking to be no warmer than the January. Ben had vague memories of the cold of an English winter, but after so many years spent in the milder conditions in Australia it had come as a bit of a shock. It was true that the climate in New South Wales wasn't constant sunshine, but the winter temperatures didn't dip to anywhere near this low.

'Probably not,' Ben admitted, trying for the third time to tie his cravat. It was a delicate item of clothing and something he had not had cause to wear until their arrival in London a month ago. However, Francesca had sent a note instructing him to dress in evening wear so here he was.

'You're playing a dangerous game.' Fitzgerald said. 'She's basically betrothed. In a few weeks, you'll have to give her up.'

'This was never going to be a long-term situation.'

Fitzgerald snorted. 'I saw the way you looked at her, Crawford, you're besotted. And I've never seen you besotted before.'

Shrugging, he concentrated on the cravat, avoiding Fitzgerald's eye in the mirror. Besotted was putting it too strongly. He admired Francesca, desired her, thought about her from the moment he woke up until the moment he went to bed, but he wasn't besotted. It would be wonderful to spend a month or two with Francesca, but he would leave her behind at the end of it. She would marry Lord Huntley and he would return to Australia.

'Be careful,' Fitzgerald said.

'I will.'

'When are you going to see your father?' Fitzgerald asked, changing the subject as if sensing Ben didn't want to talk about his complicated acquaintance with Francesca.

'He's in Yorkshire for another two weeks, I'll go back and see him when he gets home.'

His father had been estate manager to Francesca's father, Viscount Pottersdown, at the time Ben had been accused of theft. He'd lost his job and his status as well as his son, but the man was resilient and talented. It wasn't long before he'd found another position with the Earl of Harwich, initially as an assistant to the Earl's steward, but then slowly taking on more and more responsibility. He now oversaw all the Earl's estates, hence why he was up in Yorkshire at the moment.

Ben was both excited and dreading seeing his family again in equal measure. It had been so long, with only the irregular correspondence that reached Australia to link them, and he wondered if the years and their different experiences would have put too much emotional distance between them.

'Will your brothers be home?'

Ben nodded. He had two younger brothers, both of whom had been little more than infants the last time he'd seen them. They now were men in their early twenties, full grown with lives of their own. They worked for his father, overseeing the Earl's vast estate in Essex, and according to the information in his father's letters both still lived in the same village they'd grown up in.

The only two members that would be missing were his mother, who had passed away when Ben was nine from a weak chest, and his elder sister. She'd been the oldest, the one he'd looked up to and wanted to emulate when they'd been children, but his father had informed him she'd passed away in childbirth a few years earlier.

'It'll be worth it,' Fitzgerald said quietly. 'Of course it will be hard, but it will be worth it.'

'We're all different people now,' Ben said. 'Who knows what it will be like?'

'Different people, but still family.' Fitzgerald rose, looking at the clock on the wall. 'I'd better let you set off,' he said. 'Try not to break too many hearts tonight.'

'It's never my aim…' Ben said with a grin, happy they'd moved on from more painful subjects.

'Come for breakfast tomorrow,' Fitzgerald said. 'Aunt Tabitha is asking after you and Robertson is falling for the daughter of the man he hates most in the world. Not that he'll admit it yet. He needs something to distract him.'

'I'll call at eight.'

'Enjoy your evening.'

As Fitzgerald left, Ben spent a moment looking in the mirror. He looked almost unrecognisable, with the cravat and jacket on top of a pressed white shirt. It was very different to the clothes he wore while out on his farms. Although he employed hundreds of workers now he still got his hands dirty each and every day. To his mind that was the only way to run a successful business.

Trying not to think about the evening ahead, or the sense of anticipation he felt deep inside, he left his rooms. He would not give in to the more primal urges he felt every time he looked at her.

Chapter Seven

Peering out through the door of the carriage for the twentieth time, Francesca forced herself to remain calm. It was only Ben, and if he could get past her mortifying behaviour earlier that day then so could she.

As she saw his tall figure come sauntering down the steps she felt her pulse quicken and all the nerves she had been trying to suppress bubble to the surface.

'Good evening, Lady Somersham,' he said, giving a formal bow before hopping up into the carriage beside her. He looked smart and suave, every inch the gentleman even though Francesca knew he wasn't.

'We're not going far—would you prefer to walk?' she asked. The evening was cold but bright, and suddenly she realised she would prefer not to be cooped up in an enclosed space with Ben. She might do something foolish.

'That sounds wonderful,' he said, getting down from the carriage and holding out a gloved hand for her to take. She quickly instructed the driver where to wait for them before hesitantly placing her hand in the crook of Ben's arm.

'Where are we going?' Ben asked as they began to walk along the pavement. Their pace was brisk to try to stave off some of the inevitable chill and, not for the first time, Francesca felt envious of men's more practical clothing. Ben's boots and thick coat over his evening wear would keep him considerably warmer than her pretty-but-thin coat and satin shoes.

'To a dance. At the Assembly Rooms.'

She'd been unsure where to take Ben and had agonised over the decision for hours. Then she'd decided just to take him somewhere she enjoyed spending the evening.

'Ah, the famous Almack's,' Ben said.

'No, not quite,' Francesca said quickly. She felt his eyes on her as he turned his head towards her in question. 'I wasn't granted a voucher this year,' she mumbled, hoping he wouldn't ask any more.

Glancing up, she saw him frown, 'You're going to have to explain,' he said. 'I've got no idea what you're talking about.'

Sighing, she swallowed the memory of her dented pride. 'To gain entry to Almack's each week you need a ticket. To get a ticket you need a voucher which proves you are on the approved list of people allowed in to Almack's that Season.'

'The approved list?' Ben asked, his lips turning up into that smile that did strange things to her knees. 'And who decides who gets approved?'

Francesca grimaced. 'There is a group of Patronesses and they vet applicants, deciding who to grant vouchers to each year. I think the idea is that one might socialise at Almack's knowing that everyone is your social equal.'

'How dreadful,' Ben murmured. 'So why didn't you get a ticket?'

It was a deeply personal question, but from Ben she'd begun to expect no less. He wasn't constrained by the rules of good etiquette and just came out and asked what he wanted to know.

'Any number of reasons,' she said, trying to keep the disappointment she'd felt from her voice. 'Father's debts or drinking habits, our declining position as a family in society. It could be anything, really. Although I've always suspected it's because Lady Golding's husband pursued me quite relentlessly when we were debutantes and she's never quite forgiven me for making her feel second-best.'

'Something as petty as that?' Ben asked. 'It sounds like you're better off out of it.'

'Mmm…' she murmured non-committally. With her head she knew he was right. She shouldn't want to socialise with such a shallow and cruel group of people, but the snub had hurt. Knowing that she'd been judged and found wanting by her peers, whatever the reason, had injured her probably more than it should.

Every Wednesday the cream of society was off dancing and socialising at Almack's and she was excluded.

'I suppose it's hard to be pushed out,' Ben said perceptively, 'when it is something you've always been part of.'

She nodded. It was exactly that.

'Plus I love to dance and that was one of the only places I could go without a chaperon and dance without having to worry about any scandal.'

'So where are we going tonight?' Ben asked.

'When I found out I wasn't going to be granted a voucher for Almack's I looked around for other Assembly Rooms that held regular dances and I found DeFevrett's. It's not far from St James's and they hold a dance every Wednesday just like Almack's.'

It was an entirely different atmosphere as well as an entirely different clientele. Whereas Almack's was filled with the titled and wealthy all dressed in their finest, De-Fevrett's catered to the upper-middle classes. At first Francesca had felt uncomfortable and out of place, but slowly she'd realised that with all her peers spending their night socialising at Almack's there was no one to spot her attending the less well-to-do dance and had begun to enjoy herself. The first few weeks she'd persuaded Lucy Winthrow, an old friend who had once been a companion to Francesca's grandmother, to come with her, to act as an unofficial chaperon and make the whole thing a little less scandalous if she did get found out. As the weeks went on Francesca's confidence had grown and now she felt happy to attend just with Ben as her guest.

'Are you sure you're just not too embarrassed to take me as your guest to Almack's?' Ben asked, grinning at her.

'I think you'd actually go down well there,' Francesca replied. 'The patronesses seem to favour a good-looking man, even if his pedigree isn't quite as noble as some. It's me they have an issue with.'

They crossed the street and hurried towards the Assembly Rooms, Francesca's pace quickening further as she realised she couldn't feel her toes.

At the door she produced her ticket and felt the familiar soaring of her mood as they stepped inside and heard the first jaunty notes of the quartet who would provide the music for the evening's dancing.

'First drinks are served and there is the chance to socialise a little, and then the dancing will start in half an hour.'

They walked arm in arm through the entrance hall and into the ballroom proper. Around the perimeter were a few groups of people, but from past experience Francesca knew in this early part of the evening most of the guests would be gathered around the card tables in the third room.

She nodded a greeting to a few of the regular attendees, men she'd danced with and women she'd talked with. All in all most were friendly and it was certainly a more welcoming atmosphere than at Almack's.

'Who do you normally dance with?' Ben asked, eyeing the gentlemen who were dotted around the room.

Anyone who asks, Francesca thought, but didn't say. When you loved to dance as much as she did you weren't overly picky about partners.

'Just like a society ball, really you should wait to be introduced before a man asks you to dance,' Francesca said, but in fact the rules were a little looser here. She'd danced with plenty of men who she'd never met before. If her mother knew she'd be scandalised, as would the rest of society, but for Francesca the risk was worth it.

'Correct me if I'm wrong, but you take a big risk to come here. If anyone found out, wouldn't you be the subject of scandal and speculation?'

'Yes.'

'But you do it anyway.'

'I love to dance.'

If she was honest there was more to it than that. An unconscious desire to have a little freedom in her choices, to be the one to decide where she went and when. To be able to choose whether to accept or refuse a dance partner herself without always having to think whether her actions might damage the family in some way. For so long she'd shouldered responsibility for her father's mistakes, but here she didn't have to worry about any of that.

And the risk that she might get caught and exposed as a shameless widow who socialised below her class, that just made it all the more appealing.

Ben chuckled. 'You always did like taking risks, Frannie,' he said.

When they'd run around as children she'd never had a problem with taking risks, with her and Ben as bad as each other, spurring the other on to climb higher, jump further, be that little bit more mischievous. Things had been different as she'd grown up. Her mother had withdrawn more and more, leaving the responsibility of running the household and raising her younger sister to Francesca. And then her father had revealed he'd lost all the family money and it had been down to Francesca to marry well to try to save them. It hadn't worked out, with Lord Somersham almost as skilled at losing money as her father, but she'd done her bit all the same.

'Shall we get a drink?' Francesca asked.

He let her lead him to the room where refreshments were served and they both took a glass of the brightly coloured punch that was offered. Ben took one sip and handed it back to the young woman who'd served it and after tasting the artificial sweetness Francesca did the same. With replacement glasses of lemonade in their hands they wandered around the room, waiting for the dancing.

'Would you like a game of cards while we wait?' Ben asked.

'No,' she said a little too vehemently, causing Ben to look

at her with a raised eyebrow. 'No, thank you,' she said more calmly, 'But please feel free to play if you wish.'

Her heart sank a little when she thought he might. Both her father and late husband were unlucky and unskilled when it came to cards, but more importantly they both seemed to think they were much better than they were. It was just another example of their poor judgement, and Francesca had spent many a painful evening watching an increasingly desperate Lord Somersham bet money they did not have in an attempt to claw back some of what he'd lost already.

'When I have you for company?' he asked. 'A man would be a fool to leave you for a game of cards.'

'Does that charm come naturally or do you work to say what a lady wants to hear?' she asked.

'Completely natural,' he said with the smile that made her heart flip inside her chest. 'Never trust a man who has to work to give a lady a compliment.'

'I'd wager you've left a string of broken hearts behind you,' Francesca murmured.

'A gentleman never breaks a lady's heart,' he said, but from the slight shift of his eyes she knew it was true. He probably told himself he only got involved with women who understood the short-lived nature of any affair they would share together, but she would wager her only remaining set of pearls that no matter how hard they tried the women always fell in love with him.

'Only cherishes it?' Francesca asked. From his expression she could see he had never let anyone get close, let alone take responsibility for their happiness. She felt a pang of sadness. As a boy, Ben had been warm and loving, with genuine affection for his friends and family. He deserved more than passing flings, he deserved true love after all he had suffered.

'When a lady entrusts me with her heart I will let you know,' he said quietly and Francesca felt her pulse quicken and her skin flush.

'I hear the music,' Francesca said, glad for the distraction. 'Shall we dance?'

Obligingly he gave her his arm, leading her back to the main room where couples were beginning to assemble.

'How do you know how to dance?' Francesca asked.

'When I was a young boy I had an irritating young girl who would follow me around,' he said, keeping a completely straight face. 'She loved to dance and to oblige her I learned the steps to one or two of the most common dances. I merely had to refresh my memory before returning to London.'

'You used to follow me,' she murmured, 'not the other way around.'

'I remember it rather differently.'

For a moment everything was easy between them and Francesca found herself smiling a true smile for the first time in a very long while. Then the dance began and she was swept away in a flurry of steps and laughter.

Chapter Eight

As he watched her laughing and smiling Ben felt an unfamiliar tightening in his chest. It had pained him to see Francesca looking so sad at the masquerade ball and he wanted to banish for ever that despair from her eyes.

He'd only been momentarily surprised at her choice of where to take him this evening. She'd always loved to dance, but more than that Francesca had always been a bit of a rebel. Over the years she might have suppressed that part of her, but he wasn't surprised to find she still did a few of the things she shouldn't, even if it was carefully hidden from the people who might judge her.

'The mauves and greys have gone,' he murmured in her ear as they joined hands at the end of a particularly energetic dance.

'Just for tonight.' She grimaced. 'Just while no one of significance can see me and start to gossip.'

'Blue suits you,' he said, admiring the contrast of her

almost-black hair with the deep blue of the evening gown she was wearing.

'Is that a compliment, Mr Crawford?' Francesca asked.

He leaned in closer, 'Although I much prefer you in white.' He waited until she remembered the incident earlier where she'd stripped down to her white cotton chemise to get into his bed and watched her cheeks colour.

'A gentleman would never mention *that* ever again,' she said primly.

'I'm no gentleman, Frannie, and you'd do well to remember that.'

Her eyes widened a little before narrowing almost completely.

'You're toying with me,' she said. 'No one toys with me.'

'They should. It's great fun.'

'Fun isn't expected for a widow.'

'Even a widow who disliked her husband?'

'Be quiet,' Francesca hissed and Ben could see it took all her self-restraint not to punch him on the arm as she had when he'd teased her when they were children.

He was actually enjoying himself. Here in a stuffy Assembly Rooms, mixing with the snobby upper-middle classes with the woman whose father had ruined his childhood on his arm, he was enjoying himself.

'Care for some air?' he asked.

'Only if you promise to behave yourself.'

'You wouldn't like me if I did.'

She mumbled something under her breath, but allowed him to escort her through the now-crowded room to the terrace at the back of the Assembly Rooms. It was cold outside and Ben could see his breath on the air, but it was a welcome change from the heat of the room. He watched as Francesca leaned elegantly against the stone balustrade that separated the terrace from a small courtyard a few steps below. Without thinking he pushed himself up on to the balustrade, sitting on the cool stone, his feet still touching the ground.

'Get down,' Francesca hissed.

'Why?'

'You're not supposed to sit up there.'

'Who says?'

She spluttered, then regained control of herself. 'I do.'

He grinned. 'Don't pretend you don't wish you could be up here with me, sitting comfortably and resting your weary feet.'

Opening her mouth to deny it, just to be perverse, Francesca thought better of uttering the lie and pressed her lips together again.

'If you get me thrown out, I won't be very happy,' she said.

'Surely once you're married again, once you're Lady Huntley, they won't be able to deny you a voucher for Almack's,' Ben said.

She shrugged and he could tell it was a subject she didn't want to discuss, but he pushed on nevertheless.

'Lord Huntley is an earl, isn't he? So you will be a countess?'

'Can we talk of other things?' she asked, turning so her back was against the balustrade and she was looking back inside the Assembly Rooms. 'Or, better still, dance some more.'

'In a minute. I want to know why you're even considering marrying a man like Huntley.'

'You say it like I have a choice.'

Ben knew there were many reasons people got married—for money, connections, even love—but he was intrigued to know why Francesca was allowing herself to be trapped into another unhappy marriage.

'Don't you? You're a widow, a woman, not a scared young girl who has to do her father's bidding.'

'I might be a widow, but I have no independence. Lord Somersham left me no provision in his will. He was completely broke. The title and lands have gone to his second cousin, but there was no money to go with it.'

'So you still rely on your father to support you?'

She nodded.

'And that's why you have to marry whomever he chooses?'

'No.' This was said vehemently and Ben wondered whether to push her further.

'Why then?' he said. 'Make me understand.'

'My father owes a lot of money,' Francesca said quietly.

From the rumours Ben had heard that was an understatement. Lord Pottersdown had more debt than all the inhabitants of a debtors' prison and then some.

'Lord Huntley has offered to clear the worst of the debts,' she said, 'and provide a dowry for my sister.'

Ben screwed up his face as he searched for a name. The little girl had been no more than an infant when he'd been sentenced to be transported and he'd only ever seen her from a distance with the nursemaids or nanny.

'Felicity,' he said eventually.

'Yes. She's twenty and the sweetest, most wonderful young woman.'

'With no dowry.'

It seemed ridiculous to him, this business of a dowry, but

he knew in society it was one of the most important factors when agreeing on a match between two people.

'No one has offered for her,' Francesca said sadly. 'Or at least no one in the least bit acceptable. They don't want to tie themselves to our family.'

'And you feel like this is all your responsibility? To keep a roof over your parents' heads, to provide a dowry for your sister?'

'Of course it is. They're my family.'

'You deserve to be unhappy so they can live better lives?'

'Someone has to make that sacrifice,' Francesca said and it was clear from her tone that it wasn't going to be either of her parents. She was the responsible one, the one caring about the happiness and survival of everyone else but herself.

Ben pushed himself down from the wall and waited for Francesca to turn to him. She looked radiant even with the frown on her face. In the moonlight her skin was pale and perfect, contrasting beautifully with her full, rosy lips. He wanted to see her smile again, even though he felt an almost uncontrollable desire when she did. As she turned towards him her arm brushed against his and he knew from her expression that she felt the same frisson of excitement as he did every time their bodies touched. He wondered for a moment what it would be like to have her in his bed and with absolute certainty he knew it would be incredible. Part of him regretted refusing Francesca earlier that afternoon, but he knew it was only a matter of time before they would fall into each other's arms.

'Couldn't your sister marry Lord Huntley?' he asked, trying to distract himself from the spot just above her collarbone where he could see her pulse ever so faintly. It was tempting to place his lips there, to taste the sweetness of her skin, but he had to remember they were in a public place.

'No,' she said vehemently. 'That is not an option.'

He waited for her to elaborate.

Sighing, Francesca continued, 'He has a reputation—there are rumours.'

'What sort of rumours?'

'He was married before and his wife seemed to have rather a lot of accidents.'

'He beat her?'

Francesca shrugged, 'As I say, there are rumours, but who really knows what goes on behind closed doors?'

'Frannie, are you telling me you wouldn't let your sister marry this man, but you're willing to risk a lifetime of beating and abuse?'

She shrugged, but wouldn't meet his eye.

Ben let out a disgusted sigh. It wasn't his place to care, he knew that, but some part of him wanted to wrap her up in his arms and protect the girl he'd once loved.

'Let's forget this,' Francesca said, forcing a smile on her face. 'Let's dance.'

Ben could tell by the set expression on her face there was no reasoning with Francesca now so he offered her his arm. He shouldn't interfere; she was perfectly capable of making her own mistakes, but the thought of her spending the rest of her life with a man like Lord Huntley made him feel nauseous.

They stepped back into the Assembly Rooms, the temperature inside at least twenty degrees warmer than the freezing air outside. Francesca just wanted to dance, she didn't want to think about the way her life was going to be in just a few short months, she didn't want to think about the rumours that circulated detailing Lord Huntley's first wife's *little accidents* or the possessive way her future husband already looked at her. When she danced, especially when she danced in Ben's arms, she could forget all these worries and get lost in the music.

Turning to suggest they ready themselves for the next dance, Francesca stiffened, her whole body seizing up with panic. Without any explanation to Ben she let go of his arm and rushed behind a pillar, flattening her back against the cool plaster.

'I thought you wanted to dance?' Ben said casually, regarding her with a frown.

'Lord Huntley,' she hissed. 'He's here.'

There was no reason for the man who was determined to become her future husband to attend DeFevrett's—on the contrary, it should be a place a man of his class and status vigorously avoided. The only possible reason he could have for coming here was her. Someone must have seen her, someone must have told him of her less-than-acceptable behaviour, and here he was, seeking her out. Whether to reprimand her or end his association with her she wasn't sure, but she didn't want to wait around to find out.

'Looking for you?' Ben asked as he casually took a step back and cast his eyes around the room. 'So he is. He's standing by the entrance looking like someone has stolen his favourite toy.'

'Someone has,' Francesca muttered. 'I need to get out of here.'

'There's no way to sneak past. We'll have to go out through the back.'

For a moment the burden of getting out of this impossible situation didn't seem quite so heavy as she realised Ben was right there beside her.

'Move slowly, but keep your head down,' he instructed her, 'You don't want to draw attention to yourself.'

Doing as he commanded, they strolled back the way they had come, Francesca trying to keep the panic she was feeling from overcoming her and making her run, which she knew would be counter-productive. Once back out on the small terrace they paused and Ben took a moment to glance over her shoulder into the ballroom they'd just left.

'He's coming this way,' he murmured, no hint of panic or stress in his voice. Either he was very good at controlling his emotions or he felt the stakes weren't that high.

'There's no other way out,' Francesca said, looking round the enclosed area. Beyond the terrace there was a drop of a few feet to a small, square courtyard. On the opposite side of the courtyard was a wall, separating the Assembly Rooms from the street on the other side.

'That depends on how desperate you are not to be found,' Ben said, grinning at her.

She narrowed her eyes, wondering if he thought they could scoot around the back of Lord Huntley and make it to the front door while he was distracted.

'I can't be found here,' she said.

'Come on.' He grasped her hand and before she could protest had pulled her up on to the stone balustrade. Without a backward glance he dropped the few feet to the courtyard below, turning and motioning for her to follow him. Hesitating, Francesca took a deep breath, if they were trapped in the courtyard there would be a scandal of momentous proportions, it would be much worse than Lord Huntley merely finding her socialising with people not of her class at DeFevrett's. However, there was a chance, even just a small chance, that Ben could get her out of here.

It all came down to whether she trusted the man in front of her. He was not obliged to help her, but instinctively she knew he would do everything in his power to help her escape. His feelings for her might be complicated, but he was a good man, that much she could tell already from their short reacquaintance. Ben wouldn't let Lord Huntley catch her without a fight.

Hoping he would catch her, Francesca pushed off the balustrade, falling the few feet into his waiting arms. He swung her down with ease, grabbed her hand and pulled her across the courtyard.

'Ready to climb?' he asked. She nodded. It had been years since they'd last climbed together, boosting each other up haystacks or into the lofts of old barns, but as she placed her foot into Ben's hand she felt ten years old again and as if she were invincible. Deftly he lifted her up, waiting until she had hooked a leg over the top of the wall, managing to disentangle her skirts at the same time.

A shout from the other side of the courtyard made her glance back, but quickly she dropped her head so no one would be able to identify her. A small crowd was forming on the terrace, watching their escape attempt. She had to hope Lord Huntley wouldn't appear until they were out of sight.

Ben used the branches of a nearby tree to help him clamber up the wall as easily as a monkey, dropping down the other side as soon as he'd reached the top. He held out his arms for Francesca and this time she didn't hesitate to drop into them.

As her feet hit the floor he grabbed her hand and together they darted through the darkened alleyways. Francesca felt a surge of relief and an uncontrollable giggle burst from her lips.

'Do you think he saw us?' she asked, trying to get her laughter under control.

'No,' Ben said, pausing. The main street was just a few feet away, but here in the darkness of the alley it felt like they were the only two people in the world.

'My coat,' Francesca said, as the cold air penetrated through her dress, reminding her of what she'd left behind.

'I will go back for it tomorrow,' Ben promised, turning to her. Francesca's back was against the wall, the freezing bricks making her shiver, but as his eyes met hers she couldn't help but giggle again. She hadn't behaved so badly in her entire adult life.

'You're a bad influence,' she murmured.

'Perhaps,' he said and something in his eyes darkened as he looked at her. Francesca felt the whole world slow and fade into the background so the only thing left was the man in front of her. 'Frannie,' he murmured, reaching up and touching her cheek with his cupped hand.

Francesca closed her eyes as he moved towards her, knowing that his lips would find hers instinctively. They brushed against hers and inside Francesca felt a rush of elation like never before.

'Who goes there?' an annoyed shout came from the direction of the Assembly Rooms and quickly they sprang apart. Ben gripped her hand again and pulled her out on to the street. The moment between them had passed, but Francesca knew she would never be able to forget it. It had been a stolen moment in a mad evening, but a moment of perfection all the same.

'Definitely a bad influence,' she murmured.

'I wasn't the one who suggested we go to the Assembly Rooms,' he said, 'Or who insisted on getting out of there without a peer of the realm catching me.' Eyeing her with a barely repressed grin, he offered her his arm again. 'Come, let's get you home.'

They walked briskly to combat the cold and with their heads bent to try to prevent anyone from recognising them. Fifteen minutes and they were in streets Francesca recognised and within twenty they were in the small public gardens opposite her father's house.

'Will you be safe from here?' Ben asked, looking out from their hidden spot behind a tree to the darkened house beyond.

'I will…' She paused, wondering how to say everything that was clamouring for attention in her mind. And wondering if he might kiss her again before he left. 'Ben…'

'Frannie.'

'I'm sorry,' she said, feeling her heart thumping in her chest.

'Don't apologise, it was fun.'

'Not for that, not for tonight. For what my father did eighteen years ago. For ruining your life.'

He looked at her and for a moment she wondered if he might turn his back on her and walk away.

'Do you know,' he said, tucking a stray wisp of hair behind her ear, 'I had quite forgotten all about that.'

'I don't want you to hate me,' she whispered.

'I don't hate you, Frannie. I've never hated you. You didn't do anything wrong.'

'But my father…'

'Hush,' he said, his fingers coming up and brushing against her cheek. Francesca felt her heart leap in her chest and her skin tingle under his touch. 'You are not your father, or responsible for his actions.'

'I should have done more.'

'I don't hate you, I could never hate you,' he said again and as she looked into his eyes she believed him. She felt safe in his arms, content, as if she was meant to be there, and as his head lowered towards hers there was no way she could have stopped her lips coming up to meet his.

He kissed her softly, his lips brushing against hers, feeling velvety and smooth and causing a fiery heat to rise up inside her. She'd been kissed before, but never like this. Never had her entire body responded to a kiss with such passion. Ben murmured her name, kissing her again and again, until she was sure she had lost all reason.

When he pulled away Francesca felt like crying out, but just about managed to maintain some sort of composure.

'Why did you do that?' she asked, hearing the breathless quality to her voice and coughing to try to cover it up. It wouldn't do to let Ben see how much that one kiss had affected her.

'I wanted to,' he said.

Opening her mouth to reply, Francesca found she was lost for words so instead gave a short, sharp nod. She didn't quite believe he'd kissed her not once but twice now merely because he'd wanted to, but she couldn't find the words to demand a further explanation.

'I shouldn't have done that,' she said after a couple of seconds, 'I'm almost engaged.'

'Almost...'

'And I'm in mourning.'

'It was just a kiss, Frannie, nothing more.'

Feeling herself deflate a little, she tried to rally. To him it might have been just a kiss, something he went around doing all the time, but for her it had been wonderful, exquisite, and felt as though it had awoken every nerve in her body.

'You shouldn't kiss me,' she said.

'I've never been good at following the rules.' He shrugged, 'And I happen to find you very attractive.'

'But earlier...' She trailed off at the memory of him rejecting her as she lay half-undressed in his bed.

'I didn't want to rush things. If you decide to come to my bed, I'd like to think we could come out on the other side as friends. I don't want you to have any doubts, any second thoughts.'

She spluttered, her eyes widening. 'If I decide to come to your bed?' she repeated.

Ben shrugged. 'We're both adults, there's a spark between us, it is up to you if you want to pursue it.'

'I am a daughter of the nobility and the widow of a viscount,' Francesca said, focusing in on the spark of humour in his eyes. She wasn't sure if he was teasing her or if the offer was a genuine one, but she wasn't going to let herself be embarrassed any further. 'This morning was a momentary lapse of judgement. It will never happen again.'

'As you wish,' he said so calmly she wanted to thump him.

'I think I should bid you goodnight,' Francesca said, knowing she should get away from him before she said something she regretted. Or kissed him again. 'It was nice to see you have done well in life, but perhaps we should go our separate ways.'

She turned, only to have his hand dart out and catch her gently on the arm.

'What about the other seven days?' he asked and this time she knew he was struggling to keep an entirely straight face.

She looked up at him, feeling her pulse quicken. As much as she might pretend and postulate, she wasn't going to do anything to shorten the time they could spend together.

'I shall pen you a note,' she said as haughtily as she could muster, then marched off before he could say anything more.

Chapter Nine

'Lord Huntley to see you, my lady,' the butler announced and Francesca had to suppress a groan. She'd barely slept, her mind rebelling against her sensible side, and images of Ben kissing her, touching her, laying her back on the bed and making love to her, had occupied her thoughts for most of the night. The problem of Lord Huntley, and his tracking her to DeFevrett's, hadn't even crossed her mind. Now she would have to try to work out what he knew and what she would be able to get away with.

'Oh, joy,' Felicity said drily from her position on the window seat.

'Lady Somersham,' Huntley said as he burst into the room, glancing at Felicity, but barely sparing a nod in her direction. 'You have some explaining to do.'

'My lord?' Francesca tried to sound as meek and guileless as possible while the man she was probably going to have to marry paraded round the room as if he owned the place. Remembering the large debt her father owed Lord

Huntley, she realised he probably did own some of Number Twelve Park Square and a large proportion of their country estate, too.

'Oh, dear, is something amiss, Lord Huntley?' Francesca asked.

'Where were you last night?' he demanded.

'Last night,' she mused as if it were half a year ago.

'Here,' Felicity said without looking up from the book she was reading, 'With me.'

'What?' This had evidently thrown Lord Huntley and he was looking round the room as if searching for inspiration.

'We spent the evening doing a little embroidery and Francesca sang after dinner. It was a very pleasant evening,' Felicity said.

'Is this true?' Lord Huntley asked, turning back to Francesca.

'Of course. You know I'm still in mourning for my late husband. I still spend most of my evenings in and Felicity was kind enough to keep me company last night.'

'We'll talk about this preposterously long mourning period later,' Lord Huntley murmured, 'Right now I want to know why I heard reports of you frequenting an inappropriate dance.'

'Oh?' Francesca said mildly. 'And what dance is that?'

'Assembly Rooms called DeFevrett's. It caters to those of the middle class who have an inflated view of their own importance and status.'

'DeFevrett's?' she mused, beginning to enjoy herself now. 'No, I can't say I've ever heard of it. Who on earth gave you the idea I might go there?'

'A rumour,' Huntley said, frowning as if he didn't quite believe her.

'They must have been mistaken. And you think I went there last night?'

He grunted, only now deigning to sit down on the armchair that had seen better days with upholstery that had been carefully repaired more than once.

'Was there anything else, Lord Huntley?' Felicity asked. It was bordering on rude, but Francesca's sister had never had any time for the man who had initially asked for her hand in marriage before settling on Francesca instead.

'It's high time we announced our engagement,' Lord Huntley said. 'I'm fed up of all this dilly dallying.'

'The correct mourning period must be observed,' Francesca said, repeating the line she'd been using for the two months Lord Huntley had been pushing for a date. It wasn't as though she had even accepted his proposal yet, it would be bad form to do so before the mourning period for Lord Somersham was up, but everyone around her—her father, her mother and Lord Huntley himself—seemed to think the marriage between them was a certainty.

If she was honest, it probably was a certainty, but she was still hoping for a miracle before she had to formally agree to the engagement.

'How long is left?' he asked brusquely.

'Six weeks.' Only six weeks of freedom before she would have to wake up to this man every morning and promise to obey him, serve him, love him and honour him. It made her feel sick to her stomach.

He grunted again and promptly stood. 'I need to finalise things with your father. I shall call again next week—please ensure he is sober.'

'Of course, Lord Huntley,' Francesca said, knowing nothing she could say or do would have be able to influence that.

They waited until he had left before both Francesca and Felicity let out long exhalations.

'I can't believe you're actually considering marrying *that*,' Felicity said.

Francesca couldn't tell her sister she was doing it for her. If it wasn't for Felicity she might be able to finally leave her parents to sort out their own mess, but she couldn't condemn her lovely younger sister to a life of misery. Without the dowry Lord Huntley had promised to provide Felicity she might never get a proposal from a decent gentleman.

To ensure her voice didn't betray her emotions Francesca just shrugged.

'Where were you last night?' Felicity asked, sitting up on the window seat and putting her book down so she could focus all her attention on her sister.

'Just out,' Francesca said, fiddling with a frayed piece of cotton on her dress.

'At the Assembly Rooms? The inappropriate one?'

'It was just a dance,' she said, 'Nothing scandalous.'

'I didn't know you had it in you,' Felicity said, a new admiration dawning in her eyes.

'He was there,' Francesca said quietly, 'Lord Huntley. He was there looking for me.'

His behaviour terrified her a little. If he was this obsessive about her movements even before they were engaged, what would he be like when they married? Lord Somersham hadn't been a particularly pleasant man, especially as the years went by without Francesca producing the heir he so desperately wanted, but he had expressed his displeasure with his words and his obvious contempt for her. Never had he thought to control who she saw or where she went and never had he raised a hand to her.

There were rumours about Lord Huntley and how he'd treated his first wife. According to the gossips she'd often been incapacitated after some awful accident, much more often than one could expect in the course of a few years. Francesca knew she wouldn't be alone if Lord Huntley did turn out to be a cruel husband, there were many men who raised a hand to their wives behind closed doors, but that didn't soften the dread she felt whenever she thought of her inevitable nuptials.

'I take it from his appearance here today he didn't actually see you.'

'I was able to sneak out.' She remembered Ben's cool handling of the situation, the way he'd not hesitated to assist her in escaping Lord Huntley. She could still feel the pressure of his hands around her waist as he helped her down from the wall, the easy way he'd caught her and lifted her. And then, of course, there were the kisses.

The kisses that she'd been obsessing about ever since she'd returned home the previous evening. Francesca had been unable to think of anything else, no manner of distraction had worked. Over and over again she'd relived every moment, picturing how Ben had held her, how his lips had felt on her own, how her heart had hammered in her chest. Never had she been kissed like that and she knew she would do almost anything to feel the same just one more time.

'Who did you go with?' Felicity asked, pulling Francesca back to the present.

'Lucy,' she fibbed. Their grandmother's companion, when their grandmother was still alive, had chaperoned Francesca to many balls and events when her mother had been indisposed. She was now a happy spinster in her early forties who over the years had been more of a mother to

Francesca and her sister than Lady Pottersdown, who spent all her time secluded in her room.

'I would have come with you,' Felicity said with a grin.

'You, young lady, need to avoid any hint of scandal,' Francesca said in her sternest voice. Felicity was so carefree and innocent. Sometimes a little too carefree and innocent. She went through life thinking nothing bad could ever happen to her and that meant sometimes she took unnecessary risks.

Once Francesca had been like that, too, but over the years she'd been forced to step up, to be the responsible one. Their mother spent almost all her time ensconced in her bedchamber and their father was either getting them into further financial trouble with one of his doomed schemes or drowning his sorrows in the bottom of a whisky glass. Sometimes Francesca wished she could go back to the days where all she had to consider was which dress to wear or how to spend her morning, but that seemed a lifetime ago.

'Mr Crawford to see you, Lady Somersham,' the butler announced.

Francesca shot up from her chair and started to tell the butler to show Ben into another room, but he'd already stepped out to let Ben in.

'Aren't you popular this morning?' Felicity murmured, her eyes fixed on the door and a little smile on her lips.

'Good morning Fran—' Ben started, but cut himself off as he caught sight of Felicity on the window seat. 'Lady Somersham,' he corrected himself. 'And this must be Miss Felicity—a pleasure to make your acquaintance.'

As soon as her eyes met his she was taken back to the moment of their kiss before she'd left him the night before.

She remembered every vivid detail and by the smile on Ben's lips he knew exactly what she was thinking.

'I trust you are both well?' he asked. For a boy who'd spent eight years as a convict worker in Australia he did a good impression of being a gentleman.

'Very well, thank you,' Felicity said, her eyes sparkling with glee. Inwardly Francesca groaned. Her sister was always telling her to go out into the world and enjoy herself, to mix with people who made her happy and Francesca knew she would do everything to find out more about Ben and his interest in her. 'Mr Crawford,' Felicity said slowly. 'Are you the same Mr Crawford who is friends with Mr Robertson?'

'I am. Do you know Mr Robertson?'

Felicity shrugged, a non-ladylike gesture that made Francesca smile every time she saw it.

'I'm friends with Caroline Yaxley and Georgina Fairfax. I believe Mr Robertson is acquainted with Lady Georgina.'

If the rumours were to be believed, the two had been caught in a mildly compromising position and it was only the intervention of Lady Winston, Fitzgerald's aunt, who had saved the pair from much more salacious gossip.

'He is,' Ben said, barely able to keep the smile from his face. 'In fact, I am due to be attending a house party at Lady Georgina's family estate this weekend with Mr Robertson. Will you be there?'

'No,' Felicity said with no hint of malice in her voice. 'Her mother did not think me suitable.'

'Ah. That is a shame.'

'Was there a reason for your visit, Mr Crawford?' Francesca asked, pulling him back to the present.

'I wanted to return your coat.'

Francesca's eyes widened and quickly she glanced at her

sister. There was no good reason for Mr Crawford to have her coat.

'There really was no rush,' she managed to ground out.

'I thought you might be in need of it. Unless you have a whole wardrobe of coats.'

He knew very well that she didn't. Over the years she'd conserved the best-made pieces of clothing, lovingly mending them when sleeves frayed or seams became loose, but still she only had a skeleton wardrobe left now. And he was right, it was her only coat.

'Where on earth did you leave it, Francesca?' Felicity asked, her eyes dancing with amusement.

'At the Assembly Rooms,' she said, hoping her quick answer would be enough for her sister, but knowing it would not.

'How kind of you to return it, Mr Crawford. Did you enjoy the dancing last night?' Felicity asked.

'Very much so. Your sister is an excellent dancer.'

Knowing she'd been caught out in a lie, Francesca sat back in her chair and gave up. Felicity would have the details from Mr Crawford in no time, there was no point in trying to stop her. Her sister would have done well as an interrogator in the war, Francesca had never known anyone able to keep information from her for long.

In a move that surprised her, Felicity stood, executed a brief and sloppy curtsy and moved towards the door.

'Please excuse me, Mr Crawford, I've got to be…somewhere else.' She didn't even bother coming up with a convincing lie.

Left alone, Francesca tried to avoid Ben's gaze but after nearly half a minute of silence she had to look up.

'You look lovely this morning, Frannie,' he said, his eyes flitting over her face.

'Stop it,' she muttered.

'Stop what?'

'This.' She gestured to him, not really sure herself what she was asking him to stop.

'You want me to stop being me?'

'Yes. No. I don't know. Sit down.'

He did and she tried to ignore the grin on his face.

'So that was the sister you're giving up your life for,' he said as he flopped down on to the sofa next to her. He was far too close and his proximity meant she couldn't think straight. Subtly she tried to shift so their legs were not touching.

'Shush,' she said, glancing at the door. She wouldn't put it past her sister to be listening outside.

'She seems nice. Resourceful. Independent. Able to make her own decisions.'

'She's twenty years old.'

'The same age as you when you married Lord Somersham.'

'And look how happy that made me,' Francesca murmured.

'Have you asked her if she wants you to sacrifice the rest of your life for her?'

'Of course not. And it's none of your business.'

He shrugged as if agreeing with her, then leant in and started to trace a lazy pattern across the back of her hand with his fingers.

'Ben,' she said, not knowing herself if she was asking him to stop or begging him to continue.

'Frannie.'

'We can't do this,' she said, wishing she didn't believe her own words. Her body wanted to lean in to him and succumb to every pleasure he was offering.

'We can,' he said. 'We're both consenting adults, free and unfettered.'

That was technically true. She was a widow and still had not formally accepted Lord Huntley's proposal, even though in her heart she knew it was only a matter of time.

'It would be a fun way to get yourself out of marrying Huntley,' he murmured.

'Stop it.'

'Your choice,' he said, sitting back. 'Where are you taking me today?'

'I thought we could have a little break from each other today,' Francesca said sweetly. She knew she needed some distance to think rationally about the kiss they'd shared the night before. Time and distance to lock it up in a box where it couldn't ever escape and plague her thoughts like it did now.

'The sun is shining, it might be cold, but you've got your coat back. I can't think of a better time to get out in the fresh air together.'

'I find myself a little tired from last night.'

He grinned and she felt herself blushing, knowing exactly what he was thinking.

'Rest today, then,' he said. 'I'll pick you up tonight at nine for an evening of mystery.'

'Nothing scandalous?' she asked.

'I promise.'

Reluctantly she nodded. At least she would have the day to get hold of her emotions and talk some sense into herself. There would be no kissing, no discreet but passionate affairs, no wishing for something that could never be.

'Until tonight,' Ben said, taking her hand and planting a kiss just below the knuckles. 'And I promise to be on my best behaviour.'

Ben took his place at the table across from his friends and grinned. Cards were his speciality, he rarely lost a game and over the years had made a fair amount of money from his opponents. He liked to play games where you read the other players, used the skills of understanding body language and subtle changes in demeanour rather than relying on luck. He had two rules: always know when to bow out and only to play while it was still fun. He never broke these rules and as a consequence had never lost any large sums of money in a card game or felt the need to stay when he really should leave.

Sam Robertson and George Fitzgerald had seen him play numerous times and as such the three friends only ever played for fun, with no money involved. It was an opportunity to sit together, share a drink and reconnect when their lives were all so hectic.

He'd known both men for well over a decade. Sam Robertson he'd met on the transport ship on the way to Australia. They'd been two of the youngest convicts, both still children. Immediately they'd formed a friendship that had stayed solid throughout the harsh conditions of the transport ship, the cruel realities of life under the guards as convict workers in Australia, and slowly life had got better as they'd served their sentence and became free men.

Their friendship with George Fitzgerald had come a little later, when the boys had been assigned to work on his

father's farm. Mr Fitzgerald, the younger son of an impoverished baron in England, had been fair and kind, treating
the boys as people rather than animals under the yoke. One
day while working in the fields to bring in the harvest Ben
and Sam had spotted a venomous snake ready to spring
towards George. They tackled it, saving George from a
deadly bite. From then on Mr Fitzgerald had treated them
more like sons than convicts, insisting they share lessons
with George and slowly giving them the love and kindness
to make them believe there was good in the world again.
Although Mr Fitzgerald had passed away a couple of years
ago the three men were still as close as brothers. Ben found
he didn't trust many people in the world, but Robertson and
Fitzgerald he could always rely on.

'All set for the house party?' Ben asked.

'As much as I'll ever be,' Robertson replied, grimacing
as he looked at his cards.

One of the main reasons they'd returned to England after
so long away was Robertson's desire to confront the man
who had falsely accused him eighteen years ago and had
him convicted of theft. This weekend Ben had agreed to
travel to Hampshire with his friend to Lady Georgina's
house party, the daughter of the man Robertson wanted
revenge on.

Ben's main motivation for agreeing to go was to keep
an eye on Robertson and ensure his friend coped when he
confronted the old Earl, but he wouldn't deny it would be
good to have a little time away from London, some space
to think and consider what he wanted from the rest of his
time in England.

Francesca. That was what he wanted. He wanted her in

his arms and in his bed. He could deny it all he liked, but the attraction he felt for her was overwhelming in its intensity.

'How is Lady Somersham?' Fitzgerald asked mildly as Robertson stood to fetch some drinks.

'Well, I believe,' Ben said.

'You believe?'

'I'm not privy to her innermost thoughts.'

'Yet,' Fitzgerald murmured, 'I'm curious as to why you're spending so much time with her.'

Ben leaned back in his chair and ran a hand through his hair. He was curious, too. If he could understand his own motivations, it might make the whole Francesca situation much easier to contain and cope with.

'We merely want to renew our friendship, to find out what each of us has been doing all these years. And Lady Somersham has asked me to accompany her to some events,' Ben fibbed, knowing it was he who'd pushed for the eight days together. 'What gentleman could deny her that?'

'You've never wanted to be a gentleman in your life, Crawford,' Fitzgerald said.

'True.'

'Outings, eh?' Fitzgerald asked, a suggestive glint in his eye.

'Not like that,' Ben said quickly, trying to suppress the image of Francesca in his bed, the way her chemise had clung to her curves as she'd sat up, the beautiful flush to her cheeks as she'd awaited his arrival.

'Are you sure you're not in love with her?'

Ben nearly choked on thin air he was so surprised by the question.

'I've only known the woman five minutes,' he said, hearing the defensive note to his voice.

'Twenty-odd years,' Fitzgerald corrected him. 'You've only been *reacquainted* for five minutes. And in the eighteen years you've been away you haven't been able to forget about her, have you?'

'I'm not in love with her,' he ground out. Perhaps once, perhaps when they'd been children he *had* loved her in the way one could in childhood. But now he felt a myriad of other emotions, but certainly not love.

Fitzgerald shrugged. 'Fair enough.'

'What's fair enough?' Robertson asked, re-entering the room with three glasses of whisky.

'The mysteries of Crawford's heart.'

'You're going to have to let someone in one day,' Robertson said, placing the glass of whisky down in front of Ben.

'I thought we were here to play cards,' Ben said, not looking at his two friends.

'This is more important,' Robertson said, sitting down and swinging his chair back on to two legs. It was a habit he'd had since they were youths together and it still riled Ben. He grabbed the chair, set it back on four legs and ignored Robertson's grin. 'You don't trust anyone, you have affair after affair after affair and never do you let a woman get close to your heart.'

'You two aren't exactly good role models for a settled life,' Ben murmured.

'We're not talking about us. And Fitzgerald is peculiarly well adjusted,' Robertson said, 'Must have been something to do with spending his childhood with his family and not among a bunch of convicts.'

'Strange how much of a difference that might make,' Fitzgerald said.

'The next woman you have in your bed, pause for a moment and ask yourself what is stopping you from feeling something deeper for her,' Robertson said.

Ben grumbled something incomprehensible and thankfully his two friends settled back down to play cards again. He didn't need their insights into his emotions. He knew he was a little stunted when it came to initiating a deeper relationship. No doubt it stemmed from being torn from his family at such a young age. That, and his feeling that he didn't quite belong anywhere. He was a wealthy man, influential in his own way, yet most certainly not a gentleman. And class seemed to be the thing that mattered when it came to marriage. Even though he was wealthier than half the men that considered themselves the cream of society in England, he would never be deemed worthy enough or refined enough for their daughters.

He only had to look at Francesca—for her, Lord Huntley was considered a decent match, despite his age and rumoured issues with anger. Huntley had an old family name and pure pedigree and that elevated him above anything Ben could ever be. It made Ben feel sick that it was such an inconsequential thing that mattered. Anyone could inherit a family name—it was much harder to build a successful business from nothing.

He shook his head. Even thinking of a future with Francesca was ridiculous. Instead he would enjoy the eight days they had together and hope the memories would last a lifetime.

Chapter Ten

'Goodnight, Father,' Francesca called as she slipped out through the front door. To keep up the pretence she was going to a dinner party hosted by one of her widowed friends she was wearing an evening gown and thin satin shoes again, but had her thick coat thrown over the top despite it being frayed along the hem in numerous places. She wasn't sure where Ben was going to take her tonight, but she had a feeling it would be outdoors. It was easier to hide from curious eyes somewhere outside, although even just a few steps from her front door she was already shivering. The winter had been colder than usual, with snow every few weeks and the rivers and ponds in the city freezing over on numerous occasions.

Quickly she checked left and right, paranoid someone might be watching her go off to meet an entirely unsuitable man, and then hurried off down the street. Ben was waiting for her in a carriage at the corner and as he saw her approaching he opened the door and hopped down. Not for the first time she felt her insides flip when she saw him and she had to pause and compose herself before she took another step.

'Good evening, Frannie,' he said, leaning forward and giving her an entirely inappropriate kiss on the cheek. She felt the skin tingle where his lips had been and quickly tried to hide her blush.

'Behave yourself,' she admonished.

'There's no one here but us,' Ben said. He was right. On a night like tonight no one was lingering outside and all the carriages had their windows closed and curtains drawn against the freezing temperatures. 'Come inside.'

He helped her up, waited until she was settled on the seat before he stepped inside and sat down next to her. It was intimate, their legs touching through the multiple layers of clothing, but on the seat opposite was a large package taking up most of the room.

'Where are we going?' Francesca asked, trying to ignore the warmth emanating from his body. It would be so easy to sink into his arms, but she knew she would struggle to ever come up again.

'It's a surprise,' Ben said as the carriage set off.

'What's that?' She motioned to the parcel on the opposite seat of the carriage.

'A present. You will need it tonight.'

'A present?'

'Nothing extravagant,' he said, 'But I couldn't expect you to venture out on a night like tonight and not keep you adequately warm.'

Images of him tumbling her into his bed, a roaring fire across the room and their bodies perspiring from the heat they generated filled her mind and hastily she looked away.

'Can I see?' she said. It had been a long time since any-one had bought her a present. In the early days of their mar-riage her husband had bought her one or two trinkets, but nothing extravagant, and even that had stopped when their relationship had begun to sour. As he'd got more and more into debt he'd withdrawn further into himself until even a civil greeting had been too much to expect. Lord Huntley wasn't a man for presents either. To him their proposed union was a business deal, to be conducted with her father with no sentimentality involved whatsoever.

Reaching across to the other seat he pulled the package towards them, resting it on his lap.

'Open it,' he said quietly, taking her hand and placing it on the string that held the parcel together.

Pulling at the knot, Francesca opened the package, frowning as the paper fell away and a swathe of beautiful deep red material cascaded out.

'It's a cloak. A thick one. Something to keep you warm this winter.'

Francesca felt the tears building and struggled to contain them. It was the most thoughtful present. He must have seen the almost threadbare condition of her coat and of course he would know the rumours about her family's dire finan-cial situation.

'Ben,' she said, hearing her voice catch in her throat, 'it's too much.'

He turned to her, none of the usual humour or light-heart-edness in his eyes, and shook his head.

'A person needs to be warm, Frannie, it's a basic human need.'

Wondering what else he considered a basic human need, she looked down, running her fingers over the soft material.

'Thank you,' she whispered. 'It's the nicest present I've ever received.'

'Now I know you're lying,' Ben said, the grin returning to his face. 'I remember a young girl who once told me the best present she'd ever received was a baby piglet.'

Immediately Francesca smiled. It *had* been her best present. Ben had given it to her when she was eight years old. It had been the runt, unable to fight its way through the rest of the piglets to get to its mother's milk. She'd loved that piglet, nurtured and cared for it for two years as it grew until her father had declared the now almost adult-sized pig too big for the house and demanded she take it back to the farm on the edge of the estate.

'You're right,' she said, 'Porker was better than a cloak. But I doubt I'd get away with having a pig for a pet now.'

'Society wouldn't approve?' Ben asked.

'I think it would be frowned upon.'

'Perhaps you should do it anyway,' he said, his hand resting on the soft material of the cloak just an inch away from hers. 'Perhaps you should decide you don't care one iota what society thinks and do what makes you happy instead.'

'Wouldn't that be nice,' Francesca said.

'I'm serious, Frannie. People here seem to make so many important decisions on what *looks* right. Take your marriage to Huntley.'

'Proposed marriage,' she murmured the correction.

'It wouldn't make you happy. You're only doing it to save your family from the shame of financial ruin.'

'That is a pretty good motive,' she protested.

'Not good enough. Let them sell the houses. Let them sell all the land. Sell everything. Live in a little cottage somewhere. Stop spending money they don't have keeping up a pretence of wealth. Then you might be able to choose a life where you're not tied to a man with a reputation for being unkind to his wives.'

She looked down, not wanting to admit how accurate Ben was with his statement. Her father did focus too much on wanting to keep up a pretence of wealth. Their house in London and estate in the country had only a couple of rooms furnished, those which might receive visitors. The rest of the rooms were empty shells. Everything they did was to try to show the world they were *normal*, even when the act of doing it put them further into debt. On a few occasions Francesca had wondered about just running away from it all, finding employment as a companion or governess for a few years and saving up for a little cottage at the coast somewhere. If it wasn't for her sister she might have done so already. Although she knew that she would find it difficult adjusting her expectations of life. She wanted to be free, but for so long she'd lived life as a lady—as the daughter of a viscount and then Lady Somersham. To become someone who worked for a living, that would be hard to accept, even though she suspected in the long term she would be happier.

'I don't want to argue about this,' she said. 'You know why I'm doing it. Can't we just enjoy this evening?'

'As you wish,' he said, capitulating easily. For a moment she wondered why he was so concerned about her future and she felt a flurry of hope inside her. It had been a very long time since anyone had put her needs first.

They continued the journey in silence for a few more minutes, Francesca aware of Ben's body every time he shifted, every time his leg innocently touched hers.

'Are we going to one of the pleasure gardens?' she asked.

'Have some patience and you'll find out,' he said, infuriatingly not giving anything away.

'Ranelagh Pleasure Gardens?' she asked. 'Or Vauxhall, perhaps?'

Vauxhall was a little less upmarket, with a cheaper admission price, but would probably afford them more anonymity. There were rumours about what couples got up to there, with plenty of dark avenues and secret gardens, but most of it was probably grossly exaggerated. Silently she chastised herself for the bubble of anticipation at the thought of escaping somewhere private with Ben. She was a widow, a respectable lady, and in a few short weeks she would likely be engaged to be married once more. As much as she might want to be reckless, to indulge her baser desires, she knew that once again she would have to deny her own wants and needs and do what was right.

'Patience,' Ben said again and she saw the grin on his face as she glanced sideways. Patience never had been one of her virtues. She'd always wanted to know things immediately, to be told exactly what was happening.

'It's too late for a stroll in the park,' she mused, thinking perhaps it wasn't a pleasure garden after all.

'Mmm…' Ben murmured non-committally.

'And I wouldn't need a cloak if we were going somewhere indoors.'

'Unless it was very cold indeed,' Ben said, looking as though he were enjoying himself immensely, teasing her by withholding the knowledge of what they were going to do with their evening.

'It wouldn't hurt to tell me.'

'It would ruin the surprise.'

'What if I don't like surprises?'

'Everyone likes surprises. Just some people are too impatient to wait for them.'

She huffed, sat back and twitched the curtain, peering out of the window to see if she could find any clues as to where they were going.

Only ten minutes later the carriage slowed to a stop and Ben hopped out, turning to help her down before reaching up to fetch the package with her new cloak. As she looked around, puzzled as to why they'd stopped in a pleasant but quiet residential street, he draped the cloak over her shoulders, his fingers tickling her neck as he adjusted it. Francesca looked down, feeling the warmth from the luxurious garment already making a difference to her cold body.

'Ben...' she said quietly, trying to convey the myriad of emotions that were fighting for supremacy inside her.

'It's only a cloak, Frannie,' he said, offering her his arm.

It wasn't only a cloak, though. It was the most thoughtful gift anyone had ever given her.

'What are we doing here?' she asked, looking around.

'It's not quite Ranelagh or Vauxhall,' he said, smiling at her confusion, 'But I thought they might be a little too public for us to be seen together.' He paused, slid his hand into hers and then pulled her along the pavement to the quietest end of the street. 'Here. Shall I give you a boost up first?'

Frowning with confusion, Francesca looked at the wrought-iron railings that surrounded the private gardens for the residents of the street. It was like a small park, but the gates were locked and only those with keys could get inside.

'You don't mean in there?' she asked.

'Unless you're not up to it,' Ben said, a hint of challenge in his voice.

It was what they'd always done as children, challenged the other to more dangerous and more difficult pursuits, and Francesca felt the years falling away as she looked at Ben. For just one night she didn't want to be Lady Somersham, she wanted to be someone reckless and fun.

'It's you I'm worried about,' she said, moving up to test the sturdiness of the railings and feel the cold metal beneath her hands. 'You're not as young as you used to be.'

'None of us are.'

'Some of us carry it better,' she said, tapping a gloved hand on the metal.

'Cheeky minx. I wouldn't worry about me, my body has been honed by years of hard labour, while you've been sitting around idle in your drawing rooms and ballrooms.'

'How do you know I don't break into private gardens every week?'

'Sometimes I feel I know you better than I know myself,' he murmured in her ear.

She shivered, knowing everything about this evening was dangerous. There was the physical danger of climbing over the iron railings into a place they were not allowed. The danger of being caught together somewhere they had no excuse to be, but most of all the danger of being alone with a man she was finding it supremely hard to resist.

Everything in Francesca's life had schooled her to guard her virtue, to never allow herself to let her desires and emotions overcome her common sense, but here she was with a man she found incredibly attractive, allowing him to escort her into a dark and secluded garden. She knew if he tried to kiss her again she would be powerless to protest and deep inside she knew there was nothing she wanted more than to feel his lips on hers again.

'On to that tree?' Francesca asked, eyeing the railings critically. They were shoulder height, but at one corner a tree branched out over them, providing an easy route into the gardens.

'Have you got the strength?'

'Of course.' She wasn't entirely sure if she did, but was determined to give it her best try. Although she kept active, dancing while in London and walking and riding in the country, none of her pursuits required the upper body strength needed to climb a tree.

'I'll be right behind you,' he said, offering his hands to boost her up.

Placing one foot in his hand, she felt him lift her and carefully she caught hold of the tree branch, pulling herself up on to it until she was sitting comfortably with her legs dangling over the gardens beyond the railings. She watched as Ben jumped, caught hold of the tree branch and pulled himself up, the muscles straining the seams of his coat, but otherwise no other outward signs of the effort it must have taken.

Lithe and nimble as a cat he skirted along the branch, swung himself around her and dropped to the ground on the other side of the railings.

'I'll catch you,' he said, holding out his arms.

Just as she pushed herself off the branch Francesca realised she had no fear. She *knew* he would catch her, knew he wouldn't let her fall. She wouldn't jump into the arms of Lord Huntley or have contemplated trusting her late husband in this way.

'Nice work, Lady Somersham,' he said, setting her on the ground, but not hurrying to remove his arm from around her waist.

'I break into private gardens all the time,' she said, finding her footing and adjusting her new cloak. 'Climbing trees and vaulting over railings isn't much of a challenge.'

'I'll have to find something to stretch you next time,' he murmured.

He took her hand and, although they were both wearing thick gloves to protect themselves from the freezing temperatures, Francesca felt a rush of blood to her fingers at the intimacy of the gesture. Most men offered their arm or would content themselves merely with walking side by side with a lady, but Ben took her hand as boldly as if there were nothing strange in the action.

Slowly they meandered along the path, having to take care in the near-total darkness to avoid any obstacles.

'The stars look different from here,' Ben said as they paused to look up at the sky. 'You wouldn't think it, it's the same sky after all, but they look different here to how they do in the Australian sky.'

'Is it very different there?' Francesca asked softly. Ever since they'd become reacquainted she'd wanted to ask about his life, to find out what he'd been doing all these years, but she'd been too afraid. Too afraid that it might have been nearly two decades of hell because of her father and that he might resent her even just a little for it.

'I can't think of two more different places,' he said. 'England is so ordered, so structured. Australia is just wilderness. Even the settlements are nothing more than a collection of buildings.' He paused and Francesca saw his eyes softening. 'The countryside though, Frannie, that's where you fall in love with the country.'

She hardly knew anything about Australia. After learning of Ben's sentence eighteen years ago she'd tried to find out as much as she could about the country on the other side of the world, but information was thin on the ground. Hardly anyone who had been had ever come back and the reports that were published were mainly from the voyage where it was first discovered. Her imagination had supplied images of vast swathes of scrubland, dry and dusty with no redeeming features.

'It's beautiful. There's fields and farmland just like here, but so much more. There are beaches of golden sand and the ocean is brilliant blue. The mountains near Sydney are misty and cool and although I've never been the interior of the country is meant to be filled with miles upon miles of orange sand and great rocky outcrops. One day I will venture to the very centre of the country and see for myself.'

'You plan to go back?' she asked. Swept up in the passion of the past few days she'd forgotten his return to England was temporary.

'Of course. It's my home.'

'You have work there? A family?' Francesca found she was holding her breath. A lot could happen in eighteen years. Ben might be married with a brood of children for all she knew.

He laughed. 'Work, yes, a family, no.'

'And these friends you came over to England with, they're planning on returning, too?'

'Robertson and Fitzgerald. Yes. We all have farms to run.'

Francesca found her eyes widening. 'You run a farm?' She wasn't sure what she expected Ben to have been doing the last ten years after his sentence was completed, but even though he was an intelligent man she never imagined he might be making a success of his life. It took a special type of man to turn his life around after serving eight years for theft and being transported to Australia.

'I own a farm,' he corrected her. 'Actually, lots of farms.'

'How?' she asked, feeling such a mixture of emotions that she barely knew where to start dealing with them. Of course she was happy his life hadn't been completely ruined by her father's actions, but she felt a sense of loss and panic at the thought of him leaving. It wasn't her place to want him to stay, wasn't her right to miss him, but still she knew she would. In a couple of months she would be married again and he would return to his home in Australia. That was how things had to be, but it didn't mean she had to be happy about it.

'Luck,' he said, 'and a little work.'

She doubted much of it had been luck. He was a determined man and underneath the humour and easy-going attitude she would wager there was a man who worked harder than he let on.

Ben watched as Frannie screwed up her face, steeling herself to ask the next question on her mind.

'So it hasn't all been terrible?' she asked quietly. 'Not every single moment?'

He stopped and turned to her, waiting for her to lift her eyes to meet his in the darkness.

'No,' he said softly, 'It hasn't all been terrible.' It was difficult to resist kissing her. With her face turned up to his and that look of forlorn concern in her eyes he just wanted to cup her chin and kiss her until she forgot all her worries.

He had suffered greatly over the years, with the terrible conditions of the hulk ship and even worse on the transport ship, then the years of hard labour under a hot sun supervised by cruel and petty guards, but he realised in his own way Francesca had been suffering, too. It was clear she felt guilty for not being able to save him all those years ago despite doing everything a ten-year-old girl could do. Added to that were the years of unhappiness foisted on her by her father and her husband.

Ben knew he'd weathered the hard years and come out stronger on the other side and now he knew the worst of his life was behind him. Francesca still might have her hardest years ahead of her.

'I survived, Frannie,' he said softly, raising up one hand and letting his fingers trail down her cheek, 'The first few years were terrible, but I survived.'

She nodded, not able to tear her gaze away from his.

'And then life began to get better. I've got six huge farms, great friends and my freedom. No one judges you in Australia for being an ex-convict—over half the population have such beginnings.'

'But you lost so much,' she said. 'Your family. Your childhood.'

There was no way he would ever get his childhood back, but one of the main reasons he'd returned to England was to see his family. In a few short weeks his father would return home and Ben would make the journey to Essex to see the man who'd done everything in his power to show Ben he hadn't been forgotten even though he was half a world away.

'I haven't lost my family,' Ben said quietly. 'And I try not to dwell on the loss of my childhood.'

She nodded, her movements shaky.

'I always imagined the worst…' she said quietly. 'It was terrible never knowing what had happened to you.'

'Hush,' he said as she buried her head in his shoulder.

He suspected she was crying, trying to hide the tears from him, and feeling a rush of sentimentality he wrapped an arm around her and pulled her in even closer.

Waiting while she composed herself, he found his fingers trailing instinctively across the nape of her neck. It was warm under the fur lining of her new cloak and her skin was as soft as the finest velvet.

'Ben,' she murmured, emerging from his shoulder. It was phrased half as a question, half as a plea, and he knew if she looked up at him with those beautiful blue eyes he wouldn't be able to stop himself from kissing her.

Slowly she looked up and even in the darkness he could see the desire and confusion mixed in her gaze.

Ben knew a lot about desire. Since he'd gained his freedom he'd promised not to ever deny himself pleasure whenever the opportunity arose, as long as it didn't damage anyone, of course. He'd conducted numerous short and pleasurable affairs, always making sure they ended before either party became too invested in the relationship. He'd felt desire before, of course he had, but never had he wanted a woman quite like he wanted Francesca.

'Come,' he said, grabbing her hand and pulling her through the gardens to a spot of grass under the trees. Quickly he helped her unclasp her cloak and lay it on the ground, lowering Francesca down on to it before lying down beside her.

Above them the bare branches of the trees swayed in the breeze and as Ben reached out and pulled Francesca towards him he caught a glimpse of the moon emerging from behind a cloud.

Slowly, as if they had all the time in the world, he kissed

her. Beneath his lips he felt hers open, inviting him in, her arms wrapping around his back and pulling him closer.

'What are we doing?' she whispered in between kisses.

'Life is for enjoying, Frannie,' he murmured in her ear, 'Let me help you enjoy it.'

Slowly he trailed a hand inside the coat she was wearing, the threadbare one she'd kept on under her cloak, feeling the warmth of her skin just underneath her collarbone. As he kissed her she fiddled with the fastenings, opening up the coat and allowing him access to her body. At this simple gesture he felt himself grow even harder, with every nerve in his body stimulated and on edge.

Loving how Francesca moaned as he bent his head to trail kisses along the neckline of her dress, he pushed the material as low as it would go, revealing the smooth swell of her breasts. Taking his time, with Francesca's hands tangled in his hair, he kissed lower and lower. Tugging less gently, he tried to pull her dress even further down, but the material was too stiff and the fastenings too tight.

'Don't stop,' she begged, her fingers still tangled in his hair.

Underneath him he felt her hips rise in an instinctive movement, pushing against his, and in that moment he would have done anything for a soft bed and warm covers. He wanted her so badly, but even he was too much of a gentleman to expect a lady to make love on the freezing ground of a public garden.

'Soon,' he whispered, pulling away, pausing only to kiss her one last time.

As his body stopped touching hers he watched her face, waiting for the inevitable transformation. For a few minutes Francesca had been caught up in her desire, not caring that her actions were scandalous and they'd been reckless in a public place. Now, with her sensibilities returning, she would pull away from him and regret their intimacy.

Quickly she shuffled backwards, as if trying to put as much distance between her and Ben as possible. Her hand struck a tree root and she let out a cry of surprise, stopping where she was.

'What are we doing?' she whispered as she hugged her hand to her chest.

'The inevitable,' Ben murmured. Deep down he'd known all along this was where they'd end up. Not exactly here, in this private garden, but certainly in each other's arms. He'd felt Francesca's pull the moment he'd set eyes on her again and somewhere inside he'd always known that they would not be able to go their separate ways before they'd quenched the desire they had for each other.

'Nothing is inevitable,' she snapped. 'It was foolish and reckless, but certainly not inevitable.'

'Whatever you say, Frannie,' Ben said, knowing that she didn't believe her own words.

He stood, offering her his hand. For a moment she looked like she was thinking of refusing.

'It's not inevitable,' she said as she allowed him to pull her up.

'I've seen how you look at me, Frannie,' Ben said, suddenly wanting to shock her, to show her she didn't have to always abide by society's rules. 'Don't try to pretend you're anything but an eager participant. We both know I only have to kiss you here and you'll fall into my arms again.'

He kissed her on the neck, just below the earlobe, and felt her shudder with anticipation.

Quickly she pulled away, her eyes filled with anger and defiance.

'You're so arrogant,' she hissed, evidently trying to keep her voice down due to where they were despite her anger. 'You think any woman, no matter what class difference there is, will just fall into your arms as soon as you smile in her direction.'

He shrugged. 'In my experience they do.' Pausing, he caught her hand, lowering his voice to a more soothing level. 'And what's this obsession with class, Frannie? Your whole life is governed by rules and society and wanting to be perceived in a certain way. People are people, whether they are rich or poor, well educated or illiterate.'

'You wouldn't understand.'

'Try me,' he said, pulling her to face him.

She looked so lost, so forlorn that he regretted his outburst. He'd just wanted her to admit that she was just as human as he, that she had the same desires, the same needs, no matter how hard she tried to bury them.

'All my life I've been expected to behave in a certain way. To dress appropriately, to speak in the right way, to be interesting to gentlemen, but not *too* interesting. Every single day of my life I've been told again and again to conform.'

He watched her, saw the pain on her face and realised that she must have struggled with society's expectations over the years.

'A wife should run a comfortable home for her husband. A wife should conduct herself with dignity and decorum at all times. A wife should never question or nag her husband as to where he's been. A wife should provide and raise well-mannered children.'

'That's the expectation?' Ben asked.

'Yes. And I know I don't *have* to conform, but in reality I do. This is my world, Ben. If I break the rules, I'd be shunned by everyone I know, cast out. What would I do then?'

'And that's why your family are so insistent on maintaining the pretence that everything is well, even when they are in so much debt.'

'What would they do with a small country cottage? My father is a viscount, brought up to be a leader of men. He has been told throughout his life that he is important, he matters. To take that away from him would destroy him.'

'And you?' Ben asked quietly.

'Who knows? I'm not brave enough to leave everything behind and I don't want to desert my family.' She sounded resigned to her fate. 'But I don't think I care like my parents do, not about keeping up appearances. Everyone knows we are in debt anyway. I find it ridiculous the pretence we go through, incurring more debts just to make it seem like everything is normal.'

'What would society say if they saw you in here with me?' Ben asked, leaning in and placing a gentle kiss on Francesca's cheek. She didn't pull away this time, instead her whole body sank into his.

'I don't think I'd get many invitations, my social calendar would look rather bare.'

They both fell silent for a few minutes, contemplating her answer.

'Come,' he said eventually, guiding her gently along the path again, 'Let's enjoy the gardens.'

The argument that had sizzled between them was now almost entirely forgotten, but Ben knew their kiss was not. As he led her down one of the well-manicured paths he could feel her heart beating hard inside her chest. One day he would get her to see that her happiness was more important than leading a conventional life. And one day very soon he would kiss her again somewhere he wouldn't feel guilty for stripping her naked and spending the whole night making love to her.

Chapter Eleven

'Don't make eye contact,' Caroline Yaxley whispered, 'or we'll never be rid of him.'

Francesca was sitting with her sister and Miss Yaxley at the perimeter of the ballroom, thoroughly enjoying herself. When she'd been a debutante Francesca had revelled in the friendship of a close and lovely group of female friends, but over the years they'd lost contact, mainly due to her late husband's dislike of her going out and enjoying herself. Felicity and Miss Yaxley were huddled together, talking so fast about so many topics it was hard to keep up, but their faces were alight with excitement making them both look beautiful.

'He's such a bore,' Felicity said, casting her eyes down to the ground. 'I can make small talk until I'm blue in the face, but it's so difficult with Mr Witherington.'

Glancing surreptitiously over her shoulder, Francesca identified the gentleman in question—a pallid and uncertain-looking man in his mid-thirties.

'Don't look,' Felicity and Miss Yaxley whispered together, pulling Francesca round to face forward again.

'Anyway, the Duke proposed and Georgina accepted him, even though she's completely in love with someone else,' Caroline said, sighing dramatically.

They were discussing the house party Felicity hadn't been invited to the previous weekend, the one Ben had disappeared off to. *Ben.* Francesca felt the heat rise in her cheeks as she remembered their illicit embraces shared in the private gardens. She should never have been so reckless, so bold, but she couldn't bring herself to regret her actions. Every day and every night since she'd found herself thinking of him, remembering how he tasted, how his lips felt on hers, imagining what else might have happened between them had they been somewhere more private and a little warmer.

'Good evening, ladies,' a deep voice said from just behind them. Francesca felt herself stiffen and hoped her sister, with her all-seeing eyes, wouldn't notice her reaction.

'Mr Crawford,' Caroline gushed, 'How wonderful to see you.'

Feeling a momentary pang of jealousy, she wondered how well Ben knew Miss Yaxley. They'd been at the house party together and everyone knew there were different rules outside London.

'Any news on Lady Georgina?' Ben asked cryptically.

Miss Yaxley shrugged, then sighed. 'She's stubborn, always has been.'

'I have a feeling things will work out all the same,' Ben said. 'Now, ladies, you must excuse me, but I am going to deprive you of Lady Somersham's company. She promised to teach me how to dance a Scotch Reel.'

'You're dancing again,' Felicity said with a smile.

Francesca nodded, not able to do anything else. Really she shouldn't be dancing at balls until her mourning period had completely finished. It was one thing to attend as a chaperon, quite another to be seen gaily prancing around with another man on her arm while she was still meant to be remembering her late husband. Still she felt the frisson of excitement she always did when given the opportunity to dance and allowed Ben to assist her to her feet.

'How was the house party?' Francesca asked, not wanting to pry, but unable to help herself.

'A disaster. Robertson made a complete mess of everything,' Ben said with a sigh, 'He has fallen head over heels in love with Lady Georgina, but was too much of a fool to admit it and now has ruined everything.'

Although she hadn't met Sam Robertson she knew a little about him from how Ben spoke of him and the rumours that circulated in society. He and Lady Georgina were of completely different social classes and it was unlikely a romance between them could ever work out, but she felt sorry for Ben's friend all the same.

'Still, he's a lucky devil with a smooth tongue, I have a feeling he'll persuade Lady Georgina to pass over her Duke before the week is out.'

'Surely not?' Francesca asked, shocked at the idea of the daughter of an earl breaking off her engagement to a duke for a man of a much lower social class. It was the stuff of fairy tales, and romantic in theory, but everyone knew fairy tales couldn't be translated into real-life moments.

'Let's hope so. He's a good man, one of the best. I doubt I'd still be alive today if it wasn't for him. I want him to find some happiness.'

'You met him in Australia?' Francesca asked as they circled the ballroom, waiting for the announcement of the next dance.

Ben shook his head. 'On the transport ship. I'd already served almost two years on one of the hulk ships on the Thames and I was a shadow of my former self by the time we were actually transported, but meeting Robertson saved me.'

'He was a young boy, too?' She desperately wanted to know more about his life after his conviction, but didn't want him to relive the worst parts unnecessarily.

'Even younger,' Ben said with a grimace. 'I was twelve when I was convicted, he was just ten.'

'And you stayed together throughout your time in Australia?'

'We did. Our first job was north of Sydney Cove, digging a road. Then after that we were taken as convict workers to Mr Fitzgerald's farm.'

'The Mr Fitzgerald I've met?' Francesca asked with a frown. They seemed such good friends, not like convict worker and landowner.

'His father. Mr Fitzgerald was a good man. Perhaps the best man I've ever had the good fortune to know.' The words were said solemnly and Francesca could tell they were heartfelt and genuine. 'He saved me. He saved *us*, Sam and I. He plucked us from the awful abyss that all convicts stare into at some point of their sentence and taught us there is good in the world.'

'He sounds like a wonderful man.' Francesca felt the tears welling up, threatening to spill down her cheeks, and heard the thick quality to her voice. Ben had only needed someone like Mr Fitzgerald to rescue him because she'd not been strong enough to save him from her father's cruel machinations.

'He was...' Sam paused, his solemn expression turning to a grin as George Fitzgerald approached them.

'Lady Somersham,' Fitzgerald greeted her, 'a pleasure as always.'

'We were just talking about your father,' Ben said.

'Ben...' Francesca paused, then quickly corrected herself. 'Mr Crawford was telling me how he saved him and Mr Robertson.'

'Always was a sentimental fool,' Fitzgerald said with a sombre shake of his head. 'Has Crawford told you the story of why he took him and Robertson under his wing?'

Shaking her head, Francesca waited for either man to continue.

'He got it into his head those two reprobates were heroes,' Fitzgerald said, keeping a straight face, but only just.

'What Fitzgerald isn't telling you,' Ben said, cutting in, 'is he was foolish enough to nearly be killed by a poisonous snake and Robertson and myself put our own lives on the line wrestling the monstrous beast to the ground and saving his life.'

'A mild exaggeration,' Fitzgerald murmured, 'But there *was* a snake and it did spring and if it had bitten me it would have been deadly.'

'Do we regret it?' Ben asked, dodging a punch on the arm from Fitzgerald, and Francesca found herself laughing as the two friends grinned at one another.

'You two wouldn't know what to do with yourselves without me,' Fitzgerald said.

'It's true,' Ben said once Fitzgerald had taken his leave.

'He's a good man just like his father and, when Robertson and I were at our lowest, they showed us how to be human again.'

She wanted to ask more, wanted to learn every little detail about the time he'd spent in Australia, but at that moment the music started up from the next dance and Ben pulled her forward. For now she would have to content herself with that little insight into his life.

Breathless and laughing, Francesca looked radiant as they finished the dance with a curtsy and a bow. She was a wonderful dancer, her body moved instinctively and her feet never missed a step, but what really made her a pleasure to dance with was the light in her eyes, the pure enjoyment and the happiness when she was dancing to the music.

'Lady Somersham,' Lord Huntley said disapprovingly as Ben escorted her from the dance floor, looking for a glass of something cool to refresh them both.

'Lord Huntley, what a surprise. I did not expect to see you tonight,' Francesca said and Ben could hear the note of panic in her voice.

'I decided to attend at the last minute,' Lord Huntley said with a dismissive wave of his hand. 'I see you are dancing.' It was a simple comment, but his voice was loaded with meaning.

'I am,' she said after a moment's hesitation. After all, she could hardly deny it.

'My fault, I'm afraid,' Ben said cheerfully. 'I rather bullied her into it.'

Lord Huntley turned to him for the first time with an air of interest.

'I don't think we've had the pleasure of an introduction,' he said, his eyes narrowing ever so slightly. Their meeting a few weeks earlier evidently hadn't made much of an impression on the Viscount.

'Lord Huntley, this is Mr Crawford,' Francesca said. He saw her hesitate before adding, 'He is an old friend of the family, we've known each other since childhood.'

Lord Huntley inclined his head, out of habit more than politeness, but Ben saw the shrewd and calculating look in his eye.

'Mr Crawford,' he said slowly, 'I was under the impression you've only recently arrived in the country.'

'That's right,' Ben said, appraising the older man. He might appear bombastic and pompous, but there was an observant man underneath the bluster.

'I'd be interested in how you and Lady Somersham have managed to maintain a friendship with you not residing in the country,' he said.

Francesca gave a nervous laugh and Ben felt his heart shrivel a little. This was the man she was going to marry. This cruel old bully who would slowly squeeze the life out of her until there was no more vibrancy, no more free spirit. She'd be crushed under the weight of his constant disapproval. She deserved so much more than a lifetime of misery with Lord Huntley.

'Letters,' Ben said shortly. 'Lady Somersham is a fantastic correspondent.'

'I wouldn't know,' Lord Huntley murmured, looking at the woman he was determined to make his wife. 'Letters make it all the way to Australia, then?'

'I hope so,' Ben said, 'otherwise the weekly instructions I send my land steward are a little pointless.'

It would be foolish to underestimate the man standing in front of them. He already knew more about Ben than anyone else in London and that made Ben uneasy. He obviously distrusted Ben and would probably do anything to ensure he and Lady Somersham didn't spend any more time together.

'Seeing as you are dancing now, I will take the next dance,' Lord Huntley said, addressing himself to Francesca. It was said as a statement rather than request to dance and Ben saw the moment of rebellion flare in Francesca's eyes before she submitted and nodded demurely.

'Of course, Lord Huntley.'

'I'm sure you'll be going back to Australia soon,' Huntley said over his shoulder. 'It is a pity you'll miss the wedding.'

'A shame,' Ben murmured, watching Francesca's stiff posture as they walked away.

They lined up for the next dance and Ben gave a snort of disgust when the musicians struck up for a waltz. It was the most intimate of dances allowed at a society ball, a wonderful dance where it was perfectly acceptable to hold your partner in your arms while you swept them around the dance floor, and now Francesca was being subjected to dancing it with Lord Huntley.

'They don't look very well matched,' Fitzgerald said as he came to stand next to Ben.

'He's not the sort of man I'd wish upon anyone,' Ben said quietly, unable to tear his eyes from the Lord Huntley's oversized hands resting on Francesca's waist.

'Especially not someone you care for,' Fitzgerald murmured.

Ben began to protest, but found his friend had already slipped away. And if he was honest he *did* care for Francesca. Every day he spent with her, he found it harder to deny the depth of the feelings he had for her. It wasn't just desire that clouded his mind every time he looked at her, it was something much more than that.

'Don't be a fool,' he murmured to himself. Francesca had made it perfectly clear where her priorities lay. She would put saving her family from the shame of financial ruin and securing her sister a dowry above her own happiness. And that meant there was no future for them.

It wasn't even just the money that separated them. Ben was a wealthy man now, but what he didn't have was the pure bloodline a woman like Francesca was meant to marry into. He could never be truly accepted into her world, even though it was ridiculous to be separated for such an inconsequential detail.

Friendship, he told himself. That was what they'd had when they were young and that was what they were building now.

And if he hated the idea of Francesca spending even one second in another man's arms, well, he could put that down to the concern of a friend rather than jealousy.

Forcing himself to turn away, he'd only taken one step when he came face to face with Felicity, standing there beaming at him with Miss Yaxley on her arm.

'Walk with us,' Felicity requested, smiling sweetly in an expression that was reflected on Miss Yaxley's face as Ben looked from one to the other.

'For some strange reason I feel nervous all of a sudden,' Ben said, offering an arm to each of the young ladies.

'We're just curious,' Miss Yaxley said.

'How do you know my sister so well, Mr Crawford?' Felicity asked.

'After such a long time out of the country.'

'I wouldn't have thought you would remember many people from your childhood.'

Ben waited in case there was any more, his head already
spinning from the double act of Felicity and Miss Yaxley.

'Has your sister not told you?' he asked.

'She's being very coy. Apart from saying she knew you
from years ago she's been very tight-lipped.'

'Irritatingly,' added Miss Yaxley with a smile on her
face. 'But rumour would have it that you've been out of the
country for eighteen years, which would have made Lady
Somersham only ten when you left.'

'And that seems rather young for such a friendship to
endure,' Felicity added.

Ben shrugged. 'I don't know what to tell you ladies.'

'The truth,' Felicity said quickly. 'How do you know
Francesca?'

'We were friends in childhood,' he said simply.

'And...?' Miss Yaxley asked.

'And nothing.'

Felicity sighed, 'I told you, Caroline, it was too much to
hope for.'

Caroline scowled and shook her head in disappointment.
'So you haven't been corresponding all this time?'

'I'm sorry to be a disappointment, but, no...' He paused,
but realised he needed to know what they were talking
about. 'What was too much to hope for?'

Felicity waved a dismissive hand, 'Oh, that you'd been in
love with Francesca for eighteen years and had come back
to rescue her from the clutches of the evil Lord Huntley.'

Ben felt his eyes widen before he could gain control of
himself.

'Shame,' Miss Yaxley said, shaking her head.

'It would have been romantic.'

'And an answer to the Huntley problem.'

'The Huntley problem?' Ben asked, feeling exhausted by the two minutes of conversation. He wondered if the young women were always like this and realised he didn't want to find out.

'You know,' Felicity said, nodding her head towards the dance floor where Lord Huntley still had Francesca in his arms, *'the Huntley problem.'*

'No one wants Lady Somersham to marry Lord Huntley,' Miss Yaxley said dramatically.

'Well, Father does and Lord Huntley,' Felicity corrected her friend, 'But no one whose opinion should actually matter does.'

'Have you spoken to your sister about this?' Ben asked, wondering if Felicity knew her sister was mainly doing it to provide her with a dowry.

'Francesca still thinks I'm about eight years old. She won't discuss it with me—I think she thinks she's protecting me.'

'Soon it will be too late,' Miss Yaxley said ominously.

'Perhaps you could talk to her,' Felicity suggested, turning to Ben.

'I think you overestimate our friendship,' he murmured. He didn't want to tell the young woman in front of him that he had already expressed unease at Francesca's choice of future husband and been unable to sway her opinion away from the decision. 'Perhaps you should talk to her about her motivations behind the marriage.'

Felicity regarded him for at least twenty seconds without saying anything before she groaned. 'She's doing it for me, isn't she? To protect me or some such nonsense.'

'I really think you should ask your sister,' he said.

'If she's marrying that old goat purely to protect me, I will not be very happy,' Felicity said to Miss Yaxley.

'It's the sort of thing she'd do,' Miss Yaxley agreed. 'Sacrifice herself so you could have a better future.'

'I bet he's promised to provide a dowry for me,' Felicity said, pursing her lips together. 'Francesca is always talking about me marrying some nice young man and getting out of the way of Father's *ill-advised schemes.*'

'Even if it means she'll spend the rest of her life miserable,' Miss Yaxley said with a sad shake of her head.

'Thank you, Mr Crawford,' Felicity said, relinquishing his arm. 'Please excuse me, I have a sister to go and batter some sense into.'

Both young women curtsied and hurried off, their heads bent together as if they were plotting and scheming. Feeling a little dazed at the speed of the conversation, Ben moved to the edge of the ballroom, found a convenient marble pillar to lean against and took a moment to straighten his thoughts.

His eyes searched for Francesca in the crowd and he saw her finishing the waltz and curtsying prettily to Lord Huntley. Ben knew she would be angry at him for letting her sister come to the conclusion that Francesca was marrying Lord Huntley to provide a better life for her, but he couldn't have done much more. Maybe Felicity could talk some sense into her sister.

Chapter Twelve

Stretching out in one of the comfortable armchairs, Ben read through the latest letter he'd written to his farm manager, checking he'd left nothing out. There were crops to be harvested at this time of year, but knowing how long it would take for the letter to reach Australia Ben's instructions were focused more on the planting and care of the land in the Australian winter, many months from now.

He was just tucking the letter into the envelope when he heard voices downstairs and sat up to listen. Not many of the residents ever got any visitors and he was already up out of his chair and heading for the door when there was an abrupt rap.

'Good morning,' he said with a smile as he opened the door.

Normally the maid who looked after the residences in this building would come and announce any visitors, but this time it looked as though Francesca had pushed through despite the maid's protests to knock on his door herself.

'How dare you?' she asked without any form of greeting.

Ben stepped back, allowing her space to enter. Hesitating, she seemed to weigh up the options, eventually deciding this wasn't an argument she wanted to have in the corridor, so entered his rooms.

There was a mixture of anger and indignation on her face and immediately Ben knew this would be about him letting slip to Felicity the night before that Francesca was only marrying Lord Huntley out of some notion to provide her sister with a better future.

'It wasn't your right,' she said as she turned on him as soon as the door closed behind her.

'Would you care for tea?' he asked calmly, motioning for her to take a seat.

She ignored his question and didn't move towards the armchairs. With a shrug he walked past her and sat down, causing her lips to purse.

'It is my decision who I marry and why I have decided to marry them,' she said with fire in her eyes.

Ben loved her like this. She was so animated, so beautiful, not the downtrodden woman she was forced to be by other men. Francesca would never speak to Lord Huntley like this and it saddened him to think she was soon to be condemned to a life where she was the inferior one in the relationship, not allowed to speak her thoughts or air her grievances.

'Your sister guessed,' he said. 'She's a very intelligent young woman and she knows you well.'

'You could have denied it,' Francesca said.

'I wasn't going to lie. And perhaps Felicity deserves to know what you are planning on sacrificing for her future.'

'She doesn't need to know, she's just a child.'

'You were married by her age,' Ben reminded her gently. 'And I'd served eight years for theft and started building towards a better future.'

'Felicity is young and innocent,' Francesca ground out.

'I think she's more worldly wise than you give her credit for. She's been living with your parents for all these years, too.'

As he watched some of the anger left Francesca and she slowly sank down into one of the armchairs.

'What did she say to you?' Ben asked quietly.

Running a hand over her brow and down the angle of her jaw, Francesca took a moment to answer.

'This morning she came into my room with a tray of tea and toast,' Francesca said, 'And then proceeded to question me with military levels of inquisition about my motives for considering Lord Huntley as my future husband.'

'What did you tell her?' Ben asked.

Francesca sighed. 'I tried to satisfy her curiosity while still remaining vague, but she wasn't having any of it, thanks to you, I presume. She accused me of being a martyr.'

Ben laughed, picturing Francesca's overly dramatic sister calling her a martyr.

'She's not entirely wrong,' he murmured.

'I am not martyring myself for her. I'm just giving her a chance of a better future.'

'At the expense of your own.'

'I don't want to have this argument with you again. I'm angry because of what you told Felicity.'

Ben shrugged. 'I apologise for making you angry, but I'm not sorry your sister knows what you are planning.'

'You are infuriating,' Francesca said through clenched teeth.

'What if your sister doesn't want to ever get married?

What if she wants to travel the world, or work as a governess or set herself up as a merry spinster? You haven't asked her, have you?'

'Don't be ridiculous.'

'It's not ridiculous. You're sacrificing your happiness for something you don't even know your sister wants.'

'Of course she wants to get married. That's what all young ladies do.'

'Just because it is the norm doesn't mean it's what she wants. Think about it—if you could have anything, any future you desired, would you really choose matrimony to a society bore?'

Francesca hesitated 'We don't have a choice,' she said eventually. 'It's not like we can just buy up land and start a farm or go to university and learn a profession. We're women. Our options are severely limited.' Shaking her head, she took a few fortifying deep breaths. 'We're held back at every turn, told to be quiet, to follow orders, to obey others. Just look at what happened when I tried to defy my father and speak out to defend you. No one listened. Because I was a girl.'

'I know,' Ben said, a hint of conciliation in his voice. 'And I also understand the demands of society for you to conform, but some of those limits are put in place by you.'

She opened her mouth as if to protest, but slowly closed it again without saying a word. He saw the sadness in her eyes, saw the hurt and pain and uncertainty and instantly he was on his feet, wrapping his arms around her. Resting her head on his chest, she burrowed in to him and Ben felt a pang of sympathy for her. All she was doing was trying to make the best decisions for her family, despite not having many attractive options. He just wished she wasn't going to throw away her entire future in the process.

'How did you leave it with your sister?' he asked softly, giving in to the temptation to bring one of his hands up to run through her silky hair.

He felt Francesca grimace into his chest before she spoke. 'Felicity is refusing to accept any dowry Lord Huntley provides.' She sighed and shook her head. 'It's just her little protest. I'm sure when some young gentleman catches her eye she will take the dowry to smooth the path.'

Ben wasn't so sure and he could tell by her tone Francesca wasn't entirely convinced either.

'So you marched all the way over here to tell me off?' he asked, smiling into her hair.

He loved that she could be so natural with him. It was healthy to be able to voice your feelings of dismay or irritation. Although he'd never been in a relationship that lasted long enough to have first-hand experience of this, he'd had the best role models. Fitzgerald's parents, the kindly couple who had taken him and Robertson in after the boys had saved their son from the bite of a deadly snake, had been wonderful role models. The couple had both grown up in England with all the rules and expectations of society. The older Mr Fitzgerald was the second son of an impoverished baron and as such his wife was from the upper echelons of the gentry. However, years of living in Australia, surviving where many others couldn't, had meant their marriage was a partnership. It was equal, with both parties having a say in the decisions and no one overruling the other. Of course they argued and disagreed, but in a healthy way, and always they came together at the end of it to find some mutual agreement and way forward.

If Ben ever settled down, that was the sort of relationship he wanted. With a wife not afraid to speak her mind with him.

Glancing down at Francesca, he found himself imagining what it would be like to wake up to her every morning. It was a tempting fantasy, but he knew it could never be anything more than that.

'Perhaps I should show you how sorry I am for upsetting you,' he murmured and felt her stiffen in his arms.

'How would you do that?' she asked, her voice coming out as no more than a whisper.

'I can think of one or two ways.'

As she hesitated, looking up at him before nodding, Ben felt the desire almost overwhelm him. He'd found women attractive before, but never had he felt this level of desire. It was as though he *needed* to be with her, to show her pleasure and to know every inch of her.

Gently he led her into his bedroom, seeing the flush of anticipation on her cheeks and pausing to look into her eyes.

'Are you sure?' he asked. He needed to check now, when he was still lucid, still able to stop himself. Soon he would be lost in her, oblivious to everything except how their bodies and souls were meeting.

'I'm sure,' she said with an unwavering voice. He had to remember she wasn't a shy virgin, she'd been married for years and as such wouldn't be a stranger to the bedroom.

'Come.' He held out a hand, waited for her to take it, then pulled her towards the bed. Softly he kissed her, reining in some of the passion he felt so as not to overwhelm her entirely. Her lips were warm and inviting, welcoming him in, and before long he was lost. All he could think about was the woman in his arms.

Frantically he pushed at her dress, trying to expose a little more skin, but it was laced up tightly and refused to budge.

'Poor choice of clothing,' he murmured into her ear as he spun her round to fight with the fastenings. A giggle turned into a groan as he caught her earlobe in his mouth, nipping it as he fiddled with her dress.

'I didn't dress for ease this morning,' Francesca said as she caught her breath. 'I wasn't expecting this.'

Neither had he been, although he'd fantasized about this moment long enough. Every night he'd woken up hard with desire after dreaming of this.

With a swell of triumph the dress came loose and he managed to push it down to her hips. Francesca did a little wiggle to help the garment on its way and soon it was pooled around her feet. Carefully he lifted her over it, his hands encircling her waist and feeling the warmth of her skin through the cotton chemise she wore.

Ben took a moment to look at her, still far from naked with a collection of petticoats, a cotton chemise and legs clad in white stockings, and he could begin to catch glimpses of her body underneath. Forcing himself not to rush, he ran his hands over her body, loving how she inhaled sharply as his fingers brushed over her more sensitive areas.

As he kissed her again he felt her hands tugging at his jacket, pulling it off over his shoulders before untucking his shirt from his waistband.

'I'm not finished with you yet,' he said, lifting her gently on to the bed, taking his time to rid her of the petticoats before he got to work on her stockings. Slowly he rolled them down her leg, marvelling at the creamy skin underneath. She'd always been tall and her legs were long and slender, just begging to be kissed.

Underneath him Francesca sighed as his mouth met the skin of her legs and she clutched at his shoulders as he worked his way from calf to thigh. Unable to resist, he pushed her chemise higher, revealing the skin all the way to her abdomen, and carried on planting kisses as her hips writhed beneath him.

As his lips skimmed the very top of her thighs he felt her gasp in surprise as he brushed against her most sensitive place. Instinctively he knew that she had never been worshipped as she should, that her husband had never focused on her pleasure, and he felt inordinately pleased that he would be the one to give that to her.

Slowly at first he kissed her, his fingers circling and dipping as her body writhed beneath him. He could feel her hips coming up to meet him, the movement instinctive and natural, and as her breathing quickened he felt her tense, clutch hold of his shoulders before letting out a deep moan of pleasure.

Only once her hips had fallen still did he move, manoeuvring himself so he was above her, looking down into her flushed and beautiful face.

'What...?' she started to say, but couldn't seem to put her question into words.

'You deserve to be worshipped,' he whispered in her ear, kissing along the angle of her jaw and down her neck, tasting the sweetness of her skin. Quickly he pulled off his shirt and in one swift movement rid Francesca of her chemise, too, taking a moment to memorise every wonderful inch of her body.

He felt her hands on his chest, fingers dancing across his skin and delving lower to the waistband of his trousers.

Deftly she unclasped them, pushing them down and looking up into Ben's eyes at the same time.

She was beautiful, with her hair escaping in rebellious tendrils around her face, her cheeks flushed from desire and her lips rosy from being kissed.

'I want you, Ben,' she said quietly but firmly, pulling him down towards her. He loved her determination, her certainty.

Unable to hold himself back any longer, he pushed inside her, groaning at how wonderful it felt. Francesca's hands encircled his back, pulling him in further, and together their bodies began to move in rhythm. It was as though they were made for each other, they fitted together perfectly.

Again and again their bodies came together until he felt Francesca clutch at his back and tighten, a quiet moan escaping from her lips. That was enough to send Ben over the edge and for a long minute he knew nothing but pleasure.

Slowly, as his breathing started to return to normal, he lay down beside Francesca. Normally he made it a rule never to fall asleep with a woman after making love. It complicated things, gave people unrealistic expectations, but today he couldn't have done anything differently even if he wanted to. There was no way he could get up and leave Francesca alone in his bed, he had an overwhelming urge to gather her to him, to spend the rest of the day baring his very soul to her, letting her see every vulnerable part of him.

'Ben,' she said, resting her head on his chest and tracing a lazy pattern on his abdomen. 'Is it often like that?'

He kissed her head before answering.

'No,' he said. 'Not quite like that.'

As he lay there with Francesca on his chest he felt as

though his whole world had shifted. It would be difficult when he had to walk away from this woman.

Francesca must have dozed for she felt heavy and unwilling to move when she woke up.

'Good afternoon,' Ben said from his position at the end of the bed. He was dressed and had a sheaf of papers in his hand as if he'd been reading them while he waited for her to wake.

'What time is it?' she asked, feeling the panic rising up inside her.

'Only two.'

She'd slept for nearly three hours. Self-consciously she pulled the sheets up a bit higher, aware that she was completely naked under the bedclothes while Ben was sitting there with his dignity intact.

'I should be getting back home soon. I said I was going shopping with an old friend.'

Ben nodded and she felt a stab of disappointment. Part of her imagined him gathering her up in his arms, promising they'd never be parted again and whispering his undying affection in her ear. Quietly she snorted. *That* was never going to happen. Ben had made it quite clear over their short acquaintance that his relationships with women were short-lived only. He would give them affection and share pleasure, but he didn't get emotionally attached, not in a lasting way. Eight days, that was what he suggested they spend together, and after that they would disappear from one another's lives again.

As she shuffled off the bed, pulling the sheets closely around her, she wondered at the direction of her thoughts. She shouldn't be thinking of a future with Ben, her path was already decided. When she'd kissed him she'd known exactly how things were going to end up, and it wasn't with a walk down the aisle—at least not with him.

'I have seen you naked,' Ben remarked mildly, 'so if you'd prefer not to break your neck hopping around in that sheet, that would be acceptable.'

Looking at him with her best haughty expression, she said nothing. He was enjoying this—she could tell by the barely repressed grin on his face. Deciding to shock him, she stood straight, dropped the sheet and looked him in the eye, challenging him to hold her gaze.

He couldn't. Within three seconds his eyes had dropped to her body. She refused to blush, despite the heat already creeping into her cheeks, and waited for his eyes to come back up to meet hers.

'Perhaps you shouldn't have done that, Frannie,' he murmured, dropping the papers he was holding on to the floor and moving towards her.

'In your own words, you have seen me naked,' she said, finding it difficult not to sink into him as soon as he came close. 'There should be nothing surprising for you here.'

'Not surprising,' he said. 'Awe-inspiring, desire-inducing, but not surprising.'

Gently he ran his fingers over her shoulders, making her skin feel on fire and before she knew what was happening he'd tumbled her back on the bed, his mouth seeking hers.

An hour later Francesca got up again, this time dodging the hand that tried to pull her back to bed.

'I have to go,' she said with a giggle.

'Don't. Spend the whole night here with me.'

'They'll send out a search party,' she said, trying to sound stern as she struggled into her layers of clothing.

'You could send a note,' Ben suggested.

'What would it say? Don't worry, I'm spending the night with a man of questionable morals and giving him my virtue?'

'That would just about cover it,' Ben said, rolling over on to his back and grinning. 'Will anyone have missed you?'

Francesca considered and shook her head. As a widow she had a little more freedom than she had when she was a debutante. It was perfectly acceptable for her to lead her own life without informing her father of her every last move. Of course it wasn't perfectly acceptable to spend the day naked in a man's rooms, but no one would ever need to know that.

Finally dressed, she perched down on the edge of the bed, letting her head drop back as Ben came up behind her and kissed her neck.

'Do you regret this, Frannie?' he asked softly.

'No.' The word came out quickly, but she realised it was the truth.

Never before had she considered an affair, not throughout her marriage and not since her husband had passed away. It just hadn't been something she did. Although she hadn't loved her husband, she did believe in the marriage vows she'd uttered and they'd included being faithful until death.

What she didn't feel was any regret about their intimacies today. One day soon she would be married again, but until then, or more precisely until she had given her promise to another man, there was nothing wrong in enjoying herself a little.

'Do you?' she asked.

'Never.' He kissed her again on the neck and she felt the heat beginning to rise in her body. It was almost too difficult to pull away.

'I should go,' she said, standing reluctantly.

'When shall I see you again?' Ben asked.

Feeling elated that he didn't want to get rid of her as fast as possible and then never see her again, she considered.

'Felicity has persuaded Father to let her host a dinner party tomorrow night. Lord Huntley has sent his apologies so will not be there. Would you like to attend?' Too late she realised the foolishness of the invite. It was her father who had lied and condemned Ben to eight years' hard labour and transportation for theft, there was no way he would ever want to be in the same room as the man.

'It would be my pleasure,' Ben said.

As she turned to look at him she noticed a steely expression on his face and wondered what she had just done.

'Father might not even be there...' she said, trying to work out why he had accepted. It wasn't as though she could withdraw the invite now.

'All the better,' he said serenely. 'Until tomorrow, my dear Frannie.'

She rose and moved to the door, pausing as she heard his footsteps behind her. With her hand on the doorknob she turned to find him right behind her, completely naked and completely unabashed.

'Goodbye,' he said, kissing her until she forgot what she was meant to be doing.

'Goodbye,' she said once he'd released her and quickly slipped out through the door, pausing on the landing to compose herself before she made her way down to the street.

Chapter Thirteen

With great interest, Ben stood for a moment and regarded the façade of Francesca's father's house. It was a little shabby looking, with the door needing a coat of paint and the railings peeling and starting to rust. Certainly not up to the standards of the other houses in the street.

He had not hesitated in accepting the invitation to dinner, even though it would mean spending an evening in the company of the man responsible for sending him to Australia as a convict. Eighteen years ago Francesca's father had accused him of stealing a large stash of valuables from the country estate. Of course Ben had been innocent and the only item found when he'd been searched was the small locket Francesca had given him the summer before as a token of her affection, but it had been enough for the magistrate who had uprooted the twelve-year-old Ben from the family home and thrown him in jail.

Ben had begged the magistrate to ask Francesca, to hear that the locket had been given as a gift and not stolen. The magistrate had refused, but a few days later Francesca had broken free from her father's imprisonment and made her way to the jail. She'd told anyone who would listen that Ben was innocent, that the locket had been a gift, but it hadn't been enough. Francesca had been dismissed—after all, she was just a girl and it was her word against the word of a viscount.

Ben would never forget the moment Francesca was dragged away. It had been the last time he'd seen her and the moment that had sealed his fate. A week later he'd been found guilty of theft and sent first to the hulk ships on the Thames and finally to Australia.

His father had tirelessly continued to dig into the case after Ben had been sent away and in one of his letters years later he told Ben he thought it was all a scam on the part of Lord Pottersdown who, it would appear, had taken out some sort of insurance against the valuable items in his home and claimed when they had gone missing, no doubt also selling the items quietly at the same time to get double their worth.

Over the years he'd thought about Francesca's father rather a lot. At first he'd been bitter, swearing he would get his revenge on the older man, but after a while the bitterness had seeped out of him. Once Mr Fitzgerald had taken him in Ben had realised the anger he felt towards Lord Pottersdown was slowly draining away and, as he'd built himself into a success, he found he was thinking about the old Viscount less and less. It had only been Francesca who had haunted his thoughts, the girl he'd left behind.

Quickly he mounted the steps, trying to push away the entirely inappropriate memory of Francesca standing in his bedroom, looking him rebelliously in the eye and dropping the bedsheet she had wrapped around her body. That image would never leave him.

'Mr Crawford,' he said to the footman who opened the door. He was shown in to the drawing room where he'd visited previously and wasn't surprised to find the small room was already almost full to bursting.

'Mr Crawford,' Felicity gushed as she spotted him, 'What a delight to see you again. I was so happy when Francesca told me you would be attending our humble dinner party this evening.' Felicity paused, took his arm and lowered her voice. 'Has she forgiven you yet?'

Ben remembered their morning spent in his bed and grinned, 'I think she's getting there,' he said.

'Good. I'd hate to see you out of favour because of me. Now, who should I introduce you to?'

Ben surveyed the room, finding nine other people besides Felicity and himself. Some he knew, some he only recognised, but he had eyes for only one. She was standing amid a small group, listening intently to what one young woman was saying, nodding her head in an animated fashion.

'Will your parents be in attendance?' he asked, noting their absence from the drawing room.

'Father will, although I doubt he will appear before dinner. Mother is indisposed.' She spoke the words without any hint of frustration. Ben had learned Lady Pottersdown hadn't been seen at a social event since Francesca had married and it seemed Felicity had just accepted her mother's withdrawal from society graciously. 'Of course,' Felicity said, turning to Ben, 'you must know my parents if you were acquainted with Francesca in childhood.'

'We have met,' Ben said, trying to keep any hint of emotion from his voice, 'but only once so I doubt they would remember me.'

It was a white lie. He had met Francesca's parents on more than one occasion, fleeting glimpses of annoyed faces as he was chased from the house by the footmen or reprimanded by Francesca's governesses for leading her astray.

'Good evening,' Lord Pottersdown said as he appeared in the doorway, face ruddied by too much drink both today and in the past few decades. Felicity had been wrong about him waiting to make an appearance until dinner was served. On his arm he felt Francesca's sister stiffen and wondered if the older man knew how much embarrassment and suffering he brought to his children, or if he just didn't care.

'Father,' Francesca said, breaking away from her little group with a smile of apology, 'I didn't think you were joining us until later.'

Everyone was focused on the interaction between Lord Pottersdown and his eldest daughter so Ben took the opportunity to look over the man who had condemned him to transportation for the sake of a couple of hundred pounds.

Lord Pottersdown looked much older than his fifty-odd years, his face lined and sallow in complexion with the bulbous nose that gave away his habit for over-imbibing. His mid-section had long ago run to fat and his clothes bulged across his stomach. Today there was a smile on his face, but an air of panic in his eyes.

Calm, Ben told himself. He had spent years working on the feelings of hatred and resentment he had towards those who had wronged him. When he'd first been taken in by Mr Fitzgerald he had been bitter and the feelings of hatred had eaten him up every day. Slowly, with a lot of love and patience, the older man had helped Ben to see that the only person these feelings were hurting was himself. Over time he'd shown Ben how to let go of the past and look to the future, to see everything he had been blessed with and even appreciate how his difficult interlude had shaped him into the man he was today.

Still, seeing Lord Pottersdown in the flesh again brought back some of feelings of anger and hatred.

'I must go and introduce myself,' Ben said, noting Felicity's surprise, but deciding to ignore it.

Quickly he moved over to where Francesca was unsuccessfully trying to manoeuvre her father from the room without making a scene. She glanced at him with a frown and seemed to try to signal with her eyes for him to keep away. Ben couldn't do that, something was pushing him to step closer, to finally look the man who'd caused him so much pain in the eye.

'Lord Pottersdown,' Ben said, 'what a lovely home you have.'

The Viscount and Francesca both looked around in mild surprise as if they'd never been paid such a compliment before.

'Thank you,' he said. His words weren't slurred, but there was a soft quality to the consonants that suggested Lord Pottersdown wasn't on his first drink of the evening.

'Crawford,' he said, offering his hand. He waited to see if there would be any recognition, but Lord Pottersdown's eyes remained vacant. Condemning someone to transportation wasn't enough to make an impression on the Viscount, it would seem.

'Father,' Francesca said, shooting Ben a concerned look, 'why don't you step through to the dining room? I'm sure dinner is just about to be announced.'

'In a moment, Francesca,' the older man said with a dismissive wave of the hand, 'She does fuss,' he said, directing his words at Ben.

The arrival of another guest, a woman in her early forties who Ben did not know, stole Francesca's attention for a moment and Ben quickly guided Lord Pottersdown out of earshot before she could protest.

'I hear you are a man who likes a game of cards,' Ben said, wasting no time. 'Shall we have a game or two after dinner?'

He saw the older man hesitate and wondered if at last he had learnt his lesson, but after just a couple of seconds Lord Pottersdown was nodding his head, a gleam in his eye.

'I'm sure that can be arranged,' he said. 'Once the ladies retire, of course.'

Ben followed his gaze to where Francesca was deep in conversation with the new guest and he had to hide a smile. He could just imagine Francesca reprimanding her father for his reckless behaviour, even though it was almost unheard of for a daughter to speak to her father in such a manner.

'Wonderful,' Ben said, clapping the older man on the arm. 'I do enjoy a game of cards. Never have much luck, but it's the enjoyment that counts.'

Walking away, Ben fought hard not to grin. He hadn't come to England to get his revenge on the Viscount, not like his friend Sam Robertson who had been almost completely consumed by the idea of revenge against the man who had wronged him. Nevertheless, he wasn't a saint and the opportunity to toy with the man for an hour or two was too good to pass up. Ben had no doubt he would beat the older man in the game of cards and of course there would be wagers, there always were. He planned to make Lord Pottersdown sweat for a while over the amount of money he owed after the card game. In the end he wouldn't actually make the man pay up—that would only serve to hurt Francesca in the long run—but a worrying couple of weeks was the least the man deserved.

Smiling nervously, Francesca glanced again at Ben. He was up to something—she was sure of it. After she'd invited him to the dinner party she'd realised what a foolish idea it had been—it would mean her father and Ben coming face to face. Never had she expected her father to remember the young boy he'd accused of stealing the family's valuables, but she did know Ben wouldn't have forgiven her father for the awful wrong he'd done him all those years ago.

Still, so far Ben was behaving impeccably. He was suave and confident at the dinner table full of people a good few social classes above him and acted as though he'd been born to live the easy life of a gentleman. Half the ladies in attendance were already looking at him with doe eyes and Francesca suspected he would woo the other half before the night was out.

'Gentlemen,' her father said, a very subtle slur to his words that probably no one else would pick up on, but Francesca had had years of experience detecting when her father had tipped over into an inebriated state, 'a glass of port, perhaps?'

Knowing this was her cue, Francesca reluctantly stood and gestured for the ladies to follow her into the drawing room.

As she closed the door behind her she lingered for a second and felt her heart sink when her father's voice drifted through, the suggestion of a card game coming only seconds after she'd left him with the male guests. Hoping Ben would have enough sense to put a stop to any game that left her father risking too much, she stepped away, plastering a cheerful smile on her face and summoning some small talk to distract herself.

'I say, that's rather a lot of money. Surely we should have an upper limit,' a weak-chinned man called Mr Rose said, eyeing Ben uneasily.

'Anyone can withdraw at any time,' Ben said, giving the other players his easy smile. 'There's no pressure to play if you can't meet the wager.'

Four of them sat around the table, with another of the gentlemen already having excused himself, stating he was terrible at cards and withdrawing to join the ladies.

'You know, I think I might just do that,' Mr Rose said after a moment's hesitation.

'And I, these stakes are too high for my meagre income,' a cheerful man by the name of Mr Wisern agreed, standing and executing a little bow before following Mr Rose from the room.

'How about you, Lord Pottersdown?' Ben asked mildly. 'Would you like to retreat, too?'

The Viscount licked his lips nervously and glanced at the cards in his hand. Ben already knew the answer. For the older man betting seemed to be a compulsion, just as drink was. He didn't know his limits, didn't know when to stop and admit defeat. It was no doubt the character flaw that had plunged Francesca's family into so much trouble and Lord Pottersdown wasn't about to change now.

'Perhaps just one or two more hands,' he said.

'Marvellous.' Ben raised the glass of port to his lips, taking the smallest sip. He could handle his alcohol, had drunk many a hardened criminal under the table back home in his youth, but now he was much more cautious. No matter how often you drank alcohol it still muddied your senses, dulling your thoughts and affecting your ability to make sensible decisions. Still, the act of lifting his glass to his lips had the desired effect. Lord Pottersdown unconsciously mirrored him, but instead of a tiny sip he took a few large gulps of the tawny port.

Quickly Ben got into the swing of the card game, letting Lord Pottersdown win a couple of hands to boost his confidence and make him sloppy. After a few minor losses Ben waited for a decent hand of cards. By this point he could read Lord Pottersdown's face and mannerisms easily and knew when the man was confident and when he had a poor hand and was bluffing.

Now there were only two of them they were playing piquet, a game Ben had grown up playing with his father and honed his instincts to perfection over the years in Australia.

'Shall we increase the wager?' Lord Pottersdown asked after winning a moderate sum.

'Why not?' Ben said, trying not to grin. He'd been waiting for the older man to ask, not wanting to push through his wins until there was a substantial amount on the table. 'Shall we say five hundred pounds?'

He could tell it was more than Lord Pottersdown was expecting, but the Viscount clearly didn't want to lose face, and as with all reckless gamblers wherever they were in the world he thought his winning streak would continue and he'd have the chance to make some real money.

'Perhaps just for a game or two,' Lord Pottersdown said, licking his lips and glancing at the door as if expecting some disgruntled creditor to burst in and nab all his winnings from the table.

'Excellent.'

Ben dealt, watching Lord Pottersdown as he studied his cards, deciding which to discard and which to play.

Just as Lord Pottersdown laid down his first cards Francesca burst into the room. Ben didn't look up, knowing she would look either aghast or disapproving. Later he would explain, if she would let him, that he wasn't actually going to collect whatever debt her father ended up owing him, just make the old man sweat. It was the very least he deserved.

'Father,' she said, her tone clipped, and even without looking up Ben could hear the high level of stress in her voice.

'Don't fuss, Francesca,' her father said. 'Go and rejoin the ladies. Mr Crawford and I will be through shortly.'

'You promised,' she said so quietly Ben could barely hear her. What he did note was the sound of complete desperation in her voice. 'Mr Crawford,' she said, turning to him, 'my father regrets that he will have to withdr—' She was cut off by an angry Lord Pottersdown.

'Quiet,' he ordered. 'Remember your place.'

Ben had known this moment would come and resolutely ignored the small voice telling him to stand and comfort the woman who he'd held so tenderly in his arms only a day and a half ago. Later he would explain, later he would kiss the small furrow between her perfectly shaped brows until it disappeared and she forgot all her worries, at least for a short time. But right now he had a card game to win and a viscount to destroy, at least for a few hours.

Glancing up, he saw the mixture of hurt and anger in her

eyes. The hurt was aimed at him, the anger at her father, but he knew it wouldn't take much to sway it the other way.

She sat, folding her arms across her chest in a most unladylike gesture, and watched them, her eyes flitting from one side of the table to the other.

'Shall we continue?' Ben asked.

Lord Pottersdown nodded and the game proceeded. What happened next was like a carefully executed dance. Ben lulled the man into a false sense of security, quickly upped the wager and then proceeded to destroy him. After all of five minutes Lord Pottersdown was sitting with his head in his hands, one thousand pounds worse off, his normally ruddy face completely drained of any colour.

Francesca spared a disgusted glance for her father and stood. She crossed behind where Ben was standing and leaned in. 'Was that your plan all along?' she asked, her voice tight with pain and humiliation, 'Get close to me so you could destroy Father?' The words were said so quietly Lord Pottersdown couldn't hear, not that Ben thought he would take in a stampeding herd of elephants at this point.

He caught her wrist, holding firmly so she couldn't pull away, but ensuring he caused her no discomfort. 'I would never do anything to hurt you, Frannie,' he said.

Her eyes flared with anger, 'You suppose this doesn't hurt me?' she asked.

'Trust me,' he murmured. Quickly she pulled away and strode from the room, her head held high, but Ben knew as soon as she was alone she would let her calm façade crack and the tears would start to flow.

He felt a stab of remorse, but reminded himself that he wasn't actually going to call in the debt. Apart from the worry Francesca would be no worse off and, if things went to plan, his little game with the Viscount would hopefully scare the man to stop gambling at least for a few months.

'Mr Crawford,' Lord Pottersdown said, 'I…er… I am a little low on funds at the moment. All to be resolved soon, of course…'

It would never be resolved.

'A debt is a debt,' Ben said, ensuring his voice was clipped and his manner abrupt.

'Of course, and I never renege on a debt,' Lord Pottersdown said quickly.

That was definitely a lie. A big one. The Viscount owed money all over town and had a reputation for trying to weasel his way out of any small debt he could.

'One thousand pounds, Lord Pottersdown, is not an insignificant amount.'

'No, no, no, no,' the Viscount said, seemingly unable to utter any other sounds.

'And I am not a patient man.'

'If you could just give me a few weeks.'

They both knew Lord Pottersdown would only be further in debt in a few weeks.

'Perhaps there is another solution,' Ben said, tapping his fingers on the table and conjuring up a pensive expression.

'Yes, anything,' the Viscount said eagerly.

'This house must be worth a fair few hundred pounds,' Ben said, looking up theatrically at the ceiling and around the walls.

'It's the family home,' Lord Pottersdown said.

Ben shrugged and fixed a hard stare on the Viscount. 'You have a debt to be settled and so far I haven't heard how you mean to pay it.'

'Surely as a gentleman…' Lord Pottersdown said.

'I suggest in future you find out a little more about whom you're playing against before you commit to such big wagers...' He paused and looked Lord Pottersdown directly in the eye. 'I am no gentleman.'

With his whole body sagging the Viscount began shaking his head, a pleading look in his eyes. 'It was only a game of cards.'

'A wager is a wager,' Ben said firmly. 'Of course I could let it be known about town that you have reneged outright on a debt. I doubt it would take long for the rest of your creditors to become nervous and come calling.'

'No,' Lord Pottersdown said quickly. Ben wondered just how extensive the man's borrowing was. The rumours had Lord Pottersdown barely surviving, but Ben thought the situation might be even more dire.

'The house then,' Ben said firmly.

'Where will my family live? My wife, my daughters?'

'I'm not a cruel man, Lord Pottersdown. They may remain living here until alternative accommodation is found.'

'Alternative accommodation?'

'I believe there are some cheaper rooms south of the river.'

'South of the river?' Lord Pottersdown spluttered, some of the colour returning to his face. 'I'm a *viscount*, a man from a long and noble line. I can't live *south of the river*.'

'You're a man so in debt you're selling your own daughter off to a scoundrel who has a reputation for beating his wives,' Ben said quietly. He stood. 'I shall return in a week's time with my solicitor. I suggest you have yours ready and waiting. Otherwise I shall ensure the rest of your debts are called in.'

Before Lord Pottersdown could say another word Ben left

the room. Of course he wouldn't call again—instead he'd let the man stew thinking he'd just lost the family home. No matter what the old scoundrel had done to him he wouldn't see Francesca and her sister homeless.

Chapter Fourteen

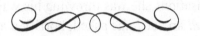

'How could you?' Francesca said as she caught up with him, grasping at his arm and pulling him to face her. She was livid, angry beyond anything she'd ever felt before, and all because of this man. Over the last few weeks Ben had got under her skin, burrowed deep and found a way into her heart. She cared for him, thought about him every moment of every day, and now she was confronted with the truth: he'd only ever been using her to get close to her father. To destroy him. To destroy their whole family.

'Hush,' Ben said, cupping her face in his hands and kissing her softly on the lips.

Francesca pulled away, aware that they were in the middle of a well-populated street and also that she shouldn't be kissing the enemy.

'Don't hush me. I trusted you. I…' she lowered her voice '… I gave myself to you.'

He smiled at her and she thought there was affection in

his eyes, but knew that couldn't be true. You didn't destroy the life of someone you cared about.

'Frannie...' he said, but she pushed on.

'Was that your plan all along? To get your revenge on my father?' She felt the tears spill out on to her cheeks. 'I know he wronged you, Ben, I wished it could be different every day of the last eighteen years, but I thought you cared at least a little about me.'

'Stop this, Frannie,' he said, still remarkably calm amid all the accusations she was throwing his way.

'Was it *all* an act?' she asked, horrified at the pleading tone in her voice. When he'd kissed her and touched her it had felt so real, so wonderful. It would hurt so much to know that for him it had been nothing more than a step on his plan to get close to her.

'No,' he said. 'It wasn't an act.'

She searched his face and thought he was telling the truth, but didn't trust her judgement much.

'But you planned this all along? Got close to me to get to my father? Always knew you would make us homeless?'

'My beautiful girl,' Ben said, cupping her face and shaking his head. 'Is that what you really think?'

She didn't know what to think. Seeing him standing here so calmly, so innocently, it was hard to believe he'd just condemned her family to losing their home and admitting to the world they were actually paupers.

'Come with me,' he said, taking her gently by the arm and leading her down the street. They were close to St James's Park, the gates just a little further down the street, and Francesca could see Ben was leading her that way. Despite what had happened earlier that evening she realised she trusted him enough to go into the park with him, even though it wasn't what young ladies did this late at night.

Once inside the park he sat her on a bench, took off his coat and draped it over her shoulders. She hadn't even noticed she was shivering after coming out without a coat.

'I hate your father, Frannie. The man ruined my life, condemned me to an eight-year sentence of transportation and hard labour for a crime I didn't commit and tore me from my family. I haven't seen my father for eighteen years.'

Still shaking with anger, she was surprised when Ben caught her chin and tilted her head so she looked up at him.

'What your father did to me deserves punishment.'

'I know.' Deep down she knew Ben had every right to seek revenge on her father, but she'd been so convinced he cared for her, even just a little. So convinced that what they'd shared was real.

'You didn't have to pretend to like me to get close to my father,' she said, feeling more morose than angry now. 'He would have played cards with anyone.'

Francesca was looking down at her hands so was taken by surprise when Ben kissed her. His lips were warm and inviting and for a moment she wished she could just abandon herself to him and forget everything that made her life hard.

'Does this feel like pretence to you?' he asked, pulling away only slightly so his breath tickled her face as he spoke.

Instinctively she shook her head. It felt real and meaningful and wonderful.

'I like you, Frannie. And I'm attracted to you. Very much so—' Ben broke off with a short laugh '—probably too much. And I'm telling the truth when I say I don't want to hurt you.' He paused again, ensuring she was looking at him, 'I'm not going to make you homeless. That was never my intention. I just wanted to put pressure on your father, to make him see there are consequences for his actions.'

'You won't go through with it?' she asked, feeling an instantaneous lightening in her heart.

'No, I won't go through with it. *He* deserves every punishment in hell,' Ben said, taking her hand, 'but you don't. In the end it would be you who would be hurt and I don't want that.'

Feeling the relief seeping through her body, she allowed herself to sag against him, his body warm and welcoming in the darkness.

'I thought…' she said, trailing off. He didn't need to know the details of all her insecurities.

'You thought I'd used you to get close to your father and that our time together was part of my revenge,' he summed up succinctly.

Even in the darkened park Francesca could see him shake his head ruefully. 'I have a bit of a reputation back home,' he said, planting a kiss on the top of her head. 'I'm known to be ruthless, a man who takes risks, a man not to be crossed in the course of my business. I'm very glad my business rivals cannot see me here.'

'Allowing my father to get away with his actions for my sake would go against the persona you've built for yourself?' Francesca asked.

'Oh, yes.'

'But you decided to anyway.'

'I couldn't help myself,' he said quietly, kissing her again, this time on her temple where her hairline ended.

'So what happened between us…' Francesca said, needing one final confirmation.

'Everything I did and everything I said was true,' he said sincerely.

Francesca felt her heart swell and knew she needed to be careful. She was beginning to care about Ben just a little too much. He'd made it perfectly clear he wasn't the sort of man to get tied down by emotions. Their dalliance together had been just that: a temporary, fleeting dalliance. The only person she would hurt if she allowed these feelings for Ben to continue would be herself.

Glancing at him in the darkness, she had a momentary flash of what her life might be like if she threw away everyone's expectations of her and ran off with this man. She could picture a life of freedom, a life of equality where she was treated as a human rather than a possession to be traded by the men around her. No doubt it would also be a life of passion.

Sighing, she pushed away the thought. Of course it could never happen—she had responsibilities, a duty to see her sister well provided for and her parents not sent to debtors' prison. And Ben had never offered anything more than a few intimate weeks. They were not of the same world; it could never work.

'Why the big sigh?' he asked as she leaned back against him, feeling his warmth engulfing her.

'No reason,' she said, trying to inject a brightness into her voice, but failing miserably.

'I have to go away in a couple of days,' Ben said quietly.

Francesca felt a tearing in her chest and wondered how those few little words could cause her so much pain. She barely knew the man sitting beside her, his departure shouldn't cause her so much upset.

'Back to Australia?' she asked morosely.

Ben laughed, 'Good Lord, no. I'm going to Essex, to see my family.'

She heard the mix of emotions in his voice, the excitement shadowed with something that sounded a little like apprehension.

'Your father is back from his trip?' she asked.

While they'd been lying in bed together a few days earlier Ben had told her of the bad timing of his arrival. A few days before his ship docked his father had been called to one of the estates he managed up north. Only now was he coming home, meaning their long-awaited reunion had been painfully delayed.

'He should return on Thursday,' Ben said, 'and he wrote he was most eager not to delay my visit any further.'

'Of course he's keen to see you,' Francesca said, picking up on the uncertainty in Ben's voice. The man next to her was strong emotionally. He'd been through so much at such a young age and come out with the ability still to care about his family and those around him. When he spoke of his father and brothers there was an uncharacteristic hesitation in his voice and Francesca knew it was not because he didn't want to see them again. Quite the opposite.

'I shall be gone for a few days,' Ben said. 'I'm not sure how many exactly. I suppose it will depend on how well the visit goes.'

'Your father will probably never want to let you leave.'

He shrugged and for a moment she was reminded of the young boy she'd once known. The image of him locked in a cell, awaiting trial for a crime he didn't commit, came to mind. He'd looked unsure and vulnerable then, too. It wasn't a side to him she'd seen much since his return.

'I need to visit Elmington Manor,' Francesca said impulsively. 'I could accompany you on the journey if you would like.'

Elmington Manor was their moderately sized property in Essex, the same estate she and Ben had grown up running around and Ben's father had once managed. She did need to visit in the next few weeks, to take her old clothes out of storage ready for when her mourning period finished, but had planned on putting that task off for as long as possible. Now, it was a good excuse to travel to Essex with Ben. She thought he needed some moral support, a friend to reassure him that his family wasn't going to reject him after eighteen years. Not that he would ever ask for it.

She saw him hesitate, wondered if he would be too proud to accept her help. Most men wouldn't want to admit they were struggling emotionally with something like this.

'You're going anyway?' he asked.

'I need to sort out my clothes for when I come out of mourning,' she said.

'Then I would be very pleased to have your company.'

In the darkness she reached out and patted the wood of the bench until her hand found his, then, lacing her fingers through his, she closed her eyes and smiled. Ben deserved a good relationship with his family and she would do everything in her power to make sure that's what he got.

Chapter Fifteen

⁓⊱⊱⊱⊱⊱⊰⊰⊰⊰⊰⁓

The morning was crisp and clear as Ben waited on the out-skirts of London at their agreed meeting point. He was on horseback, wrapped up in his thickest coat with his warm-est gloves on his hands. Although he wouldn't ever admit to anyone in Australia that he missed his homeland, the cold, snowy winters in England were something he'd found him-self dreaming about in the heat of the Australian summer.

In the distance he could see a carriage approaching and smiled ruefully. He knew Francesca would like nothing more than to be up on horseback riding alongside him, but she was tied by the expectations of society. A young woman did not ride from London to Essex on horseback when there was a carriage at her disposal. It wasn't the done thing, no matter how much she wanted to.

Shaking his head, he wondered what more he could do to help her break free of those restraints, to show her the world wouldn't end if she didn't conform to the expectations of a group of people she didn't much like anyway.

'Good morning,' he greeted Francesca as her carriage came to a stop beside him. The coachman looked pale and miserable to be out in such icy weather and was blowing on his hands impatiently.

'Good morning. Would you care to join me?' she asked, motioning to the seat opposite her in the carriage.

'I have a better idea,' he said. 'It's a beautiful morning, why don't you come and join me?'

'I don't have a mount.'

'This beast is strong enough to carry both of us for a while,' Ben said, enjoying the widening of Francesca's eyes as she realised what he was suggesting.

'You want me to come and ride with you?' she asked.

Suppressing a grin, Ben nodded. He loved the look of disbelief and mild indignation she got on her face when he suggested something that wasn't a societal norm.

'You never used to be scared of horses…' he taunted her.

'I'm not scared of the horse,' she said calmly, 'it's the man on its back I'm cautious of.'

'I promise to behave.'

'I don't think you know how to behave,' Francesca grumbled, but Ben saw her edging off her seat. He grinned, loving how easily he could read the woman in front of him. Deep down she wanted nothing more than to vault up behind him and feel the wind whipping at her face as they raced off ahead of the carriage. It was only years of conforming to what a well-brought-up young lady *should* do that was holding her back.

'Put up your hood and if anyone passes lower your head,' Ben said. 'Then no one will recognise you.' He could tell she was almost convinced. 'I'll let you sit in front,' he said eventually, knowing she wouldn't be able to resist that offer.

'Really?' Francesca asked, her eyes lighting up.

'If that would make you happy.'

Within a fraction of a second she was out of the carriage and inspecting his horse.

'How do you have a horse?' she asked, stroking the beautiful grey animal's nose with the affection of a girl who grew up in the countryside.

'Lady Winston, Fitzgerald's aunt whom we stayed with when I first arrived in London, she arranged for us to hire a mount each.'

'How generous,' Francesca murmured.

'She is. Outspoken and forthright, but unbelievably generous. Do you need a leg up?'

Placing her booted foot into his hand, Francesca pulled herself up on to the back of the horse, settling herself on its back. She was wearing a plain grey dress with a full skirt and her cloak over the top, not the most practical items for riding a horse, but Ben could see she would just about manage to sit sideways in front of him.

'Are you sure the horse will be able to manage both of us?' she asked.

Quickly he pulled himself up on to the horse's back, settling himself behind Francesca and looping an arm around her waist to support her.

'I've never ridden like this before,' she said, gripping the reins. From the tone of her voice he could tell she was smiling and wondered when making her smile had become quite so important to him.

He was barely listening to her words, distracted by the contour of her waist under his hand and the warmth of her body pressed against his.

'We shall meet you at the King's Head,' Francesca called to her coachman, who grumbled something inaudible in return.

With a squeal of delight she threw her head back as he spurred the horse on, and Ben made sure he allowed it to pick a nice steady speed that it would be able to maintain with an extra rider on its back.

Ben relaxed back, glad of the distraction of having Francesca with him. When she was in his arms he thought about things less, worried less. Carefully, ensuring he did not surprise her too much, he leaned forwards and placed a kiss on her cheek, feeling the fur from the inside of her new cloak tickle his lips.

'What was that for?' she asked, glancing round, but not able to quite meet his eye and keep her balance.

'For coming with me.'

Ben knew she'd seen the worry buried deep inside him, that she'd sensed his unease and nervousness at seeing his family again after so long and had offered to accompany him to distract him on the journey and offer what little support she could.

It was a kind gesture, one that showed their friendship had blossomed again despite all that had gone before. Friendship…and something more.

Ben had thought the day they'd spent in bed together might slake his desire for Francesca, but in reality it had only heightened it. Before when he'd felt an attraction towards a woman a night or two in their arms had been enough to fulfil that so he could move on. Now, despite having had Francesca in his bed, he still thought about her almost every waking moment. And sleep didn't give him much respite either. The dreams…

'Tell me about your family now,' Francesca said, leaning back into him and warming his body with her own.

Ben took a moment to collect his thoughts. All he knew of his family had been from his father's letters, but seeing as they lived half a world apart he had been kept remarkably well-informed.

'Do you remember my brothers?' Ben asked.

There was a moment of hesitation before Francesca replied, as if she were trying hard to recall people from a long time ago.

'Thomas and William,' she said eventually.

'That's right.' Two boys who would have grown into men in the intervening years. Thomas had been eight when Ben was arrested and Ben had fond memories of playing with his younger brother, but William had only been four. No doubt his youngest brother wouldn't remember him at all.

'They both work with Father and they still all live in Elswyre. Thomas was married, but his wife died in childbirth a couple of years ago. He has just the one son. William is still young and unattached as far as I'm aware.'

'And your father?'

This was one of the things Ben was most apprehensive about. Never in his letters had his father mentioned remarrying, but Ben wondered if that had been to spare his feelings when he was so far away. Their mother had died soon after William was born, wasting away for no apparent reason, going quickly from a healthy young woman to a shadow of her former self before passing away one night. His father had always blamed a weak chest, but in reality no one knew why Ben's mother had died. Ever since then their father had become everything to them. Through his own grief the older man had helped his children find their way in the world without their mother as well as taking on all the jobs his wife would ordinarily have done. To Ben he was a true hero, a man he'd looked up to and wanted to emulate. Part of his discomfort at the idea of finally going home centred around wondering if that had been a fantasy built up by a child or if it was the truth.

'I don't think he's ever remarried.'

'How extraordinary,' Francesca murmured.

It was extraordinary. He'd been a relatively young man with a good job and three children to look after. There wouldn't be many in his position who wouldn't find another wife to share the load.

'Enough,' Ben said, not wanting to think about how he might slot into a family he hadn't seen for eighteen years. 'Let's canter.'

In front of him he felt Francesca adjust her grip on the reins and lean forward ever so slightly before urging the horse on. As they picked up speed he heard her let out a little cry of pleasure and he noticed she didn't even tense as another carriage passed them on the road, the occupants looking out disapprovingly. If he could get Francesca to embrace her true nature, to realise she didn't always need to conform to society's expectations, before he left for Australia, then he would be happy.

Not happy, the little voice inside his head insisted. He tried to ignore it, focus instead on the woman in front of him and how her body felt pressed against his. He didn't want to have to examine how she made him feel emotionally. It was enough to admit that he still desired her, without acknowledging that he would find it hard to leave her behind. She'd burrowed her way under his skin and lodged herself treacherously close to his heart.

Silently he shook his head. He wasn't meant for a long-term relationship, he was better suited to short flings, dalliances where no one could get hurt. To commit for life to just one woman, that required a level of mutual trust he just didn't have.

It didn't matter anyway. In a few weeks Francesca would probably insist on marrying the odious Lord Huntley in some misguided attempt to save her sister. Even knowing her motivation, it hurt him more than he wanted to admit, the thought that she would choose Huntley over him.

Chapter Sixteen

Although it was only a little after three o'clock in the afternoon when they entered the village of Elswyre the sky had already lost its brightness and the sun was dropping ever lower.

'I'll escort you home first,' Ben said, knowing his voice was clipped and tense, but unable to help it. He felt nervous, more nervous than he had done for years, and he was torn between wanting to run to his father's house to reunite with his family and wanting to stay away in case it wasn't everything he'd hoped for.

They were sitting in the carriage, giving Ben's horse a rest after he'd carried them both for over twenty miles.

'There's no need,' Francesca said, patting him on the hand as if he were a small child, 'I have the carriage and the maid will be waiting for me.' She hesitated, as if unsure whether to continue. 'I could come with you,' she said eventually.

He frowned, the offer unexpected.

'Only if you want me to. I don't want to impose. I just thought it might be a little difficult, seeing your family again after so long and you might want someone by your side. I completely understand if you don't. I'm probably the last person you want for moral support.' Her words came out in a gush and for the first time in the last hour Ben found himself smiling.

'That's a very kind offer,' he said. He was just about to reject it, to send her on her way to Elmington Manor to begin the arduous task of sorting out her clothes for when she came out of mourning, but he found himself hesitating.

His family knew Francesca's father was responsible for Ben's conviction and subsequent transportation so she might not be the most welcome. Even so, he felt the warmth of her body by his side and knew he drew strength from her being there.

Silently he shook his head. He shouldn't need anyone to give him strength. He'd survived false imprisonment, two years on the filthy hulk ships, the perilous crossing to Australia and nearly six years of hard labour under the hot sun. From that dark time he'd risen and built an empire of some of the most successful and productive farms in Australia. Ben knew he was strong, knew he was a survivor, but right now he felt like a scared young lad.

'Thank you,' he said quietly, not able to admit how much he needed her in this moment.

They continued their journey through the village in silence, Francesca must have sensed his need to prepare for the reunion ahead and the familiar sights from his childhood were overwhelming. Not much had changed in nearly two decades. The high street still had the same small collection of shops, with only a couple of new shopfronts added. The village square looked identical to when Ben had last run around it with the other village children and the church still dominated Elswyre with its towering steeple and impressive stone exterior.

He leaned out of the window of the carriage, calling for the coachman to stop. The last bit of the journey he wished to do on foot.

Hopping down, he turned back to assist Francesca, wondering if he was making a mistake in allowing her to accompany him. It should be family time, all about the reunion, but he was unable to send her away. He wanted her reassuring presence by his side, her warmth, her kindness, her calming attitude.

They crossed the village square, going past the oldest houses in the village and turning off into a narrow street. His father's house, the house Ben had grown up in, was the second on the left.

It was quite an impressive size, especially for a working man. Years ago, even before Ben was born, his parents had inherited it from a wealthy aunt of his father's. It had been the reason they had moved to Elswyre and led to Ben's father taking the job as land steward for Lord Pottersdown.

He felt Francesca slip her hand into his and only then did he realise he'd frozen, stopped in the middle of the road, unable to take another step.

'He's your father, he loves you,' she murmured quietly, applying a little pressure to his hand to get him moving again.

Ben took another step, then stopped again as the door to the house was thrown open.

'Ben?' a clear voice called out.

It was unmistakably his father. Eighteen years and the

man hardly looked any different. His once-dark hair was now filled with a smattering of grey and his face had acquired a few more lines, but apart from that it could have been exactly the man who'd hefted Ben up on to his shoulders during one of their long walks across the fields or told him a bedtime story while tucking him in at night.

'Father?' Ben said, hearing the layers of emotion in his voice. Beside him he felt Francesca step back discreetly, letting father and son have their moment.

With outstretched arms his father rushed towards him, pulling Ben towards his chest and embracing him for ten seconds before pulling away to study his son's face.

'My, you've changed,' his father said, 'although in some ways barely at all. It is good to have you home. I've been waiting for this day for eighteen years.'

The tears were flowing freely down his cheeks and Ben felt his own well up in his eyes. His father grasped his arm, leading him inside, seemingly unable to stop touching him as if scared Ben might disappear at any moment.

'Thomas,' Ben said, catching sight of his brother as he stepped into the hallway. 'And William.' He embraced the two men, memories of their childhood together flooding in and almost overwhelming him.

'Good to have you home, Brother,' Thomas said.

'We've been waiting for this day for a long time,' William added.

They were both big men, tall with broad shoulders and rich, dark hair and eyes just like their father. Ben favoured their mother more in looks with his green eyes, but the family resemblance was obvious.

'Come in, sit down, we have so much to catch up on,'

Ben's father said, ushering them in to the comfortable room filled with armchairs and sofas at the front of the house.

Inside a little boy played on the floor, setting up line upon line of toy soldiers and moving them while babbling away happily to himself. Thomas's son, Ben supposed, the one his brother had sole care of since he'd lost his wife.

'My boy, Benjamin,' Thomas said quietly. 'We call him Benny.'

'I'm very pleased to meet you, Benny.' He felt a little stab of emotion at the thought of his brother wanting to remember him in this small way, giving his own son Ben's name.

The little boy grinned, then went happily back to playing his game.

Sitting down, Ben felt the familiarity of the house and for a moment he was back in those carefree days of his childhood where he was loved and cared for and thought everything in the world was good.

Realising he should introduce Francesca, he glanced at his father. The man was reasonable and forgiving, but he didn't know how he would react to seeing Francesca after all this time.

'This is a friend, Father,' he said slowly.

'I know who she is.'

Ben glanced at Francesca, saw her cheeks redden, but she didn't back away and held the older man's gaze. Ben realised just how uncomfortable it must have been for her to suggest coming here with him today, but she'd done it anyway. For him.

The silence stretched out for nearly a minute, before Ben's father crossed to Francesca and took her hand.

'You're welcome in this house,' he said.

'Thank you,' Francesca said quietly. 'I'm sorry—'

Ben's father cut her off with a shake of his head. 'No need for that. You did everything you could, it wasn't your fault no one listened to you.' He glanced over at Ben with a hint of question in his eyes. 'And it would appear my son does not hold a grudge. We're happy to have you here.'

He motioned for Francesca to sit on the sofa next to Ben while a middle-aged woman bustled into the room, carrying a tray with a large teapot, cups and a cake ready for slicing.

'How are you, Father?' Ben asked. The older man looked well, his face was tanned and had a healthy glow, probably from all the hours spent outside.

'I'm well, Son. All the better for seeing you.'

'And your journey from the north?' Ben asked.

'As smooth as can be expected.' His father's voice was smooth and melodious and Ben felt the warmth inside him as it took him back to his childhood, the days where he was happy and carefree. 'But enough about me, I want to hear about you. What have you been doing since you've been back in England?'

Glancing at Francesca, he wondered how to answer that question. He could hardly tell his father he had been caught up pursuing a woman he had no right to be interested in. She was bound for marriage, albeit an inadvisable one, and he would one day soon return home to Australia.

'I travelled with George Fitzgerald and Sam Robertson,' Ben said, knowing his father would be aware of the two men from his letters to England that often spoke of the friends who were almost brothers. 'And while I awaited your return I stayed with them in London.'

Ben didn't miss the speculative glance his father flashed at Francesca as he digested Ben's words.

'Tell us about Australia,' William said, his eyes wide and his tone enthusiastic.

'It's a wondrous country,' Ben said. 'Harsh and danger-ous, but beautiful at the same time.'

'You've come to love it?' His father asked.

'Yes. I hated it for the first couple of years, until Mr Fitzgerald...' Ben trailed off, not sure how his father would react to hearing the name of the man who'd stepped up and taken Ben under his protection, becoming a second father in many ways.

'A man I will always be eternally grateful to,' he said qui-etly. 'I wished I could be there with you each and every day, but in my absence I'm just glad to know someone watched out for you, someone cared for you.'

'He did, Father. He was a good man.' Ben paused, re-membering for a moment the man who had taken him and Robertson into his family. Only when he glanced at his brothers' eager faces did he continue with his descriptions of Australia. 'It seemed a dusty and cruel country when I first arrived and for many months I hated it. It was only when I'd served the first few years in Australia, when they deemed me trustworthy enough to work on the farms rather than do the hardest of the jobs—building roads—that I began to actually *see* my surroundings.'

'Is it very dangerous? All the strange creatures and wild natives?' Thomas asked, his honest and open face clouded with concern.

'There are some dangerous creatures. Snakes that will kill with a single bite. Spiders the size of a dinner plate, but we never had any trouble from the natives.'

'And you actually like it out there?' Thomas asked, in-credulous.

'It's wild and untamed,' Ben said, trying to convey the allure of a land that was so vast and beautiful, but in a way completely different to the rolling green hills of England. 'The beaches are stretches of golden sand and inland the farmland is beautiful and bountiful. There are mountains and deserts and everything in between.'

'You'll go back?' his father asked quietly. There was a wealth of emotion hidden in that small question. Ben opened his mouth to answer, felt the words unable to come out. Beside him Francesca sought out his fingers with her own and squeezed, trying to reassure him. It was a tiny movement, their hands hidden under the layers of her skirt so no one else could see, but Ben felt the strength flowing from her into him.

'Of course you'll go back,' his father said, shaking his head. 'Your life is there, everything you've built for yourself.'

But not his family. And not Francesca.

Ben blinked at the thought. He'd never considered staying in England before, never even thought it was a possibility. For so long he'd been apprehensive about seeing his father again and meeting the brothers he hadn't seen since childhood, he hadn't thought much past it. This meeting was the culmination of his plans and now the future stretched out, empty and open, full of possibilities.

'I suppose I will have to,' Ben said quietly, glancing at Francesca.

That was one thing he should be certain of: his future wouldn't include Francesca. He might like her, care for her, spend his nights dreaming of having her soft body beside him, but he was not a man meant to settle down. Ever since his first dalliance with a woman he'd found it hard to imagine spending a lifetime with someone. Every time anyone even began to get close, he found he felt the beginnings of panic—the thought that if he started to care for someone, they might be wrenched away from him.

His friends always joked that one day he would fall head over heels in love and then the object of his affection would end their affair as he had with dozens of women before. Surreptitiously he glanced sideways at Francesca. Only now was he beginning to realise that it was Francesca, and the way they'd been pulled apart all those years ago, that had made him the way he was. Even if he didn't like to admit it, losing Francesca had shaped him into the man he was today—a man who knew he could never settle down out of fear of losing the one he loved.

Suppressing a grim chuckle, he shook his head. It didn't matter anyway; the object of his affection, the only woman who had ever come close to his heart, was steadfastly insisting on marrying a man who would make her miserable.

'Perhaps something might persuade you to stay,' Thomas said, casting a knowing glance at Ben and Francesca.

Ben shifted uncomfortably. His brother's remark was just a little too astute for comfort.

'I should leave you to your reunion,' Francesca said, her cheeks delightfully pink, but whether it was from the warmth of the roaring fire or her understanding of the knowing, but wrong, glances being exchanged across the room.

'Come to dinner,' Ben's father said, 'Our table is only humble, but you are most welcome at it. We eat at seven.'

'Thank you,' Francesca said quietly and Ben could see she was overwhelmed by the invitation from a man who should rightly hate her.

Standing, he escorted Francesca to the door, pausing as she pulled on her cloak and gloves.

'Enjoy them,' she said, standing on tiptoes and planting a kiss on his cheek. 'You deserve every moment of this.'

He watched her leave, realising that although he was back with the family he'd yearned for all those years he spent apart, he felt as if something were missing as she walked away.

Chapter Seventeen

'Tell me everything,' his father said as they strolled side by side around the village, their breath floating in an icy vapour and their posture stiff to try to combat the cold despite the thick coats they were wearing.

It was hard to know where to start. How did you compress eighteen years of life into a few short hours or days? Ben had written to his father over the years, long letters describing his situation, his successes and the people who surrounded him, but he knew it wasn't like hearing it first-hand.

'Tell me about your life now,' his father said, seeing Ben hesitate.

'I'm happy, Father,' Ben said, watching the older man nod in satisfaction. 'I'm my own master, I make my own decisions and my own mistakes. Australia is a curious land, over half the population are ex-convicts, but still it seems like a land of opportunity. Any man can rise up and become successful, no matter his past sins.'

'And your farms are thriving?'

'Very much so. Or at least they were when I left.' In total Ben owned seven farms, stretching out over a vast area in eastern Australia. The first he'd been given by Mr Fitzgerald the elder, a present when he'd turned eighteen, although legally he hadn't been able to take control of it until he'd served out his sentence two years later. That small parcel of land had flourished under his careful management and soon he had borrowed against it to buy more land. Ben took risks, but always calculated ones, and his strategy had paid off. He was now one of the wealthiest landowners in Australia and had a mixture of arable and cattle farms that provided him with an income that surpassed his wildest dreams.

'You have someone trusty looking after them?'

Ben thought of the man he'd left in charge, dependable, safe and certainly trustworthy. 'I do,' he said, but even he could hear the hesitation in his voice.

'You find it hard to let someone else look after things and make the decisions?' his father said with a knowing smile, 'You were the same as a lad.'

'I expect to make mistakes,' Ben said slowly, 'Everyone does. To plant a wrong crop one year, to move the cattle somewhere the water supply is dwindling, but they are *my* mistakes.'

'You find it hard to let go, to give up the responsibility...' his father paused and Ben felt his eyes on his face '...to trust?'

Hesitating only a second, Ben nodded. He'd forgotten how astute his father was, how well he read people and understood them with just a few hours in their company.

'And how about your personal life?' his father asked.

'Have you found someone special to share all this success with?'

An image of Francesca flashed across his mind, but
quickly he suppressed it.

'No,' he said, trying to be abrupt and put an end to that
line of conversation.

'That is a shame,' his father said, patting him affectionately on the arm, 'A companion, someone to share the highs
and lows with, is the biggest blessing you can have in life.
Apart from your children, of course, but one could argue
it is difficult to beget one without the other.'

'You never remarried,' Ben said quietly. The question as
to why had been on his mind for so long. It had been impossible to ask in a letter, but still he had a burning need
to know why.

'I loved your mother with all my heart,' his father said.
'She lit up my world. I've never found anyone I care for the
way I cared for her and it would be cruel to marry again and
expect a woman to settle for anything less than the whole-
hearted love they deserve.'

'Were you ever tempted? When we were young?'

'To give you another mother of sorts?' his father clari-
fied. 'No.' He laughed good naturedly. 'I supposed myself
to be enough for you all.'

'You were.'

'But you do not have my excuse,' his father said, turning serious again. 'You have not loved and lost, so what is
holding you back?'

Ben couldn't answer.

'Perhaps the one you want is somehow off limits to you?'
his father prompted. 'Perhaps you've been holding back

from loving anyone while you wait for the one your heart truly wants.'

'Father...'

'It's obvious to see, just as it was when you were a child.'

Again he opened his mouth to start denying the attraction and feelings he had for Francesca, but his father stopped him.

'You loved her then, do you remember that?'

Ben shook his head. He'd thought of Francesca like a sister, like a best friend, nothing more. They'd only been children.

'Oh, it was an innocent sort of love, I have no doubt, but you loved her. Put her before yourself every time. I had visions of you two growing up and running off together, to escape her disapproving parents. But life worked out a little differently.'

'Just a little,' Ben murmured.

'I'm a hopeless romantic and I suppose I believe there is one true love for all of us out there,' his father said, stopping in front of the church. He motioned for Ben to go into the churchyard before him and then looped around in front, leading his son a few steps to the neatly kept grave. 'Your mother made me the happiest man alive. I would hate for you to miss out on that feeling.'

'She doesn't think of me that way,' Ben said, his mind filling up with images of Francesca's face lighting up when she saw him, her chin tilting for the illicit kisses, the light in her eyes as they discussed politics or agriculture or London gossip.

'Nonsense. I've only seen the two of you for a few minutes together and even I can see she's hopelessly in love with you.'

'A little infatuation, perhaps,' Ben conceded.

'Love,' his father insisted.

'She's practically engaged to another man.'

His father shrugged. 'Does she know a life with you is an option?'

With widened eyes Ben shook his head, trying not to let his complete surprise show on his face. It was funny how a parent, even one you hadn't seen for so many years, could pull down all the walls you'd built to protect yourself and render you speechless within a few minutes.

'She has some notion of saving her sister from a disastrous marriage by providing a decent dowry and stopping her father's creditors from destroying him completely.'

'She always did take on other people's problems,' his father murmured.

'So even if I did ask her to take a chance on me, she couldn't.'

'You could provide the dowry,' his father said quietly.

Ben blinked, wondering why he hadn't thought of that. It was simple, and infinitely better than Francesca being married to a man she hated for the rest of her life. Not that he was thinking of doing it so he could be with her...

'You have the funds.'

'She wouldn't...' Ben was unable to finish the sentence. The thought of being with Francesca was too good, too risky. What if he took away all the barriers and she still said no?

Still, the idea of waking up to Francesca in his bed every morning, taking her out on week-long trips to inspect his furthest farms, producing a brood of wild-haired children who looked just like their beautiful mother, that was tempting.

He watched as his father crouched down beside his mother's grave.

'She would have wanted you to find love.'

He remembered his mother, but not well. There were images of a beautiful woman who was always smiling, who took time from running the house to play and laugh with her children. He remembered cuddling up to her for bedtime stories and helping her knead bread in the kitchen.

Crouching beside his father, Ben laid a hand on the cool stone. His childhood seemed a whole lifetime ago, sometimes even a life that hadn't belonged to him.

They stayed in the graveyard for another few minutes, Ben paying respect to his mother at the grave he thought he would never see.

'I'll let you be alone with her, follow on when you're ready,' his father said eventually.

As he watched his father walk away he sat down on the cold earth next to the gravestone and lowered his head.

'What about you, Mama?' he asked. 'What do you think I should do?'

Of course, there was no answer, no flash of divine inspiration. Instead Ben reached into the neck of his shirt and folded his fingers around the locket that rested against his chest. Francesca's locket—the one he'd been accused of stealing all those years ago. He'd worn it every day of his sentence. At first he told himself it was a reminder of how little things can change the direction of your life completely, but now he wasn't so sure. It had been a piece of the girl he'd loved, his only connection to her.

He smiled ruefully as he thought back to the day he'd been dragged from the county gaol to the magistrate's house before he was due in the courtroom for his short trial. Francesca's locket had been lying on the desk in the magistrate's study, glinting up at him. He'd slipped it into a pocket before he could even reason through his actions and kept it with him ever since.

His fingers brushed over the warm silver and he closed his eyes. There would be no answers here. This was a decision his mother couldn't help him with. Perhaps his father was right, perhaps he had been alone for too long. Perhaps he needed to stop being scared she would reject him due to their differences in class, or would somehow be taken away from him. Instead, perhaps he needed to find a way to make the woman he couldn't stop thinking about his.

Nervously Francesca knocked on the front door. She had spent the remainder of the afternoon with Ginny, the only housemaid left at Elmington Manor. Ginny was in her thirties, an age at which most housemaids had moved up or moved on, either to more senior household positions or to marriage, but neither seemed to appeal to the mousy woman and she stayed at Elmington Manor for a pittance of a wage and her room. Consequently the house was not in a great condition, but Francesca had cajoled the inherently lazy housemaid into opening up her bedroom, airing it off and flicking away the worst of the dust.

Tomorrow she would tackle the task of getting her old dresses, the ones in colours other than blacks and greys and mauves, out of storage.

Here, outside Ben's father's house, she felt nervous. Her stomach was roiling and her palms felt hot and sticky inside her gloves. It meant so much to her for Ben's family to like her, even when she knew she would probably never see them again. When they were younger Ben's parents had been kind and welcoming and level-headed, a lovely anti-dote to her chaotic family, and it would appear his father had not changed one bit.

'Lady Somersham,' Mr Crawford said as he opened the door, 'Welcome, come in.'

'Please call me Francesca,' she said.

'Ben is with his brothers,' Mr Crawford said, 'They're talking land management. Would you have a couple of minutes to spare for me before we find him?'

'Of course,' Francesca said, the nerves rearing again. She didn't know why Mr Crawford would want to talk to her in private, but she felt like a naughty child, probably because the last time she'd seen him before this afternoon she'd been ten years old and always getting into trouble with Ben.

'Come through to the garden.'

He led the way, taking her through the warm hall and out through the door in the kitchen to a garden that smelled of wet earth and herbs even at this time of year.

'How have you been, Francesca?' Mr Crawford asked, as he motioned for her to have a seat on a little bench that looked out over the grass.

'Well, thank you,' she answered, remembering all the times she'd come for lunch in this happy home as a child and all the times she'd wished it was her home.

'I'm not making small talk,' Mr Crawford said, and even in the darkness she could tell he was smiling. 'How have you really been?'

She hesitated. It wasn't the done thing to air all her woes to a man she hadn't seen for eighteen years, but Ben's father had a soothing way about him that made her want to spill every disaster and every uncertainty in her life.

'Ben said you were married,' Mr Crawford prompted, 'although he hinted it wasn't the happiest of unions.'

'Father arranged it,' Francesca said. She sighed and gave in to the urge to talk, no matter how improper it was. 'Lord Somersham was never violent, but when that is the best you can say about your late husband it is hardly a ringing endorsement, is it?'

'You were unhappy?'

She nodded. Although for years she'd tried to pretend she was content, tried to accept this was what she had been born for, she had never been happy in her marriage.

'Yet you are considering marrying again, another man you do not care for.' He said the words so quietly it took Francesca a moment to absorb them.

'I must,' she said, 'My family…'

Patting her on the hand in a fatherly fashion, he shook his head. 'It is a poor state of affairs when a child has to be responsible for her parents. And the consequences of their actions.'

It was true, but there wasn't much she could so about it.

'If you were my daughter, your happiness would be paramount.'

Francesca laughed, trying to hide the bitter edge. So many times as a child she'd wished this man was her father instead of the drunken gambler that resided at Elmington Manor.

'I think you would be happier if you married Ben,' Mr Crawford said.

Francesca almost choked on the air she was breathing.

'Mr Crawford…' she said, but didn't know how to continue.

'You would,' he said with a shrug. 'You love him. And love is a decent foundation to base a marriage on.'

'I barely know him,' she protested.

'Nonsense. You were inseparable for years.'

'Two decades ago.'

'People don't change.'

'Of course they do. I've changed.' She thought sadly back to the happy, carefree girl she'd been as a child and knew that person had been slowly eroded away until the woman she was today was all that was left.

'Not really,' Mr Crawford said and even in the darkness she could see him smile. 'Oh, maybe on the surface,' he conceded, 'but deep down, that core inner person, that will never change.'

They sat in silence for a few minutes and Francesca wondered at the warmth and love in the heart of this man. No wonder Ben had managed to survive such a terrible experience in his childhood. He had solid foundations built by his parents, foundations of love and self-belief and confidence in his decisions.

'Have a think about it,' Mr Crawford said. 'Consider whether you want to spend a life with a man you don't care for or take a chance on love.'

He stood before she could reply, turning and walking back towards the house. Francesca felt the tears slipping down her cheeks. Whatever she'd expected to find here it wasn't this wonderful kindness. Mr Crawford had taken a precious few seconds away from his time with his son to talk to her about her future happiness. Her father wouldn't ever do such a thing—half the time she suspected he didn't even see her as a person, just a commodity to be traded— yet here was a man she had last seen eighteen years ago and he was trying to advocate for her future happiness.

Love. Was that what there was between her and Ben?

Until now she'd been too scared to call it anything but affection, but perhaps it was love. She felt her whole being lift whenever Ben was close, thought about him constantly when they were apart and could only truly be happy when they were reunited again. Thinking back to the day they'd spent in his bed, she felt a now-familiar tingle of desire, but that wasn't all there was.

You've loved him for years, the little voice inside her head said. Surely it couldn't be true. She hadn't been able to forget Ben, but she'd always put that down to the terrible way they'd been torn apart.

'I see my father has been spreading his wisdom.' Ben's voice came from somewhere behind her.

'He is a very persuasive man,' Francesca murmured.

Ben sat on the bench next to her, looping an arm around her back and pulling her closer in a supremely intimate gesture.

'He thinks I am denying myself love and affection,' Ben said, grumbling in a way that told Francesca he probably agreed with his father, but didn't quite want to admit it. 'What did he want with you?'

'He was concerned about my future happiness,' Francesca said carefully. She wasn't ready to admit her feelings for Ben yet, not when she wasn't sure herself what they actually were.

'Then he has got some sense in him. *Everyone* is concerned about your future happiness.' He paused, then shook his head. 'I'm wrong. Everyone should be concerned about your future happiness, but your family seem incapable of thinking of anyone but themselves.'

They were harsh words, but Francesca couldn't protest, it was the truth.

'Except your sister. She's a decent human being and doesn't want you to sacrifice your happiness for hers.'

'What would you have me do?' Francesca asked, a little sharper than she'd planned. 'If I didn't marry Lord Huntley, what would you have me do?'

'What would you want to do?' he asked, searching her face.

Run away with you. She couldn't say the words, even though she realised it was the truth.

Instead she shrugged, feeling his eyes on her and not knowing how to respond.

'We'd lose the house, the estate. Father's creditors would finally lose patience, I'm sure. I would have to find work, perhaps as a governess.'

She'd always wanted children, but after the unsuccessful years with Lord Somersham she doubted she would ever have any of her own. Perhaps being a governess wouldn't be too bad.

She saw a flash of disappointment flash across Ben's face and knew he despaired of her putting social appearances first, before anything that really mattered.

'You'd make a fine governess,' Ben said.

'And what about your relationship issues?' Francesca asked.

'I'm working on them.'

'Really?'

He chuckled. 'Well, I will certainly try to. A man doesn't like to be told he has flaws.'

'Do you think…?' She paused to take a deep breath. 'Do you think one day you might have a meaningful relationship?' she asked, knowing it was a deeply personal question.

'Who knows? I wouldn't like to promise anything I couldn't be sure to deliver.'

Francesca looked up sharply, unsure if what he was saying had a deeper meaning, whether he was talking about their situation, or if she was reading too much into his words.

'Come inside, let's have dinner. Perhaps tomorrow things will be clearer.'

Allowing him to take her arm as she got to her feet, Francesca felt a wave of sadness wash over her. Mr Crawford was right, she did yearn for a future with Ben, but there were too many obstacles, too many things keeping them apart. Added to that, he hadn't ever mentioned staying in England, not for her or anyone. Soon he would sail back to Australia and out of her life, and she couldn't build their relationship up into something it wasn't or it would be even worse when the time came for him to leave and for her to get on with her normal life.

Dinner was a cheery affair. Ben was sat in the place of honour at the head of the table, with Francesca on one side and his brother Thomas on the other. Further down the table his father and William sat, and even Thomas's young son Benny had been allowed to stay up as it was a special occasion.

For the first time in years he felt at peace, as if his homecoming had dampened down the turmoil that was always raging inside him.

'Ben came home covered in soot with dust all over his clothes.' His father was telling a story of one of Ben's exploits from his childhood, his face glowing with happiness.

'I remember that,' Francesca said slowly. 'You were convinced you could climb the chimney in the dining room at Elmington Manor, but the butler caught you before you were even halfway up and thrashed you with a carpet beater.'

'If I hadn't been caught, I would have been able to climb that chimney,' he said, grinning.

'Nonsense. It was too tall and even then you weren't *that* agile.'

'I was like a cat. Probably even more lithe than a cat.'

'I think you have a touch of selective memory,' Francesca murmured as his brothers laughed. 'You were always falling off things. *I* was the better climber.'

'You were not,' Ben said, gesturing with a fork loaded with peas. 'The number of times I had to catch you or rescue you...'

'You're remembering it wrong. I always had to catch you.'

'I'd have squashed you.'

'You were quite a scrawny boy...'

'I don't know what you're talking about,' Ben said, grinning, 'I was a strapping lad, made of muscle.'

An unfamiliar sensation was washing over him and Ben realised it was contentment. Here, with Francesca by his side, surrounded by his family, he felt content. Perhaps he needed to consider what was important to him going forward. He might have built a life for himself in Australia, but was it the life he wanted?

'I want to propose a toast,' Mr Crawford said. 'To my boy, finally you're home. We've missed you more than you'll ever know.'

Ben looked around the table, seeing the happy, open faces and wondered whether he was being a fool even considering going back to Australia.

Perhaps his brothers would grow tired of him, resent

the return of a man who'd they had thought long lost to the other side of the world, but there was no indication of anything like that yet. And his father was ecstatic to have his eldest son back home.

He had a lot of decisions to make and right now he didn't know where to start.

Chapter Eighteen

Feeling like a naughty child once again, Ben pulled back
his arm and threw another pebble at Francesca's window. He
hoped he had the right room—when he'd last been at Elmington Manor she had still had her bedroom in the nursery,
but this was the only room on the first floor with a hint of
a candle burning behind the curtains.

Another pebble left his hand and made a satisfying tapping sound against the window pane, this time resulting
in movement in the room. The curtains twitched and he
held his breath as Francesca looked out. Her hair was loose
and untamed, the sleekness she had managed to maintain
throughout the day long gone now, and she was dressed in
a billowing cotton nightgown that made her look like someone from the last century.

Opening the window, she peered down at him.

'You could have knocked at the door,' Francesca said, an
amused half-smile on her lips.

'And woken half the household?'

'There's only me and Ginny here, Father dismissed all the rest of the staff a couple of years ago.'

'Why use the front door when you can climb through a window?'

'What makes you think I'll let you through my window?'

'You can't resist my boyish charm or my devilish good looks.'

Francesca snorted, but motioned for him to come up anyway.

'I'm only letting you in because I want to see you climb up here.'

Although Ben had kept fit over the years, with his boxing and regular riding across the Australian countryside, scaling walls was not something he'd done for a very long time and it took a particular set of skills. Still, he wasn't about to admit defeat and go in through the front door.

Using the ground-floor window and a convenient metal pipe that ran down the edge of the building, he climbed, gripping on to Francesca's windowsill within a mere few seconds. Using all his strength, he pulled himself up, tumbling into the room with a loud crash. Francesca sat perched on the edge of her bed giggling.

'Easy,' Ben said, wiping the grime from his coat before shedding it and placing it over the back of a chair. It was much warmer inside than out and the effort of the climb had already warmed his muscles.

'I suppose it's not a chimney,' Francesca murmured.

'I'm happy to go downstairs right now and prove to you I can climb that chimney,' Ben said, starting for the door.

'You barely fit then and you're four times the size now.' She laughed. 'Although I wouldn't mind seeing you with your head stuck up the chimney.'

Ben turned and closed the window, latching it shut. The remains of a fire glowed in the grate and as he pulled the curtain he felt peculiarly warm and contented.

'I received a letter from the seventeen-eighties and they want their nightgown back,' Ben said.

Francesca looked down. 'I'll have you know this is the height of fashion.'

'The height of fashion from thirty years ago.'

'I wasn't expecting to receive any visitors,' she said primly, 'and it keeps me warm.'

'I could keep you warm,' he said, raising an eyebrow suggestively and making Francesca burst out laughing.

'Is that why you came? To defile an innocent and upstanding widow?'

'Do you know where I can find one of those?' he asked, taking a step closer.

'I was perfectly virtuous before you came back.'

'A man can't help being irresistible,' he said with a shrug, now close enough to loop his arms around her waist and pull her slender body towards him.

'You always were too confident for your own good.'

'There's no such thing,' he murmured, catching her earlobe between his teeth and feeling her body react in his arms.

Bunching the thick cotton in his hands he pulled the offending nightgown up and over Francesca's head, much more satisfied when he discarded it on the floor behind him and turned back to her now-naked body.

As her hands pulled first at his jacket and then his shirt he kissed her, stopping only when he needed to lift his garments over his head or step out of his trousers. Their bodies entwined they tumbled back on the bed.

Slowly Ben ran his hands over Francesca's body, feeling her rise up to meet his touch and hearing her moan with anticipation and pleasure. Everything about her felt right, she fit perfectly against him and Ben had never felt this level of desire with anyone else in his life.

With passion and tenderness, they made love. The moment Francesca cried out with pleasure she looked into his eyes and Ben felt something in his chest tighten.

Love, that was the word his father had used. Turning over and pulling Francesca into his arms, Ben felt her warmth and the reassuring beating of her heart in her chest.

'I come out of mourning in three days,' Francesca said quietly. It must be almost a year since Lord Somersham had died and Ben knew she couldn't stretch out her mourning period any longer. 'Father will accept Lord Huntley's proposal on my behalf.' They'd also now had all the eight days together they had promised one another. At the thought, Ben felt consumed by panic.

He didn't say anything. With Francesca in his arms he didn't want to think about losing her.

'Once I return to London...' She trailed off, but Ben knew what she was saying. Once she returned to London she would not be able to see him again. An illicit liaison was one thing when she was merely a widow and had not yet promised herself to someone else, but Ben knew she would not break a vow to be faithful to another, no matter how much she wanted to.

'Don't marry him,' Ben said quietly.

'Ben, we've been through this a hundred times. I have to.'

'No, you don't.'

'My sister, my family.'

'I'll provide the dowry for your sister,' he said.

Francesca stiffened and then turned over to face him.

'I'll even sort something out for your odious father if it stops you from having to marry Huntley.'

'You don't mean that.'

'I do, Frannie. I can't stand the idea of you being unhappy for the rest of your life.'

'I couldn't let you do that.'

'Why not? I have plenty of money. I can't see a better cause to spend it on.'

'And in return?' she asked, her voice coming out as barely a whisper.

Ben closed his eyes for a moment. He wanted to ask her to be his, to marry him and spend her life by his side. The words wouldn't quite come out, though. He felt selfish asking, as he knew he might not be able to give her what she deserved. He would be asking her to give up her status, her friends, her family. She would no longer be the widow of a viscount, but the wife of an ex-convict, albeit a wealthy one. He knew those things mattered to her, but he just didn't know how much.

Taking a deep breath, he pushed on.

'You would be free,' he said, stroking her cheek. 'You could choose to marry or not, choose the sort of life you lived.'

He watched as she swallowed, saw the nervousness on her face. 'A life with you?' she asked.

'Marry me,' he said, pushing away all his doubts. He wasn't great at taking risks, but how could he hold back from asking her when they both clearly wanted it so much?

She searched his eyes with her own and Ben felt a bubble of nerves as he realised she hadn't answered him yet.

'Are you sure?' she asked. 'I don't want you to ask just

because you think otherwise I will throw my life away on Lord Huntley.'

Ben grinned. He was going about this all wrong. No woman deserved to be proposed to like this. Sitting up, he turned Francesca to face him and took her hand in his own.

'I love you, Frannie,' he said. 'And I know you love me.'

'I always imagined my marriage proposal to be a little less arrogant...' Francesca said, trying to keep the smile from her face.

'Is that a yes?'

'Yes.'

Ben kissed her, feeling the soaring of his heart and wondering if this was what he'd wanted all along. Deep down he knew Francesca was one of the main reasons he'd returned to England, alongside seeing his family again, of course, but he'd told himself he had just wanted to see his friend, to make sure she was happy. Now he was beginning to wonder if he'd deluded himself all those years and if in fact he'd loved her all along.

'I feel like I'm in a dream,' Francesca murmured as she pulled away, looking into his eyes, 'and I don't want to wake up.'

'This is no dream, Frannie, this is the rest of our lives.'

Despite his words he agreed with her, this evening *did* have a dreamlike quality to it. He hadn't set out to propose to her, his words had been spontaneous even if the idea of spending the rest of his life with Francesca by his side had been circling in his head ever since his father had suggested Ben might be happier if he gave in to the feelings he had for her. In just a few short moments he'd completely changed the course of his life.

Never had he imagined sharing his life with anyone.

Whenever he'd pictured his future it had always looked the same as the past few years: a successful business obtained through relentless hard work, pleasing but short-lived affairs, and keeping everyone at arm's length, deep down too scared they might be wrenched away from him.

'Is it possible to be this happy?' Francesca asked, her voice muffled as she spoke into his chest where she'd buried her face.

He knew the next few weeks would be difficult. Francesca would have to break the news to her family that she was not going to abide by their expectations and marry Lord Huntley. No doubt there would be harsh words and recriminations, but it would be worth it. Soon the drama would be behind them, Francesca would be free of her responsibility to her family and they would be husband and wife.

'Where will we live?' she asked.

'Do you mind?'

Slowly she shook her head. It would be a lot to ask to insist she leave her family and friends behind for an entirely new life in Australia, especially when Ben wasn't sure if he could do the same to his family once again. Perhaps they would be better settling in England, although then there would always be the pull of her father's antics and no getting away from the responsibility Francesca would feel towards her parents even after they'd done so little for her.

'There's no need to decide yet,' Ben said, stroking her hair. 'It is enough we know we'll be together. We can work out the details in time.'

'I shall have to tell Lord Huntley,' Francesca said, her fingers dancing across his abdomen distractedly.

'I'm more than happy to break the news,' Ben said with a

grin. He would take satisfaction in informing the Viscount he had better start searching for a new wife.

'I'm sure you would be, but it should come from me.'

'Whatever you think best, although you don't owe that man anything.'

'I suppose not.'

They both fell silent. Ben's head was spinning with plans for the future. Right now he couldn't quite believe he'd actually asked Francesca to marry him, or that she'd said yes. His life was on such a different trajectory to what it had been even a few hours earlier and he felt like he needed some time to adjust. No doubt Francesca felt the same.

He sat up, but quickly Francesca's hands coaxed him back down.

'Stay,' she whispered. 'Who can protest if we're to be married?'

'It might give your maid a shock if she finds me here in the morning.'

Francesca grimaced. 'I doubt she'll be up before us. She's not used to having anyone residing at Elmington Manor, it's been so long since we opened the house up.'

With a satisfied smile on his face, Ben settled back down next to the woman he was going to marry.

Chapter Nineteen

It had been a week since Ben had proposed. A week of blissful happiness. They'd spent the time in Essex, long mornings in bed followed by leisurely afternoons riding out to visit Ben's family. Francesca could see the change in Ben and often wondered what had been the catalyst for it. There was no doubt that his reunion with his family, and with his father in particular, had changed him, but she also thought their own plans for the future might have played a role in the shift in his outlook.

From the little he'd told her and a substantial amount of reading in between the lines, Francesca had worked out that Ben had never allowed a woman to get close to him before. There had been affairs, and plenty of them if she read his expressions correctly, but no one he'd allowed close to his heart. She was in a privileged position and she was determined not to jeopardise his trust in her.

For her part Francesca swung between being wonderfully content to worrying about how she was going to break the news to her family and Lord Huntley. Of course they wouldn't approve. She was risking her future, all their futures, on a man who would never be accepted by society. It didn't matter that he hadn't committed the crime he'd been sentenced for, or that he was now a very successful and rich landowner, all that would matter to the people close to her was that he was not of their class.

Shaking her head, she reprimanded herself. Over the years, since making her debut in society and then marrying Lord Somersham, Francesca felt as though her true identity had been slowly eroded away. She'd been browbeaten into believing the trivial things in life were the most important. If you were told time and time again that it mattered what clothes you wore, who you were related to and were judged on how pretty your curtsy was, then you began to believe these inconsequential things were actually important. Since Ben had reappeared in her life she had felt some of the lies she'd been told over the years washing away and her true self re-emerging.

Still, it would take some time for all her society-induced behaviours to be modified and she still felt nervous about telling anyone of her decision to leave the world she'd always known and set up life with Ben instead.

Francesca was under no illusion that she would be required to leave everything she knew behind. Once she married Ben she wouldn't be accepted by the same social circle, she'd be excluded and shunned. It was a shallow and cruel reaction, and she shouldn't mind, but it was just like when the Patronesses had excluded her from getting a voucher for Almack's—she felt hurt and betrayed by the idea.

Perhaps it would be easier to start afresh in Australia. In Australia, Ben assured her, there wasn't the same prejudice.

A man was admired for making his own way in the world, not for the family name he started with. They could build their lives together with no preconceptions, no expectations or interference from someone else.

She wasn't sure whether Ben was ready to leave his family again, though—after seeing them after so long—he'd started to cultivate a lovely relationship with his father and brothers. It would be extremely difficult to leave them behind, knowing he might not ever see them again.

Francesca's feelings on leaving her family behind were just as complicated. She'd miss her sister without a doubt, but her parents she had mixed emotions about. Her mother had been mentally absent for so long that Francesca had half-forgotten what it was like to have a proper conversation with the woman and her father was a selfish and impulsive man who'd put his own desires and urges above his family, almost rendering them destitute in the process.

Still, they were her family. She might hate how her father treated her, hate how he had been so selfish all those years ago to accuse Ben of theft when in reality he'd sold the family valuables to give him more funds for his gambling, but he was still her father. She could hate how he'd acted all these years, but she couldn't hate him.

Part of her wondered how it would feel to have parents invested in her happiness. For them to congratulate her on her impending union because they knew it would make her happy rather than thinking only of how it would affect them.

Francesca dawdled for another moment after the carriage had pulled up outside the front of their town house, fiddling with her skirts and summoning up the courage to go in and tell her parents her decision to marry Ben, not the man her father had chosen for her.

She wished she'd taken Ben up on his offer to accompany her, but when he'd suggested it she had told him it was best if she broke the news gently, on her own. Of course her father would be irate and her mother would probably tell her how selfish she was being, but it would be nothing that Francesca hadn't been dealing with her entire life. Throwing Ben's presence into the mix would make things worse.

Instead she'd made a detour on her journey, dropping Ben off at his rooms before returning here. They still hadn't finalised their plans as to where they would be living when they started their life together, but Ben had torn himself away from his family to give her the support she needed with hers.

Sighing, she resigned herself to an ugly few minutes once her parents found out her plans, summoned her courage and allowed the coachman to help her down from the carriage.

She was barely up the steps before the door had opened and her father loomed in the doorway.

'Get inside,' he said, his voice tight with anger.

Francesca swallowed, feeling the scratchy dryness of her throat, and wondered if he knew already of her plans.

Roughly, he took her by the arm, his fingers digging in even through the thickness of the luxurious cloak Ben had bought her all those weeks ago. He manhandled her into his study, a room that was barely furnished, like so many in the house. There was an old desk and two chairs, nothing more, and Francesca was pushed forcefully to sit in one of the chairs.

'After everything I've done for you,' her father hissed, his face so close to hers that she could feel his breath on her cheeks. He'd been drinking, of course he had, but he wasn't yet inebriated. The anger was coming from a place of sobriety.

He pulled back, crossing the room to turn the key in the lock before slipping it into his pocket.

'Father,' Francesca said, trying to sound reasonable.

It was hard when she was cringing inside. When she was a child he'd beaten her a couple of times, when her minor misdemeanours had coincided with his episodes of particularly bad fortune, causing him to react poorly to any irritation, but he hadn't raised a hand to her since she'd become a young woman. Right now he looked as though he might murder her.

'Don't call me Father. You have no right. A *daughter* treats her father with respect. A *daughter* honours and obeys her father. A *daughter* does not scheme and collude with criminals behind her father's back to defraud him of what is rightfully his.'

Frowning as she tried to decipher his words, Francesca started to shake her head slowly.

'Don't shake your head and act all innocent,' he hissed. 'I know exactly what you've been up to. Using that criminal to defraud me out of my house. To take the roof over your own family's head for your own gain.'

Slowly understanding dawned. This wasn't about her engagement to Ben. It was about the wager he'd made with her father and the resulting agreement that he would take the house in lieu of payment.

'I knew nothing about the wager,' she said, 'but he won't go through with it.'

It was as if her words didn't even penetrate her father's mind. He curled up a lip in disgust, brought back a hand and slapped her squarely across the cheek. The sound of the blow reverberated in Francesca's ears and her head snapped back. Yelping involuntarily from the shock and the pain, Francesca recoiled. Never had she expected her father to act like this.

'And then I find my whore of a daughter is out prostituting herself to the very man who wants to ruin me.'

'Ben isn't going to ruin you, Father,' she said, her hand cupping her cheek. 'You did that to yourself a very long time ago.'

'So you don't deny it?'

Francesca tried to rein herself in, but something had been unleashed inside her. 'I don't deny I've spent the last week with a man I am not married to. I don't deny we've been intimate and I don't deny I've loved every minute of it.'

She saw her father raise his hand again and tried to stop herself from cowering away. These were only physical blows, she would recover, she told herself, but still she felt her arms raise up and her body jerk away.

'We're going to be married,' she blurted out, her eyes still closed in anticipation of the slap.

'No, you're not,' her father said. 'He's a dirty criminal. A thief, a liar, a cheat.'

Francesca laughed, seeing her father as he truly was for the first time; a man to be ridiculed.

'Don't laugh,' he said, raising his hand again. Francesca refused to cower and looked him directly in the eye.

'Eighteen years ago you ruined a young boy's life and you have the audacity to call him a liar and a cheat.'

Her father laughed, a mirthless chuckle that scared her more than a raised hand could ever do. 'He was nothing, a nobody. A necessary sacrifice to save one of the greatest families in England.'

'He wasn't a nobody,' Francesca said, shaking her head in disgust. 'He had a family who loved him and a future that could have contained anything.'

'He was the son of a servant. A troublemaker. *A nobody.*'

Francesca looked at her father with disbelief. For her entire life she'd been making excuses for him, telling herself that he'd only done this or that because he didn't know any better. Now she could see she'd been wrong. Her father wasn't a bumbling fool, circumstances hadn't got the better of him, he was a cruel and petty man.

'I didn't recognise him at first,' her father said. 'Even when he came here and sat at my table I didn't recognise that runt of a child I sent to Australia.'

'Do you really have no remorse?' Francesca asked with disgust, but her father didn't seem to hear her.

'I invited him to my table, played cards with him and all he did was deceive me.'

'Hardly a crime, unlike what you did to him when he was a child.'

'Did he tell you he was planning on taking the house from me?'

Francesca nodded, not even bothering to try to explain again that Ben wouldn't have gone through with it. Her father wasn't listening, too caught up in his own monologue, too busy justifying his own heinous behaviour by condemning another.

'You probably laughed at me while you whored yourself to him,' her father said, picking up his glass and taking a gulp of the port that was filled almost to the brim. 'Well, I shall be the one laughing now.'

Feeling a spark of unease begin creeping through her

body, Francesca tried to stand, but was jolted back down as her father pressed a forceful hand against her shoulder.

'What have you done?' she asked, her eyes flicking to the locked door.

Her father smiled, a malicious grin that showed his port-stained teeth and made Francesca feel sick inside.

'I hear the punishment for an ex-convict found to be stealing again is much harsher. Perhaps even the noose.'

'No,' Francesca said. 'Please, Father, whatever it is you've done we can still put it right.'

'I'll not have that boy take my house from me,' her father said, 'or make a fool of me through my own daughter.'

She stood, lunging at her father, trying to grab the key to the door from the pocket he'd deposited it in, but despite the alcohol he'd imbibed already this morning her father was surprisingly quick.

'All these years,' Francesca said as he gripped her wrists, bruising the delicate skin with his fingers, 'I've made excuses for you, I've made allowances. All these years I've told myself you aren't evil, just desperate, but I can see now I was so wrong.'

Her father didn't deign to answer, instead gripping her by the shoulders and pushing her along in front of him. With the key she'd tried so desperately to get her hands on he opened the door, but before she could even think about escaping he pushed her roughly towards the stairs. When Francesca fought him every step of the way he picked her up, tossed her over his shoulder and started to ascend the stairs.

On the first floor he made a turn, bypassing her room and starting for the stairs that led up to the smaller rooms once used by the servants when they'd employed more than the bare minimum a house needed to get by. Out of the corner of her eye Francesca saw movement and raised her neck to see her mother's gaunt face peering out of the bedroom she hadn't emerged from for years.

'Mama,' she called. 'Help me!'

Francesca felt her heart break a little as her mother steadfastly refused to meet her eye, instead closing the door quietly on the situation in the hallway.

On the second floor her father, panting and gasping from the effort of carrying her when he did not normally engage in any physical activity, threw open one of the doors to an empty servant's bedroom and flung her unceremoniously inside. Before she had even had chance to get to her feet he had closed the door and locked it.

With a sinking heart Francesca rattled the handle. The door was solid and well made and unlikely to give way no matter what she did to it. Quickly she crossed to the window, wondering if that might provide her with an easy escape route.

It was locked and the glass thick, and the window itself small. Hardly an ideal window to escape through. Slumping back against the wall, Francesca let her head drop into her hands and allowed the tears to fall. To think she'd been worried about leaving her family, she'd felt guilty about going back on the agreement her father had made with Lord Huntley to provide a little money in exchange for her hand in marriage. In accepting Ben's proposal she'd thought she was letting her family down.

All these years she'd made excuses for them. For her father who was selfish and cruel and her mother who hid herself away from the world, not rousing herself from her bedroom for anything at all.

She thought of Ben, the man who'd built a good life despite what her father had orchestrated against him. Now who knew what fresh lies her father had organised? It wasn't fair on him and it was all because of his acquaintance with her again.

Shaking her head, she told herself not to be ridiculous. It was her father's doing, not hers. She needed to learn when to accept responsibility for things and when to realise it was others at fault. It was her father who had done these things, both eighteen years ago and now.

Wiping away the tears, Francesca stood and crossed to the window again. She couldn't change what her father had done, but she could work on a way of getting out of this situation and helping the man she loved.

Chapter Twenty

Ben ducked and weaved, landing a couple of punches on his opponent before backing away again. Today he felt light on his feet, as though he were flying through the air rather than walking on the ground, and his reaction time was nearly half what it normally was.

He dodged a couple of punches, landing one more on his opponent's chin before the man on the edge of the ring called time.

Ben shook hands with the other man, grabbed the cloth offered to mop his brow and crossed over to where George Fitzgerald had been watching him.

'I can't believe you're getting married, too,' Fitzgerald said, 'and to a lady. First Robertson and now you.'

Sam Robertson had set sail for Australia just before Ben had left for his trip to Essex with the beautiful Lady Georgina as his companion, despite her being due to walk down the aisle and wed a duke that very same day.

'There must be something in the air,' Ben said with a grin. 'It'll be you next.'

Fitzgerald grimaced. 'I hardly think so. How did it happen?'

Ben grinned, unable to stop himself. He still didn't really know how it had happened. One minute he'd been quite content conducting a passionate affair with his childhood friend and the next he'd decided he wanted to spend the rest of his life with her. Shaking his head, he knew that wasn't quite true. The feelings had been there for a while, he'd just needed some help to figure out exactly what they were.

'My father gave me some good advice,' he said slowly. 'He told me to look to what would make me happy and stop living in fear of having things taken away.'

'That is good advice,' Fitzgerald murmured, 'Especially for a man who doesn't trust anyone.' He looked unusually serious with a thoughtful frown on his face.

'Do you disapprove?' Ben asked. His friend's opinion was important to him. For so long Fitzgerald and Robertson had been like brothers to him, they'd been through so much together, and he wanted Fitzgerald to like Francesca.

'Good Lord, no,' Fitzgerald said. 'Any woman who can have you even think about settling down must be worth her weight in gold.' He paused, his expression turning serious. 'I just want you to be happy and it would seem Lady Somersham makes you happy.'

'She does,' Ben said quietly.

'I knew that was why you'd never forgotten her.'

'What do you mean?'

'You loved her all along,' Fitzgerald said simply.

Ben opened his mouth to protest, but slowly closed it again, considering his friend's words. For eighteen long years Francesca had haunted his thoughts. He'd assumed that was because of the dramatic way they'd been ripped apart without any natural closure to the relationship, but there might be some truth in Fitzgerald's words. Perhaps his love for her as a child was what had driven him back here.

'You are a romantic,' Ben said, shaking his head. It might be the truth, but he wasn't about to admit it. Eighteen years was a long time to be in love with someone without even knowing it yourself.

'So where will you live?' Fitzgerald asked. 'Here? Australia? Some neutral third country?'

Ben shrugged. 'We're not sure.'

'She's reluctant to leave her family?'

'Maybe. But I'm reluctant to leave mine.'

'The reunion was everything you hoped for?'

Ben nodded, remembering his father's happy face when he'd first set eyes on the son who'd been absent from his life for nearly two decades. He wasn't sure if he was ready to return to Australia yet, knowing that he might not ever be able to make the trip to England again.

'And your brothers were happy to see you?'

Ben had often wondered if his brothers would welcome him after so long. He'd read the story of the prodigal son in the Bible when he was a child—there could always be resentments from those who'd been at home all along when a brother returned. It was possible they wouldn't like him barging into the family, changing the dynamics.

'They were. There was no resentment, no hostility, just pure happiness that I'd made it home.'

'Take your time over the decision,' Fitzgerald said as they ascended the stairs from the boxing club. 'There's no need to rush. I'm sure you and Lady Somersham will be happy wherever you decide to be, but you don't want to regret your choice.'

Ben was just about to open his mouth to reply when a smartly dressed man crossed the street towards them. Behind him trailed four well-built young men. He'd seen enough of the world to know trouble when it approached.

'Do you know them?' Fitzgerald asked in his ear.

'No.'

'I'd say you've upset someone.'

Ben would have to agree. The sombre expressions of the men didn't hint at good news.

'Mr Benjamin Crawford?' the smartly dressed man asked, looking from Ben to Fitzgerald and then back again.

'That's me.'

'If you would come with me, sir, no fuss.'

Ben felt the hairs on the back of his neck stand on end at the sense of déjà vu. He might not know this man's name or where he came from, but he was certain he was a magistrate.

'Who are you?' Ben asked, trying to work out what he'd done and coming up with nothing.

'Mr Francis Poole, magistrate and Member of Parliament.'

'And why should I go with you?' Ben asked. He wasn't about to flee, there was no point. If he was accused of something, they wouldn't let him get away. The magistrate probably had a few more men stationed at various points nearby. Ben was fast on his feet, but he knew when he was outnumbered.

'You have been accused of a heinous crime,' Mr Poole said, his eyes scrutinising Ben, as if trying to work out if he were facing off with a dangerous man.

The pieces all started to fall into place. 'By Lord Potters-down, no doubt,' he murmured to Fitzgerald.

'I have the authority to take you into my custody and search your premises.'

'What is it I'm supposed to have done this time?' Ben asked. He felt uneasy. It didn't matter if he was guilty or innocent, that didn't seem to concern the system of law in England overly. Once you had been falsely convicted of a crime you didn't commit and sentenced to hard labour and transportation you lost faith in the justice system.

'Theft,' the magistrate said, motioning for two of the brawny men he'd brought with him to approach Ben.

'Unlikely,' Fitzgerald said calmly. 'The old man is desti-tute and in debt, he doesn't have anything worth stealing.'

'A search of your rooms will either prove your innocence or condemn you,' Mr Poole said.

'Lord Pottersdown has a habit of planting evidence,' Ben said calmly. Inside he didn't feel calm. Part of him wanted to run, to flee and find the first ship to take him from this country, but he knew it would be pointless.

This time he had to stay and fight, to clear his name and put a stop to Lord Pottersdown's ridiculous attempts to blacken his name.

With a rush of concern he thought about Francesca. She'd returned home alone to tell her family she wasn't going to be marrying Lord Huntley and would instead marry Ben. No doubt the news wouldn't go down well and Ben wondered if he should be concerned for Francesca's safety. Surely her father wouldn't harm her. He hadn't before, but the old man was desperate, believing he was about to lose his house and have his debts come crashing down around his shoulders. Silently Ben cursed himself for making the Viscount believe he would take the town house from him—no doubt it was that deception that had triggered the old man to think about retaliation.

'Go and find Francesca,' Ben instructed Fitzgerald. 'Make sure she's safe.'

'And you?'

'This isn't my first time in custody,' Ben said grimly.

'Take care, I'll be back as soon as I can.' Fitzgerald paused, looking at the magistrate. 'Where will you be holding Mr Crawford?'

'The cells at Giltspur Street Compter.'

'That's ridiculous,' Fitzgerald protested. 'He's not a common criminal.'

Ben shook his head ruefully. Cells were much the same wherever you were held. Dark, filthy and full of hungry rodents. If he had anything to do with it, he wouldn't be staying long so it didn't much matter.

Lord Pottersdown might have got away with falsely accusing him once, but he'd been a child then, helpless and naïve. Now he was a man of the world with nearly twenty years of experience of dealing with the most hardened of criminals. This time he would fight every step of the way.

'I'll come with you,' Ben said, giving one of the brawny men a hard look until he stepped a little further away.

'Good. We don't want any trouble,' Mr Poole said.

'Have you been a magistrate long?' Ben asked.

'A few years.'

'Then you should know when a story is a load of twaddle,' Ben said, shaking his head.

'Lord Pottersdown is a respected man…'

'He's a desperate man with more debt than either you or I can begin to imagine and a vendetta against me.'

'A vendetta?' Mr Poole asked mildly.

'I'm going to marry his daughter and he does not approve, and there was a little matter of a gambling debt he was unable to pay.'

Ben did not think it would help his case if he mentioned the man had falsely accused him before. The magistrate probably wouldn't look too kindly on the information that his suspect was a convicted criminal. For theft.

'And his daughter would be...?'

'Lady Somersham.'

'And she'll confirm all of this for you, will she?'

'Yes.'

'Then it sounds like you have nothing to worry about, Mr Crawford. If you would just come with me while we sort everything out.'

Ben walked alongside the magistrate, the brawny enforcers keeping a few paces behind, but looking ready to pounce if Ben as much as put one foot wrong.

'Is this your address?' Mr Poole asked as they stopped outside the building that contained his humble set of rooms.

'It is.'

'Shall we go up together?' Mr Poole suggested reasonably.

Ben used his key in the door and allowed the magistrate to ascend the stairs first, before he followed, closely trailed by the silent guards.

Inside Ben's rooms looked just as he'd left them a few hours earlier to go to his boxing club. At first sight nothing had been disturbed and for a moment he was filled with a hopeful relief that Lord Pottersdown hadn't managed to actually plant anything to back up his story of theft.

'Do you mind?' Mr Poole asked, motioning to the rooms.

Ben shook his head. The question was just a courtesy from a polite man. Whatever his answer the magistrate would still search his rooms, still pull the clothes from the wardrobe and throw over the bedclothes. That was his job and responsibility.

While the other men searched Ben sat in his chair and watched. He cursed himself time and time again for goading Francesca's father, for poking him like a sleeping bear with the threat of losing his London home. It had been unnecessary and indulgent and now had sparked a chain of events that Ben had very little control over. He just hoped Francesca was safe and could come to his aid as soon as possible.

If they believe her, the little voice in his head said. Quickly he tried to silence it. Francesca was a grown woman now, a respected member of society, not a ten-year-old girl. The magistrate would have to believe her.

'Could you tell me what these are, sir?' the magistrate asked, holding up a bag in one hand, a bound stack of books in the other.

'I don't know,' Ben said slowly. They weren't his and they certainly hadn't come with the rooms.

'Lord Pottersdown reported three very valuable books missing alongside some assorted items from the house.'

'He's run out of jewellery to plant,' Ben murmured. It was a sorry state if all you could find to plant in a man's house was a few books and a couple of almost worthless trinkets. 'I did not take these items,' he said louder, for the benefit of the magistrate.

'How do you explain them coming to be in your rooms?'

'Perhaps my fiancée left them behind,' Ben said, trying not to let the frustration become apparent in his voice.

'Take him to the cells' Mr Poole instructed one of the

men who'd accompanied them. 'I want to go and talk to Lady Somersham and see if we can get this mess sorted.'

The cell was dank and filthy and smelled of urine and decay. He wasn't the only one in it, two huddled figures sat in one corner, whispering softly to one another. Another man was closer to Ben, his broad face suspicious and nervous.

'Good afternoon, gentlemen,' Ben said as he settled with his back against the wall. 'Lovely day to be spending in prison.'

Three sets of eyes regarded him, trying to work out if he was a threat or someone to be exploited.

The damp walls, repulsive smells and less than salubrious company took him back the early days of his incarceration. He'd been kept in the county gaol cell until he'd been convicted, which hadn't been too bad, but after that he'd spent nearly two years incarcerated on a hulk ship moored on the Thames, awaiting transportation. It had been one of the grimmest periods of his life and he refused to go back there.

He had to believe Francesca would come through for him, that she would confirm her father's nefarious plan to wrongfully accuse Ben again and he would be released. Still, it sat heavily on him that once again he was having to rely on someone else to get him out.

For a moment he closed his eyes and thought of his father. He'd be devastated by the news that Ben had been arrested again, but no doubt he would come and fight for his son. Ben knew he was blessed to have a family as supportive as his and, sitting in the darkness, he knew he could never leave them behind again. Once this was over he would start making plans for a new life with Francesca, but he would also see if he could incorporate his family into that life too.

'What did you do?' the suspicious man asked, sidling closer.

'Nothing,' Ben answered with a grimace. 'I'm innocent, of course.'

The man laughed, a cackle that turned into a cough. 'Aren't we all?'

Chapter Twenty-One

Francesca slumped down against the door and felt the tears begin to flow. Until now she'd refused to cry, wanting to instead conserve her energy for more useful pursuits. She'd been determined to escape and had spent the last six hours clawing at the door, the window, the skirting, anything that might allow her to be out of this awful room and find her way to the man she loved.

There was a pit of dread in her stomach. She knew her father had something awful planned for Ben and she knew that, when faced with the word of a viscount or the word of a convicted criminal, the law would always side with her father. Even if it was obvious he was a lying scoundrel. It was just the way the world worked.

Despite her very best efforts, and with cracked and bleeding fingers, she just hadn't been able to find a way out. The house might be needing a coat or two of paint, but it was irritatingly well built.

Francesca wiped the tears from her cheeks and listened

at the door. Her best hope was to wait until Felicity came home from her shopping trip with her friends and then shout as loud as she could and hope her sister could let her out before their father stopped her.

There was nothing, no sounds downstairs, no footfalls coming up towards her. Just a silent house.

Wishing she had never come home, she pictured Ben's face, heard him whisper the reassurances she needed to hear. One day soon this would be over and they would be together again, ready to start their new life together.

Francesca turned back to the door and started pulling at the lock again, trying to work her fingers underneath it. In the hours she'd been in here it had only budged a very small amount, but she would keep going until she came up with another plan. For a moment she paused, pressing her ear to the door and wondering if she heard voices downstairs somewhere, but the noises were too faint. Deciding she had nothing to lose, she shouted anyway.

'Help,' she screamed as loudly as she could. 'Help me.' She repeated it a few more times before falling silent to listen. The walls and doors were thick, but surely if someone was there they would hear her screams.

Francesca waited for a minute, then tried again, hearing her voice cracking as she screamed and shouted, this time pounding on the door with both her fists.

'Help me. Let me out.'

Again she waited and listened, but the house was completely still and silent. Feeling the tears spill on to her cheeks once more, Francesca turned back to the lock.

She was still in shock, unable to believe her father had treated her so poorly. She'd known he was a selfish and small-minded man, but until now she'd always made excuses for his cruel deeds, telling herself he'd done things out of desperation or only when his judgement was clouded by alcohol. Now she could see him for what he really was—a cruel and vindictive man only interested in self-preservation. She felt embarrassed by how she'd made excuses for him over the years, even by how she hadn't acknowledged properly the heinous way he'd treated Ben all those years ago.

'I'm sorry, my love,' she said, knowing that now the scales had truly fallen from her eyes. Never again would she put her father above the man she loved, or above anyone else for that matter. He deserved everything that happened to him, for no doubt the weight of his debts would come crashing down very soon. All she needed to do was make sure she and her sister weren't present when that happened.

Sparing a thought for her mother, Francesca felt the sadness mount. Although they lived in the same house and had done ever since the death of Francesca's husband, she'd seen her mother only a handful of times. Instead of being a source of wisdom and affection, her mother hid away in her bedroom, unwilling to engage in the world, standing by while her daughters struggled.

Still, she didn't know what her mother had endured over the years. Perhaps the self-imposed isolation was her only way of dealing with it.

Deciding that no matter what happened she would do her very best to get as far away from this house and her cruel father as possible, Francesca renewed her efforts to escape. Ben needed her and it was time to put him first. It was time to stop worrying about how society would judge her for her actions and do whatever it took to save the man she loved.

* * *

Ben sat across a rickety wooden table and looked the magistrate in the eye. Something was wrong. Right about now Francesca should be here, explaining the connection between them and clearing his name. Instead there was just the magistrate and two well-built men who looked as though they were hoping for trouble.

'I am charging you with theft,' Mr Poole said as soon as he'd made himself comfortable. 'You will appear in court within the next two weeks.'

Ben shook his head, his vision momentarily going blurry. There was a tightness in his chest and a momentary feeling of helplessness.

It only lasted a few seconds, then he rallied. He wasn't a boy this time, wasn't an innocent who could be pushed around and manipulated by the powerful men.

'Have you spoken to my fiancée?' he asked.

'Lady Somersham?'

'Yes.'

He expected the magistrate to shake his head, to make some excuse about not being able to find her. That was the only explanation for this turn of events.

'Lady Somersham denied any connection between the two of you. She informed me that you had been childhood friends before your conviction for theft eighteen years ago and, since returning to England, had persisted in making a nuisance of yourself.'

'No,' Ben whispered, feeling as though he'd been punched in the gut. 'That's not possible.'

'It seems you have been spinning quite a fantasy, Mr Crawford. You almost had me believing you.'

Ben barely heard the magistrate's words—his blood was

pounding in his ears and a grey mist descended over his vision. It just wasn't possible. They were setting him up. He didn't know if the magistrate was working with Lord Pottersdown or if Francesca's father had found a way to deceive him, but he knew Francesca would never betray him, not like this. She'd fought for him when she was just ten years old, she would fight for him now.

'No,' he said again. 'No, no, no, no, no.' Each utterance was a little louder than the last until he was shouting the word. One of the men the magistrate had brought with him pushed Ben back into his seat roughly, before he'd even realised he was standing.

'I shall see you at your trial,' Mr Poole said, exiting the room quickly now he'd said all he had to say.

Ben barely felt the rough hands that pulled him to his feet and dragged him back to the filthy cell. He didn't hear the rasping of the key in the lock or the receding footfalls of the guards. All he could think about was Francesca's beautiful face, how she sounded when she laughed, the unruly mass of hair as it cascaded down her back.

He wanted to hold her, to feel her in his arms one more time, to smell the sweet honey scent of her hair and to feel the softness of her skin under his fingers.

'Ben.' Fitzgerald's familiar voice roused him from the fitful sleep he'd sunk into. Through the small grate on the door he saw his friend and wondered how much he'd had to bribe the guards to let him in.

The sound of the key in the lock lifted Ben's spirits momentarily, but when Fitzgerald stepped in, rather than the guard to let Ben out, the hope dissipated pretty quickly. He was alternating between wild despair and forced optimism, but right now he knew he needed to get a grip on himself and take control of the situation.

'It's not looking good,' Fitzgerald murmured as he embraced his friend. 'We might need to get you out of here another way.'

'I'm worried about Francesca,' Ben said, pacing backwards and forward.

'You need to worry about yourself.'

Ben gave a dismissive wave of his hand. It was true things weren't looking good for him, but he was a survivor. One way or another he would get out of here and be a free man again.

Fitzgerald fell silent for a few minutes. 'I haven't been able to find her,' he said slowly. 'I didn't want to worry you.'

'The magistrate says he's spoken to her, that she's confirmed her father's story.'

'But you don't believe him.'

'Francesca would never betray me.'

'Then her father has probably locked her away somewhere,' Fitzgerald said. 'The magistrate will not be reasoned with. He says he has the testimony of Lord Pottersdown and Lady Somersham and they both confirm that you've been loitering and making threats. So either the magistrate is crooked, or has been tricked by the Viscount.'

Ben shook his head in disbelief.

'The items found in your rooms would not be enough to convict you alone,' Fitzgerald said, 'but with a statement from Lord Pottersdown I think it will convince a judge.'

'And the fair and unbiased justice system steals another ten years of my life.'

Fitzgerald cleared his throat and Ben registered the unease in his friend's eyes.

'The noose?' Ben asked, involuntarily touching his neck.

'Perhaps. It is a second offence and no doubt Lord Pottersdown would be calling for the harshest punishment. You know the importance of connections in a case like this. The magistrate will probably roll over and do whatever the Viscount asks.'

'That old bastard took eight years of my life, he's not going to get the rest of it.'

'I won't let that happen,' Fitzgerald said grimly. 'There are a couple of guards susceptible to a bribe. If we move fast, I think we could have you out of here tonight and on a ship for France at first light.'

'My cellmates inform me they don't check the cells between midnight and dawn,' Ben said.

'Then that will be the best time to move. Be ready.'

'I can't go without Francesca,' Ben said. He wouldn't leave her behind, wouldn't get on that ship without the woman he loved.

'You might have to,' Fitzgerald said grimly. 'I can always find her and send her on at a later date, but you will have people at your heels. You know how they don't like to lose a prisoner.'

'I can't go without her,' Ben repeated. He was imagining the worst, of Francesca scared and alone, locked in a dark room thinking that everyone had forgotten her. Once before he'd been forced to leave her in England—he wouldn't do it again.

'I'll see what I can do.'

'Thank you,' Ben said, embracing Fitzgerald.

'We'll get you out of here. In a couple of years' time we'll be sitting on the veranda at home laughing about this.'

Ben wasn't so sure. He had no doubt he would escape.

The guards were underpaid and slow and Fitzgerald was a cunning man with a deep purse. Perhaps in a few years, once he and Francesca had managed to establish a life for themselves in Australia, he would feel less anger and hatred towards the man who was trying to steal his life for the second time, but he wasn't so sure.

'Keep your head down until tonight,' Fitzgerald said, banging on the door of the cell to let the guard know he was done.

As the heavy door closed behind his friend Ben slumped against the wall. He'd be leaving England once again as a criminal, even though neither time had he done anything wrong. Only on this occasion he'd also be an outlaw, a wanted man, no longer welcome in the country where his family resided.

It would devastate his father and Ben felt a new surge of anger at the thought of once again being wrenched away.

Chapter Twenty-Two

A soft noise from outside the door made Francesca sit up. She pressed her eye against the keyhole to see if it was someone who might help her in her attempt to escape or if it were her father. She'd been locked in the room for over eight hours and outside it was already dark. Perhaps her father had come to his senses and would let her out, let her leave to check Ben wasn't harmed by whatever scheme her father had planned.

'Felicity,' Francesca almost sobbed as her sister opened the door.

'Shh,' her sister warned, indicating the stairs. 'I had to wait for Father to fall asleep to get the key, but he's only dozing so keep quiet.'

Francesca embraced her sister.

'You need to go,' Felicity said, her face screwed up with worry. 'I'm not sure entirely what happened earlier, but Father had one of the maids dressed up and impersonating you to some man who'd called round. I only returned home when he was leaving, but it seemed very strange.'

'Impersonating me?' Francesca asked, wondering if her father had gone completely mad finally.

'I got the impression he was a magistrate,' Felicity said.

Understanding began to dawn. Although she didn't know the details of what her father had planned for Ben, she realised she'd been locked away so she couldn't let the truth out to the magistrate when he came calling. Her father's word would not be disputed and once again it would be enough to condemn Ben.

'Thank you,' Francesca said, giving her sister one last hug before she turned and hurried to the stairs.

'Good luck,' Felicity whispered.

Francesca dashed downstairs, grabbed her cloak, quietly opened the door and ran out into the street. She had a small amount of money on her, enough to find an empty hackney carriage and instruct the coachman to take her to Ben's lodgings. Throughout the journey she felt a mixture of nerves and anger. She didn't know what she would find, if anything, when she got there, but she had the feeling it wasn't going to be anything good. Her father had surpassed himself this time in his attempts to ruin as many people's lives as possible.

The rooms were dark with no sign of a candle burning behind the curtains, but Francesca hammered on the door all the same. It was opened almost immediately by a severe-looking woman who ushered Francesca inside and closed the door quietly behind her.

'What do you want?' the woman asked, looking Francesca up and down with irritation.

'I'm looking for Mr Crawford,' she said.

'You and half of the magistrates in London,' the woman grumbled. 'This is a respectable establishment with a good reputation, or it was before one of my rooms was ransacked and a guest dragged out in chains.'

Francesca knew the woman was exaggerating, but felt the panic well up inside her.

'Where have they taken him?' she asked.

'And he still owes this month's rent.'

'Where have they taken him?' Francesca repeated.

'Prison. To await trial, no doubt. Apparently he's a thief. Stole from some hoity-toity lord.'

'Which prison?' Francesca asked, her patience wearing thin.

'How am I supposed to know?'

Without another word Francesca turned and reached for the door handle.

'Giltspur Street Compter,' a soft voice called out as Francesca opened the door.

'Quiet,' the severe-looking woman said, shushing the young maid.

'Mr Crawford was a good man,' the maid said defiantly. 'He'll likely have been taken to the Giltspur Street Compter, that's the closest.'

'Thank you,' Francesca said, giving a nod of gratitude to the young maid.

'Good luck.'

She was out through the door and rushing back towards the carriage within seconds and instructed the coachman to take her to the prison.

Pacing up and down the small room, Francesca tried not to panic. The walls were dank and the smell from the cells wafted in through the open window when the wind blew in the right direction. When that happened she felt nauseous and wondered how the men coped being kept in such foul conditions.

She had arrived at the prison a little over half an hour ago and demanded to see Ben. There had been a scuffle among the guards as they realised they were talking to a lady of wealth and influence, but eventually someone had agreed to fetch the prison warden who in turn had listened to her story and sent a guard to find the magistrate.

Now she waited, wondering how Ben was coping being locked up in a place like this again. He was a strong man, with reserves that even he wasn't aware of, but being falsely accused of a crime he didn't commit again, and being taken to a place like this, must be dredging up some painful memories.

'Good evening,' a tall thin man said as he entered the room. 'I'm Mr Poole.'

'Good evening, Mr Poole. I'm Lady Somersham.' She noted the look of confusion that crossed his face, but pressed on. 'I think there has been some mix up with Mr Crawford. I understand he has been accused of stealing from my father.'

'Forgive me, Lady Somersham, but I am finding it a little difficult to take this all in. I met a Lady Somersham, a Lady Francesca Somersham, at Lord Pottersdown's house earlier today.'

'You met an imposter,' Francesca said. She wondered if he would believe her, wondered if he would dismiss her as the imposter instead, but was relieved to see understanding dawning on his face.

'An imposter?' he asked.

Francesca wondered who he had used. Perhaps Lilly the

maid, who might be able to fit into Francesca's clothes, but her speech was pure working class.

'My father locked me in an empty servant's room this morning and kept me there ever since. I assume he paid someone to pretend to be me when you visited.'

'Is that so?' Mr Poole asked. 'And why would an upstanding gentleman like Lord Pottersdown do that?'

Francesca tried not to snort. Upstanding was not a word she'd used to describe her father for a very long time.

'Mr Crawford played a game of cards against my father. He won and my father could not honour the wager between them. Knowing of Mr Crawford's lower station in life, he thought to save himself the humiliation of losing his house to pay the debt by accusing Mr Crawford of stealing some items.'

'I'm finding it hard to believe...'

'That a man of his station would sink so low?' Francesca asked, shaking her head. 'He has the most to lose.'

'I understand you have a close personal relationship with Mr Crawford.'

'I do. We are engaged to be married.'

'And do you know anything of Mr Crawford's villainous past?'

Francesca laughed grimly, 'Of course, if you could call it that. Again my father planted evidence and accused Mr Crawford of stealing from him, when in fact nothing had been taken.'

'There was evidence, I understand.'

'A locket. My locket. That I'd given him as a token of our friendship.'

Mr Poole leaned back in his chair and laced his fingers

together as if contemplating the information Francesca had provided.

'You want me to believe that Mr Crawford has been set up, twice, to be accused of crimes he did not commit, by your own father.'

'It's the truth.'

Francesca could see some small part of the magistrate believed her. There must have been something he hadn't been happy with during his investigation, some doubt that niggled at him.

'I need to look into one or two things,' he said. 'Would you care to wait, Lady Somersham?'

'Of course.'

'I'll see about having some refreshment sent up.'

Mr Poole stood and made his way to the door, pausing before he opened it.

'You understand these are serious allegations against your father,' he said quietly.

'I understand.'

Francesca knew that, although bearing false testimony was a crime, her father would never have to stand up in court and answer for his actions. He was too well protected by his title and the family name.

She waited for well over an hour, wondering exactly what Mr Poole was doing with the time and hoping that he was astute enough to uncover the truth now he had more of the facts available to him. A guard with questionable personal hygiene brought her a dirty cup of water which Francesca smiled her thanks for, then left untouched on the small table. Even if it had been the finest wine she wouldn't have been able to touch it, her stomach was roiling inside her as she wondered what the next few hours would bring.

When the door opened again she felt a mixture of hope and dread as she saw Mr Poole enter.

'Thank you for your patience, Lady Somersham,' he said, 'I would like to extend my apologies for taking so long to verify your story. I hope you understand my need to check all the facts.'

'Of course,' Francesca murmured.

'I have spoken to your father...' Mr Poole grimaced '... or attempted to. He was a little the worse for wear.'

Francesca held her breath in the hope that in his drunken stupor her father had revealed the extent of his crimes against Ben.

'And I spoke to various members of your household. Their accounts have led me to believe that Mr Crawford was charged in error.'

Francesca felt the relief crash over her at his words.

'I have asked a guard to bring Mr Crawford up here and I will arrange the necessary documents for his release.'

'Thank you,' Francesca said quietly, knowing that Mr Poole had been more than conscientious. Many magistrates did not bother investigating the crimes they were supposed to look into, instead enjoying the privileges of the title without doing any real work. They were lucky that Mr Poole seemed to take his job seriously and wanted to see justice, not just make his own life easy.

'I am sorry for any inconvenience caused.'

'Thank you,' she repeated again.

Feeling her heart pound in her chest as the door opened, she watched as the warden entered the room and whispered in the magistrate's ear. She peered out into the darkness, half-expecting to see Ben in the shadows, waiting to be escorted into the room, but there were just two nervous-looking guards.

'What do you mean you can't find him?' the magistrate asked quietly, but not so quietly Francesca didn't hear every word.

'It would seem...er...that the prisoner has escaped.'

Francesca frowned. She was pretty certain they were talking about Ben.

'Where is Mr Crawford?' she asked in her haughtiest voice. Sometimes the years of mixing with only the most entitled people became useful, now she was a woman not to be refused an answer.

'Have you checked everywhere?' the magistrate asked.

'Yes, sir, everywhere. Twice.'

'Lady Somersham,' the magistrate said, 'it would appear your fiancé has escaped from prison.'

'Shall I send out the hue and cry? Gather the guards for a manhunt?' the warden said, a gleam of excitement replacing the embarrassment that had been in his eyes.

Mr Poole considered for a moment.

'For an innocent man?' Francesca interjected quickly.

'A man who has escaped our custody,' the magistrate corrected her.

'A man you were just about to release,' she shot back.

'Stand your men down,' Mr Poole said after a long pause. 'Mr Crawford is no longer under arrest. Although I would like to speak to him,' he said, directing his last comment at Francesca. 'Please ask him to present himself so we can get this mattered cleared up for good.'

Francesca nodded, knowing persuading Ben to voluntarily step into a room with anyone official would be a hard task. He was probably booking a passage back to Australia right now, eager to leave the country that had nearly falsely convicted him for a second time.

'I will take my leave, gentlemen,' Francesca said, feeling a mounting panic. She didn't know where to find Ben, but she did know she only had a limited time. He would still think he was a wanted man, a man who had to flee the country immediately. She knew he wouldn't want to leave her behind, but he might not have a choice.

Chapter Twenty-Three

Ben paced across the drawing room, covering the space within five seconds before turning back and heading in the opposite direction.

'You boys and your dramas,' Lady Winston murmured from her position on the sofa.

After escaping the prison in the dead of night he'd been whisked away by Fitzgerald to his aunt's house, with his friend reasoning that the connection with Lady Winston would not be known by the warden or magistrate, and in any case they would think twice about storming into the house of a woman of his aunt's status.

'I need to go to her. I need to find her,' Ben said. Ever since his escape he hadn't been able to think of anything but Francesca.

'You need to lay low until the ship sails at dawn,' Fitzgerald said.

'The boy isn't going to go without his love,' Lady Winston said, directing an admonishing glance at her nephew.

'So you might as well stop trying to persuade him and find Lady Somersham.'

'If they catch you...' Fitzgerald said.

'They won't catch me. They probably don't even know I've escaped. They had no reason to check the cells.'

'Where might she be?' Fitzgerald asked, bowing to the pressure to stop trying to persuade Ben to leave with or without Francesca.

'There hasn't been enough time for her father to take her to the country, so he's most likely got her locked up in his town house somewhere.'

'You want to pay him a visit?'

'I can't see any other way,' Ben said, knowing it might result in him being captured, but unable to think of another way to get Francesca.

'You're mad,' Fitzgerald murmured.

'Are you coming?'

'Of course I'm coming. I'm not going to let you roam the streets on your own, you lovesick fool.'

Lady Winston cackled and smacked her hand on the arm of the chair. 'Wonderful. You go get your girl. And don't get caught.'

Ben gave a nod, then strode from the room, not needing to turn to know Fitzgerald was right there beside him.

Lord Pottersdown's town house was only a few streets away, but they took the carriage all the same just in case they needed to make a speedy exit. Ben sat flicking the curtain back and peering out of the window, all the time hoping to catch a glimpse of Francesca, even though he knew she had no reason to be wandering the streets.

'So I take it you'll be returning to Australia, then?' Fitzgerald asked as they weaved through the empty streets.

'My hand has been forced,' Ben murmured. He hadn't been able to decide where he had wanted to build his life with Francesca. In Australia he had his home, his farms, his livelihood and his friends, but in England he had his family. Now it looked as though that decision had been taken from him. Even if he somehow managed to clear his name, he wouldn't be able to stay here. Twice he'd been arrested for crimes he didn't commit. He wouldn't ever be able to live a life here without always looking over his shoulder, without wondering when he might next be hauled in by a magistrate.

'Perhaps it is for the best,' Fitzgerald said. 'A new start for you and Francesca.'

Ben nodded. It might be easier for Francesca away from the eyes of society. They could be together without the judgement of the people she had spent her life socialising with. This way they would be free to build their life together without worrying what anyone else thought.

Before Ben could answer, they pulled up outside Lord Pottersdown's town house and both men looked out uneasily.

'How are we going to do this?' Fitzgerald asked.

'Storm the house, find Francesca, get her out and make a dash for the docks.'

'You make it sound so simple.'

Ben shrugged. He didn't know what they would do if Francesca wasn't being kept somewhere in the house.

'Let's go.'

They jumped down from the carriage and approached the door, Fitzgerald knocking and Ben standing to one side so he wouldn't immediately be seen by whoever answered the door.

A maid opened the door, peering out through a little crack, and giving Fitzgerald a suspicious look.

'Mr George Fitzgerald,' he said, holding out a card, 'Sorry about the late hour, but I had a message from Lord Pottersdown.'

The maid opened the door a little wider to accept the card and at that moment Ben stepped forward, planting his foot in the way of the door so it couldn't be closed.

'Good evening,' he said, slipping inside before the maid even had chance to blink.

'Quiet,' a woman's voice hissed from the end of the hall-way. For a moment Ben thought it might be Francesca and his heart soared, but then he realised the silhouette was too petite, the voice not quite the right tone.

'Where's Francesca?' he demanded, watching as Felicity hurried forward and closed the door behind them, dismissing the maid with a scowl.

'Isn't she with you?' she asked, sending a bolt of dread through Ben's stomach. 'Father locked her up in one of the upstairs rooms. I let her out when he passed out a couple of hours ago. She left to go and tell the magistrate the charges against you were false.'

There was a loud snore from one of the downstairs rooms and they all jumped, but the snores continued and Ben cautiously stepped forward to peer in the room. Lord Pottersdown was fast asleep, his head lolling back at an uncomfortable angle. Quietly Ben closed the door, holding the handle to minimise the click.

'I need to find her,' Ben said, feeling increasingly desperate with each passing minute.

'Did they release you before she arrived?' Felicity asked.

'They didn't release him,' Fitzgerald explained, watching Ben closely as he prowled up and down the hallway.

'You escaped?'

'I've had dealings with the English justice system before,' Ben said. 'I wasn't going to put my faith in it a second time.' He paused, then made a decision. 'We need to trace the route between here and the prison. Francesca has to be somewhere on it.'

'I hope you find her,' Felicity said, a sad little smile on her face. Ben realised that the woman in front of him knew she might never see her sister again, but she still wanted him to succeed none the less. 'I'll stay here and keep Father distracted if he wakes up.'

'Thank you.'

Francesca felt as though time was running out. She'd first checked Ben's rooms, but of course he hadn't been foolish enough to return there after his escape from prison. Next she'd headed for Lady Winston's town house, knowing Ben might have sought refuge with the aunt of his friend. Lady Winston had flung open the door herself when Francesca had knocked and quickly sent her on, telling her that Ben had gone to find her at her father's house. Now she was nearly back to where she had started, but was dreading what she might find if her father had woken to find Ben barging into the house.

Just as she rounded the corner into her street, she saw a familiar silhouette bounding down the steps in front of her father's house. Inside her chest her heart skipped a beat and she felt a rush of relief suffusing through her.

'Ben,' she called, not caring it was the middle of the night and they might wake the neighbours.

She watched as he turned and looked at her, watched as the smile of relief lit up his face. Francesca broke out into a run, her feet sliding across the damp paving stones, and flung herself into the arms of the man she loved.

'Frannie,' he murmured into her hair, kissing her again and again wherever his lips could find skin.

'I thought I'd lost you,' she said. 'Again.'

'Never.'

'I was so scared. I can't believe what Father did to you.' Even as she said the words she realised it wasn't true. For so long she'd been making excuses for her father, but the reality was he was a cruel and heartless man who only cared for his own needs. 'How did you get out of prison? I went there and they checked the cells and you weren't anywhere to be found.'

'I escaped,' he said. 'I wasn't going to wait for the law to condemn me again.'

'I'm so sorry I couldn't come sooner. Father locked me up in one of the upstairs rooms. Felicity released me, but only once Father had passed out. I came to find you as soon as I was able.'

'I know,' he murmured, bending down and cutting off her sentence with a long kiss. She felt all the panic and stress of the last twelve hours begin to melt away. 'We will have time to pick apart what happened once we're on the ship, but right now I'm a wanted man. We should leave.'

Francesca shook her head, smiling at the man she loved. 'It's all explained,' she said quietly, taking his hand in hers. 'I told the magistrate everything—how Father lied and planted the items you were meant to have stolen, how he owed you a lot of money with the gambling debt. He believed me and has decided not to pursue any of the charges against you.'

Ben looked at her with astonishment for a moment.

'They're not chasing you. The magistrate asked if I would bring you to him to sort out the formalities, but you're a free man.'

With one hand, he stroked her cheek, 'I love you, Frannie,' he said softly, 'But I think you've been duped. Magistrates don't just drop charges on a woman's word.'

'He listened to me, looked into the things I was saying and he believed me.'

'I can't risk it,' Ben said, glancing at Fitzgerald. Francesca saw his friend shake his head out of the corner of his eye. 'There is a ship sailing in two hours. We'll be in France before they even have chance to mount a proper search for me.'

'There isn't going to be a search,' Francesca said. 'We can stay here, there's no need to flee.'

Ben shrugged, 'Perhaps not. Perhaps you found the one magistrate in England who believes in the law and doing the right thing, but I'm not prepared to risk my life on it. If they catch me, Frannie, it might be the noose.'

She fell silent. She understood his concerns. Eighteen years ago he'd been innocent as well, but that hadn't saved him from an eight year sentence, transportation to one of the harshest countries on earth and the end of his life in England. Still, they didn't have to leave everything behind this time. The magistrate had *assured* her he would drop the charges against Ben. They could stay in England at least for a while, work out how they wanted to live their lives.

'Come on,' he said, gripping her hand.

'I can't just leave,' she said.

'Of course you can.'

'My family...'

He looked at her with disbelief. 'The family that locked you up and tried to have me hanged for theft?'

'I can't excuse my father,' she said, 'but I can't just leave them like this, without saying goodbye, without making sure they will survive.'

'I'm leaving, Frannie. I'm sailing for France and then on to Australia.'

She shook her head. Part of her wanted to take his hand and go with him without any further protest, but she knew there was no need to run.

'We can stay here, make a life for ourselves,' she said. It wasn't that she was averse to the idea of living in Australia—it was just everything she knew was here. In England she knew how to live, how to socialise. Surely she would flounder elsewhere?

'Are you still worrying what people will think of you?' Ben asked with exasperation in his voice. 'If you leave, are you worried that your family will sink under their debts and the family name be dragged through the mud?'

'Of course I'm worried about my family,' she said, a little sharper than she'd intended.

'But are you worried about your family, or are you worried about how it will look when the scandal breaks? Damn it, Frannie, none of that matters.'

She shook her head. She knew none of that mattered, but she still couldn't quite bring herself to leave everything behind.

'Perhaps it's me you're ashamed of,' he said quietly. 'If you marry me you won't have a title, you'll just be the wife of an ex-convict.'

'I don't care about the title,' she said. 'And you are a finer man than any duke or earl.'

'Think about what you want,' he said, some of the harshness fading from his voice. 'Do you want status and a place in society, or do you want a simple life with a man who loves you?'

Ben watched as she turned away, walking back towards the house, and he felt his heart break in two. He had never thought she would actually choose to stay in England. He understood it would be difficult for her to leave her family, he'd had first-hand experience of having to do just that, but he thought she would do it for him.

'We have to go,' Fitzgerald said quietly. 'The ship...'

Ben nodded, but didn't move. He couldn't leave without her. Once they'd been ripped apart and it had been the hardest time of his life. Eighteen years he'd tried to live without her and hadn't succeeded, and, now he knew her intimately, he couldn't imagine his life without her.

'Frannie,' he called out, his voice sounding pleading even to his own ears. She was already up the steps and inside the house.

'You can't miss that ship,' Fitzgerald said, manoeuvring Ben closer to the carriage.

He pictured her face, the way her eyes lit up when she smiled, the softness of her lips and the unruly hair that tumbled around her shoulders. Even though it hurt so much to see her walk away, he *had* to try one last time to persuade her to come with him.

Quickly he darted forward, bounding up the steps and striding in through the door. Inside he came to an abrupt halt. Francesca was standing there embracing her sister, both women crying softly.

'Go, you fool,' Felicity said, giving Francesca an encouraging smile.

'Frannie,' Ben asked, hardly daring to hope. 'I thought...?'

'I lost you once,' she said, her face serious. 'I'm never losing you again.'

He reached forward for her, pulling her close to his chest and kissing her deeply. Ben felt like singing, like shouting with joy from the rooftops.

'I might not agree with how you want to leave the country,' Francesca said, 'but I will go to the ends of the earth with you rather than have to spend time without you ever again.'

'And your family?'

'Leave them to me,' Felicity said grimly.

'Felicity...'

'You need to stop worrying about me,' Felicity said to her sister. 'I'm not a child any more.'

'You can't stay here...'

'I'm not planning to, not long term. I have arranged a position as a governess. In Devon.'

Ben felt his eyebrows raise in surprise. It was a bold move for the daughter of a viscount.

'And in the meantime?' Francesca asked.

'I've been placating Father for a long time,' Felicity said. 'I'm sure I can sidestep his rage for a few more weeks.'

'Perhaps I could suggest an alternative,' Fitzgerald said. 'My aunt is always bemoaning the lack of company. I'm sure she would be pleased to have you stay until things are a little more settled.'

Felicity only took a moment to consider, nodding her

head to the suggestion and seeming not to mind she would be leaving with only the clothes on her back for now.

'Good, that's sorted. Now we need to get you to that ship.'

Ben gripped Francesca's hand. He felt a surge of hope for the future. This wasn't quite how he imagined leaving England, but what really mattered was the time he'd spent here. The wonderful days with his family, getting to know them again and realising how much they cared, how much they had always cared. Perhaps one day he might return— if Francesca was right about the magistrate believing her, then in a few years they might be able to come back for another visit. Or maybe he would persuade his family to make the trip to Australia.

Then there was the woman standing beside him. Francesca. His Frannie. He would traverse the world a thousand times to find her.

He waited as she glanced back over her shoulder, expecting to see sadness in her eyes as she turned around, but instead there was a glimmer of anticipation.

'I love you, Frannie,' Ben murmured, realising that he had everything he wanted standing right beside him. Wherever they were in the world it didn't matter, as long as they had each other. 'We will build a new life together,' he murmured. 'A family of our own.'

Epilogue

Ben stood hand in hand with Francesca, watching the big ship come in to the bay. Three days they'd made the journey down to the port area, knowing it would be soon that the ship carrying Ben's family would arrive, but not knowing the exact date. Today they'd been in luck, with the tall masts in view even as the sun rose over the shimmering sea.

'I can't believe we're all going to be together,' Ben said, shading his eyes as he watched the ship's slow progress.

It was like a dream come true. For three months he and Francesca had been back in Australia. He'd loved showing her the land he now thought of as home, the rich fields, the vast expanses of farmland, and further afield the hazy blue mountains and beaches framed by long stretches of golden sand. They were happy here. Francesca had slipped easily into the role of an Australian landowner's wife and most days would ride out with him to solve the problems in the furthest corners of his land and to keep the farms ticking over. He could see she didn't miss the world of London society, the balls and the expectations to always be presented perfectly with impeccable manners. Here things were different. You were respected for your hard work and self-made success, not a title inherited from a grandfather.

'I wonder how they found the voyage?' Francesca murmured, watching the ship as it neared. Now they could see the tiny figures racing about the deck as the sailors prepared the vessel to dock.

He and Francesca had made that same voyage, setting out a year ago. The long months on board had flown by, a much different experience than the first time he'd sailed from England to Australia when each day on the transport ship had seemed like an eternity. With Francesca by his side the voyage across the world had been enjoyable.

'Come with me,' Ben said, taking her hand. It would still be over an hour until the ship had safely anchored and the unloading of the passengers would begin. Although he was eager to see his father and brothers, Ben had a different motive for bringing Francesca out here today.

They wandered through the streets of the settlement. It had changed in the time Ben had been away, becoming more organised, more permanent. It was as though the people of Australia realised they were here to stay and were finally building something more solid than the camps that had welcomed them when he and Sam Robertson had first arrived nearly twenty years ago. Despite this it was still small, still a town you could walk through without needing to stop and take refreshments even in the heat of the summer. They climbed a small hill and once they were at the top Ben pointed to the land in the distance.

'See that there,' he said, indicating the wild area between

the settlement and the hazy blue mountains in the distance. 'I've put in an offer for five thousand acres.'

'Five thousand...' She shook her head with a small smile on her face. Even after the months she'd spent in Australia she still seemed surprised at the vast areas of land available to be farmed.

'I thought I would gift it to my father and brothers, let them have some land of their own to manage.'

'That's very generous,' Francesca said.

It was the least he could do. Ben still couldn't believe his father and both his brothers had given up their lives in England to come join them out here in Australia. In fact, they'd jumped at the chance. Ben had sold Australia as a land of opportunity and he knew his brothers were eager to see what they could make of themselves in this fledging country. His father was just pleased to have all the family together for the future.

'When Mr Fitzgerald gave me my first parcel of land on my eighteenth birthday it was a wonderful feeling. Like someone believed in me. He wasn't asking me to work for him, to report to him, he was trusting me to make a success on my own.'

'And you want to give that to your brothers.'

Ben nodded. He turned slightly so they were looking at a stretch of land to the west.

'That area there is for sale, too, although I'll have to get in before Robertson claims it,' Ben said. The land in question was a strip between where his farms started and his friend's land ended. They both would enjoy being direct neighbours, whoever owned the land. 'I thought I might put in a bid for it. For the future.' He looked pointedly down at Francesca's midsection and she bit her lip.

Slowly her belly was beginning to swell. When she'd first tentatively mentioned she thought she might be pregnant neither had dared to hope. Francesca had been married for such a long time to Lord Somersham with no sign of a pregnancy, she'd long ago resigned herself to the fact that she couldn't have children. They'd discussed it before their wedding and Ben had assured her he did not mind. That had been the truth—he'd rather have Francesca even with no hope of children than a future without the woman he loved. However, when she'd missed her monthly courses not just once, but three times, and when she'd started finding certain smells utterly nauseating, Ben had begun to hope.

Just last week a doctor had confirmed the pregnancy, putting her about four months along.

'I still can't believe it,' Francesca said, her face lighting up as she thought of their unborn child. Only a few months ago Robertson and his new wife, Georgina, had given birth to a beautiful baby girl. Francesca visited at least once a week and Ben had seen the longing in her eyes every time she came home. Now, they were going to be blessed themselves.

'Is this how you ever envisaged your life?' Ben asked.

Francesca shook her head. 'A little over a year ago I was resigned to a miserable marriage to Lord Huntley and a life of dull domesticity.'

'Do you ever regret it?' He often wondered. For him he had just returned to his old life, with the added bonus of the woman he loved by his side. Francesca had given up so much more.

She turned to him and stepped closer, reaching out for his hand.

'Not for even a single second.'

Ben grinned. Only a certain type of woman would be suited to the rough and adventurous life Australia offered, but Francesca had loved every minute of it. He felt like the most blessed man in the world. He had a collection of successful farms, his family arriving to start their lives out here and the woman he loved to share each wonderful moment with. And soon they would have the only thing they'd never even hoped to wish for, a child to complete their family.

'Good. The voyage is too far to take you back to England.'

Playfully Francesca punched him on the arm, giggling as he caught her wrists and swung her round to kiss him. Then, arm in arm, they started off back down the hill to watch the progress of the ship bringing Ben's family as it made its way into Sydney Cove.

* * * * *

NEW RELEASE

BESTSELLING AUTHOR

DELORES FOSSEN

Even a real-life hero needs a little healing sometimes…

After being injured during a routine test, Air Force pilot Blue Donnelly must come to terms with what his future holds if he can no longer fly, and whether that future includes a beautiful horse whisperer who turns his life upside down.

In stores and online June 2024.

Subscribe and fall in love with a Mills & Boon series today!

You'll be among the first to read stories delivered to your door monthly and enjoy great savings.

WE SIMPLY LOVE ROMANCE